BITTER PILL

A novel by Peter Church

Catalyst Press

Pacifica, California

For further information, write Catalyst Press at
info@catalystpress.org

In North America, this book is distributed by
Consortium Book Sales & Distribution, a division of Ingram.
Phone: 612/746-2600
cbsdinfo@ingramcontent.com
www.cbsd.com

In South Africa, Namibia, and Botswana,
this book is distributed by LAPA Publishers.
Phone: 012/401-0700
lapa@lapa.co.za
www.lapa.co.za

First published by Burnett Media, South Africa in 2011.

FIRST EDITION
10 9 8 7 6 5 4 3 2 1
Library of Congress Control Number: 2018964506

ISBN 9781946395207

Cover design by Karen Vermeulen, Cape Town, South Africa

THE PICK-UP

It's ten to ten in the Mother City, and the bars on the Claremont strip are a blur of action, booming music, and heaving students shouting to be heard.

"Shots! Come on!"

It's Rick, with the puka shell necklace and Dirty Skirts T-shirt. He's a madman after one tequila, now he's onto his third. On one hand he balances a tray sloshing with five shooters; with the other he grabs his share of the spoils.

"Let's go, people!"

Angie can't say no. She throws her head back and downs the golden liquid in a single swallow, then wipes her mouth and prepares for the lurch as it reaches back into her throat like a fist.

Lily Allen's instant classic is playing: *Fuck You.* Patrons are pointing fingers at one another and mouthing the words as a luminous-green strobe draws squiggly lines across the walls. Rick puts his hands under Angie's hair and pretends to stretch it out.

"No more! Please, Rick!" Angie tugs on his sleeve and suppresses the impulse to retch.

Angie Dean is cute. Sexy, sassy, and eighteen, youthful bust straining a sleeveless tank top, white jeans tight with promise. Bikini tan stripes contrast against her golden skin. She's in the Blue Venus Nightclub and Bar with a handful of varsity mates, first-years like her, most of them from residences just a short drive away. This is their stomping ground; has been for the last couple of months since they arrived at varsity, freedom and fantasy beckoning. Inside the bar Angie, and her clique are safe on the marble floors and in amongst the crowds, while the outside menace of the Mother City's street wolves is avoided, forgotten.

Angie clutches a silver handbag under her arm. She's hoping to hook up with a third-year student she met earlier on Llundudno Beach.

"We gotta do town," yells Angie's friend Zoe, mouth to ear. She's been seeing Fabian, in the black V-neck sweater, but she plans to break it off tonight. There are too many opportunities to be tied down right now, just when a girl's discovering the big wide world.

"What's the hurry?" says Angie. Downtown at Elevation, the action only gets started at midnight.

"We're gonna get so bent!" screams Rick, jogging on the spot.

Angie scans the bar for her date. Surely he wouldn't stand her up? She can't see him anywhere, checks her phone for the third time in a minute.

No messages. Where could he be?

"What's with the phone thing, Angie?" asks Colin. He's trying to look cool in a striped polo shirt. He's been keen on her since they met in O-week but she pretends to be oblivious. *Colin is so average.* Still, she doesn't mind having him around—usually. She pulls a tight smile, shakes her head, blonde hair gleaming under the downlight. Zoe frowns at her but Angie ignores the gesture. She sums up the body density in the club: maybe there's a long queue outside, she figures.

Two-for-one drinks run until ten o'clock, so it's no surprise the Blue Venus is overflowing with the young set. The Wednesday-night special is the perfect mid-week stress-reliever—ideal for first and second-years living the endless varsity party. In a sunken dance area, kids fueled by cheap alcohol sway to the music. Rihanna's latest comes on, and Fabian holds his iPhone above his head with Shazam running so he can get the name of the song. He likes to copy playlists of popular club DJs and then pass them off as his own.

"Hey Angie!" A girl brushes past the group clutching a Smirnoff Spin.

Angie recognizes her as a friend of her little sister. In the shiny orange light, her face glows. Sweet sixteen, not even in matric. The girl giggles as Angie waves back at her. She wears a skimpy dress. *Geez Hayley, that's not a dress, it's a waistband!* Angie remembers being sixteen. Fake IDs and stuffed bras. *Every year it's getting younger and wilder. Now they go out drinking on a school night. Slutty is the new flirty.* Some of her sister's friends were on the pill at fourteen, boyfriends staying over and sleeping together with parental consent.

"Hey Angie, you coming to town?" Colin touches her elbow cautiously.

"Town! Town!" shouts Rick.

Zoe's just spotted Rick popping a pill, the booze and the amphetamines intensifying his feverish antics. Time to get out of here. "You coming, Angie?" she says.

Angie and Zoe have been friends since school. Southern Suburbs private-school princesses, lucky to sneak into residence at UCT, the University of Cape Town—that's what connected parents are for. Seems like yesterday they were dreaming about this independence: no chaperones or organized lifts or curfews, no parents to worry about where they were going or what they were up to or waiting up until they got home. Now it's just their advice ringing in their ears—*Stick together. Stay with your group. Don't do anything reckless*—which they are free to ignore at their pleasure.

Angie checks the time then looks around the bar anxiously. Shit. She knows she can't hold back the gang for much longer.

The barman leans across and taps Rick on the shoulder. "Another round for you guys?"

"Wow, man, that's just mental service!" Rick spins around, running his fingers through his hair in time to the music.

Angie looks at the barman, who raises an eyebrow at her. He's got a cute smile.

"I'll have one," says Angie. The barman winks at her. Another round will buy her a few more minutes.

Rick shrugs his shoulders then plants a wet kiss on her cheek and nods to the barman. "Hit us!" he says, smoothing a spot on the counter.

The barman lines up the shot glasses, spins the bottle, and pours: one, two, three, four, five. He pushes the shots across, passes Angie hers individually.

"For the sexy thing," he says with a grin.

Angie smiles. She feels like a goddess. The barman is at least twenty-two.

"Come on, Angie!" Zoe says and they intertwine arms then slot back their drinks.

"Oh—my—god!" they cry in unison, bent in half, then bouncing up together like a spring. The music pulsates through their bodies, reverberates through the bar counter.

"Awesome!" says Rick as he tries to put his arms around them. He staggers back against Colin who pushes him away irritably.

"I want to go," says Zoe. "We definitely need to get to town."

The guys shuffle towards the exit. Zoe grips Angie's arm.

"You coming?"

Angie grimaces. *I want to stay.* Decision time.

"I think I'll stay," she says.

Zoe hesitates. "You sure, babe? What if he doesn't pitch?"

Angie removes a tube of apricot lip gloss from her bag and puckers in anticipation. She'll give him an hour. She's got the phone number for Rikkis taxis in her cell just in case. And the cute barman keeps looking in her direction.

"He'll be here."

Angie Dean screams.

She's not wearing her top and she can feel her bra straps being tugged off her shoulders by rough hands—a guttural laugh and the scuffing of feet as her body is manhandled from behind—balance lost and she keels from her knees onto her side. She's in a gravel parking lot, wedged between two cars—nothing makes sense.

"Help me!" she screams again. But only a moan escapes her lips. She sees a car guard sitting immobile on a steel drum in the distance. She wants to signal to him but her vision keeps blurring and he vanishes into the night.

What's going on? How did I get here?

Her befuddled mind can't work it out.

I don't want to be here. I wish I'd gone to town with Zoe.

The rough hands yank on her bra, but she can't lift her arms in defense —they feel like lead oars.

"No," she moans, the word expanding like a long drone in a tunnel. "No..."

She feels subdued and terrified at the same time. Terrified by the man assaulting her, by the croaking sound of her voice, by her inability to react.

One hand now works on the buckle of her belt.

"No, please."

She manages to cover the hand with hers, but it's tossed away like a rag—the buckle is open, now the hand works at the buttons of her jeans. Angie summons up all her efforts to concentrate on what's happening to her. She feels fatigued but she knows it's not a dream. Something very bad is happening to her but she can't resist it. Instead, she is floating, disconnected, helpless. Her attacker looms in front of her; she becomes aware of his heavy jutting chin in front of her face, tries to identify him— but she can't focus for more than a moment.

Suddenly she's on her back, the night sky above her—no pain, just an awareness of her head hitting gravel—her jeans are being pulled off.

"Please," she says, her voice a mile away, as a part of her realizes what's about to happen. She wants to sleep.

Then another voice.

"Hey you! Leave her *now!*"

The words echo from the distance, yet are firm and clear. The man springs to his feet instantly. Who is it? Angie can make out two figures above her, squared up like crows competing over a kill.

"What the fuck you pulling?" Angie's assailant hisses.

"Just back away and get out of here." A woman's voice, firm and in command.

Angie hears the metallic click of a gun being cocked.

"OK, OK."

Footsteps disappear into the night as arms reach down and tuck under Angie's armpits, lifting her into a sitting position. The woman materializes

---

in front of her, seems older, grey hair tucked under a tight scarf.

"Please help me," says Angie softly.

"Don't worry, sweetheart, everything's going to be just fine."

The woman moves lightly around her slumped form, shimmies up her jeans, buckles her belt, works her bra into place. Then she retrieves Angie's discarded top, dusts it off, and pulls it over her head. She works quickly, her guard up, on the lookout.

"There we go. Now, where's your handbag?"

Angie registers the question, but can't answer. She doesn't know. Her handbag has her phone, her purse, her driver's license—which she only got three months ago.

"Don't worry, we'll find it. Think you can stand?"

The woman moves behind Angie again, hands under her armpits and pulls her to her feet. In the process she spots the handbag, which has slipped underneath a car.

"There it is."

Angie Dean sits up suddenly. She screams. Someone is touching her arm. The man recoils at her reaction, steps backwards. Angie looks about, terror in her eyes.

She's in a gravel car park; she recognizes it as the parking lot around the corner from the Blue Venus. A security guard shines his torch into her face.

Angie feels like someone just awakened from an operation, her heart beating uncertainly. She hugs herself; her body is ice cold.

The guard remains motionless, confused by his discovery.

Angie runs her hands down her body. She's fully dressed. Her silver handbag is on the ground beside her.

"What have you done to me?" she screams at the guard, who retreats another step. Angie rises to her knees, gravel embedded in her elbows, clutching her handbag tightly to her chest.

"What have you done to me?" she says again, quieter, this time to herself. Her voice shakes; her breathing comes in short, sharp gasps. She looks at her watch. *Can that be the time?* She has no idea where she's been or how she got here.

"Lady, can I help you?" the guard says eventually.

"No!" Angie reacts instantly. "Just leave me alone!"

She pulls herself to her feet, looks around as though frightened of what she might see. She picks out the red neon light of the Blue Venus bar and staggers in its direction. The last revelers of the night are leaving. As she makes her way unsteadily along the road, she fumbles in her bag— her wallet is there, her bank cards, her cellphone; nothing seems to be missing. *Must call a taxi.*

Twenty minutes later, the Rikkis taxi stops in the bus shelter outside the girls' residence, Tugwell Hall. Angie is nauseous, her body shaking uncontrollably. But her physical symptoms pale in comparison with the strange terror she feels inside. Something monstrous has happened to her. Her legs are numb; she can barely move.

On Angie's cellphone are two messages from Zoe, one shortly after midnight:

woo hoo elevation going off! how romeo?

The second an hour ago:

u home? let me no what happnd u badgirl

The taxi driver watches her in the rear-view mirror. "I said thirty rand, please." His words are brittle, as if he deals with countless cases of young girls out of their depth. To him she's just another drunk passenger, possibly about to vomit in his car.

Angie forces her legs to move, pays the driver, and hurries in through the revolving doors.

"Everything OK?" asks security at the front desk.

Angie gasps inwardly, says nothing, presses the lift switch repeatedly.

"Come on, come on," she mouths silently, rubbing the goose bumps on her exposed arms. She notices her gold bangle is missing. *My bangle...*

The lift opens and she enters quickly, catching a glimpse of herself in the lift mirror. Smudged with mascara, the face that stares back is ashen and frightened. Her white tank top is dirty. She keels forward and retches, the output a pale-yellow dribble.

"Oh my god," she says, wiping her mouth.

The lift halts at the third floor and Angie runs down the passage to her room. The door isn't locked. Her roommate, sound asleep, doesn't budge as she throws her bag on the bed and fumbles for a towel.

She leaves her handbag in the room and hurries back down the passage to the brightly lit bathroom, falls against the basin, her body heaving. She hasn't eaten anything since lunch the day before.

Turning the taps on full, she splashes handfuls of water on her face, then steps back to examine herself in the full-length mirror. Relief floods through her chest as she runs her hands down her body over her breasts to her crotch. No bruises, no scratches; everything looks normal, feels normal.

But still.

She suddenly needs to pee. She steps into a stall, undoes her belt, unzips her pants and pulls them down. A loud gasp as her legs buckle and she lunges forward, grabbing the edge of the loo seat as she falls to the floor.

Her panties are on inside out.

THE LIMERICK

Robbie Cullen splashed water on his face. His head still ached.

He'd managed to make it up to campus for fourth and fifth lectures, but the effort had been altogether pointless—he'd hardly heard a word, let alone taken any notes, so he'd traipsed back down to res for a decent meal and a shower. He'd have been more productive if he'd stayed in bed till lunch time sleeping off the hangover, he reflected ruefully. And even without the headache, he was distracted.

Last night he had met a girl. Fallon. He couldn't get her name out of his head. That cleavage. And those dark and broody eyes. And then their easy conversation. She'd said she was a trust-fund kid, that she was finishing off a law degree; she must have been a couple of years older than him, at least.

The bathroom was empty, quiet except for the rumbling of the geyser in the roof. Robbie dropped his towel and stood before the mirror that stretched horizontally across the communal ablutions. He still had a long rake mark visible across his chest, the result of a weekend rugby match, the first of the season.

Robbie had an easy smile, pale-blue eyes, and light-brown hair that needed a cut. His looks came from his mother's side. She'd always told him it was both a blessing and a curse—she was probably right, he reflected.

His impulsive father, Milton Cullen, had struggled to handle the attention his wife's looks attracted. A chicory and pineapple farmer in the Albany district of the Eastern Cape, he was old-school: the family lineage could be traced back to its 1820 Settler roots. Slow with words, Milton Cullen used knuckles to protect his turf. Robbie had tried hard not to follow too closely in his father's footsteps. It hadn't always been easy, but he'd just about got it right.

Robbie leaned closer to inspect his complexion in the mirror, his image cut in two by a rusty stain. He touched a mark on his cheek, moved quickly away from the blemished reflection.

He pictured his laughing, dancing mother. His moody, reclusive father. The gene map was no blueprint for behavior, he thought. Robbie hadn't touched another girl during his relationship with Melanie, nor threatened a rival. Like the alcoholic's son who never drinks. Well, not the greatest analogy, he thought ruefully, rubbing his temple.

Melanie, his ex, was also a farmer's child, from the same district, chicory and dairy. After six years together she'd been as much a part of his family as he of hers. *Her mother had cried when she heard they'd split up.* Robbie fiddled with the elephant-hair bracelet on his left wrist: an old anniversary present.

It was time to stop hoping Melanie would come back to him, he resolved. Time to focus on the practical challenges of the year: midyear exams coming up, a job next year—and hard cash.

Cash. He was almost at the point of placing an advert in the Classifieds: "Student. Will do anything legal for money."

His father had wanted him to study Agriculture at Cedara near Howick. But Melanie chose music at UCT. Decision made—all he had to do was pick a degree. So where exactly was a BSc in Computer Science taking him now?

Robbie's thoughts wandered. He suddenly found himself picturing the black lace of Fallon's bra, the curves of her breasts underneath. Six years with the same girl...

A loud voice startled him.

"Nice ass! You been working out?"

Dennis le Roux, a fellow Kopano inmate, appeared behind him, threw his towel over the shower railing and balanced his shampoo bottle on a basin. Denny was a gangly Mechanical Engineering student with curly brown hair, a gummy grin, and eyes that moved like goldfish in a glass bowl. He was also a part-time barman at the Blue Venus in Claremont.

"Muay Thai," replied Robbie automatically, snapping back to reality.

"Muay Thai, indeed," said Denny making a mock-karate pose. "Just know it's working for me."

"Piss off, you perv." Robbie laughed. Muay Thai, the art of eight limbs. After several unsavoury incidents involving students over the last year—muggings, stabbings, even a murder—Robbie took his classes quite seriously. And it was useful pre-season training for rugby. He wasn't the only student who thought self-defense skills would stand him in good stead if a thug came for his cellphone. His instructor was worried about his temperament, though. Every time he took a blow, he'd lose his rag and fly in with flailing fists—Melanie's soothing effects dissipating, perhaps. He had compassion, endurance, courage, and honesty, his instructor said. But patience was the missing influence. Robbie respected the advice, so he supplemented his skills with a can of Bulldog Mace whenever he went out.

Denny disappeared into a toilet cubicle, the *Varsity* newspaper in hand. "So what's up, boykie?" he asked as he closed the door. "Big night out?

"Well, I'm totally boxed today if that's what you were looking for."

Robbie stepped into the communal shower area, turned the tap, and squeezed a dollop of Radox shower gel into his hands. He tried to focus his thoughts. Cash. Study. A job next year. His father said there was a place for him on the farm. *No way I'm going back to Albany.*

He scrubbed under his pits then rubbed gel vigorously into his scalp, as if trying to wash his mind clear.

Don't think about the farm. Don't think about Melanie.

His thoughts returned to the previous night at Blue Venus.

Fallon.

Why did she leave so suddenly?

Denny flushed and emerged from the cubicle, mumbled something.

"What you say?" Robbie asked over the roar of the shower.

"I said, did you find any talent out last night?"

Robbie finished rinsing his hair, turned off the tap. Could never be bothered wasting time in the shower. He grabbed his towel, wrapped it around his waist, and made his way to a basin.

"Funny you mention it," he said, rummaging around in his toiletry bag. "I had...fumblings in the Venus."

"What? Fumblings with your penis? Can it be true? Who's the lucky lady?"

"Erm, not sure exactly," Robbie said, a little embarrassed. "Some chick. Didn't get her name." He avoided mentioning Fallon.

"Hectic, bru. Everything happens in the Venus. Man, I love that place."

"Said with the commitment of one of its most well-loved barmen."

Denny worked on Tuesdays and Fridays.

"Full on. So is our heartbroken farmer boy about to cash in on years of frustration?"

Robbie ignored the comment, dipped two fingers in a tub of Prep cream, and lathered up his face. Maybe a shave would give him a fresh start to the day. Or the week! He positioned his old Gillette Mach 3 below his right sideburn and dragged downwards. He needed a new blade.

"Hey! You heard about a chick called Angie Dean?" Denny asked.

Robbie nodded his head. "Think so." Hot little first-year from Tugwell; one of his mates had hooked up with her at some stage.

"Story goes her drink got spiked in the Venus last night," Denny continued.

"No shit?"

"You wouldn't know anything about this, would you, Casanova?"

"Hey man, I had eyes for one girl only."

"Of course you did, hotshot. What was her name again?"

Robbie laughed. "Fuck off. So what happened?"

Denny explained what he'd heard; rumors going around that she'd woken up in her room without her bra or panties; everyone talking about it on Upper Campus, cops involved—but no one was sure whether she'd actually been raped. "Apparently she's a basket case today."

"Geez, news travels fast," Robbie said, trying to think if he'd spotted her in the club the night before.

Denny guffawed. "Spiked drinks—can you credit it? And check out the irony." Denny held up the *Varsity* in one hand. "They've even got tips in this week's paper about how to tell you've been spiked."

"Yeah?"

Denny started reading. "'One. Your drink tastes odd.' Your drink tastes odd? Hmmm, barman, do you think my triple cane and cream soda tastes odd?" He mimed downing a glass of liquor, then shrugged. "'Two. You can't think straight.' Seriously? This is advice?"

Robbie smiled and shook his head; he was busy on his neck, trying to finish up around his Adam's apple where the grain was all over the place.

Denny continued: "'Three. You behave wildly.' Check. 'Four. Uncoordinated movements.' Check." He imitated a burst of dance-floor gyrations, swinging his arms around like a manic policeman conducting the traffic. "Wait, there's more: 'Five. Blackout.' Hey presto! I've got it. Who spiked our drinks at the German School Beer Fest?" He stumbled against the bathroom wall and mimed throwing up in a basin.

Robbie rolled his eyes and rinsed off the excess shaving cream.

Denny calmed down, took a deep breath. "I know, I know. 'You always make fun of everything,'" he said, in mock seriousness.

You always make fun of everything. Pretty much summed Denny up. Everything was a joke; nothing ever serious. But he was good company.

"You ever met this Angie Dean?" Denny asked.

"Maybe once or twice. I know who you're on about," said Robbie.

"Apparently Tony Beacon was with her at the time. You know him, right?"

Apparently. Great word. You could place it before just about any statement and deliver up the wildest rumor in the guise of bald fact.

"Sure. The Tonester." Robbie nodded. He knew Tony Beacon well—well enough to know he didn't need to go around spiking girls' drinks. He had so much cash falling out of his pockets it was more likely to be the other way around.

"Seems everyone's in on this Mickey Fun," said Denny.

"What?"

"You know? Mickey Fun, Mickey Finn. It's the name they're giving to drink spiking now. Slip her a Mickey."

"You've lost me, Garmin."

"What? You've never heard of Mickey Finn? He was an olden-day pickpocket or something."

"If you say so, dude."

Denny kicked off his towel and stepped into the showers. He chose the same one as Robbie had; the only one with an unblocked rose.

"Seems like Mickey picked the front pocket," Denny laughed. "Get it? Picked the front pocket?"

"Hilarious," Robbie replied. "Weird to think I might have walked past Angie last night. It's a pretty grim day when a guy needs to drug a girl to have sex."

"Yeah, yeah," said Denny. "Says the stud from last night."

"Hey, it's not like I went home with the chick."

"More's the pity. We would have so much to talk about right now." Denny poured the shampoo straight from the bottle onto his head, patted it into his hair with clumsy hands. "Never fear, let me entertain you with a limerick."

"Oh Jesus," said Robbie. "No, thank you."

Unperturbed, Denny boomed out loudly:

"There was this girl, Angie Dean,
Who knew not where her pussy had been."

Robbie zipped up his toiletry bag, gave his face a last look in the mirror. He caught the reflection of Denny mid-thought, working on the next couple of lines while rubbing shampoo into his head. He shook his head again and made his way to the door, Denny's verse disappearing in the steam behind him.

"She claimed late at night,
In terrible fright...
That she'd revealed all to a person unseen."

THE EXECUTIVE

Usually, Julian Lynch played golf on a Thursday. His regular fourball always teed off at Steenberg just after lunch; it was one of the highlights of his week and it necessitated a busy morning in the office to free up his afternoon.

Today, though, he'd left work just before ten o'clock without telling his secretary where he was going.

His secretary, a plain-looking girl by the name of Christine, had noticed his choice of an open-neck short-sleeve shirt rather than the usual white or pale blue monogrammed shirt and tie. "Casual day?" she'd joked when he arrived. But he hadn't answered.

Christine was unlikely to advance her career much beyond administering basic clerical duties and she was content with that fact. Now, with her boss apparently gone for the day, she stole into his office, careful to shut the door behind her, and switched on his computer to consult his online calendar. For some reason, he'd always refused to synchronize his calendar with hers, an irritating habit that regularly left her appearing misinformed as a result—and served as justification for her habits of sneaking through his files.

Lynch's Windows password was "Holly"; she'd used it often. She opened Outlook and then checked his calendar.

```
10:15      Holly
13:00      Golf
```

Holly.

That was odd, Christine thought. Surely Lynch's daughter would be at school?

She had worked for Lynch at the Green Point offices of Premier Marque Asset Management for nearly two years and she still couldn't work him out. He intrigued her and frustrated her at the same time. Or perhaps he intrigued her and the job frustrated her. Work had always frustrated her; it just wasn't her thing.

Their relationship was formal, yet relaxed enough. His instructions were always clear, his conduct professional. He followed a set routine and answered all his own emails. She knew about his divorce, though not from him, and she knew not to ask about his personal life.

But she did wonder.

She scanned Friday, which listed the weekly management meeting, then closed Outlook. On impulse, she clicked on Internet Explorer and checked the history of sites visited. She had snooped on her boss many times before. As usual, his history was blank. Did he even use the Internet?

So what's he like?

Under cross-examination from other staff, Christine would always defend her boss. She was that type of assistant. He had a right to privacy, she'd say, which was ironic given her own inquiring tendencies.

And then she'd wonder why he never had a girlfriend.

It had occurred to her that he was gay, and that perhaps that's what ended the marriage—but she'd laughed at the thought. He…didn't look after himself well enough.

He was unusual-looking. Tall and thin with scraggy hair. A slim, lanky version of Ozzy Osbourne, she'd decided once. Except for the smile. And that voice which always maintained its single pitch—almost a monotone. Different glasses too. She'd always wanted to date a rock star, but couldn't quite imagine Julian Lynch with a black vest and a rat on his shoulder.

Lynch's desk telephone rang.

"Hello, Julian Lynch's phone," she answered.

"Lynch."

No niceties. She recognized the voice of one of the Johannesburg directors.

"He's not in, Mr. Kenwood."

"Get him to phone me."

The call went dead. That was Premier Marque, Christine thought. Kenwood knew exactly who she was but couldn't be bothered to greet her, just assumed she'd know who he was. She scribbled down a quick message and left it neatly on Lynch's keyboard. He was in demand; something about an offshore scheme involving all the directors. She liked it when he was in demand.

Christine swiveled on Lynch's worn leather chair and wondered if he was coming back to the office before golf.

After three years, Christine still couldn't decide whether she liked him or not. She certainly thought about him a lot; told herself it was because she admired his love for his daughter.

She flicked through the unopened correspondence in Lynch's in-tray, recognized the bimonthly VAT return; a Post-it attached included a note in the distinctive ink of Lynch's fountain pen: "Contact Sonya from SARS." She didn't know who Sonya was.

Outside of work, her boss was very predictable. He had his golf and he had his young daughter, Holly. He never revealed any other clues to his private life, just his tee-off times at Steenberg and news about Holly. When he spoke of her, it was the only time his voice lifted out of the monotone range.

Not that he offered up information. Like blood from a stone, Christine would tell her colleagues in frustration. But when she wanted to see that he was human, she'd point to the glass-framed photo of Holly on his desk and ask after her. And Lynch would lower his pen and raise his head and smile, and then tell her about Holly playing netball or Holly and her friends or Holly's latest school-concert performance. She remembered the way he'd described Holly's arched hands while she played the piano. And then he would smile again and get back to his work, and Christine would smile too and return to her desk, satisfied.

Lynch's previous secretary still worked for the company and Christine had once asked her opinion of him. She'd said the same: nice-ish, consistent, private. "Impenetrable" was the word she'd used. She'd known the attorney who handled Lynch's divorce; said it had dragged on for ages. Holly had been an infant; the wife had blocked Lynch from seeing his daughter.

From time to time, Christine scanned Lynch's emails, but there was never anything interesting. He must have another computer at home, she figured.

On another occasion, she'd asked him whether he wanted to join her and a group of friends at the Waterfront for drinks after work. He'd looked up at her and flashed a smile, pink gums visible as if his teeth were too short. She'd thought he was pleased and about to accept, but he returned to his work and shook his head without reply.

Now he was gone for the day and he'd left her with nothing to do.

Holly.

Perhaps there was something at the school. But he'd never put her name in his calendar before.

Leaning back in his chair, she remembered that moment when he'd turned down her offer for drinks. And if he had said yes? she wondered to herself. What might have happened then? What if they'd ended up talking casually at the bar? What if, with the courage of a drink or two, she could have got him to open up to her? What if all he needed was some human comfort and in a moment of madness, they got a room together?

Christine laughed out loud at the thought. She'd never had much luck with men. She closed down Lynch's computer, took a moment to compose herself, and returned to her desk to play solitaire.

⊗

Meanwhile, outside the grounds of St Augustine School for Girls in Claremont, Julian Lynch parked his red BMW and checked the time on his Rolex. Ten past ten. In five minutes he'd hear the bell ring and the girls would filter out into the grounds for first break.

He hoped to catch a glimpse of Holly.

He needed to see her.

DARK VIDEO

On the other side of the world—another hemisphere, another continent, another time zone—a swarthy middle-aged man leaned back in his Aeron desk chair, reading the morning paper.

"Honey!" Carlos De Palma heard his wife call out. "I'm just heading out to the shops, going to get us some pork ribs for tonight!"

Carlos didn't reply, just folded his copy of the *Seattle Times* neatly and placed it on the desk in front of him.

She was back, kid and all. Said her parents were driving her crazy; said she missed him. Carlos knew the little tramp was just running short on cash, could see right through her. Her lawyers' attempts at a settlement had proved futile—because they were *his* lawyers. It wasn't the first time she'd left.

But *c'est la vie*. He appreciated her chutzpah, her balls. Maybe that's what he'd liked about her in the first place. That and her...cleanliness.

They'd got it on a few times since her return. Make-up sex. He'd been gentle and paternal; she'd been the vixen. Raked his back with her claws and squeezed her knees into his sides so hard, he had purple bruises below his ribcage.

Who says a little smack now and again doesn't work things out?

Carlos pushed back his chair and strolled across the studio office, stood directly in front of the mirror. An advantage of body hair, he thought, makes you look old when you're young and young when you're old.

His appearance belied his age: no lines on his forehead or around his eyes; his hair thick, black, and curly. Much curlier if it weren't cropped, short back and sides.

Beep.

A sound emanated from the security console mounted on the wall. Carlos flicked to the front-entrance monitor. The guard was talking to someone outside the house: a boy on a bike, probably the kid who delivered the *Times*. He wasn't sure why he continued to get it; could read it just as well online. But there was some vestigial pleasure to be gained from the real thing—archaic and unwieldy, yet tangible and real, a temporary relief from the digital world in which he operated.

He flicked off the console and returned to the desk, tabbed to his email inbox, scrolled quickly through a list of emails, stopping at one with subject line: Cape Town.

Carlos was the man behind Dark Video. Or rather, he *was* Dark Video.

After years of online wheeling and dodgy dealing, he'd discovered his true calling on the back of the rise of online video-sharing sites such as YouTube and Watchit. He'd quickly realized there were certain videos that most people wanted to watch—and then there were certain videos that some people would *pay* to watch. Indeed, the right people would pay substantial amounts for the right material, and he used a network of content gatherers and creators around the world—his "mules"—to gather content, which he then sold to an equally dispersed coterie of wealthy and suitably twisted clients. His history of murky online dealing gave him ready access to both mules and clients; others he sought out through the many video-sharing sites he laced with spyware and Trojans.

Carlos's success had come in developing a small market for profession-al-quality material, tailor-making videos to suit particular clients' tastes. The material had to be genuine, no acting allowed. "Show the fear," was his motto. And the rich, sick fat cats in Tokyo and Frankfurt and Buenos Aires lapped it up.

In the last five years, he'd built up a veritable digital empire from the comfort of his Aeron. There was no need to physically meet with anyone, be it his clients, his mules, or the select hackers and IT specialists he involved from time to time to develop his systems. It was simply informa-tion being transferred: downloads, uploads, financial transactions—ones and zeros zipping around the world. The magic of the Internet.

But the Internet was fallible, a fickle mistress, always mutating, always demanding more. Clients came and went on a whim and he had to strive constantly to both keep up with the race and watch his back—from com-petitors, from the FBI, from whoever was out to get him. Times were tough; Dark Video was on a downer at the moment.

Cape Town.

Carlos hesitated before opening the message.

Cape Town was a hotspot of action for his line of work—a perfect schizophrenic location: modern-city infrastructure and steeped in foreign money, but loaded with glorious scenery and compromised Third World potential. A Shangri-la for creeps and pervs; a new Bangkok and a mine of opportunity. But its strengths were its weaknesses.

Two years previously, just as a new team of mules he'd acquired had started submitting top-quality videos, they'd self-imploded, victims of their own productions. This hadn't surprised Carlos, it wasn't uncommon—but it had been regrettable, particularly as it came shortly after they'd secured him one of his greatest cash cows yet, a fifteen-minute clip called *Men In Grey Suits*. The climax was outrageous: high-quality shots of a young man—one of the team, in fact—being savaged by a great white shark.

But that team had been dangerous, caused hassles. They'd called themselves the Gorillas, were too smart for their own good. The brains behind the operation had come close to tracking down Carlos to his Yarrow Point mansion, had had visions of claiming the Dark Video mantle for his own. Carlos had been one step ahead, as he always was, and the errant players of that particular team had been dispatched to the hereafter in good time. But they had vexed him. Cape Town vexed him.

Now, he had a new mule, someone with potential. A text had arrived that morning.

WAITING INSTRUCTIONS?

Carlos considered his reply, his fingers measured perfectly over the keyboard of his MacBook Pro. His return text would be bounced around the computer ether until all trace of its origin had vanished—standard procedure.

Ping.

A reminder popped up on his computer screen, interrupting his thought process: he had an appointment to call a client, arranged the previous evening. He was annoyed; didn't need the distraction now. But he was fastidious about responding to clients; they had no way of getting in touch otherwise.

Getting hold of Carlos was a complex arrangement. The Dark Video website floated as a Trojan with no permanent address and no contact details, except for a pseudo email address that changed daily. Potential clients emailed the address and, once their details had been authenticated, Carlos would provide the sender with instructions for a secure conversation over Skype, each call a unique transaction requiring invitation and authorization. He'd chosen Skype despite warnings that its voice-over Internet could be tapped. Carlos knew better. Skype was a black box and his encryption keys were impossible to retrieve. With one hundred seventy million anonymous users around the world, who cared anyway?

Carlos fitted his Bose noise-cancelling headphones over his ears, then brought up Skype on screen and scrolled to the relevant contact, a small-time client with the username Bruno. A flashing red x in the right-hand corner confirmed his voice-distortion software was enabled, and a small stub of black masking tape covered the eye of the webcam. He pressed the green phone icon.

"Carlos! How are you today, my fine friend?" Bruno said. Bruno's real name was Bernard Jones. Carlos knew him as a shyster lawyer who lived in Manhattan; had his work and home address recorded on his contact database. He made a point of digging up background information on his clients whenever he could. They all prized their anonymity, would be horrified to know how much he knew about them. Carlos liked to think of it as his insurance information. Beyond that, he knew the important information by heart: clients' names and code words, their "thing," the amounts they owed.

Carlos crinkled his nose and snorted. Bernard Jones was not his fine friend. He was small fry, and he owed him a thousand dollars. The amount didn't matter; it was the principle, the insult. But in the turmoil of the current markets, Carlos realized the importance of holding on to one's client list.

"I'm well, Bruno. What can I do for you?"

Bruno laughed. It was conspiratorial and irritated the shit out of Carlos.

"What is it?" Carlos asked again, just as Bruno started talking. Their sentences slapped together like two waves, cancelled each other out. Carlos rolled his eyes. The frustration rose.

He tabbed back to his iCal daily planner. Empty for the rest of the day. And the week. It invariably was. He had no routine, no appointments. He could sit at his computer all day and command his operation.

He clicked on the Cape Town message in his inbox. It was lengthy, in minuscule Helvetica font, which annoyed him because he couldn't read it without his glasses.

Bruno tried again. "I've been having some fun on XtremeUltra.com," he said. "You need to move with the times, Carlos."

"Good for you," Carlos replied. He didn't take the bait. XtremeUltra sounded like rubbish. Still, he was nothing if not thorough. He wrote "Bruno" on a notepad on his desk, then alongside it "XtremeUltra."

"So how's the *Jaws* video going?" Bruno asked. "Still being picked up?"

Carlos clicked irritably on his mouse, highlighting the Cape Town email and boosting the font to 16 point. Bruno's fishing about compounded his annoyance. Carlos knew he was itching to see the clip, had been since the day he first let his clients know about it two years before. But it was still popular and still way out of Bruno's price range—especially when the chancer had a bill outstanding. Carlos visualized the underwater shot of the enormous great white appearing from the depths of the Atlantic Ocean, hitting the kid in the water like a freight train. He usually didn't allow himself to obsess over any of his videos; like a drug dealer, he avoided using his own product. But he'd made an exception for that one; it still took his breath away. He imagined Bruno in the kid's place; the thought brought a smile to his face.

"Bruno, I'm afraid you have an account outstanding, so I'm not sure that particular film is, er, viable for you," Carlos said.

"Oh, I'm not into blood and gore, just asking."

Bruno ignored the update on his liability; Carlos ignored Bruno's lie.

"So what's it you like again?" Carlos asked. Blood and gore was top of Bruno's fantasy list, but he refused to pay for the good stuff, made do with low-quality car crashes and the like. Was always arguing he could get the material free off the Net. He would do his absolute nut for *Men In Grey Suits*, Carlos knew, but he couldn't even scrape together a thousand fucking dollars.

What a waste of time.

Carlos had had enough of Bruno. He tore the top page off his notepad, scrunched it up and tossed it in the wastepaper basket. As the lawyer in Manhattan mumbled an answer, Carlos interjected: "Listen, Bruno, pay your goddamned bills before you decide you need to speak to me."

He pressed the red phone icon to end the session. "Don't need this shit," Carlos said aloud.

Truth was, he was concerned. Dark Video was struggling. There were always ups and downs—that was built into the business plan—but he felt he'd dropped off the game in the last year. Websites broadcasting unimaginable filth had taken over the Net: sex and death and obscenity readily available at the click of a mouse. Once again his markets had been destroyed by pirate sites and free access, and he was battling to differentiate himself from the crowds. The tastes of the big spenders had changed and he was struggling to keep up. Even his own material was being hacked from careless clients, becoming instantly valueless, despite countless precautions. Regular clients had fallen off the face of the earth. Some hadn't transacted in over six months.

Carlos was incensed. He'd used all available channels to complain bitterly to the powers that be about the lack of online protection, about the freely available filth, but the Web had a life of its own. Sites would appear and disappear, their owners and creators invisible, beyond the reach of his intimidation.

Beep.

The security console sounded again. He checked the monitor and toggled through ten viewpoints that covered his property. It was quiet. Must have been a bird on the sensor. Or a raccoon.

Carlos returned to his desk, flicked on a giant LED TV that looked like an electronic wall. Breaking news: appalling scenes of a high-school shooting in Norway flickered across the screen.

Who needs Dark Video when you have CNN?

Everything seemed to be colluding against him. He flicked over to Fox News. The face of Hollywood super-agent Cy Gold flashed across the screen. Reporters had microphones in his face, asking him about rumors of another A-lister meltdown. Carlos watched intently as Gold turned on the charm, smiling, shrugging his shoulders.

The scrolling headlines flashed Cy Gold's latest Twitter post: *Get the latest f***ing news, before it gets you.*

"Damn him," Carlos cursed out loud. Gold's account had thousands of followers, his website hundreds of thousands. He was raking in the cash from online advertising, his site's click-through rates boasting ballistic returns. Carlos could hardly attempt to claim Google advertising revenue on the Dark Video site. It didn't even exist.

Carlos knew he needed some magic.

His hunt for the legendary videotapes of serial killer and rapist Paul Bernardo had drawn a blank. The search had cost him a small fortune: archives, courtroom records, bribing personnel involved in the trial. He'd even tried to track down Bernardo's wife and accomplice to the Antilles, where she'd reportedly moved after getting out of jail.

His Caucasian mules had produced five independent shoots of atrocities in Georgia, but the footage ran like a war documentary. The bids from clients were peanuts, not worth the embarrassment.

One client had posted a million-dollar request for the original footage of the accidental killing of Brandon Lee in the movie *The Crow*. No trace.

Another was offering big money for a snuff movie in which a recognized actor was deliberately killed. Carlos had briefly considered taking out some B-grade hack. Maybe Eric Roberts. Or Lou Diamond Phillips. Madness.

At least he still had his sense of humor.

Not too long ago, Dark Video had been hot news in select Hollywood circles—inertia generated by whispers of serious fetishes captured on video. Snuff, necrophilia, bestiality. It was a fashion industry. Summer blue was winter red. Wealthy clients signed on, searching for forbidden fruits, chasing that perverted dragon. At one stage, Carlos added over three hundred clients in three months. But straight sex and death was no longer enough to hold the attention of the virtual chic. With so much free material on the Net, the taste of the big spenders had changed.

Carlos was running out of ideas. But he did have one smart new concept on trial. Perhaps the Mickey Finn Club was the future, he mused. He returned to the Cape Town email, addressed the keyboard, and began typing a reply.

CAMPUS PANIC

At that precise moment, the warden of Tugwell Hall Student Residence glared across the table at the burly Afrikaans policewoman.

"I'm not sure you are affording this situation the respect it merits," she said pointedly. "The student involved is clearly quite traumatized, and this is not the first such incident to happen to a female resident of UCT. Something must be done. This is a serious incident. We expect action."

Alongside the warden, the University of Cape Town guidance counselor and representatives of two other female residences, Baxter and Fuller, nodded in agreement.

Captain Maryka Vermaak sighed and took a sip of water from a polystyrene cup. Here she was wasting her afternoon playing cry-on-my-shoulder with snotty-nosed university students and their righteous guardians, when she had a never-ending case list of *real* problems to deal with. Sure, she had sympathy for any woman who suffered at the hands of a man— and she made it her duty to tear apart every woman-hating rapist and abuser she could—but what did these spoiled kids or their wardens and counselors know about the *egte* rape and assault cases she encountered on a daily basis? The self-involvement of the affluent always amazed her.

"Certainly, Mrs. Eachus, I understand your worries but you must also understand that I have to deal with the facts," said Vermaak. She spoke slowly and deliberately, in a heavy Afrikaans accent. "Like we have established, the lady, er, Miss Dean, spent a day in the sun, she ate no lunch, and she drank three or quite probably more shots of tequila in less than an hour, plus a number of Smirnoff Spins and"—Vermaak paused, looked down at her notes, then up again—"a double vodka and lemonade."

Vermaak had nearly thirty years in the force; had seen it all, the old and the new. Her man had been killed in township unrest up north in the late eighties, but she bore no grudges—figured there was no point. Over the years she'd found herself specializing in crimes against women. When she had transferred from Vereeniging to Cape Town, she'd made a new start in the Peninsula Narcotics and Sexual Offenses Squad, but it didn't matter where she was because the expressions on the faces of drugged and abused prostitutes were no different: they were the same anywhere in the country—or the world, she imagined. Haunted faces of beaten women appeared in her nightly dreams, but they no longer bothered her. She reluctantly accepted her work as her calling, and anything to do with women and drugs was passed her way.

The guidance counselor cleared his throat. He felt uncomfortable, the only man in the room. "Yes," he began. "There was certainly alcohol involved, but..." He stopped himself short and fumbled with a file on the table in front of him.

Vermaak pulled out a pack of Marlboros from the breast pocket of her blue police shirt; slowly tapped out a cigarette while maintaining eye contact with the counselor. Earlier he'd given her a dirty look when she'd lit up. *Doesn't anyone smoke any more?*

"Now what drink exactly does she say was spiked again?" Vermaak asked without sarcasm, her face emotionless. She lit her cigarette, discarded the match back into the box; she was used to not being offered an ashtray.

One of Vermaak's functions involved controlling the drug flow in Cape Town bars and nightclubs. Controlling was the wrong word, she always said; *monitoring* was more accurate. Once the primary supplies were established, it was virtually impossible to stop things at the user end of the cycle. Success required targeting weak links in the chain, but that was someone else's responsibility. So she watched and reported and did what she could with her limited resources.

The warden flicked a disapproving glance at the counselor. It was hard to argue with the policewoman's logic. A recent university-sponsored research project found that in one hundred seventeen allegations of drink tampering over the previous three years, not one could be proved to in-volve a slipped sedative or illicit substance. In most cases, if not all of them, it was simply a case of too much booze. Still, the warden was no fool and she had a good rapport with the girls; this incident didn't feel right, and it came on the back of several others in recent months. Only a week before, another first-year student had ended up in Groote Schuur getting her stomach pumped after a night out in Claremont.

"Look, Captain," the warden said. "She didn't say which drink was drugged. Of course not. But she did say that she was raped, which is the issue here. It's irrelevant whether she was drunk or her drink was spiked or if she was stone-cold sober. *Something* has happened, and I am concerned—we are all concerned—that a pattern is emerging and that our students are being preyed upon in bars and nightclubs."

The counselor and other wardens again nodded in agreement. Vermaak shifted on her plastic chair and coughed. She'd already explained the problems—besides the quantity of alcohol she'd willingly consumed, Angie Dean had not gone to a police station after the event and no rape kit had been administered. Not that she blamed the girl; the process was often as traumatic as the original incident. But Angie Dean had even refused to be examined by a private doctor during the day and, most tellingly, she bore no external injuries. As a result, there was nothing of practical consequence that could be done. Any further efforts on the case would, she knew, just be a waste of time and resources. That she had managed to spend a couple of hours on the case the day it was reported was a minor miracle in itself.

"With all respect, Mrs. Eachus, I've seen women drugged and raped," she said. "When I spoke to Miss Dean earlier, well..." She had interviewed Angie for twenty minutes the day after the incident. The girl had been showered and red-eyed. She tried to get her point across: "Look, you're talking black eyes, hair ripped out, torn clothing, bruises, cuts, swollen genitals. It's a *gemors*. A mess." She paused for a moment. "It's not love-making." She took a long drag, looking from face to face before continuing. "Don't mistake what I am saying. We take all sexual offense allegations very seriously and I am sure your student might have had something happen to her. But in all likelihood if something happened we're talking about a one-night stand. A boy she maybe regrets the next morning."

The counselor cleared his throat. Vermaak thought one of the wardens was about to get up and leave in a huff. She was weary of her audience, their attentive eyes and worried faces. She could give them something to worry about if they really wanted to know. While they saw the mountain and the beaches and the wonders of the city, she was transfixed by a city outgrowing its structure and culture, overrun by opportunists and dealers looking to profit from the afflictions of others, and clogged by a culture of gang violence and drugs.

And somewhere on top of that septic cupcake were the pretty little scholars of the town, with their flashy cars and parents' money, running amok: drinking and driving, abusing recreational drugs, having sex in shopping-mall toilets, spreading their homemade pornos online and by cellphone. These weren't real problems.

"OK, let me explain," Vermaak stated firmly, keen to wrap things up. "You ever seen date-rape drugs? *Nee?*"

She reached into her bag and fished out a half jack of vodka and a bubble wrap of tablets.

"Flunitrazepam. Otherwise known as Rohypnol. You've all heard of it? Street name: roofies or roach or rope."

Vermaak showed them the wrapper. The small tablets were a dull green color, scored into four sections.

"Myself, I call them forget-me-nots." She emptied the last drops of water from her polystyrene cup, then popped a single tablet from its packing and dropped it in. "They are manufactured by a Swiss company for short-term sleeping disorders." She added a shot of vodka to the cup and looked up mischievously.

"Purely for *demonstrasie* purposes," she said, turning the cup to her audience to display the resulting concoction: the liquid had turned a pale-blue color.

"You see, Rohypnol is specially manufactured to turn blue when added to a beverage, specifically to counter drink-spiking activities. It's also very bitter when mixed with alcohol. Anyone want a taste? *Nee?*" She stood up, walked to the window and tossed the liquid onto the grass outside.

"It's not so easy, hey? What I am trying to show is that there is a lot of"—Vermaak searched for a word, couldn't find it—"crap going about. These kids drink too much, and then when it goes bad and they make a mistake, they say they've been spiked."

"But Angie remembers being taken somewhere," the counselor tried once more.

"When you're pissed, you remember anything. Too many movies, too many stories, too many other nights of drinking. We imagine perverts hiding behind pillars with syringes under their coat. Normally it's their buddy. Or it was no one. Maybe it was a dream."

Vermaak held up the halfjack of vodka. "This stuff added to beer and tequila or whatever"—she flicked her index finger and pinky in front of her eyes—"makes you *poegaai* very fast." She returned the vodka to her bag.

"Yes, but surely there's some form of investigation you can attempt," the warden persisted. "You are police, what about some *police* work? The nightclub, security cameras, someone must have seen something?"

The big policewoman sighed. "We have limited resources, I'm afraid. And even if they saw someone, what could we do? You know how many convictions for drink-spiking and rape I've seen in the last ten years? None. Not one. Can't even remember when last they got one into court."

Vermaak's cynicism belied her dogged duty to the job: she had already visited both the Blue Venus and the manager's house, recent photograph of Angie Dean in hand. She hadn't been surprised to discover that no one remembered a face among hundreds, or that the CCTV camera over the entrance was out of order. She'd covered this all with her audience.

"Mrs. Eachus, we haven't even established that the girl was, in fact, raped."

Vermaak knew that even if Angie Dean reported the rape, the chances of her following through to trial were minimal. In a country with one of the highest instances of rape in the world, she would inevitably end up withdrawing the charges, like so many other victims with far stronger cases—with reliable testimony, with witnesses, with a suspect even.

Vermaak was tiring of the subject. The club and student party scenes were swimming in illicit substances, most of them used knowingly. Hers was a pointless battle here; best she took herself elsewhere where she could be of some genuine assistance, however small.

"Look," Vermaak said. "I'm not saying nothing happened. But what can I do more? The girl says her underwear was on the wrong way round, that she felt bad this morning—but what can I do with this information? You know what most of these cases are?" Both the counselor and the warden avoided the policewoman's penetrating gaze. "The man tops up your *dop* before you finish and then next thing you know, you're on your back. *'n Dronk vrou is 'n droom in die bed*, isn't it? You just have to say no to that. The girls must say no. I watch my glass, so I know how much I've had. They must do the same. Then no regrets."

The university counselor fiddled with his glasses; the three wardens looked at each other in silence. There was little point in antagonizing the big policewoman any further.

"Now you said there were other instances," Vermaak said, removing her jacket from the back of her chair. "Anything with some solid evidence I can work with?"

"Well...no, they're just stories I've heard," said the Tugwell warden.

Vermaak smiled. "Ah yes, stories."

THE MICKEY FINN CLUB

Carlos could smell the faint aroma of pork ribs permeating the crisp climate-controlled air of his office. It annoyed him. The kitchen door should be closed, odors confined to their space. The wife should know better. He disliked domesticity, preferred a world connected by wire, without smells or reality.

The Mickey Finn Club.

He leaned back in his Aeron chair. The more he thought about it, the more it made sense. Got to keep up with the times, as that piece of shit Bernard Jones had so annoyingly reminded him.

Nobody owned the Mickey Finn Club. It was simply a network of barmen working together to boost their income by spiking drinks. Or rather, it was several networks operating in suitable locations around the world. Party towns, where drinking and revelry were par for the course and where the local policing skills couldn't keep up with the pace. Like the online world, the Mickey Finn Club had a life of its own. You just had to know how to tap into the system.

Carlos had already made his first tentative steps in three locations: Rio de Janeiro, Ibiza, and Cape Town. The challenge was two-fold. First he had to ensure his mules were trustworthy and competent. It was one thing putting together a high-quality film, a finished product; it was another dealing in kidnapping to order. And secondly, he had to convince his clients in those areas to buy into it. Forget video, he told them, forget the passiveness of watching the unsuspecting victims; now you can play. Now you can *be* the video.

It was a very selective market: clients looking for unattainable girls who existed outside the influence of fat wallets and powerful position. Young girls who still believed in the virtue of love; whose boyfriends were lifeguards and waiters and students, vocations irrelevant. Girls who were pure, naive, innocent—who hadn't already been hardened in the school of life.

It was early days, but Carlos was signing orders. He was considering separating the service from Dark Video and repackaging it under the label Lucid Dream. Give it some marketing shtick. He, Carlos, was the dream-maker offering the client the opportunity to create his own fantasy scenario using young girls made willing with the slip of a pill.

Beep.

His cellphone sounded. An appropriate interlude to his thoughts: a transaction confirmation for a job going down in Cape Town tonight.

But there were drawbacks to the Mickey Finn Club. It carried a new contingency, a product that required physical delivery. And with that came all sorts of risks. By definition of its very looseness, the Mickey Finn Club was difficult to control. There were so many people already tapping into the networks that it was difficult to track the opposition, from solo players to larger operations, his direct competition. There was also the possibility that his clients might consider venturing out on their own. He would have to rely on their obsession for privacy, their unwillingness to be compromised. And he would have to keep the closest of tabs on his mules.

In the recessive video business, some of Carlos's mules were already trying to cut him out of the loop; shopping their material about, looking for better deals. The big news networks and gossip websites had become primary buyers, happy to score a scoop even if it meant blurred censor spots covering "offensive material." Inevitably, their "breaking news" would be quickly followed by widespread online pirating; anyone with a search engine could download videos and images free of charge.

One of Carlos's UK teams had recently set up a married MP, got him on film buggering a rent boy in a five-star hotel. It was Dark Video "hometown" material, but they'd sold it to the local tabloids and it had spread like wildfire. The pictures were published unedited; the video even made it on to YouTube for half a day before the complaints registered.

Carlos had been incensed. His big hitman, Samuel Chester, a.k.a. Chestwound, had been dispatched to give the errant British mules a swimming lesson in the Thames. He recalled Chester's message on his cellphone:

```
But alas I wuz no swimmer, dropped em
in the foaming brine.
```

Classic Chestwound MO. The memory raised a rueful smile. It was more money down the tube, another content source blown.

Carlos's email pinged. Bruno requesting another Skype call. He deleted it. That worthless lowlife was becoming a nuisance. Pestering him. Boasting of his disloyalty. Disrespecting him by not settling his tab. He considered having him taken care of.

When it came to being messed around, Carlos believed in the certainty of sanction. But he wasn't the goddamned mafia; he couldn't go around wiping out everyone who ticked him off. He needed to get a grip on things.

Carlos checked the security monitor again. He toggled through the screens: garage, front garden to the lake, back garden to the gate, outside street.

The anticipation of the enemy arriving unexpected at the door sent cold shivers down his spine. Nobody knew where he lived, not even Samuel Chester, his long-term associate. But his unseen foes always worried him; there were many players around the world who would be happy to see him gone, and he hadn't come this far by letting his guard drop.

He knew that it was near impossible for anyone to link the Internet persona Carlos De Palma to his quiet Yarrow Point residence. And yet the Gorillas gang had seemingly come close two years before. What had he missed? And would Samuel Chester be there in time to lay the next pretender to rest?

Of his three Mickey Finn trial locations, Cape Town was showing the most promise.

South Africa was topical. Cape Town had just been voted the top destination to visit in the world, tourists loved the place. It was magic.

Tainted magic, perhaps.

The South African police had recently arrested a Dark Video client in Durban, gone public with the filth on his computer. Jacker, his top tech man, had learned that the bust had come about after an anonymous tip-off. The modus operandi was similar to a client bust in Tokyo only a week earlier.

Jacker handled Dark Video's technical and security work—the loading of Trojans, cutting through firewalls, jail-breaking cellphones, developing and adapting useful programs and utilities. He knew his stuff. But Jacker couldn't explain where the tip-off came from.

Must be coincidence, figured Carlos, wondering if there was another content provider involved, lacking Dark Video's strict security measures. He suspected the Mickey Finn concept had made it up to Durban and his client had been playing an independent operator.

Carlos had never been to South Africa. Hadn't been anywhere in recent years, actually; international travel was a risk. But he knew enough about the place. Johannesburg, the City of Gold, loaded with flashy mining money: three big clients with specific tastes. Durban, hot and sweaty, some kind of African madness in the air, he'd been told: he'd had two wealthy Indian clients, now reduced to one. And Cape Town, loaded with nouveau Eurotrash trying to keep a low international profile while spending their ill-gotten pounds and euros as injudiciously as possible. Some old money too. A dozen clients and a world of opportunity.

With the long fingers of a piano player, Carlos caressed the keyboard and checked his email.

Then, almost out of force of habit, he kicked off a custom-designed virus checker and scanned his hard drive for any suspicious ailments—a process he repeated at least twice a day. You could never be too safe.

Satisfied, he stood up and picked up two ten-kilogram dumbbells from a weights rack in the corner of his office. He stood in front of the mirror mechanically lifting his arms in alternate curls. The repetitions were slow and deliberate.

There was not a single photograph of Carlos in the studio office, or in his bedroom or anywhere else in his Yarrow Point mansion. His wife had put up photographs of her and their child, but he allowed none of him. He didn't believe in recording images of oneself.

As a young man, Carlos had believed in only one God: himself. He believed in life and death; that each night he died, his bed a grave, and that each morning he woke fresh and new, reincarnated, attached to the previous soul only by memory. Photographs were reminders of a person who no longer existed. He bore his past self neither resentment nor gratitude.

He didn't want to look back, except to learn from any mistakes, so he'd stopped thinking about who he was. Twenty years of anonymity had blurred his real persona anyway; what existed was the person who rose from his bed each morning. His wife regarded him as a dotcom millionaire and he wasn't about to disabuse her of the notion. As long as no one linked the real-life character that existed in his physical shell with the online purveyor of dark material and twisted visions, he was happy.

"Honey!"

It was ironic, reflected Carlos, still pumping the dumbbells. She was his only connection to reality, yet he never missed her when she ran off home to her folks.

"Honey! The ribs are ready!"

Her high-pitched voice grated. He hoped the kid wouldn't be at the table, face smeared with barbecue sauce.

Carlos replaced the dumbbells, noticed the crumpled piece of paper he'd thrown in the wastepaper basket earlier in the day. He leaned down to retrieve it, unfolded it. Goddamned Bruno. He made a snap decision. "Samuel Chester to collect," he wrote on the top of the page in perfect handwriting. He placed the note in his in-tray and walked out of the office.

Come to think of it, I could do with some ribs.

WEDNESDAYS

It had seemed an interminable wait, but the two weeks had finally passed. He made the call.

"It's Julian," Lynch said, holding the Motorola to his ear and looking out the sitting-room window into the vast grounds of his Bishopscourt home.

"I can't talk right now," said the woman. Lynch had met her on two occasions. He thought her voice didn't match her haggard appearance. "Is there a problem?"

The house, set among two acres of overgrown garden, had changed little since being built by Julian Lynch's father, Bobby, in the early 1950s. Back then it had been an elegant mansion, but the years were showing. Modern appendages had been patched on haphazardly—satellite dish, electric fence, security cameras, a guardhouse fashioned from the original tool shed—yet the house itself remained largely unchanged a half-century later, and the Cape winters had been unkind. Shutters hung on rusty hinges, swollen doors creaked. The roof had virtually disappeared under a layer of moss.

"No problem," he said.

The woman was listed on Lynch's contacts under the name Diva. No surname.

He walked from the sitting room through an interleading door to his study. His long legs gave him an elegant gait, as if practiced.

A longcase clock stood like a sentry against the wall, two meters tall. The clock was older than the house; two sets of weights and the hanging pendulum were visible inside the cabinet. The study resembled a mad professor's library, disordered books spilling from the racks and stacked on the floor.

Lynch sat down in the leather chair behind his desk. A large framed picture of a young girl in her early teens held pride of place amid the clutter of papers and books in front of him. Holly. Lynch looked at the photo and smiled. It had been cropped to exclude his ex-wife, Sandy, though her arm was visible around Holly's shoulders.

In front of the portrait was a smaller hinged double-frame: in the left window another picture of her with "DAUGHTER" inscribed below; in the right him and "FATHER."

Holly was the apple of Julian Lynch's eye, his princess. She had always reminded him of his sister, Estelle; they had the same lonely eyes. In the last couple of years, he had grown particularly fond of Holly. Sandy, on the other hand, was his nemesis, the overprotective dragon who did whatever she could to keep Holly from him. It amazed Lynch how embittering a divorce could be.

"I'm going to have to phone you back," Diva said over the phone.

Lynch wiped his fringe from his eyes. A note on his desk from the maid explained there was no more storage space in the garage. He decided he'd park his car outside.

"I'm sorry, what did you say, Diva?" Lynch asked.

"I said I'm going to have to phone you back," the woman repeated. He could hear voices in the background.

"Sure."

Lynch placed his cellphone in front of him, looked around the room.

He was faintly aware that he'd let the house go since Sandy had left him. He saw it as a form of penance; the house was a monument to happier times. In public, however, he kept up appearances.

The Lynches had been a prosperous Cape family for several generations, and he had learned from an early age not to let the name down. Strife comes everyone's way, his mother had explained to him as a boy. It was inevitable. How a man handled it was his measure. So, he dressed well enough when he went out, kept his BMW in reasonable nick. His position as Financial Director at Premier Marque Asset Management carried suitable status. And he was sociable with a small group of colleagues, went for the occasional drink, had a regular golf fourball—wasn't ashamed to call them his friends. He even went on the odd date, though he always struggled toward the end of the evening. He found women his age... transparent. And of course he could never bring them home; they would doubtless be unimpressed by the state of the house.

Lynch twirled the ring finger on his left hand between thumb and forefinger. It had become a habit since he'd discarded the gold band that once symbolized his marriage. He'd prised off that little piece of metal with a cake of soap and sent it to Sandy, a farewell gift. What else was he meant to do with it?

The divorce itself was not a resentful affair, though it had gone on a bit. Julian was apathetic, barely able to express an opinion. His disinterest in the final disintegration of his marriage had surprised his ex-wife and their mutual friends, but it was only later that Sandy turned into the disapproving, obstructive bitch that he had to deal with these days.

How long ago since they separated? Ten years? Twelve? And see how she behaves now!

Lynch stood up, pulled down his tie, threw his jacket over the back of his chair. In the corner of his study, a trap door was set into the floor-boards. He lifted it and descended carefully down a wooden staircase into the wine cellar below. He pulled a cord and a single bulb above his head illuminated the narrow chamber. The shelves were filled with empty wine bottles, a legacy of the days when Bobby Lynch entertained Cape Town's elite. Lynch nudged an empty cardboard box with his foot and scanned the shelves for any unconsumed bottles. There was not much left: just a few old bottles of Nederburg Cab scattered among the empties, and a box of Château Libertas on the floor in the corner. Not exactly Château Lafite; those days were long past.

Lynch sat down on a bench and sniffed the damp air. If he were to spend any money on the house, he thought to himself, this might be the room he started on. It felt right to him, had potential.

A black-and-white photograph hung from the wall opposite the racks, centered inside a collage of newspaper cuttings. He pulled the picture off the wall and held it close to his face. His father in a baggy dark suit with flares, his mother in tennis dress, Julian in shorts, shirt buttoned to the neck, long white socks and sandals, '70s hair. In the photograph, his father was about the same age as he was now: 40. His sister hadn't been born yet.

Lynch replaced the photograph, then moved along the racks, systematically sliding out bottles and replacing them, searching for a full one. Prior to his divorce, he had regularly replenished the cellar with purchases of new wine. Cases at a time, good stuff. There wasn't much to show for it now, other than the empty bottles that he meticulously kept, just as his father had.

Each time he uncorked a bottle, some buried emotion was released.

He extracted a mouldy 1984 Château Libertas, removed the foil and prodded the cork. It was soft and crumbly. He held it to the light, imagined the trapped liquid nestled in the damp and dark, years of reductive aging. It had been down here for two and a half decades.

He replaced the bottle, climbed the ladder into the study and closed the trap door.

It was Wednesday. He didn't drink on Wednesday.

BAD DRUGS

"Up the revolution, comrade!"

Robbie stood in the doorway to Denny le Roux's room, sizing up his friend's attire: grubby white cheesecloth pants held up by a string belt, faded Ché Guevara transfer on the front of a chocolate-brown T-shirt, Converse tackies. His room was a national disaster, clothes strewn everywhere, air stale and boozy. Denny had worked last night at the Blue Venus.

"They named a fucking road in Durban after this dude," Denny replied brightly, pulling on the sleeve of his T-shirt. If their lives were a comic strip, Robbie thought, Denny's character would be permanently encapsulated in a bubble of buzzing flies.

Robbie would be the average Joe. He wore jeans and a checked shirt over a white T-shirt, plastic slip-slops. At school he'd worn a uniform; nothing much had changed.

"Come on, man, let's get some chow," said Robbie, making off down the corridor. Seven in the evening, time for dinner, then perhaps a couple of frames of pool.

"Guevara said that blacks spend all their money on frivolity and drink," Denny declared as he followed Robbie, closing the door behind him. "What a legend! No wonder they honored him."

Robbie ignored the comment. He couldn't be bothered with politics. Neither could Denny, for that matter. Indeed, the Kopano residence demographic was highly representative of the new South Africa, so where was the bother? They were a generation too late, as his father so often told him. His old man had been a reservist in the SADF, said he'd fought the bloody Russians in Angola.

The two students descended in hops into a noisy dining hall, grabbed trays and utensils.

"How you hanging, motherfuckers!" said Denny to no one in particular. Heads spun around.

They joined the queue of students waiting to receive their dinner from silver servers. Some were on their way in from late lectures; others, like Denny and Robbie, on their way out.

A first-year in the queue was paging through that afternoon's *Cape Argus* as he waited. Denny looked over his shoulder and recited a headline: "Norwegian shooter declared sane." The gunman who had run amok with an automatic weapon in a junior-school playground somewhere outside of Oslo a couple of weeks back had been declared fit to stand trial.

Denny whistled through his teeth.

"Twelve dead. And we think we've got problems," he said.

Robbie tapped his tray against his chest. The clatter of plates on trays and feet on the shiny floor made the dining room sound like a railway station.

"Hey! Apparently Angie Dean got baby-proofed," Denny announced, folding his arms and looking across the dining hall.

"What?" said Robbie.

"You know? Angie Dean? The chick who got date raped a couple of weeks back. They apparently put some substance used to sterilize large animals in her drink." Denny fiddled with his crotch and filled his cheeks with air.

The student with the *Argus* turned around. "Progesterex," he said. "It's a hoax."

"What do you know, young Padawan?" said Denny, shaking his head in mock sympathy. "So innocent, so naïve." Denny patted the first-year on the head with one hand while calmly appropriating his newspaper with the other.

"Check it," Denny said, showing Robbie a picture of the Norwegian playground killer—nice-looking, black baseball cap. Denny looked at Robbie then back at the photograph. "Psycho assassin looks a bit like you, I reckon. You harboring any ill feeling we should know about?" Denny raised a pantomime eyebrow—always the joker.

"What's the opposite of disgruntled?" Robbie asked, throwing his mate off. He took the newspaper from Denny, offered it back to the first-year in front.

"I'm done with it, you can keep it," the student said.

They reached the head of the queue. Denny gratefully accepted three slices of limp roast beef before loading up on potatoes and veg. Robbie was happy with half the amount, avoided the mashed pumpkin—its orangeness was near luminous. They sat down at an empty table.

"Progesterex, huh? You've got to be careful," Denny remarked.

"I think the kid was right," Robbie replied. "Progesterex is some made-up drug, an email hoax or something. Doesn't even exist."

"Well, that's besides the point," said Denny, unfazed. "What I'm trying to say is there's so much bad drugs going about these days. In the old days, drugs were cool, they were pure."

Robbie ignored him, speared a roast potato.

"Those were the good old days," Denny rattled on. "Drugs were straight out available. They gave you cocaine for a toothache. Issued the stuff as lozenges. For kids!"

Robbie looked up.

"Cocaine for kids? You talk such shit, dude."

Denny put his hand on his heart; indignation gave way to sincerity.

"In the old days, I swear it. Sherlock Holmes lived on coke; it's in all his books, you can read it yourself."

Denny smoked pot regularly—like half the kids in res. He also took Ecstasy on occasion—not quite as popular but not unusual. The most frequently abused drug was still alcohol.

"Then there's Horse. Our grannies nailed it for their coughs," he laughed. "Fucking cocaine wine made from cocoa leaves. Can you imagine that? Two chardonnays with cocaine, please barman!"

Robbie ignored him, turned his attention to the *Argus*. He scanned the smalls for any cash-generating opportunities.

"Opium for asthma," Denny pressed on, unabated. "MDMA for psychotherapy."

Robbie turned to the sport pages.

"Anyway, I just wish we could have grown up in a cleaner age, when our drugs were the real thing. Not cut with rat poison and baking powder and other crap. You know, real coke, pure as the driven snow, the stuff that Keith Richards lived on. 'Cos if he were kicking off his career today, he wouldn't last five years. Or MDMA just as is. Life would be so much easier."

Denny's address seemed to be at an end. Robbie's weather-beaten Nokia beeped with appropriate timing. He frowned, pulled it from his jeans pocket. It said:

FALLON

Robbie's heart skipped a beat. Two weeks later. He hadn't expected to hear from her again.

She'd attached her number with an electronic business card.

"Who's that?" Denny asked. He shoveled creamed spinach in his mouth.

Robbie tilted the screen face towards him.

"Fallon? Sketchy name," Denny said through the food. "What's she like?" Before Robbie could reply: "Two tits and a catcher's mitt. You gonna fuck her?"

"Funny man," said Robbie, shaking his head and rolling his eyes. He looked at Fallon's number then saved it. He'd been out of the dating game for so long.

"See that guy over there." Denny pointed out a student in a blue

Heineken vest. "He was at the Blue Venus with Angie Dean. Colin something."

Denny spoke with his mouth full, his teeth in a trench war with the food inside.

"I thought you weren't there."

"I wasn't. Friend of a friend was. Knows him."

Robbie snorted and looked at the student, then glanced around the room—mostly men, a sprinkling of loyal girlfriends looking fresh and shiny. Melanie often used to eat meals with him here.

"Said she was wasted!" Denny emphasized, looking in Colin's direction.

"Figures," Robbie replied.

"Dodgy number," Denny said, staring at Robbie, still chewing. He pointed his knife. "Your mate, china. Beacon. Was either him or our friend Colin over there, I reckon." He nodded his head in time with the pointed utensil, then shoveled in another dollop of spinach. "What you think, huh?" He rubbed his stubbled cheek, hard bristles protruding like tubers on an overripe potato.

"Geez, who knows, man?" Robbie shrugged. He had spoken to Tony Beacon who denied knowing Angie Dean, was more interested in making plans for the upcoming long weekend. "I heard she was back in lectures last week already. Maybe she's just an emotional chick who got too pissed."

"I don't reckon. Not the first incident from what I hear," Denny said. "Some guy out there's cashing in on his Rohypnol supply—and I think we're missing out. Haha!"

Robbie put down his knife and fork. "Christ, Denny, you're going to make a first-class father someday."

"Sorry, couldn't resist it." Denny burped and rocked back on his chair.

Robbie shook his head and scrolled through his contact list to a name, pondered what to do about it.

Fallon.

THE USUAL

Julian Lynch tapped an impatient forefinger on the desk. It was getting late. Diva should have called back by now. He wanted assurance that everything was in order, that his Wednesday wouldn't be spoiled.

Ever since Carlos from Dark Video had contacted him to offer a new service, three months earlier, he was a transformed man. Now Wednesday night was his favorite night of the week. His special night. He lived for it. Every second Wednesday, that is. He had to show restraint; had to be careful not to overindulge.

Tomorrow he would pace the fairway with a spring in his step, his secret burning. He would listen to the banter of his fourball and chuckle at the pathetic attempts of his golfing buddies to convince each other they were still young and virile and desirable. If only he could tell them *his* secret.

His cellphone remained silent. Lynch took a deep breath, visualized it ringing, visualized Diva informing him that arrangements had been made and all was on schedule. He swiveled his chair to face his computer; the screen saver showed still images from his favorite videos, a constantly mutating collage of nudity and nature.

He had never gone for anything too hardcore. Of course he'd seen his fair share of pornography, but who hadn't in this online age? It just never fulfilled him. He felt it wasn't right. Preferred the subtler stuff. Younger girls, fresh-faced and naïve. Videos that captured genuine emotion.

But they were hard to come by. It had always been a problem—until he found Dark Video. Or perhaps Dark Video had found him. Such good services. So...specific to his needs.

His favorite clip was one called *Forest Frolic*. The thought of it energized him. He shifted his mouse, the screensaver vanished, revealing his desktop. The background wallpaper showed tiled images of the American teenage singer Miley Cyrus photographed by Annie Leibovitz. Lynch had never understood the controversy they had created. Just beautiful shots, he'd thought.

He clicked on a short cut on his desktop. Windows Media Player sprung to life. The words "Forest Frolic" materialized from a dark background. Lynch took a deep breath and leaned back in his chair.

Early morning, forest scenery. Close ups on the bark of a tree, leaves, sunlight appearing through the branches. Cut to a long shot. A girl appears jogging on a footpath, pine trees to her left, vegetation to her right. The only movement is her bobbing figure approaching from the distance. Cut to another shot. Much closer. Tree trunks intermittently obscure the girl's progress. She is young and pretty, white vest, blue cap on her head, headphones in her ears. She continues past the hidden cameraman, head down, unaware.

Lynch knew the video by heart, had watched it religiously at least once a day since he had first downloaded it a year and a half before. Carlos had told him he would enjoy it. Carlos could never know just how much.

The ambush and abduction was well-edited.

A flash of movement as the three attackers pounce. One wears a red top, hood up, its brightness prominent against the colors of the forest. The girl, surprised, is initially submissive, thinks it's a misunderstanding, tries to continue on her way. Then a struggle as she's lifted off the ground, quickly blindfolded. Legs kicking, body squirming, she's carried into the trees past the camera.

Lynch appreciated the production; whoever had put it together knew what he was doing; realized that it wasn't about the action. The wide-angle footage of the girl being forced to undress was his least favorite part of the clip—he would have preferred less involvement from the other characters—but it passed in a flash of cuts: running shorts off, vest, bra. Then the truly sublime shots once the men had disappeared.

The girl sits on a bed of pine needles, her back to a pine tree, hands behind her head, naked except for her running shoes and a blindfold. The camera focuses in, shows a close up of her face, her lips trembling; lingers on her breasts, the cleft between her legs. Her body is wracked with fear. Then back to her face as her arms eventually drop and tentatively remove the blindfold.

Lynch froze the video on a close-up of the girl's tear-streaked face. He was entranced by the beauty of it all. So much potential. So much for his imagination to work with. He didn't even need to let the video play out because he had a crystal-clear vision of it in his mind: how she nervously got to her feet, gathered her top and quickly pulled it on, located her jogging shorts hanging from a branch just out of reach. The close-ups of her pert little bottom as she jumped in vain. Then a passing jogger coming to her assistance, helping her retrieve the shorts by balancing on his shoulder—some levity to conclude proceedings, then the closing credits—"A Dark Video production"—as he escorted her away.

Lynch struggled to pinpoint just why he found this clip so mesmerizing. So many reasons. The girl was just perfect. But perhaps the kicker was that it was shot in Cape Town. He was sure of it; recognized Newlands Forest, had walked the same route himself. He'd even ventured out to try to find where the filming took place; believed he'd found the abduction spot, but could never be sure about the strip scene, about the exact tree she had leaned against.

Lynch gazed at the girl's face. He wondered what her name was. Whether he'd encountered her in real life. Maybe they'd been in a shopping mall together. Or they'd driven past each other in traffic. Maybe he could meet her one day. It wasn't such a far-fetched idea.

A surge of excitement shook Lynch from his reverie. He needed to talk to Diva. He rang the woman again. After two rings, he was cut off.

He picked up a three-pack of new Titleist golf balls from his desk. The flexibility of Lynch's job enabled him to play golf every Thursday morning with his regular group. He had done so for years, and he had purposefully scheduled his recent Wednesday evening arrangements for the night before. They had revitalized his golf game—the guys had even commented. If only they knew his inspiration.

The grandfather clock chimed once on the half-hour. Lynch paused and checked his old Rolex, an heirloom, not quite as old as the clock, but one of his father's favorites nevertheless. He noted a one-minute difference, loosened the crown on his watch and shifted the minute hand. They were probably both inaccurate, but he preferred them to coincide.

The woman phoned back.

"Sorry about that," she said. Then straight to the point: "The usual?"

Lynch laughed. He put on his black-framed reading glasses and inspected the branding on the golf balls.

"Mr. Lynch?"

"I love your casual tone," he said chuckling. "The usual. Diva, this is anything but usual, you know?"

"Yes, of course," said the woman.

"What about the same girl?" Lynch asked, ignoring her shallow indulgence.

A brief silence.

"As last time? That's not possible," she eventually responded.

Lynch laughed again. "I'm the client. There are other operators out there, you know?"

This time the silence was more drawn out.

"Mr. Lynch, I assure you we offer the best service available. But I can't do that. It would attract too much attention. We don't want to create unnecessary risks—for us or you."

"Fine, fine," he said. "Just thought I'd check. Eleven pm again?"

"Thereabouts," she replied.

"OK." He was about to end the call. "Oh, one more thing," he said, looking at the paused clip on his computer screen. The girl from Newlands Forest. "If I give you a picture, would you consider an order?"

"I don't understand," said Diva.

"I have a picture of a girl who I…like the look of. I would be willing to pay extra. It may take time, I understand. Would you consider it?"

"But, how would—"

"All I'm asking is this. If I give you a picture, will you try to find the specific girl? She's a local. It's as easy as that."

"Right. Well, it may be possible. I'll have to check with—"

"Of course!" Lynch interjected. He loosened the belt of his trousers. "No commitments, of course. I'll give you the picture tonight. Now, speaking of which, make it special!"

Lynch ended the call, slipped the phone into his right pants pocket, and removed a set of keys from the left. He unlocked the single drawer of his desk and retrieved a hard-cover journal with golden binding on the spine.

Carrying the journal, he marched into the sitting room and sat down on the sofa, removed a Parker fountain pen from the top pocket of his shirt, and turned to a fresh page.

The thick burgundy-colored curtains were drawn. The room, furnished with antiques, smelled musty and uninhabited, its couches and chairs in need of recovering. Framed paintings on the walls portrayed no discernible theme: flowers in Flanders, an old fishing vessel, a family crest, a map of ancient Arabia. Years of Lynch family acquisitions, though nothing recent.

Lynch filled in the current date at the top of an empty page, then returned the Parker to his pocket and flipped back to a page dated two weeks previously.

The text began with a careful inventory of a girl's clothing: pale tank top, white brassiere, white jeans, black panties, silver sandals. Tracing his finger across the flowing cursive of his handwriting, he sounded out each word in a whisper. Alongside the various items, he recorded the size and manufacturer. Small, Woolworths; 34B, Triumph; 28 waist, Levi's; small, Woolworths; unknown.

Lynch had also compiled a profile of the girl based on the contents of her handbag. He'd gathered she was a student, a social smoker, liked animals. A single photograph, printed on his Canon Pixma, was glued to the right hand corner of the page.

Lynch had also photographed her clothing, but those were stored with a copy of the girl's ID on his computer in a folder bearing her name: Angela Dean.

The remaining text documented his thoughts and reflections in neat paragraphs.

> *She tasted salty—this was in keeping with evidence of sand I found under her shoes. Presume beach and not washed. Social conventions prevent her remaining with me. But I'm sure she would be grateful to have someone as appreciative as me in her life. I could make her life so much easier. It would be much better—without struggle.*

The final comment on the page read simply:

> *I could tell how much you wanted me.
> And I you! In your subconscious you will hold our moment precious, until we meet again,
> I share your unspoken desperations.*

Lynch felt warm. He closed the journal, placed it on the coffee table in front of him. He retrieved his cellphone from his pants pockets and accessed a profile via a short cut. He pressed CALL.

The phone went to voicemail, an automated message.

"Hi, uh, Holly, it's Julian here, your father. Um, you should try to record a personal message on your voicemail, it's much nicer. Anyway, just phoning to say that I haven't spoken to you in a while and I'm thinking of you. Hope all is well at school. Bye now."

He stared at the phone for a while then checked the time on his Rolex. Getting on for 8 o'clock. A good three hours to kill.

STEPPIN' OUT

Bernard Jones, an associate in the law firm of Rosenthal, Lanier & Rifkind, followed the post-lunch stream of workers back into the lobby of the Bank of America Tower in midtown Manhattan. He'd allowed himself a fifteen-minute break—long enough to make it out the building and get himself a hot dog from a stall on the edge of Bryant Park, but too short to find a decent place to sit and put his feet up. So he'd scoffed it and drained a Coke while standing, before heading back in—all the while tapping away on his BlackBerry. Bernard Jones prided himself in always being connected. Email, Facebook, Twitter, Google+, Skype, LinkedIn, Hashable—he monitored all his accounts relentlessly. It's how you got ahead, he told people.

The young lawyer hesitated in the building lobby. He needed a leak, but his offices were on the 62nd floor. Glancing at the restroom sign, he figured he'd make it OK and joined the scrum of bodies jostling for the elevators. He preferred the privacy upstairs anyway.

Two minutes later, Jones sighed contentedly as he watched his thick stream of urine disturbing the white naphthalene balls in the men's room on his floor. Cock in one hand, the BlackBerry in the other, he smiled and imagined filming himself pissing—he could have the clip online in minutes.

The restroom door swung open and a figure stepped up to the urinal on his left. Jones shifted his gaze back to his phone, checked his email again. He wouldn't want to be accused of eyeballing someone else's pecker.

The man cleared his throat.

Bernard Jones glanced askew—the newcomer was a huge black man in a dark suit. Why did he choose the urinal right next to him when there were three other empty ones? He couldn't help a quick peek down: the man hadn't undone his fly.

"Hello Bernard," said the man. "Thanks so much for picking this particular lavatory and not the real busy one in the lobby. That coulda made things awkward like."

Jones shook himself and straightened up. "Yeah, do I know you?" he asked, turning towards the basin. He placed his free hand under the tap; the sensor registered and the tap released a short flow of water. He didn't bother rinsing the hand holding his phone.

The man appeared alongside him. He was enormous.

"Carlos sent me," said Samuel Chester.

Bernard froze. *Carlos. Dark Video.* He felt his blood rushing.

"Should I know you?"

Chester looked at himself in the mirror. "You owe Carlos a thousand dollars," he said to his reflection.

Bernard straightened up, looked Chester in the face for the first time. What the hell was going on here, he thought. *He* was the client. What was Carlos playing at having some Neanderthal debt collector approach him at work for a measly thousand dollars?

He summoned up his best court-room confidence. "I don't know what you're talking about, buddy," he said calmly. "And no offense, but you're harassing me in my place of work."

"Nice place." Chester smiled, looked around.

"Yeah, it's great, and the security is pretty good here too." Jones made for the blower to dry his hand. Chester placed a hand on his shoulder to stop him.

"Let's not make a fuss, Bernard. Or is that Bruno?"

"Look, mister, you better leave me the fuck alone or I'll slap a harassment suit on you so fast you—"

The hitman grabbed Bernard Jones by the throat, lifted him off the ground, and thrust him up against the tiled wall in one fluid movement. The young lawyer's BlackBerry clattered to the floor; his feet shimmied back and forth above the ground.

"Light he was and like a fairy," Chester sang softly, looking his victim in the eye.

"What the fuck you doing?" Jones rasped. One of his shoes came off. Chester thrust his huge face forward.

"And his shoes were number nine," he continued the song.

"Please, man!" Bernard implored.

As suddenly as he'd grabbed Jones, Chester released him. He fell to the floor, cowering, but the hitman quickly pulled him to his feet. He straightened his collar, smoothed down his lapels.

"Now Bernard," he said quietly. "Carlos provides you a service and if you don't pay, well, that's just disrespectful. How is he meant to run a business knowing he's being disrespected?"

Jones was flushed red, tears welling in his eyes. He looked despairingly at the door, willing someone to walk in at this moment—then he noticed the key in the lock. His assailant had clearly done this before.

Chester held him firmly by the shoulders. "Ain't no one coming, friend," he said.

"I can write you a check," Jones stammered.

"Heh-heh," chuckled Chester. He reached into Jones's suit pocket, removed his wallet and looked inside. "Would you look at that? There must be fourteen hundred dollars in here. Lotta money to be carrying around, Bernard. So many dangers in the world, never know what could happen. But it must be your lucky day 'cos I understand fourteen hundred's exactly what you owe."

"What? You just said –"

"Shhh, Bernard. A little extra for my efforts, you understand?"

Chester counted out fourteen crisp hundred-dollar bills, leaving a crumpled fiver and a couple of ones, then replaced the wallet and smoothed down the frightened lawyer's suit front once more.

"So the message from Carlos is this. We your agent, Bernard. Don't go cheating and disrespecting on us and not paying your bills, right? Now promise me here that you'll be a good boy. Shake on it."

Bernard Jones offered his trembling hand. Chester consumed it with his enormous paw and flashed a fat grin.

"Then the miner forty-niner soon began to peak and pine," the hitman concluded his tune. He slapped Bernard's cheek lightly. "Don't make me sing the next verse to you, darling Clementine."

With that, Chester bent down and retrieved Bernard Jones's BlackBerry off the tiled floor. The screen had cracked but the phone worked. He managed to navigate to the camera.

"Smile!"

Jones did as he was told, then watched in silence as Chester attached the photo to a new email, addressed it to Carlos, and fired it off into the computer ether.

When he was done, Chester laid the phone neatly next to the basin. "I'll be taking my leave now, friend. Best you clean yourself up before you follow me," he said, winking and pinching his nose. Jones had crapped himself.

A continent away, in Seattle, Carlos's MacBook Pro announced with a ping the arrival of a new email. It contained one word in its subject line: "Done." Carlos clicked on the attachment and a photograph materialized: the tear-streaked face of Bernard Jones, also known as Bruno, back to a tiled restroom wall. Half an air dryer was visible to one side. Carlos couldn't repress a surge of laughter. The picture was priceless; the world's worst passport photo. He clicked the print button, then tacked the resulting A4 copy to his pinboard, sniggering again as he did so.

Carlos seldom allowed such levity in his life, but he felt emboldened now. As he pumped a set of handgrips, he wondered how conventional businessmen would rate his managerial skills. Not many CEOs of a multimillion-dollar corporation would employ the services of a highly skilled debt collector for a measly thousand dollars outstanding. Carlos was no righteous mafia don but he'd had enough of people like Bernard Jones; the principle here was actually important. Carlos wouldn't even see any of the money recovered; he had Samuel Chester on retainer, but piffling spoils from a job like this were his to keep. Luckily Chester lived in Brooklyn; otherwise the operation would have actually cost him money.

Nevertheless, he was pleased with the result. At six-foot-four and three hundred twenty pounds, Samuel Chester was pure intimidation. Word would get around; he'd see to it. Don't fuck with Dark Video. And besides, the picture was a hoot.

Back to serious business. It was time for the monthly systems reboot. Carlos closed down his MacBook, unplugged it, and placed it on the floor beside his desk. Tomorrow, he would remove the hard drive then, after he'd earned himself some brownie points from the wife cooking pizzas in the wood-fired oven, he'd toss it on the coals. The laptop would go in the bin.

Carlos pulled a brand new MacBook from its packaging, booted up and completed the installation of a fresh operating system. He loaded two programs off a flash disk and connected to a remote proxy. He then used tailor-made software to test whether anyone had tried to interrogate any of the thousands of pseudo connections that fed back from the proxy to the thousands of fake servers and workstations he'd created. Of all those connections, only one was his real link.

He was up and running again. The process had taken less than twenty minutes and it was as if nothing had changed. Carlos remote-checked his closed-circuit cameras to ensure the online feed was working; he could check the same CCTV images that went to the security console mounted on his office wall anywhere in the world, as long as he had an Internet connection.

He toggled through the various viewpoints. All in order. Next, he translated a new Google email address and checked his mail. Three new messages.

An encrypted message from Jacker informed him that the arrested Dark Video client in Durban in South Africa had been released, his computer equipment impounded. And a spam message invited him to attend a conference in Los Angeles. Funny, Carlos thought; he can remove virtually all trace of his existence from cyberspace but he still gets spam.

Regrettable though it was, the Durban incident came with the territory. And the sense of satisfaction that came with seeing that smarmy dipshit Jones having had the bejesus scared out of him remained. He looked up at the printout of the terrified lawyer's face and smiled again. He would remove it before the end of the day—it was disturbing his meticulous pinboard—but for now it pleased him.

On a whim, Carlos typed XtremeUltra.com into his Google Chrome web browser. Almost instantly, a pop-up appeared on his monitor.

WANNA FUCK?

The thumbnail depicted a woman with hair tailing down to her breasts. Cheap rubbish, Carlos thought. And the website itself wasn't much better: the usual celeb sex videos—most of them deliberately released as free PR by the talentless starlets in action—and an array of porn clips, from straight-up amateur and professional scenes to gangbangs and midgets and animals and pregnant women. Carlos suspected that if he hunted around the site for long enough, he might discover a back-door code that would give access to the really nasty stuff, but he couldn't be bothered.

He shook his head. This game was fast losing its mystique, if there was any left to lose. There was a certain class about the old days—the clicking whir of the projector, its searching blue light floating through the smoky room like a lantern on a misty night. Soft-lit porn that told a half-decent story. Or jumpy images of blackened terror shimmering on a retractable screen, if that was more to your taste.

But those days were gone.

Now it was instant gratification. Click, click, click. One image of gratuitous nudity overlaying another. Pimply kids with sticky hands tabbing between windows, opening, closing, jerking off without an ounce of wonder in their minds.

What had happened to the class? To the big rollers?

Carlos needed a break. He headed down to the kitchen, flicked on the kettle. Then he changed his mind and decided to grab a cup of coffee down the road.

He strode along the tree-lined 11th Avenue, passed a number of coffee stops before opting for Caffe del Latte on a whim. It was quiet. Privacy was never overrated. After checking his image in the window—short dark hair, lacy white shirt, moustache and glasses—he pushed open the door, approached the counter, and examined an illuminated display board.

"Cappuccino," he ordered.

"To go?" the barista asked. She was pretty.

He paused. "No, I'll have it here."

While he waited for his order, Carlos thought about mortality. Since he never dreamed during sleep, and sleep to him constituted a death each night, perhaps he would dream in ultimate death, that last day when he would not wake and his existence would expire. He wondered what those dreams in real death would be like.

He received his cappuccino, resisted the urge to add sugar, and savored the first taste, sharp and bitter.

A lone customer got up and left. Carlos and the barista were the only two people remaining. The barista lifted the counter and began to wipe down the tables with a wet cloth.

"You look familiar," she said to him.

Carlos smiled. "I don't think so," he said.

She straightened up, a hand on her hip.

"Really? You a movie star?"

"Sure," Carlos replied with a laugh.

The barista giggled and continued to clean.

"My name's Dino Velvet," Carlos joked, enjoying the sound of the name, the sleazy producer of porn videos from the movie *8mm*.

The barista screwed up her eyes.

"No," she said. "Maybe not."

Carlos sipped the cappuccino.

He imagined that the reason for his lack of dreams was because he was alive and he had no time for them. Not dreaming implied that he didn't experience the phase of sleep described as Rapid Eye Movement. He believed that, instead of the daily two hours of REM activity, when the brain of a normal individual operated in a similar state as when awake, his brain would use this time to reorganize the vast mass of information and knowledge he stored in it.

Like a defrag.

Perhaps this enabled Carlos to reuse the space that others wasted on feeble emotions such as guilt or remorse. He had no time for either. Each day life presented its challenges and one could not be sidetracked by indecision.

To prove his point, a few years back Carlos had mounted a night-vision digital camera with over six hundred minutes of recording time on a tripod beside his bed. He had filmed his sleep each night for a period of a week. The footage confirmed that he barely moved during slumber. He invariably awoke in the same position as he fell asleep.

The barista finished her sweep of the tables. She ducked under the counter.

Carlos took another sip of his drink, the chocolate taste of the cooling cappuccino pleased him. Two customers entered the café and peered up at the menu displayed above the barista's head.

"Name's Velvet," Carlos chuckled to himself.

He was enjoying his trip; he made a mental note to visit this coffee shop again.

DROP-OFF

A silver BMW X5 slipped behind Wynberg Park, ducked under the freeway, and ascended at speed into Bishopscourt. A girl in a frilly lace top lay slumped to one side in the back seat, resting her head in the lap of another woman.

"Take it easy," the seated woman said to the driver as she dialed a number on her cellphone. Grey strands of hair protruded from the scarf that covered her head.

"We're close," she said to the recipient of the call.

The car glided through the leafy suburb where mansions hid behind high walls and electric fences and the roads were silent.

"Turn here," the woman said.

"I know, I know," the driver replied. He muttered under his breath.

He slowed and turned into a stone driveway, cameras on either side of a solid metal gate. A dirty white wall reinforced by a row of pine trees hid the property behind it from the road.

The driver's electric window hummed as a uniformed guard approached the car, handgun visible in his hip holster.

"Delivery for the property owner."

The guard nodded, flicked his remote control, and motioned the car through the electric gate. He tried to catch a glimpse of the occupants of the X5 as it swept past him, but the windows were blackened and the car quickly disappeared up the dimly lit driveway.

Half a minute later, the X5 halted in front of the colonial-style house. The woman passenger opened the door and helped the girl in the frilly top to climb out.

"Come on," said the woman, glancing sideways at the surveillance camera mounted above the front door. Her head bowed, she hooked her arm behind the girl's back and shuffled her slowly across the dusty driveway towards the front door, where the owner stood waiting.

"Welcome," said Julian Lynch.

The girl flopped onto the bed in the master suite.

Julian Lynch looked down on her. He smiled, showing both upper and lower teeth. He removed his black-framed reading glasses and placed them on the bedside table. The girl smiled back and stretched her arms towards him.

"Where am I?" she slurred.

He stroked her forehead and undid the first two buttons of her frilly white top. Her hand closed over his.

"Stop it," she giggled. She had a silver memory bracelet fitted with links: her star sign, Gemini, a white opal heart, the letters MAC.

He withdrew his hand, smacked it with the other. "Naughty, naughty," he said.

She giggled again and rolled over onto her stomach.

"I'm sooooo tired," she drawled.

A strategic tear in her black jeans showed a flash of pink panties. Lynch ran his hand across the fabric, felt the electric charge of lust and desire shoot through his veins.

His Motorola cellphone beeped:

All in order?

He thumbed back.

Perfect

Lynch tossed the phone on the desk, took the wooden stairs down to the kitchen, didn't bother with the light. He removed a smoothie from the fridge—Mango flavor—took a long sip. He loosened the cufflinks on his shirt. It had, as usual, been a long wait, but in the course of the evening he hadn't had a single alcoholic drink. He never did on a night like this.

Lynch closed the door of the refrigerator. In the darkness, he nearly tripped over a stack of newspapers. He cursed. He'd told the maid to store them in the garage.

The grandfather clock sounded, issued a string of twelve chimes. Lynch checked his Rolex. *Running a little behind schedule, but all's well that ends well.*

An adrenaline tremor squirted through his body as he considered that upstairs, a beautiful young girl waited for him. And she wouldn't spoil it by asking for money.

He wiped his hair from his face and replaced the plastic smoothie container. Breathing deeply, he paced up the stairs and returned to the bedroom.

The girl was still on her stomach on the bed.

Lynch tucked his shirt into his pants, dimmed the lights, lifted the zone controller and arrowed through the playlist. He had short-listed five possible songs; now he had to decide. He settled on Dido. He bit down on his lower lip, strummed on an imaginary guitar, felt the thrill fill his veins like morphine.

No risk, no comebacks.

Lynch sat down alongside the girl, picked up her silver handbag, and removed a pink purse. Cute, he thought, and opened it; inside a picture of her, bright eyes, haircut like a pudding. He removed the picture and placed it carefully on the bedside table, closed the purse. He located her green ID book and perused the details.

"Hello, Marianne Aletta Combrink," Lynch said.

He transcribed her surname, forenames, country and date of birth onto a pad of paper. She was old enough to vote in the 2009 elections. When he had more time, he would transfer the details to his journal.

No driver's license. The woman said they'd picked her up in Claremont.

He turned her handbag upside down and turned his attention to the contents. *Lip gloss.* Two sticks, red cherry and apricot. He brushed some sand off the white duvet onto the floor. She'd obviously been to the beach at some stage—like the last one. Hadn't cleaned out her bag. He smiled to himself. Attention to detail was his forte. And patience. In the absence of more conventional icebreakers, a handbag told him so much about his date. *Smints.* He thumbed one out of the green-topped container. *Eyeliner, a pen, and a set of keys.* He jangled them, inspected the Donald Duck key ring. *A single tampon.* He paused, looked at the girl; he hadn't considered that, but it didn't matter. *A hairbrush.* Lynch removed loose hair from the brush and placed it on the bedside table alongside the photograph. He gathered the remaining items and returned them to the bag, replaced the purse, and pressed the studs of the bag together.

Lynch ran a hand through his greasy hair. After work, he'd removed his suit pants and pulled on a pair of jeans, kicked off the shoes, didn't bother to remove his collared work shirt.

No perfume in her bag?

He lifted her arm and sniffed, starting at her wrist and moving along to her armpit. The act aroused him. Her arm flopped down when he let go.

"Marianne, I'm Julian," he said. Then he frowned. Dido was wrong. Too haunting. Marianne was a Gemini. Like the Unabomber. He fiddled with the remote, skipped until he found the song he was looking for: *Dani California* by the Red Hot Chili Peppers. It wasn't the lyrics; it was the rhythm. It made him feel powerful.

"Is that better?"

He rolled the girl onto her back, pressed his ear against her breast.

Pump. Pump.

Her heartbeat was regular, no sign of distress. Her eyes were closed, head sunk into the plump white pillows. He licked his finger and ran it along her lips, held it to his nose. Cherry. He repeated the action, this time smudging her eye shadow and running a line along her neck. He pressed his thumbs lightly against her throat, applied some pressure.

Marianne Combrink moaned and her eyes flickered open.

"Ssshh," he said. He loosened the grip, slipped a hand smoothly inside her top and cupped her breast. It felt warm and unfamiliar.

Risk free.

He increased the volume of the music, then removed the hand from inside her blouse, worked it between her knees, the other at the buckle of her jeans.

"Now *this* is the fucking badlands," he said quietly to himself.

THE PROPOSITION

The Claremont strip shimmered under the streetlights.

Inside the Blue Venus, Robbie Cullen stared at the black dots on the tiles above the urinal. Beyond the bathroom, the club was cooking, the cacophony of excited voices almost drowning out the music.

Robbie straightened up and zipped the fly of his faded Lee Coopers. He thought of Fallon waiting for him back at the bar. He pictured her dark eyes, her preening eyelashes like feathers, her full lips; he could almost feel the heat of her body.

Robbie rubbed the elephant-hair bracelet on his left wrist as he made his way to the basins, glanced across at his image in the mirror. His eyes were red, hair tousled; a red-wine stain marked his yellow T-shirt. He adjusted the striped beanie on his head, felt the room vibrate. The whole place seemed to be moving.

"Pull yourself together, buddy," he said aloud.

A stocky guy with forearms bulging sized up alongside him. He wore a Sharks rugby top with cut-off sleeves. Robbie flicked him a look; he seemed too old to be having fun in the Blue Venus.

"What'd you say?" The rugby guy addressed Robbie's image in the mirror.

"Nothing." Robbie sensed the latent aggression, dropped his head and made a show of washing his hands. An even six foot, Robbie was slim and athletic and knew how to handle himself, but he was in no mood for stirring trouble. Having courage meant knowing your fear, he'd always rationalized.

He finished up quickly and left, the swing doors slamming back and forth behind him.

Pressing back into the heated amphitheatre of the Blue Venus, he checked his pockets—a few notes and some shrapnel; less than R100. He wiped his mouth on his sleeve and returned to the bar. The air smelled of beer and spray-on deodorant.

Fallon sat at the bar, her back to him. He placed his hand on her shoulder and she quickly turned, her mouth slightly open, lips glossy.

"Drinks," he said over the noise of the club.

She wore low-cut jeans and a black stretchy top, navel exposed. Tilting her head, she swept her curly black hair aside with a practiced flick, shifting her curvy body on the bar stool.

Pity Denny was not on duty tonight; he'd be good for a few free shooters.

Robbie fumbled in his back pocket for cash. He was never flush; never had been. Food and accommodation came courtesy of his res; otherwise he made do with a monthly allowance of R1,000 from his parents and tried to earn a little extra during semester breaks, running deliveries for the father of a friend. Not particularly lucrative.

"I'll get it," Fallon said. She removed a purse from the black Gothic handbag that hung over her shoulder. A barman appeared as if on cue.

There were twenty-plus seats against the bar at the Blue Venus, a line of patrons waiting to be served, four barmen operating. Robbie didn't recognize any of them tonight. No problem though; Fallon seemed to have things under control.

"The same," she told the barman.

Robbie raised a hand to protest. "You can't pay for everything," he said, embarrassed. She closed a cool hand around his wrist.

"Can. Will," she said, turning to watch her order being poured.

Robbie noticed the guy in the Sharks jersey at the bar counter, a few patrons over. He could see the man was a fighter: football-shaped head glinting in the light, hard emotionless face, salt-and-pepper goatee. *Grey in the beard, devil in the head.*

A gang of teenagers bounced past, faces shining and energy in their steps. The Blue Venus seemed to have become the in place for the six-teen-to-twenty-year-old set. They made Robbie feel ancient. He shrugged them off.

"You really a trustafarian?" he asked Fallon as the drinks arrived. Castle lager for him, tequila for her—to go with the bottle of Pongracz she'd bought on arrival.

"I have some vices," she laughed, holding up her purse. It was bright red and in the shape of a vampire coffin, a Nordic cross on the leather and a silver chain attached to the zip.

"Nice purse," Robbie said.

"Cheers."

Fallon downed her shot without lemon, then topped up her glass of sparkling wine. She took a sip and turned her attention to him.

"So let me guess. You're a student."

"As charged," Robbie replied, raising his bottle. "But I told you that last time."

She leaned back to size him up. "Definitely not commerce with that dress sense. But can't be doing arts either. Please tell me you're not another bloody ambulance chaser?" She feigned a hand on her mouth, waiting for a reply.

"Lawyer? You crazy?" he replied. "Computer science."

She raised an eyebrow, then took his right hand in hers to inspect it.

"Mmm. A cyborg? Clean fingernails, no keyboard grease. This is something of a turn-up for the books."

Robbie shifted on his stool, his hand stiff in her cool hold, stomach turning strangely as he caught the scent of her vanilla perfume. The sensation was new, almost overwhelming.

"So what's your story?" Fallon asked. "You don't *look* like a computer geek." She released his hand, ran her eyes down his chest.

"Looks can be deceiving," Robbie shot back, trying to keep it cool, struggling. "I play rugby, you know. For UCT. Besides, what do I look like?"

"Hard to say, really." Fallon winked at him, then rummaged in her bag for her cellphone. Robbie noted the illuminated screen: new message. He looked away to give her a moment, caught the Sharks guy staring. Robbie gave him a nod and a two-finger wave.

"I might have a proposition for you," Fallon said, gaining his attention once more. "Could be up your street, something you may find interesting."

Robbie tracked the movement of her lips, aroused by the way she formed her words, her sentence a continuous stream, no pauses. He watched her closely, could see the base mask on her face, pupil pinpricks in her brown eyes. She was nothing like Melanie. He noticed a thin silver ring in her belly button, wanted to reach forward and pull her towards him.

Robbie restrained himself. He lifted his Castle and took a sip, willing himself to keep it together, keep the girl interested. Fallon looked at her watch and then across the bar. She stood up.

"Tell me, Robbie," she said. "Do you like fun?"

Robbie paused. It seemed an odd question to ask, like something out of a movie. He had grown up on a farm, spent his school days at St. Andrews in Grahamstown; the girls he knew didn't ask questions like "Do you like fun?"

"If you have to think about it..." Fallon patted his cheek.

"What sort of fun?" he asked quickly.

She gestured flamboyantly with her hand. "If you have to ask..."

Out the corner of his eye, Robbie noticed the Sharks guy detach from the counter and move in their direction. He gripped Fallon's wrist, suspended in midair.

False alarm. The guy walked harmlessly past.

"Thank you," Fallon said coolly. Robbie released her and she disappeared in the direction of the bathroom.

Five minutes later, she hadn't returned. Robbie wondered whether she'd brushed him off, if he'd fluffed his chances with the beautiful girl.

"Do you like fun?"

Why hadn't he had a witty retort to her question? he wondered. He finished the last sip of his beer, noted Fallon's half-drunk bottle of Pongracz.

What the hell.

Robbie went looking for her.

He followed the direction in which she'd left, waited for a moment outside the Ladies then popped his head in the door. A girl at the mirror gave him a dirty look. No sign of Fallon.

He walked past the loos into a thin passage leading down to a restricted staff area. A tall guy with streaked blond hair blocked his path. He looked like a surfer: deep tan, braided white shirt unbuttoned halfway, silver brooch on his breast.

"Staff only," he said. He was good-looking, with a cold smile.

"Did you see a friend of mine?" Robbie asked. He took a chance: "She came through here."

The surfer shook his head dismissively. Behind him were two doors leading off the passage and a metal door at the end, sealed with a lock bar.

"Can I take a look?" Robbie tried to ease past.

"Fuck off, bra!" The surfer was suddenly animated, pushed him back roughly.

Robbie balled his right fist, but restrained himself. He closed his left hand around the canister of Bulldog pepper spray in the pocket of his jeans. But he backed off, turned away.

"Up yours, dipshit," he said under his breath.

"Hey, man," someone said. A pixie-looking chap, with spotty skin. "I saw them take a girl. She *is* through there."

Robbie grimaced, turned back to the surfer. He felt a surge of heat and anger through his veins, clenched the canister in his pocket.

"Look, buddy, I know one of the barmen here," Robbie said. "Denny—"

The surfer grinned and widened his stance. He raised an arm, gesturing back into the club. "You heard me, bra," he said slowly. "Fuck off."

Robbie recognized the onset of his rage. He hadn't felt it for years. Hadn't been involved in a fight since first year.

Patience.

He made to leave.

"There's a back entrance. Down the alley," the pixie whispered.

Robbie retraced his steps into the bar, pushed through the throng, exited via the main entrance. As he jogged along the pavement and turned into the alley, he heard the sound of empty bottles being knocked over and a woman cry out in pain.

Fallon!

He pulled down his beanie and scaled a rusted iron gate, jumped down, feet clattering on the cement.

In the hooded light, a figure emerged from the darkness.

"What the hell's going on here?" Robbie said loudly, trying to interpret the scene in the dim light, each word resonating in the narrow alley. A tangle of drainpipes ran down the damp walls on either side. He was suddenly aware that he was trapped. He froze, took his bearings, realizing that every instant was crucial.

The unidentified man strode aggressively toward him. Behind him, Robbie could see another figure under a light outside the rear door to the Blue Venus. He made out a black-and-white rugby jersey, then a woman in the shadows. She screamed.

"Fallon!" Robbie shouted.

"You're fucking toast, man!" The first figure advanced; suddenly there was a baseball bat in his hands, raised.

Robbie stopped thinking, let the blur of instinct assume control. He feigned forward, then jumped back as the first strike passed within a ruler length of his chest. The miss opened up the batter's stance, allowing Robbie to jam the Bulldog canister into his face and spray, letting fly a debilitating pepper stream that hit home like a liquid bullet. His attacker grimaced and fell to one knee, bat clattering on the cement. Robbie stepped in quickly to deal a second blast from above, directly into his right eye from a hand's-length away. The man cried out in agony as he writhed on the floor.

In a flash, Robbie sidestepped the fallen attacker, advancing, attention focused on the second man. He moved to his right, the Sharks jersey now clearly discernible in the half light.

"Let go of her!"

The man shoved Fallon aside and lunged toward Robbie, something metallic glinting in his hand. Robbie moved quicker, using the lighting to his advantage: dark into light against light into dark. Robbie went for his attacker's face with the Bulldog as his weapon sliced into air.

"Fuck sake!" The Sharks man clutched his face with one hand, thrashed the air with his knife in the other. Robbie stepped off his right foot then off his left to deliver a kick to the knee with the bottom of his shoe. He followed it up instantly with a high-swinging elbow to the ribs, feeling the clean connection and the ugly exhalation of air and energy.

His Muay Thai teacher would have been proud.

Robbie grabbed Fallon by the forearm and pulled her into the doorway. He kicked against the metal door. The lock bar shifted and the door opened. Behind it the surfer with the streaked hair moved forward.

"Hey, what the fuck..."

Pepper spray struck him in the face, and Robbie leaned in with a hard shoulder, smashing him to the floor as they dashed past. Warm air consumed them as Robbie pushed Fallon into the crowd of the Blue Venus. He stopped to take stock for a second, pocketed his mace, placed his hands on Fallon's shoulders and looked her in the face. Her cheeks were flushed red, tear-streaked, the strap of her black handbag wrapped around her neck. He unwound it and lifted it over her head. Behind them he could make out the surfer pulling himself to his feet, rubbing his eyes.

"Come with me! Keep moving!"

Robbie led Fallon through the throng of bodies.

Get out. Don't look back.

Fallon staggered. Robbie steadied her, an arm around her waist, another on her shoulder. They shuffled toward the entrance.

"Hey!" The bouncer sized up Robbie as they reached the front door. Students were spilling out in the street with their drinks, others trying to jump the queue to enter. Fallon's legs buckled, her eyes were streaming, nose bleeding.

"She got wasted," Robbie said, not stopping. He hoisted her over his shoulder, ignoring the whistles, and carried her quickly to his car.

Robbie gunned his rusty blue Mazda Sting down Newlands Main Road, checking the rear-view mirror through swollen red eyes. He'd hardly noticed the residual pepper spray until he caught a glimpse of himself in the mirror.

They were in the clear.

Fallon's head flopped against the headrest, her seatbelt holding her steady.

"Are you OK?" he asked. He leaned across and wiped her face with his sleeve.

"Mmm." Black tear lines ran down her cheeks. Her neck was raw from the handbag straps.

"Where're you taking me?" she said.

"Police," said Robbie, nodding his head firmly. "We'll go back with the cops."

She shook her head. "Please take me home," she said. "Jesus, it hurts."

"What hurts? We must report those—"

"No! Take me home! Please."

Robbie clenched the steering wheel.

"Did they drug you?"

She shook her head. "I'm fine. Please just take me home, Robbie. You don't understand."

"Understand? Understand what? Hey, I know someone who was drugged in that place—it must be the same guys!"

Fallon turned towards him, gripped his arm. "*Please* take me home, Robbie. I will explain."

"Fine."

Robbie followed her directions along Main Road past the Rondebosch Police Station, turned right at the fountain and crossed over Belmont Bridge.

"Turn here," Fallon said, guiding them through Rosebank. They stopped in a quiet cul-de-sac alongside the southerly railway track. Her apartment block was wedged between the Liesbeeck River and the railway line, a depressing paint-peeling court surrounded by a formidable green fence with electric cabling. Wooden postboxes were stuffed with junk mail.

"Here," she said, rummaging through her bag for keys.

As he pulled her from the car, Robbie noticed a dark stain on the passenger seat.

"You're bleeding," he said, leaning in to feel the sticky liquid on the car seat. "Shit, Fallon, you're bleeding. What the fuck did those guys do?"

Without responding, she slumped down alongside his car, rolling on to her uninjured side. Robbie lifted her off the pavement, hands supporting from beneath, the blood seeping from the back of her jeans. He helped her towards the entrance.

"Which one?" Robbie asked, jangling the keys in one hand. Fallon took the keys from him and fingered the opener; the pedestrian gate clicked open.

"Up the stairs," she mumbled, staggering forward.

"Let me," he said, lifting her into his arms. She didn't resist.

"Number 15."

It was a three-room furnished apartment: lounge, kitchen, and en-suite bedroom; cheap furniture and curtains, an empty suitcase in the lounge. No television.

Robbie moved her, half-carrying, half-dragging, through to the single bedroom, felt her groan as she flopped onto the bed, front first.

"OK, let's see how bad it is," he said, reaching around to unfasten her jeans and working them down to her knees. He grimaced as a sticky mess of congealing blood was revealed, spreading from her panties and down the back and inside of her left thigh.

"What's it look like?" she mumbled.

Robbie hesitated a moment, then slipped two fingers under the seam of her panties, pealing them aside and into the cleft of her ass. He noticed a faded lightning strike and sun tattoo flush on her inner thigh, was briefly embarrassed by the sudden wave of arousal that ran through his body.

"Erm, shit. Not good."

It was a deep gash, running diagonally just below the tattoo, the length of a box of matches, edges jagged and open.

Robbie moved quickly. In the kitchen, he found a bucket and filled it with warm water. Using a face cloth and towel he'd located in the bathroom, he cleaned the wound and dried it, pinching the edges of flesh together tightly. Fallon moaned in pain. When he released his fingers, the wound gaped open again.

"This is going to need stitches," he said. "And a tetanus shot if you haven't had one. How'd you get it? Barbed wire or a fence spike or what? Or..." Robbie recalled the metallic object in the second attacker's hand.

"I don't know, something. I'm fine. No stitches," Fallon replied. "Just bandage it. Check the bathroom cupboard."

Robbie returned to the bathroom and opened the cabinet above the basin. He scanned the shelves: dental floss, mouthwash, Panado, various hair products, perfume, a roll of bandage.

"This isn't going to work," he called out.

"I don't care," she said firmly. "Do what you can."

He found what he was looking for: needle and cotton.

"I can stitch it," he said, returning to the bedroom.

"Jesus, if you must."

She lay on her stomach, face in the pillow.

He sterilized the needle with the mouthwash, then got to work, starting from the left, the needle struggling through the flesh. Last time he'd played doctor, he'd stitched the dogs on the farm. Not that hard, really.

"One," he said, as the needle exited the other side of the wound. "Two...three..."

Fallon pressed her face hard into the pillow as Robbie drew the stitches —eight in total—and then dabbed the wound with the damp facecloth.

Not bad, he thought, admiring the zigzag pattern.

He filled a glass with tap water in the bathroom and returned to the bedroom with a couple of Panados.

It was a stark room, with two ugly paintings of countryside scenery on opposite walls, a single yellow lamp fitting in the center of the room, a lamp shade with butterfly patterns on a narrow table by the bed. The room didn't suit her, thought Robbie.

"You looking at my ass?" said Fallon, unmoving, still on her front.

He was now.

"Here, take these when you can," he replied.

Robbie picked up Fallon's soiled jeans, noticing the expensive horse-shoe label on the back pocket: True Religion. He laid them gently on the edge of the bed and sat down next to her. Her body tensed as he touched her forehead then relaxed as he ran his fingers softly through her hair.

"My foot hurts where I kicked that fucker," she said.

"I'll get some ice."

In the kitchen, he opened the fridge. A smiley-face Butler's pizza box held a half-eaten medium feta and avocado. An unbroken six-pack of Hunter's Dry cider rested on the bottom shelf. Old jars of pesto, salsa, sweet chilli and mayonnaise adorned the side rack, but the central shelves were otherwise empty—more the fridge of a student than a trustafarian, thought Robbie.

Robbie removed an ice tray and closed the door. An assortment of magnets retained Mr. Delivery tokens, rates for Nanucci, the local laundromat, a letter to tenants. Nothing personal.

Robbie heard a car pull up in the street outside. He stopped and listened. Except for the hum of the fridge, the flat was silent.

Then a loud ring from the intercom.

Fallon appeared in the doorway in her red panties.

"You've got to get out of here!" she said urgently. Her face was pale and tense. She looked much shorter without her shoes.

"What's going on?" Robbie asked. He put down the ice tray and patted his pockets, checked that his car keys and the Bulldog were in place.

"Look, you've just got to go." She hobbled as quickly as she could to the front door to unlock it, turning to him. "Go down the back steps. My boyfriend...he'll never understand. Please, Robbie! Quickly!"

Robbie moved toward the door.

"Boyfriend?"

"I'm sorry."

He looked her in the face, her cheeks still marked with mascara, hair unkempt across her eyes. It suddenly hit home that this was dangerous and unprecedented territory for him. *Jesus, I was up against a guy with a baseball bat tonight!* Still, as he turned to go, he realized he desperately wanted to stay.

"Wait!" Fallon called.

She stepped forward on tiptoes, placing a hand on his cheek and delivering a full kiss on his mouth.

"Now go."

CLEANUP

Julian Lynch stretched, stripped the sheets off his bed, and walked barefoot across the worn Saxony carpeting into the bathroom, closely inspecting the bloody stain that had faded to a pale-brown color.

That was a first.

He bundled the soiled linen into the wash bin, lifted the toilet seat and urinated, one hand directing, his weight shifting from one leg to the other.

In the steamy cabinet mirror, he gazed at his unshaven face and the red blood vessels inside two black eyes that stared back at him. A chill ran down the back of his neck as black-and-white memories of a distant yesteryear merged with the color image in the glass.

He looked away and checked the time on his Rolex. The Dark Video operator had been late in attending to the disposal of the girl.

Another, less pleasing first.

Lynch flushed and closed the shower door, let the stream rain down on him. By the time he emerged, condensation ran from the tiles as in a damp cave. He gave the wash bin another look.

Better not leave it for the maid.

Wrapped in a towel, he carried the sheets down the wooden stairs through the main living area into a wide, farmhouse-style kitchen. Used wine bottles, mostly reds, lined the shelves and a large cardboard box blocked the exit to the outside door. A section of ceiling skirting had peeled away and hung untidily down the wall.

He pressed the sheets against his face, savored the illicit scents before stuffing them into the washing machine. An electric hum and the sloshing of water signaled the rapid disposal of evidence.

An hour until dawn, yet Lynch felt electric, more inspired by the last six hours than he'd ever been in his life. He dropped the towel and pulled on a long-sleeved vest, feeling like he'd shaken off a dusty coat, emerged from a swim in icy waters.

Half-naked, he retraced his steps across the living room and into his study where he stopped before a blinking monitor. He screwed up his eyes in the dim light, his slouched image reflected in a wall mirror. His legs were too long for his torso. He reached down and patted his crotch, his bent penis hanging like a tap between his legs.

Stepping over a cardboard box of books, he sat down before the monitor and clicked the cordless mouse. Microsoft Calendar opened automatically on 17 April, the morning jammed with staff performance reviews, an afternoon insert for Thursday golf. A recurrent appointment with the club masseur was arranged for Friday afternoon.

His silver Motorola rang. He knew it would be the Dark Video hag.

"Everything OK?"

Lynch leaned back in his chair, an afterglow of tension releasing slowly from his muscles.

"Diva. Well, yes…"

"Thank you," she said curtly and cut the call.

Lynch stared at his silent phone. He wanted to talk, to share his thrill with someone. But no one besides the woman could ever know of it, let alone understand the visceral, life-giving energy that it extended to him.

He closed his eyes and ran over the events of the night in his mind. For forty-five minutes, he sat calmly, eyes shut, a half-smile on his face, as light began seeping in through the windows. Finally, the electronic buzz from the mounted zone player distracted him. There was one in each room—white aluminium speakers with built-in amplifiers. Their presence looked alien, incongruous in the crumbling colonial house.

He picked up the controller to the wireless system and replayed the last song. *Dani California.* Last night had passed too quickly; he wished he could have kept the girl longer. He listened until the chorus and then muted all the zones.

Looking up after replacing the controller, his image reflected again in the adjacent mirror. Black hair flopped over his ears, the split fringe like two drawn curtains. His eyelids were wet and heavy.

Lynch looked away quickly and held his hand under his nose. He could still smell her, the musky scent of her sex on his skin. The memory ignited a fuse. In his head, the Chili Peppers were upping the ante, showing their teeth.

He slid his hand along the curved base of a bronze statuette, a bust of Hertzog, then picked up a silver charm bracelet and twirled it in his hand.

He'd taken it off the girl.

MAC.

He fingered the individual initial charms on the bracelet. It would serve as record. Along with the two semen-caked tissues he'd used to wipe her down, before dragging her into the shower and cleaning her off with the shower hose.

He toed his bare foot against his golf bag. The gleaming silver heads of his Titleist clubs seemed to be inviting him to select one. He put down the bracelet and drew out the three-iron.

This new game is dynamite.

It occurred to Lynch that he may be addicted. He needed to take care, not get too carried away.

Once a fortnight only.

There was no space to swing the club. He shifted a pile of books.

Would it be so bad to increase the frequency?

He lifted the club above him and brought it down slowly, touching the head against the leg of his desk.

He needed to talk to Diva and discuss options. Not all of the girls delivered to date had been to his taste.

But this last one...

He slid the club back into his golf bag. They were playing Steenberg as usual tomorrow. Lynch had shot 36 on the back nine last time around.

Pulling his vest down, he pushed his chair back and returned to the kitchen, opened the washing machine, and removed the wet linen. The stain on the sheet was still visible on close inspection, the white of the sheet now a light pink.

"Shit," he said, stepping back and considering the problem with hands on hips. Water pooled on the floor beneath the sheets.

He opened a cupboard and retrieved a large plastic bag, stuffed the sheet inside.

The clock chimed the hour—Westminster Quarters, two strokes. Lynch checked his Rolex and confirmed it was spot-on.

SUSPICION

Carlos woke from a dreamless sleep, rejuvenated and inspired. A positive sense that something good was about to happen ran through his veins.

After completing his morning plyometrics—consisting of sit-ups, push-ups and walking lunges—he toweled himself off and digested an Interpol report listing Dark Video as a global Internet crime syndicate. Carlos laughed at the appropriateness of the term; Jacker had hacked the confidential document from the hard drive of a French police commissary who was employed as an Interpol liaison officer.

The beauty of the Net.

The authors of the report lamented the lack of cooperation between countries in the ongoing policing of online felonies, as well as the corruption in specific police forces that continued to prevent meaningful progress being made. It warned that transnational syndicates were using technology to forge links with one another.

"'When good gains an inch, evil adds a yard,'" Carlos read out loud. He chuckled at the quote, from an unnamed source at the FBI. "I like this!"

Carlos believed in staying close to his adversary. Interpol's huge database recorded Dark Video as a criminal organization, but the fields storing the organization's member details—fingerprints, DNA, addresses, passport and identity numbers, criminal records, known associates—were all empty. Not one name listed.

Carlos smiled when he saw this. He was aware, and had documented, a number of FBI attempts to break into his network. They posed as clients, hired hackers, had even tried to sell him illicit video material. But the Feds were always fishing, and he'd always managed to stay one step ahead. And since they weren't even aware of what his crimes were, the commercial pirate sites attracted most of the FBI's investigative resources.

Still amused by the many fruitless attempts to pin him down, he connected to Dark Video and tested the login script. The Dark Video website operated as a parasite; it stuck to its host site like an undiscovered tick. Every couple of months, Jacker would move the website to another host. Carlos would double-check the links and protocols to ensure the move went smoothly and undetected. He preferred not to leave anything to chance.

Carlos whistled contentedly as he moved his own Internet connection link to one of over a thousand pseudo connections that dangled from Dark Video's host. Happy that his virtual security was intact, he retired from the office to make his preparations for the day.

He showered and groomed himself, then dressed in a pair of waist-hugging black jeans and a tight black T-shirt. Checking his watch, he noted that his wife would have taken the kid to pre-school and probably be having a coffee in Bellevue Square round about now. She'd be back in half an hour. He confirmed her location on his GPS tracker then phoned her to be sure, listened to the noise of the mall in the background.

"Everything OK, honey?" she asked.

"Perfect," he said, ending the call.

In the kitchen, Carlos opened the fridge, contemplated breakfast. Nothing took his fancy. He thought about the pretty barista in the coffee shop on 11th Avenue. She'd thought he was a movie star. The memory brought about his second smile for the morning. He closed the fridge, whistled to himself.

"I know what I want," he stated aloud. He'd decided to take a stroll to the Balcker's speciality store.

Carlos felt secure, desirable. On his game. Moving leisurely down the aisles, he filled a trolley with luxury items: smoked rainbow trout, a French brie, Castelvetrano olives, Tall Grass baguettes, Pommery Champagne, a decent Bordeaux.

At the till, the cashier checked him out, he was sure of it. She had a pokey face and an unflattering haircut—but always nice to know he still had it.

"You live around here?" she asked.

Carlos paid with $100 notes. He smiled at her. "Sometimes," he answered and winked.

Walking home, he felt an urge to greet a passer-by. Yarrow Point was his home. Perhaps he'd run for city council next year. He laughed at the thought.

The experience reminded him that he occasionally missed exposure to real people, with warm breath and blinking eyes. He'd spent too long in the dungeons of this business. In a month's time, he would turn forty-five. Half his life, he figured, was over—the best part. Or the worst?

Carlos sprayed the monitor with isopropyl solution then wiped it with a microfiber cloth. He appreciated aseptic cleanliness. But it didn't improve the quality of what he'd been sent.

Bzzzt.

A buzz from his security system distracted him. Sometimes he needed to remind himself that physical safety was as important as virtual security. There had been two break-ins last month in Yarrow Point.

He checked the security cameras then removed a pistol-shaped device from a drawer. He turned it on, fiddled with the controls, and examined its small monitor. This Interceptor device enabled Carlos to sweep the entire residence for intrusive devices. He twisted the frequency and scanned a wide range, stopping when the monitor isolated each of his external security cameras. No foreign broadcasters in this house, he concluded, turning off the equipment and replacing it on his desk.

"Honey!"

He heard his wife call, then silence.

This really irritated him. She'd call and then say nothing. No question, no command. She'd wait for him to go looking for her. He pushed his chair back, lifted the handgrips in his right hand and squeezed in and out.

"Honey!" she called again.

He traced the shrill call to the bedroom.

"What?" he said, pumping the handgrips.

His wife looked up, painting her nails, cotton wool between her toes, chewing gum. A copy of the latest *People* magazine was open on the bed.

"What's the matter?" he asked. His right hand began to cramp. Carlos ignored the pain, pumped in and out.

She batted her eyelids slowly.

"Well?"

Something was fucking wrong, thought Carlos. Here she was looking like a skanky starlet, not the prim princess he'd married. He had an inkling that something was up. But he'd checked her cellphone and her accounts thoroughly, all within the last fortnight. Had a detective play a bit of follow-the-Porsche. Nothing.

Perhaps she loved him. He could never be sure.

Carlos's right hand was screaming in pain. He stopped pumping, set the handgrip on the bedside table and rolled out his wrists, listening to them crack.

"Carl," she whined, stretching like a cat, arms out above her head. Her breasts didn't move. "Why don't we ever go anywhere?"

He recognized the tone.

"Let's go somewhere, baby."

"Where?" he said, flatly. His name—real or alias—may not be linked with Dark Video in any way, but Carlos had a pre-Internet past that precluded international travel from much of his plans. The FBI had a long memory; even local flights were a risk he preferred to avoid.

"Somewhere exotic. The East. Or Africa," his wife said, beckoning him to the bed. She didn't know the actual names of holiday destinations. With all her family money, Carlos knew she'd never left the United States except for a trip to Niagara Falls when the viewing boat she was on possibly crossed the international boundary. She thought Africa was one big "place."

"You ever heard of Belgium?" Carlos asked on a whim. He picked up the remote and pointed it at the TV. "You must watch this movie."

"Of course I know Belgium," she said, only half-lying. Somewhere in Europe. A town or a country? Next to France?

"Maybe I'll take you there," he said.

"Why there, baby?"

"There's this great movie."

Carlos flicked on the 40-inch Sony LED opposite their bed and scrolled through his media center, eventually locating the film in question. *In Bruges*. He had watched it three times already. Best gangster movie he'd ever seen. He fancied himself a real-life Ralph Fiennes.

DISCRETION

Two days after the Bulldog pepper spray had been his savior—and he'd spent a surreal ten minutes stitching up Fallon's ass—Robbie couldn't get the events of that night out of his head. Or the resulting questions.

What had happened to Fallon? And why hadn't she wanted to bust those Blue Venus shitfaces?

He'd intended to discuss it all with Denny, but he hadn't been around; busy with university work for a change.

There was something about Fallon. Who was she? A trust-fund kid just having a good time? Not likely, Robbie concluded. Her apartment hadn't made sense; not hip enough. Fallon's Facebook page listed her occupation as a criminal lawyer. Then what was with the ambulance chaser comment? A double bluff? His instincts were telling him to cut and run while he could—but then why did he want to see her so badly?

The morning after, he'd received a text:

Thank you for helping me.

That was it. In the meantime, he'd kept getting flashes of Fallon lying on the bed, his hand on her leg, one side of her red panties pulled up.

Lucky boyfriend.

Then, out of the blue, Robbie returned to his residence after Friday lectures to find her waiting in the corridor outside his room.

He tried to act nonchalant; let her in and closed the door behind, kicked a T-shirt and a pair of boxers towards the corner of the room. "Sorry," he apologized.

"Have you told anyone?" she asked, looking into his eyes. No pleasantries. She wore a grey pantsuit, dressed for success.

"No." Robbie told the truth. He was suddenly glad he hadn't seen Denny.

Fallon seemed visibly relieved, dropped her guard. She placed her handbag on Robbie's desk, exchanging it for a fingered copy of *CelebSpot* magazine. Last month's issue.

"You read this stuff?"

"Not mine," Robbie replied. "Ex-girlfriend. She liked it."

Fallon replaced the magazine and looked at a copy of *The Big Issue*. Homeless people sold it at street intersections. Sometimes Robbie would end up with two of the same edition.

"You want to sit?" he asked.

Robbie's room had limited seating options: the bed, the chair at his desk, the wooden counter down the wall or the ledge under the window.

"I'll pass."

She tossed *The Big Issue* aside, scanned his room. On the back of his door was a dartboard; hanging from one of the six darts, a leather necklace with a shark's tooth. She smiled.

Robbie felt awkward, but he recognized the same feeling in Fallon. A small relief.

"You want some, uh, tea or coffee?" He pointed to the kettle on the counter. Alongside it were a Ricoffy tin and a box of Five Roses tea. A poster of the Stormers rugby team looked down from above. Pride of place belonged to a second-hand bar fridge. "Or a beer?"

"No thanks," she said. "So, you like it in res?" she asked.

Most of the students who'd started with Robbie had vacated the residence, moved into student houses in the neighboring suburbs of Rondebosch, Rosebank, Mowbray and Observatory, dragging clothes for cleaning to the pink Laundry Lady, or Wash 'n Web, eating home-cooked bowls of noodles, buying groceries past their sell-by date at the local supermarket. Robbie had a bursary from Altech, which paid residence fees, not for digs.

"It'll do," he answered.

The awkwardness wasn't going anywhere. And yet the more he was aware of it, the more he wanted her. She looked sharp and sophisticated in her suit; her high heels gave her extra height. Normally she would be right out of his league, but the knowledge of her wounded behind, and the fact that he'd tended to it only two nights previously, leveled the playing field. He wanted her to drop her pants so he could take a closer look at his handiwork.

"Not a man of many words," she remarked, smoothed a hand along his crumpled duvet.

He smiled. "How's your ass?"

She touched her rear. "Want to see it?"

Robbie grinned. "Sure. But don't you think your boyfriend would object?"

She smiled, chose not to answer. "Bit of a fighter, Robbie?" she said instead.

Robbie shook his head.

"You handled yourself pretty well the other night." She took a step towards him, squeezed his bicep.

"I was lucky," he said.

The Bulldog pepper spray canister was hidden in the top drawer of his desk. He'd need to get it refilled.

Robbie didn't enjoy fighting. At school in Grahamstown, he had never hesitated to defend his honor because he was brought up to believe that that was the only way. But somewhere along the line he'd realized there was always one more fight, and it was better to walk away. Melanie had helped him see that.

"What was all that about anyway?" Robbie asked.

For the second time, she ignored his question. She stepped back, looking around the spartan room absent-mindedly, circled him. "I need a special favor. Two in fact."

He nodded, noting her businesslike approach, the sentences clipped into words—the come-on he thought he'd noticed gone; no longer that sexy Blue Venus drawl.

"The first: discretion," she said, looking intensely into his eyes.

"I can do that."

"Look, I know I owe you some answers. But it's very sensitive. I'm sure you've done some homework."

"Ambulance chaser, huh?" he replied.

She offered a wry smile. "Look, just be discreet and keep a low profile. I recommend you give the Blue Venus a wide berth."

Robbie frowned. It was the same advice he would give her. But she was right. People knew him.

"I was wearing a beanie so I think I'm good. Who were those guys in the alley? That surfer guy?"

Fallon gripped his arm. Her long fingernails were painted red. "Look, it's under control. But you need to steer clear of the place for a while."

Robbie shrugged. "I've been thinking, Fallon. That whole business with Angie Dean. Is it related, I mean, to what happened to you?"

"I'm sorry, Robbie. I want to tell you. But..." She patted his cheek, opened her handbag, a demure grey leather number, and removed an envelope.

"My people want to thank you," she continued. "For helping me."

"What the hell? Your people?" Robbie suppressed a laugh.

"There's five thousand in there," she said. "Take it."

"Five *thousand*?" His face reddened. "Holy shit, Fallon, I can't take money from you. Who the fuck are *your* people?"

Robbie was suddenly feeling very uncomfortable.

"Special forces," she replied cryptically, offering the envelope.

"What? You some sort of police?"

Fallon nodded once, didn't say anything.

Robbie withdrew his hands. "Look, I can't take money from you," he repeated.

She placed the envelope on his desk. "Robbie, don't be modest. I... We want you to have it. It's a guarantee."

"How so?"

"For discretion. You need to stay away from the Blue Venus and forget what you saw. We're involved in an extremely sensitive undercover operation. I have authority to incur expenses in protecting our interests."

Robbie eyed the envelope. Five thousand rand would make a big difference in his life right now.

"I'm very serious," Fallon continued. "This could be a life-and-death situation. You must never refer to what happened. And don't tell anyone that you know me."

Life and death?

Robbie was floored.

"Uh, I....People saw me meet you," he told her. "The first time. At least two of my friends know your name."

"That's fine. We met. Nice guy. Nice girl. Nothing happened. If you see me, it's like, 'Hey, where did I meet you again?' Not sure. Maybe mistaken. OK?"

He nodded, recognizing the reality. Felt suddenly foolish. Clearly this wasn't going to blossom into any form of romance.

Special forces? Geez!

She looked casually around his room. "No female touch?" she remarked.

"Unfortunately not."

"Oh? Sad story?"

"My girlfriend dumped me."

"She'll be back."

"Oh, I don't think so. She's got a new boyfriend. Picasso the painter."

"Fidelity was not Picasso's strong point."

Robbie didn't get it, but he smiled.

Without warning, Fallon stepped forward into Robbie's space. "You have eyes like big blue swimming pools, you know?" she said. "They really are beautiful."

Robbie felt his stomach drop.

She leaned into him and kissed him lightly on the lips, a wave of her vanilla perfume washing over him. "Goodbye, Robbie."

She'd done it again.

Robbie didn't say anything as she left. Couldn't say anything.

Only after she'd gone did he realize that she hadn't told him what the second favor was.

SCOPOLAMINE

Julian Lynch waited for the man at a table by the window. The Pump in Green Point was packed as usual; a two-week waiting list for reservations, even for lunch.

"You ready to order, sir?" The waitress appeared to flirt with him, flicked her hair, eyelids fluttered.

"Call me Julian," he said, eyeing her, greedy. His smile opened to reveal both upper and lower teeth. He wore a regulation grey suit with a striped tie. "I'm waiting for someone."

"Kay, Julian. I'm Kim. I'll be looking after you today. You just shout." She spun around, wiggled her bum.

Lynch scanned the eatery: the architecture exposed red brick walls and metal ceiling beams; the clientele were mainly men in dark suits, huddled forward, in earnest discussion. He was mentally recounting the minutes of the morning's financial meeting at Premier Marque's offices when a figure stepped up in front of him.

"I'm Kryff."

The man called Kryff pulled out a chair and sat down without shaking hands. He wore a dark-grey V-necked jersey even though it was warm outside. Lynch observed him carefully as he took his seat; his guest did not meet his eye.

Kryff had a narrow face with thin brown hair, a sharp pointed nose and pencil moustache over a small mouth. He looked to be in his early forties and was slight of build.

"How did you get hold of me?" Lynch asked.

Kryff sniffed and fingered his moustache with thin fingers. He picked up a knife and inspected it.

"It's a small world," he said.

He cleaned the knife with a napkin; repeated the procedure with a fork. When he looked up, he blinked his eyes as if the light were painful. They were the eyes of a jackal, thought Lynch.

He observed his guest closely. They had never met before, had only spoken once on the phone and exchanged a few text messages.

The previous Wednesday night, the Dark Video woman had failed to deliver. He had clearly told her he wanted to play every Wednesday now. Lynch, livid and desperate, had left an unflattering voicemail on her phone. Then several more. The following day, seemingly from nowhere, he'd received a phone call. At first he suspected blackmail, then he realized Kryff was offering a service in competition to Dark Video. At a competitive price.

"No seriously," persisted Lynch. "How did you find me?"

"Competition gets careless," sniffed Kryff.

Like Carlos's Dark Video operative, Kryff exploited the underground operation of barmen called the Mickey Finn Club. Orders were pre-arranged by operatives acting for clients, or occasionally by the clients themselves. A money transfer starting at R5,000 generated a reference number for an "accredited" establishment. To initiate a transaction, the operative would quote the reference number to a contracted barman and point out the target. The barman would slip the target the chosen drug. Roofies usually. And that was it. No guarantees. The rest was up to the operative.

Kryff screwed up his eyes against the light and scanned the restaurant.

The tables at The Pump were well spaced. The room resembled an industrial loft, mirrors and large framed portraits of angels softening the look.

Lynch followed Kryff's gaze across the room. He seemed to be looking at a table of three men deep in conversation.

"Clients of yours?" Lynch joked. Kryff did not look like he frequented restaurants like The Pump.

Kryff shook out his napkin and smoothed it over his trousers. The waitress, Kim, returned with a bottle of mineral water. It had already been opened. Lynch sent it back.

"You get my request?" Lynch said.

Kryff craned his neck to the specials chalked up on a framed board then briefly perused the menu. He looked back at Lynch.

"Yes. I recommend a new product from Columbia," Kryff said.

"Oh," said Lynch, curious. Lynch had been doing some exploratory homework. On YouTube, he'd admired a barman's sleight of hand while slipping a roofie into a Vodka and apple juice. He'd had to pause the clip second time round to see that it had actually happened.

"We've had problems with roofies and GHB," Kryff said as if reading his mind. "You can never be sure of the quantity. A young girl in Germany died from an ill-judged dosage."

"Really?" said Lynch, intrigued.

"Not the first. And other disasters. Vomiting, defecating. Not really conducive to the entertainment a person might be looking for. You understand?"

Lynch nodded.

"So this Colombian pill..." Lynch began.

"Scopolamine," interrupted Kryff. "It inhibits the formation of memory. Even under hypnosis, they don't remember what happened."

Kryff sniffed twice, touched his nose with his index finger. He removed a glass phial from his pocket, slid it over to Lynch. A piece of paper was fixed to the tube with an elastic band.

"...because the memory never recorded it."

Lynch removed the note attached to the phial, glanced at it briefly then tucked it into his shirt pocket. He left the phial on the table.

"The victim never remembers?" Lynch repeated.

"Victim?" Kryff replied.

Lynch chuckled.

"Sorry. The beneficiary! Whatever your term of choice."

Kim was back with an unopened bottle of mineral water and traces of a sulk. "You gents ready to order?"

Lynch chose vitello tonnato. The menu described it as roast veal drizzled with anchovy sauce. Kryff pointed to the calamari.

"And for mains?"

"Later," said Lynch.

She nodded. Kryff looked straight ahead as if transfixed by the patterns on the wall behind Lynch's back.

"Can I open it?" She pointed to the mineral water, checking Lynch for consent.

"I'll do it."

"And I can't interest you in anything from our wine list?"

Lynch raised his hand, palms forward. Kryff ignored her.

"Thank you, gents," she said, turning to go.

Lynch noticed the length of her cocktail dress. She wore no stockings and her legs were white and blotchy. Still, he thought she was sexy: big boobs on a narrow waist, small pouting lips, a hint of chubbiness on her cheeks. He could work with that.

"Right, the beneficiaries," Lynch took up the thread. "We do them a service. Only they don't know it." He patted his pocket. "So, this new Sco- whatever? Tell me about it."

"Scopolamine. Also called Devil's Breath. Legend has it they used sco- polamine to drug the slaves of deceased Inca kings and bury them alive."

Kryff was a character from the fringes, a grey man without attachments or accoutrements. Almost without history, as far as anyone knew. His birth date had passed three days ago but he was unaware of this fact; it was thirty years since he had celebrated a birthday and even then it was the incorrect date. He had done his time in the netherworld of society, where any vestiges of moral direction he may have acquired in foster care in rural Aliwal North were reduced to dust.

He had no memory of his parents. In his early teens he had run away to Johannesburg where he'd scraped a living on the street as a male prostitute going by the name of Eric—in those days an even less desirable profession than today. One day he'd escorted a wealthy client to Durban and decided to stay, employed first at a petrol station and later as an apprentice in a garage. For ten years before his arrest, he had worked without any ID as a mechanic in an autoworks.

He'd come a long way since then. He'd come a long way since his first venture into the drug-rape business, in fact.

"So scopolamine isn't actually new," he said. "Been around for centuries. But this latest concoction is certainly innovative. And more efficient. Perfect for your requirements."

Kryff stared down at his hands, folded on top of his place mat, as he spoke.

"Hold on a second. Why did they bury the slaves?" Lynch asked.

"Bury the slave? So they could never leave their master. So that the king would always have his servants with him. The Nazis used it too. You know, Mengele? Some interesting experiments. And the CIA, of course."

After serving his time in the early '90s, Kryff had emerged into a new era of human rights. He'd received a new identity and a hypothetical second chance. But he quickly destroyed the new identity, moved to Cape Town, and assumed the name of Johannes Kryff, a Dutch immigrant who had died in the city in 1995. Having fallen off the system, he'd breathed new life into the deceased Kryff.

Lynch didn't know any of this. No one did, except Kryff. But Lynch wasn't interested in Kryff's past; he was interested in what he could offer him right now.

"Jesus Christ. Mengele? The Angel of Death? And the CIA? This sounds like interesting stuff. Is it easy to get hold of?"

"Grows wild around Bogota. A tree called borrachero. And in Ecudaor." Kryff recited the facts without falter. He reached forward and touched the thin phial. "Legitimate medical uses."

Lynch recalled that he had read an article on the stuff during his online investigations. Sensational stories were doing the rounds. In Brazil, hookers rubbed it on their breasts, drugged the punters, and robbed them blind. The clients willingly gave what was asked for.

"Thing is, they seem perfectly fine throughout," Kryff continued, driving home the sale. "They're not groggy or limp or out of it. It's just that they're

...impressionable. And they don't remember anything the next day."

This was the answer, Lynch knew. A twilight sleep, the victim would be a lucid zombie, compliant to any suggestion.

Kryff allowed a faint smile. He knew he had secured another client.

Under his new identity, Kryff had found employment in Cape Town in a sex store in Long Street called Strictly Adult, selling cheap toys to bored women and pornography to shady lowlifes. He'd quickly realized he had found his niche.

And then, one rainy July morning, his luck had changed. Shortly before closing time, a breathless client had entered the shop requesting a stripper for a party. Kryff realized it wasn't an average bachelor party. He located a candidate off the beat on Kenilworth Main Road and agreed a price. In a single swoop, Kryff had a new business venture.

"So how do you take it? By licking?" Lynch asked.

"Yes, that's a way," Kryff replied, without meeting his new client's excited gaze. "It's very versatile. You can use it in chewing gum, for example."

"And what's its medical use?"

"Motion sickness, apparently. In lesser doses."

Kim returned with the starter portions, checked the water, and forced a smile. Lynch noticed her smudged mascara, concluded she'd rubbed her eye. He shook his head as he watched her mince away. He wondered what she'd be like on scopolamine. He wanted to lift her skirt, see what type of underwear she was wearing.

Kryff paid no attention to the waitress. He held the knife and fork in his thin, brittle fingers and sliced his calamari steak into four quarters.

"You want her?" Kryff asked, angling his head towards the departing waitress.

He speared one portion of calamari onto his fork and raised it to his mouth.

Lynch grinned and tested his veal. This was what he was looking for. The next step....Being able to order your date.

"Is that a service you provide?" Lynch asked.

Kryff shrugged. "Tonight?"

Lynch checked the date. Monday. "Wednesday."

Kryff nodded again, noting the excitement in Lynch's voice. Kim cruised by their table and Lynch nodded at her, smiling.

Kryff had little interest in sex. Like any successful drug dealer, he didn't partake in the addiction he traded in. After prison, he had avoided all forms of sexual contact. Fellow prisoners are particularly severe on sexual offenders. Especially when there are children involved. Kryff's only attraction was to a nonexistent young boy called Eric. He was Eric. And that boy was long gone.

"You need to tell me how," said Lynch. "Maybe I'll give it a try myself." He held up the glass phial.

"I would be careful," said Kryff.

The drink spiking game was becoming more difficult. Undercover police, bouncers on duty, more cameras, photographs at entry and exit, water jugs covered with lids, unattended drinks removed. The surest way around the crackdown was the inside job—the advantage of the Mickey Finn Club.

"How much do I need?" Lynch asked, ignoring the warning.

Kryff raised one bony finger, chewed slowly.

"One what?"

"There's five milligrams in the vial," Kryff said.

"And with that they'll be controlled?"

Kryff nodded.

Kryff's first client had lived in Muizenberg. He'd transported the hooker in his faded-red Ford Sierra. She was colored, early twenties, chatty in the car, bright-eyed, unfazed by the assignment. On delivery, the client had paid him a thousand rand, which equated to nearly half his monthly salary at the time. Afterwards, he'd given Kryff an envelope containing another thousand. This, he explained, was for Kryff to return the girl to Kenilworth afterwards.

"I've something to ask you," Lynch said. He put down his utensils and removed a folded photograph from his pocket, passed it to Kryff. It was a still captured from his beloved *Forest Frolic* video.

Kryff inspected the photograph with detachment. He nodded as he chewed, showed no emotion. He forked another quarter of calamari, paused.

"Who is she?" he asked eventually.

"She lives in Cape Town. Probably a university student."

Kryff chewed his mouthful and stared at the photograph. He was making a mental image. Although he'd received no schooling beyond the age of twelve, he was able to memorize faces.

"You can get her?" Lynch asked.

Kryff returned the photograph face down. The back of his scrawny hand was riddled with veins, the manicured fingernails providing no evidence of his previous occupation in a grimy motor garage. The social worker in Durban called them "sex pest hands."

"Won't you need it?" Lynch asked, folding the photograph.

"Put it away," said Kryff, shaking his head. He licked the sides of his mouth, knife and fork held like a surgeon.

"Can you get her?" Lynch asked again.

Kryff continued to chew, looked down, nodded.

When Kryff had fetched the hooker from Muizenberg, he'd realized she was drugged. He drove her to Kenilworth, inserted R500 into her purse, laid her down in a quiet side street and drove away. That was his first transaction—eight years ago now.

A waitress bustled past and brushed Kryff's chair.

Nowadays most of Kryff's clients lived in upmarket suburbs. Although he specialized in supplying working girls—who he considered actresses rather than victims—the big-money clients were only interested in amateurs. To them, it was the difference between a canned lion shoot and the real thing. Although Kryff wasn't averse to drugging the girls himself, he usually availed the services of the Mickey Finn Club.

"What do you do with the girls?" said Lynch, placing his knife and fork neatly together. "Afterwards? You've never had any comebacks, have you?"

Kryff removed the serviette from its ring and dabbed his mouth. A small smile touched the edge of his mouth.

"As long as they're clean," Kryff replied. He put down his knife and fork. The trace of his smile disappeared.

"Ever had any problems?"

"Problems?" said Kryff. His hands were in his pockets, jangling his car keys. "What business does not have problems?"

Kryff's Sierra had delivered promise and fetched problems for four years. It had been reported on a number of neighborhood-watch websites, but he'd never been stopped. He'd reckoned the boot was a Pandora's box of intermingled DNA traces. When he'd got rid of it, he removed the number plates and abandoned it in Langa, keys in the ignition. The insurance claim covered the down payment on a white second-hand VW Polo. By that stage, he could have afforded something better, but he preferred to keep a low profile. Every second car on the road was a white Polo these days, it seemed.

Lynch leaned forward; Kryff smiled again, obliged.

"Take a girl called Mary," Kryff said, his expression changing, voice becoming purposeful. "Anterograde amnesia differs from person to person. So assume that our young lady vaguely remembers being..." Kryff paused. He'd spent many late nights behind the counter at Strictly Adult researching his business. He had tested the drugs personally, recording the memory affects. "Being interfered with. She arrives home. Hysterical. Her friends press her to report the incident to the police. Bad move! That ordeal is worse than the original trauma. The police put her through the post-rape process, get out the kit, take swabs—but they reveal nothing. Because you've cleaned her. The police remind the victim how busy they are, that the majority of date-rape cases are caused by alcohol." At the term "date-rape," Kryff wiggled two fingers on each hand. "Management at the pick-up spot agrees. They don't want aspersions cast on their establishment. Silly girl, she's had too much to drink."

Kryff had learned the technical side of his trade from an elderly Afrikaans-speaking man called Van Rooyen, who had worked at the Maitland Crematorium. Van Rooyen had been a regular customer at Strictly Adult. They weren't associates in the true sense of the word, or even friends, but a symbiotic relationship had developed—only halted when Van Rooyen had died from lung cancer two years before.

Kryff picked up his fork and retrieved another quarter of calamari. Kim the waitress removed Lynch's plate, raised her eyebrows. Lynch waved her away.

"Can I ask you a question?" Lynch said. Kryff motioned with his hand to continue. "Do you fear death?"

Kryff narrowed his eyes. At first it appeared as if he would ignore the question. "No," he answered abruptly. Then with annoyance, "Why? Do you?"

Lynch hesitated. He hadn't expected to be countered.

"For some death is a remedy," said Kryff before Lynch could respond. He pictured Van Rooyen, his once ruddy frame reduced to skeleton, every breath a labor. Van Rooyen had believed that God was "fixing" him.

Lynch frowned. *For some death is a remedy.* It made sense to him. Reminded him of his father.

Lynch looked out the glass front of the restaurant, noticed a vagrant walking by. He imagined Kryff in decrepitude, gaunt face, nose twitching like a rat.

"Getting back to the business," Lynch said. "What if there is, er, a problem? With the girl."

"Like she's broken? We don't encourage…"

Lynch waved his arms.

"No, no. I mean, like she remembers something. She starts to talk."

Kryff widened his eyes.

"If I think there's going to be a problem…" Kryff paused for a moment. "Well, then I remedy her." His upper lip curled over his teeth and he rubbed his thin moustache. He looked Lynch in the eye for the first time.

Lynch glanced about, suddenly paranoid of eavesdroppers, but Kryff had spoken softly.

Kryff had never kept count of his deliveries, but he'd recorded each death for which he was responsible. In the first six years, there were four, all street workers; three female, one male. His associate Van Rooyen had disposed of the bodies at the crematorium. With a better quality of client, extreme measures were unnecessary. Which was all very well. After Van Rooyen's death, disposing of bodies had become problematic. It was one thing removing a nameless street sex worker, whose disappearance would hardly be investigated; another getting rid of a victim sourced from the upmarket establishments served by the Mickey Finn Club. Since he'd started using their service, there'd been no need. But the contingency had occurred to Kryff.

Kryff placed the knife and fork together on the plate, wiped his mouth and stood up. He preferred not to stay for the main course.

"Wednesday then," he said. "We'll see you then." He pointed to the phial of colorless liquid on the table. "Don't forget your medicine."

SURPRISE

Robbie was impatient at the wheel of his Mazda as he headed out of Cape Town. A car in the right lane slowed his progress. He weaved into the left lane, accelerated and overtook, then whipped back into the right again.

Robbie wasn't easily hurried—but a long weekend in Plettenberg Bay, money in pocket...

For the first time in months, he felt carefree and happy. He couldn't wait to be there.

He lifted the hem of his T-shirt and wiped the perspiration. Even with both windows open, it was hot. What he wouldn't give for an air conditioner. Or a new car.

He wrenched down a gear and decelerated into Somerset West. Ahead, Sir Lowry's Pass loomed, but traffic wasn't too bad; he'd be up and over in fifteen minutes. He had beaten the N2 rush hour; Plett was five hours away.

At the traffic lights, Robbie took the last sip of his now-warm Coke, tossed it into the passenger seat footwell alongside an empty hamburger box. He repositioned the fan, so that the steady stream of warm air blew on a different part of his body. Nothing helped. But he didn't care.

Fresh exhilaration swept over him. A long weekend at Tony Beacon's mansion in South Africa's premier holiday resort ranked high in the fun stakes.

He rapped his hands on the steering wheel. He knew he wouldn't be coming if it weren't for the windfall. A cool five thousand rand from Fallon. Perhaps he should become a bodyguard.

Robbie cranked up the volume and removed his shirt. Billy Idol rocked White Wedding from the speakers, a track siphoned off LimeWire. The lights turned and he skipped out of Somerset West, then buzzed the Mazda up and through the pass, U-bends navigated like a fairground ride.

"Don't die on me, baby. One more time, I promise." Robbie urged his car along, one hand on the wheel, one on the dash. He turned down the volume and listened to the engine roaring.

A weekend with Tony Beacon. The Tonester.

Robbie liked Beacon. Figured he was cool. Something always happened at Tony's place. He'd met him on a school rugby tour to Johannesburg in his matric year, hooked up with him in Plett at the end of that year, reconnected at varsity in Cape Town. Beacon had a simple outlook on life: fun, fun, fun. Who said money didn't buy happiness?

The quilted landscape flashed past as he descended into the Botriver Valley, aloes loitering around farm gates, burnt-out farm houses in dry fields—early autumn but in dire need of rain.

Tony Beacon's last few weeks had been rough, though. The university had called him in and quizzed him about Angie Dean. She had been having flashbacks. Remembered a barman from the Blue Venus. One of her friends had mentioned Tony's name, how he was meant to meet her. Now people were talking.

Goldfish followed Billy Idol on random selection. Robbie relaxed and swayed his shoulders back and forth to the beat.

He thought about the tall blond surfer at the Blue Venus.

Fuck off, bra!

He'd wanted to question Denny about him, and about the Sharks bugger in the back—but he'd kept his tongue. He was staying out of it as he had promised. Discretion was worth an envelope of two-hundred-rand bills.

Still, he wanted to know the truth.

Had someone been trying to drug Fallon? Was she a decoy for a police sting? An undercover agent?

My people want to thank you.

Then five thousand rand.

Pleasure, he thought. And yet...

Robbie slowed behind a large 18-wheeler truck with a sticker on its rear declaring that it didn't drive in the yellow line. The truck shifted onto the shoulder of the road and Robbie sped past, flicking his emergency lights. The truck flashed his lights; Robbie waved a bare arm out the window.

He'd chatted to Tony Beacon last week.

"Here's the agenda," Beacon had explained. "First, bring fuck-all. Except yourself. If you've got a chick then bring her, otherwise just come play. But don't bring one, if you know what I mean? Why have one when you can have a smorgasbord, huh, Robbie?"

He'd asked Tony about the Angie Dean rumors.

"Jesus, Rob. Hectic! They kept asking why I didn't call her," Tony had replied. "Fuck sake! I forgot. She's not the only fish in the sea! Know what I mean? But seriously, I felt bad, but I chatted her up on the beach, nothing more. Anyway, drugging a chick—sorry, man, not my style."

"And not like you need to, dude," Robbie had added diplomatically.

"You said it, brother. Bang!"

A row of tatty flags strained forlornly in the wind at Dassiesfontein, but the landscape marched swiftly on—Caledon, Swellendam, Wilderness, Knysna—and as he approached his destination, the blue of the Indian

Ocean sparkled in anticipation. The sign for Plettenberg Bay welcomed him and he hung a right at the circle, exiting the N2 and descending down the hill toward the sea. The Beacon house was situated just off Central Beach. He parked outside, a broad grin on his face as he stepped into the salty air, stretching out the strains of the drive.

Tony Beacon greeted him in a silk gown that flapped open, revealing white boxers. He stood expectantly on the veranda, watching him walk up the drive, one arm around a girl in a tiny blue bikini, the other holding a B2 air rifle at his side. He aimed the gun in Robbie's direction and fired off a shot, the pellet zinging off the bricks a meter to his left.

"Hey man, shit! You could take my eye out!" shouted Robbie, hopping to the side. Tony laughed and skipped down to meet him in the driveway. They clutched hands, African style, then hugged.

"Just welcoming a brother to my house!"

The same height as Robbie, Tony Beacon had a round head with a number-one haircut, a gold stud in his left ear. His eyes twinkled. It was hard to imagine him without a smile. Robbie gave him the once-over, noticed he was wearing white hotel slippers.

"Meet my minx!" Beacon declared, gesturing with a wide arm to the girl in the blue bikini still on the veranda. "For the time being," he followed up under his breath.

"Sylvana," said the girl, offering a token wave.

Robbie sucked in his breath and repeated her name twice. He wasn't good with names.

"She's a local," Beacon added, as if it had consequence.

"I'm from Russia," Sylvana countered, offering first one cheek then the other as Robbie came up the stairs. He'd never met a Russian before. He thought immediately of his father. He'd be blown away; he used to believe the Reds were going to take over Africa.

She was taller than him, French-looking with shaggy hair. Her lips were bright red and thick, almost swollen, as if bees had stung her.

"I thought it was Romania? Ha! You're full of surprises, baby. And you've met Vuka," Tony said.

Vuka waited with Robbie's suitcase. His real name was Mativuka. He had speckles of blood on his white shirt.

"You get all the feathers out?" Beacon asked him. "I shot a guinea fowl. Fuckin' believe that?"

Robbie stared at the gun. Beacon's eyes danced mischievously. He related the story: he'd pulled his rental car onto the shoulder of the N2, aimed into a stray group of guinea fowl, and pipped one in the head with his first shot. The others had flown off squawking in dismay while Vuka climbed the fence, finished off the job with a sharp wringing of its neck and returned with a feathery mass.

"Vuka thought it was a chicken," Beacon laughed. "Funny, hey!" He slapped Robbie on the back.

Judged by the company you keep, Robbie thought ironically. *Denny would have loved this.*

Beacon checked the time on a watch the size of a small kitchen clock. "You gonna roast the big chicken, Vuka?"

"Nkhulu nkukhu," Vuka answered.

Of Zulu descent, he had proud broad shoulders and his smile revealed pearly white teeth. He wore simple cotton pants and a collared shirt.

"A bad scene," Robbie muttered, melodramatic. He didn't need any reminding. On the school rugby tour at a party at the Beacon's place in Dainfern, he remembered Tony Beacon feeding a bonfire with antique heirlooms. Tony was the son of Fergus Beacon, the tissue magnate— apparently he'd been just as wild in his younger days.

"Follow me," Beacon gestured. They ascended a flight of stairs into the hallway.

Upstairs, an integrated lounge and dining room led through glass doors to a gigantic patio with a view over Central Beach into the bay.

"Choose a room," Beacon said, pointing down a set of cement stairs into a dark corridor. "There's a pack of bodies in this fucking house. Careful you don't lie on anybody. Just yet..."

Downstairs, a warren of inter-leading rooms presented themselves off a long passage, each room with its own door opening outside, sea or garden facing. The walls were decorated with framed collections of pansy shells and turquoise paintings of the sea.

Robbie walked past two bedrooms and turned into a room with pale-yellow walls and a sash window opening onto the downstairs porch. Reed grass mats covered aged teak floorboards. He did a quick pat test on the four-poster bed, checking the mattress, then took in the view out to the garden for a moment.

This would do nicely.

At the door, Vuka placed Robbie's bag on the floor, bowed and disappeared into the corridor. "Hey, Vuka. *Enkosi*," Robbie called after him in gratitude.

Robbie whooped and leaped onto the bed, lay there, hands behind his head. It was all rather romantic. He twirled his elephant-hair bracelet, wished that...

No!

He jumped up and threw open a double door leading to the garden, a narrow green strip of lawn, private, surrounded by thick bougainvillea. In the center of the garden, a single royal palm stretched upwards like a giant umbrella. This was some of the most expensive real estate in South Africa.

The view from the deep, white-railed sash windows projected into another bougainvillea bush. A wicker basket of rolled-up towels perched in the corner of the room. Matching fluffy white robes hung behind the door, slippers below.

Pity I don't have a date...yet.

Someone walked past the open door, a girl with dark hair.

Robbie looked up, sucked in his breath. Fallon.

LOTUS FLOWER

The heavy burgundy drapes were drawn. Outside, the Lynch property was unlit and, except for the perimeter wall, unprotected. The guard was gone. Lynch had caught him stalking about the house and peeping in windows; had terminated his service with Protection & Surveillance the following day. One staff member remained: the maid, Florence. In the glory days, there'd been six maids and three gardeners. Not to mention the stable boys.

Bobby Lynch had owned horses. The dilapidated stables still stood at the far end of the Bishopscourt property. Now they were stuffed with bottles and cardboard boxes. The riding gear—saddles, harnesses, bits, his mother's jodhpurs, boots—were all stored out there somewhere, too, but hadn't seen the light of day in decades. Lynch had other preoccupations these days.

Inside the house, in the lounge, he looped the leather handle of a riding crop around his wrist and ran it down the spine of a prostrate girl, halting in the fine hair at the base.

He tickled the tongue of the crop across her ass. He'd wanted Kim, the waitress from The Pump. The idea of made-to-order was an exciting improvement on his standing arrangement with Dark Video. Instead, Kryff had delivered some tart covered in tramp stamps, an earring through her left eyebrow. The replacement was spread-eagled naked on his sofa. Lynch was livid; the new arrangement with Kryff was meant to be a step forward, not backwards. This was amateur. All his anticipation wasted.

He picked up a digital camera, held it in one hand, the crop resting on the girl's ass.

Flick.

He lifted the crop, brought it down gently.

Flick.

There were a number of unwritten laws of the game. Rule one: never physically harm the girl. Both Diva from Dark Video and Kryff had repeatedly stressed this.

Competition gets careless. Lynch recalled Kryff's words from their meeting. It worried him. Who else knew? If he told Carlos about the negligence, he might have to tell him about Kryff. Carlos didn't seem the understanding type.

Lynch put down both crop and camera, placed his hands on his hips, formulating his plan of action.

BITTER PILL

He was frustrated.

It seemed an age now since sweet Marianne. The previous week Diva had failed to deliver; now Kryff had served up this horror show. Lynch cursed. Another wasted Wednesday night. How was he supposed to face his golf game tomorrow? How was he supposed to face the day even?

The girl's clothes lay in a pile on the floor. Turquoise vest, short black mini skirt, black high-heeled shoes. No underwear, no bra. Such a disappointment; he always enjoyed the act of removing the panties....She wore heavy black eyeliner and a strong, almost overpowering perfume. Probably a paid hooker for all he knew.

And she'd been dropped off without a handbag.

Lynch tried to phone Kryff again. No answer.

He paced through to his study and removed his journal from the bureau. An unopened package, a delivery from Amazon, lay on his desk. He swept it to one side, replacing it with his journal, as he sat down in his leather chair.

Lynch was fully dressed; only his tie and jacket removed. His monogrammed white work shirt looked grey in the light of his desk lamp, the collar frayed, pale-yellow perspiration marks under the armpits.

He fumbled for his reading glasses and opened the journal. Through the double doors, the girl was still visible on the couch in the lounge.

Is she even worth an entry?

He regretted cancelling with Dark Video.

The grandfather clock struck once. He checked his Rolex: 11:30 pm.

He considered calling Diva. Was it too late?

Mind racing, Lynch flicked through the pages of his journal—seven entries, Angie Dean and Marianne Combrink, the latest. It was plastered with pictures, items taken and sticky-taped to the pages—a piece of gum, a lock of hair, inscriptions, sketches. A wooden decoupage box contained an inventory of larger items: bangles, a perfume bottle, an Alice band. He leaned back in his chair, absorbed in his frustrated reflections.

His eyes fell on the unopened Amazon package. Impulsively, Lynch ripped it open and removed the content, a paperback. He grunted softly in satisfaction; he'd been waiting for *The Strange Case of Patty Hearst* to arrive for some time now. The granddaughter of the American publishing icon William Randolph Hearst, Patty had been kidnapped at the age of nineteen by a bunch of militant left-wingers calling themselves the Symbionese Liberation Army. After two months' captivity she joined the movement, going on to take part in several bank robberies. Lynch was particularly interested in the way she had succumbed to Stockholm

Syndrome, the condition in which a kidnap victim falls under the spell of her capturer. He already owned a number of other Patty Hearst books; had read *The Trial of Patty Hearst* several times.

A low ring from his workstation attracted his attention. His heartbeat accelerated. He recognized the ring: Carlos from Dark Video.

"Hello Carlos," said Lynch, attaching headphones and talking into an attached microphone. "How can I help you?"

"Courtesy call, Julian. How are you doing?"

Lynch wiped a bead of perspiration from his forehead. Carlos seldom pursued direct contact. In the early days, yes, when the subject of his obsession was changing with regular frequency. But once he'd settled into routine, the calls stopped.

"Erm, all's well. Thank you."

Julian decided to keep it short. *He* was the client. No need to panic. He waited for the time gap to fill and Carlos's encrypted voice to answer.

"OK. That's fine then. No problems?"

"None," Julian replied immediately and adjusted his rimmed spectacles. He pinched his left ring finger between his right thumb and forefinger.

"Why?" Julian asked, instantly regretting the question.

"No reason, no reason," said Carlos. Then after a short pause, "It's Wednesday night there, isn't it?"

Lynch removed his handkerchief and wiped his brow. The long fringe hanging over his forehead masked teenaged acne scars. He could feel streams of sweat running down the inside of his shirt.

The girl on the sofa moaned. In a moment of detachment, Lynch hoped she wouldn't vomit on his sofa.

"Oh," he said, trying to gather himself. "Yes, I see what you're asking. It's month end. Big presentation to the board tomorrow. No time to play, unfortunately."

"No need to explain," Carlos replied immediately. "Just checking our service was up to scratch. No problems with the operator."

"No, uh, no problems....Uh, actually. Yes, I think I should mention it. Last week, I had an order that was not fulfilled."

He stared at the naked girl on the couch and his fury returned. From the next room he could make out the lotus flower tattooed on her lower back, the words DIVINITY, FERTILITY and WEALTH inscribed above.

"Really?"

"Yes. I informed Diva of my dissatisfaction."

Lynch wondered whether he should press home his complaint and ask Carlos about the photograph of the girl in the forest. Decided against it.

Now wasn't the time. Now he wanted compensation for his disappointment.

"Diva? That's not acceptable service, I'm afraid. I must express our sincere apologies. I will have a talk with Diva."

Lynch's mind was racing. Somewhere in the depths of his muddled, angered thoughts, he wished that Carlos could simply interpret his desires and offer him his *Forest Frolic* angel. Wasn't it obvious that this is what he needed? But Carlos was offering him nothing meaningful. And Lynch could not express the roiling emotions within. He did what he always seemed to do in stressful situations; he backed off.

"I have no issue, Carlos. These things happen. It's not an everyday service, I suppose."

"Thank you for your understanding. I will follow up and ensure we are back on form. Swiftly."

"Thank you, Carlos."

The connection terminated.

Lynch removed the headphones and sat staring at the screen. He looked around the room. Carlos couldn't read his desires, but it seemed as if he could see into his house. Did he know all along there was a low-class good-for-nothing whore lying unconscious in his lounge—arranged by Kryff?

"Fucking Kryff," he cursed.

He tried to call him again. No answer.

Lynch strode back into the lounge, kicked at the drugged woman's clothes. He felt nothing for her. She may as well be dead.

He picked up the crop and poked it at her rear. He'd photographed her tattoos, thought about sketching them in his journal—then laughed scornfully at the idea.

Fucking Kryff.

He'd been wrong to give another operator a look-in. At The Pump he'd been sucked in by the opportunity to actually talk to someone else about his desires and needs. The Dark Video woman never made conversation. And Carlos was all business. But Dark Video understood the product he desired; Kryff was just some hacker.

The giant grandfather clock clicked over and began to chime. Midnight. Lynch had a vision of his father sitting on that very couch, counting out the chimes, shaking his head at him, ashamed of what he'd become.

Dong.

Fuck you!

He wouldn't keep this one even if he could.

Lynch picked up the crop, grimaced, looked at the girl's prone body then brought it down as hard as he could on the back of her bare thigh.

Dong.

Another stroke, diametrically across the lotus flower.

Dong.

He counted out twelve strokes. If she didn't respect her body, why should he?

The clock fell silent. Red welts were appearing on the unconscious girl's body.

"Ha," Lynch smirked. "Let's see you clean this one up, Kryff."

SUCKERED

Bodies in brightly colored costumes baked on the sugary sands fronting the Beacon residence. To either side, old-money mansions loomed like grand sentries. The sun reached center point.

"Nice baggies, boykie." Tony Beacon mocked Robbie's black rugby shorts. He tugged on his own quick-dry costume patterned with silver daggers, declaring, "Zanerobe. Only the finest Italian swimwear for the Tonester."

Central Beach was speckled with Hobie Cats, with waves shuddering off the orange-stained Lookout rocks and thumping hard on the shallow banks. A flotilla of paint-peeling fishing boats lazed beyond the breakers inside the Blind Rocks. Though they were regular attendees, they seemed out of place offshore from the affluent suburb.

Robbie had been introduced to Tony's various female guests but he struggled to remember their names, preferred to make an association. Chewing Gum, Pearls, Chinese Eyes. Sinead, the bald girl. And Amber, in the honey-colored thong.

"Do my back?" The girl who'd been chewing gum all morning gave Robbie a coy look and passed him a tube of Tropical Blend, then turned and waited. He thought her name was Carrie.

He adjusted his peak and smoothed cream gently over her shoulders

The previous night, Robbie had retired early, feeling suddenly exhausted by the long drive. Perhaps it was more than just the drive, it had occurred to him when he awoke that morning. How else could he have slept through the booming bass that must have rumbled through the house all night? But he'd managed a forty-five minute run along Robberg Beach while the others slept and now he felt revitalized, ready to go.

He worked the cream down the girl's back, stopping at the seam of her bikini bottom, then running both hands up her flanks. He finished by wiping a finger across the top of her ear.

"You're the best," she giggled.

Robbie wiped a smudge of cream from his elephant-hair bracelet. It was nearly three months since Melanie had dropped him for Picasso, he thought. Time to move on.

Shielding his eyes from the sun, Robbie scanned the beach. Fallon stood at the water's edge in a one-piece black swimsuit, a blue scarf wrapped around her waist, her raven-black hair flowing like a mane. A stocky, well-built man stood behind her, arms folded, a tight Ferrari cap covering his scalp. The boyfriend.

Hardhead, Robbie named him.

Fallon had had a quiet word with him the night before, asked him to give her a wide berth, to avoid even talking to her. There were enough people in the house that they could steer clear of each other without a problem, she'd explained. Robbie hadn't liked it, but he'd had to shrug it off.

Robbie looked away. Nearby, several of Beacon's friends played beach bats and threw Frisbees. Robbie knew one or two of them. Otherwise, the beach was surprisingly empty. In the distance, the Beacon Isle hotel looked like a giant beehive, a verdant stretch of grass clearly visible out in front, marked with deck chairs.

"Are you, like, the Beacon of the Beacon Isle Hotel?" the girl with the Chinese eyes under a large straw hat asked Tony Beacon.

"No, but I can, like, show you the beacon of Tony Beacon if you'd like."

He pretended to pull at the drawstring of his dagger-patterned baggies. Sylvana tossed a handful of sand at him.

"Tony!" she scolded in a thick accent.

Beacon winked at her, then tugged at the tight leather string of her blue bikini top. It was invitingly loose.

"Hey, my man!" Beacon's attention was diverted as he spotted Vuka lugging a large blue cooler box through the soft sand. He opened his arms wide in anticipation.

Fallon and her boyfriend sauntered up the beach. Robbie watched out the corner of his eye as the boyfriend picked up a towel, shook it and laid it out for her. The lightning strike sun tattoo he had noted previously on her inner thigh had faded away.

Robbie felt a thrust of desire.

Shit! Got to be discreet.

The combined flesh on display was beginning to get to him.

The boyfriend leaned over to place his towel alongside hers. Muscles bulged all over his body: abs, quads, and mountainous biceps. Plus a tight black Speedo.

"Everyone's met Fallon, right?" said Tony to no one in particular. "And Frank?"

"Ferdi," Fallon corrected.

Tony caught Robbie's eye.

"Yeah, sorry, it's Ferdi," he corrected, opening the cooler box. He briefly inspected the contents then closed it again. "Thanks, Vuka."

"Who wants a, uh, water, ginger ale, Spin, vodka orange, more water?"

"Can we trust you?" someone called Pete quipped. Sinead and Pearls giggled.

"If you ask for a single, Tony pours you a triple," Sinead said.

"Just ask Angie Dean," Pete added. Everyone sniggered.

"Hey!" Tony Beacon waggled a finger at the group. He was smiling. "Uncalled for!"

A low wall, made of stone taken from the original whaling station in the area, surrounded the patio of the Beacon house. A Perspex shield, protecting the house from the prevalent southeaster, was drawn back.

Robbie lay on a teak recliner. One of the girls—Amber—darted up the steps from the beach, yelping, a guy in red shorts behind, flicking a towel at her backside. Robbie spotted Fallon rinsing herself under the outside shower, but diverted his attention just in time, as the Chewing Gum girl slipped into his lap, a film of fine sand on her elbows. Robbie now thought her name was Callie, not Carrie.

"What you reading?" She turned his book around, a Stephen King novel with a ghoulish cover. "Oh. Nasty."

"Passes the time."

She bounced up and down in his lap. "I feel like doing something... exciting," she whispered in his ear.

Robbie lowered the novel. A shudder of electricity passed through his body. It had been more than three months...."Oh really?"

He looked past her to Fallon, stroking her hair beneath the shower.

Carrie/Callie followed Robbie's gaze, straightened up. "Why don't you ask her bust size while you're at it?" she said, pulling the paperback from him and whacking him over the head.

"Huh?"

"Bastard!" she said with a smile and hopped off his lap.

"Hey! It's not like that—come back!" Robbie implored as she danced inside.

He let her go, wasn't sure what he wanted. Figured he had to play it cool either way. Besides, he was enjoying the Fallon show.

Fresh from the shower, Fallon peeled her costume straps from her shoulders, wrapped a towel under her arms, a second towel around her head like a turban.

She looked up and locked eyes with him. Robbie held her gaze.

You have eyes like big blue swimming pools, she'd told him.

Fancy a dip?

"Ahem!" Carrie/Callie cleared her throat. She'd been watching Robbie through the glass doors.

Robbie lifted the melted remains of a glass of Coke, sipped at the straw, tried to get back into Stephen King but couldn't.

Sylvana and Tony Beacon took Fallon's place beneath the outside shower. Tony yanked the cord of her bikini top. Sylvana let out a mock protest, but allowed it to fall to the floor. Her breasts pointed upwards like ski jumps.

More electricity.

Carrie/Callie returned with a glass of Oros. She had a fresh piece of gum in.

"Nice view?" she asked. She had a good body; nineteen years old and firm. Robbie decided she wasn't his type.

The view of the garden extended to the blue horizon. Robbie felt he could sit forever and watch the day unfold. In paradise, worrying about university exams and the cost of living seemed irrelevant. But the amount of naked flesh he was being exposed to was starting to take its toll.

Not far from the raunchy shower, Fallon wiggled her bathing costume off beneath the towel. Robbie shut his eyes and pictured it in his hands.

"Full on!"

Robbie was pumped up as he emerged from sea. Behind him, hollow waves barked as they pitched and hit the shallow bank at the Wedge. The sun was sinking fast, a melting orange ice cream. In the distance a school of dolphins made its way to some unknown destination.

Robbie ascended the narrow steps from the beach in energetic leaps, skinned his wetsuit on the veranda and made his way inside to his windowless en-suite bathroom for a shower. Water dripped from his nose and his ears ached, courtesy of an exhilarating three-hour bodyboarding session. He found the light switch in the darkness and turned on the taps, waited for the energizing heat of the water to come.

Though he was enjoying the weekend break, he'd concluded that Tony's guests were not his type. They were aliens bonded by secret privilege, and that privilege had a few downsides. For example, it relied on others having less of it—others like him.

As if to emphasize the point, a heavy metal track began pounding through the ceiling from the living area above. Not his cup of musical tea.

But he could hardly complain: he had a great room in a mansion with a perfect beach at its doorstep. And he had Fallon to distract him.

As he immersed his head under the warm rush of water, an image of her wet body, fresh from the ocean, entered his head. Since the night he'd met her, she had provoked intense and strange feelings in him.

Is this more than lust? Is this what happens with the first girl you meet after breaking up with your long-term girlfriend?

They had hardly said a word to each other all day. And yet every time they walked past each other, he felt electric.

Robbie had used this shower before, when he'd stayed in the house for a week after matric finals. Beacon had invited his bratpack down from Joburg for Plett Rage, South Africa's answer to Fort Lauderdale and Spring Break. The invite had been extended to Robbie and Melanie. His father had stumped up for two tickets on the Baz Bus.

It had been, as it always is, a week of mayhem. Bikini contests and foam parties at a strip of up-market clubs with faux-exotic names like SuperClub and Cubar Libre were the order of the night. Robbie had been seventeen at the time, an Eastern Cape farmer's son, not entirely prepared for the assault on his vision of the way the world should be. Sex, drugs, and alcohol were the fuel of the rage; one big party after another, participants blissfully unaware of any other reason for existence. *El-party continua!* they'd cried.

While he'd enjoyed letting loose with copious amounts of alcohol, Robbie hadn't really "got" matric rage. Now that he was single, it was starting to make more sense. All the young and virile bodies on show.... So what if they weren't his "type"? Maybe it was time for him to test other waters.

He pulled at the elephant-hair bracelet. Six years. Like part of his skin...

The shower thundered, heat penetrating his sea-chilled skin. He felt invigorated, cleansed by the session in salt water.

He lathered shampoo into his hair, closed his eyes tightly as the suds ran down his face.

Then the light went out. Even with eyes fast shut, he could sense the blackness behind his lids. A power cut?

No. The heavy metal played on. Above the drum of the shower and the beat of the music, he could just make out the creak of the door and click of the lock.

"Who is it?" he said loudly, hands still in his shampoo-filled hair.

"Shhh," said a voice as the shower door opened.

A body pressed up against his chest.

"Whoa! What the—?"

Robbie tried to rinse his hair and open his eyes at the same time. In the darkness, he couldn't see a thing. A hand reached between his legs.

"Jesus!" he protested. Was it Chewing Gum?

He sensed it wasn't her. His body didn't seem to care either way.

She released her hold, pulled his hands to his sides and gripped both wrists, then put her mouth against his ear and whispered something Robbie couldn't hear.

He laughed, played along.

Still holding his wrists, she slid down his chest. Before he could process what was happening, her mouth closed around him and he felt the heat of her tongue on his shaft. His arousal was complete, the thrill inducing an involuntary shudder.

"Hey," he said without much protest.

His mind raced. What was going on here? Was it OK? He could have easily broken free of her grip.

His heart pounded. He tried to remember the girl's actual name. Was it Carrie or Callie? She'd wanted to do something exciting—did this qualify?

But it couldn't be her. He'd felt her breasts again his chest. Too big.

His mind raced trying to work out what was going on. Could it be Fallon? He wanted it to be.

Do you like fun? she'd asked. Fallon.

She released the grip on his left wrist, used her free hand to anchor his cock as she worked her mouth slowly and rhythmically up and down. The hot water crashing on his head seemed to accentuate the exquisite sensation in his loins.

I can stop this, he thought.

If you have to think about it...

He abandoned resistance. Ecstasy spread throughout his body. He wanted to feel her tongue on him and his hands on her ass and her breasts and be inside her all in the same moment. The hot steamy room, the pitch darkness, the excitement of not seeing her face or her crouched, naked body—it all intensified the pleasure. Right then, nothing else mattered. If the lights went on....If everyone in the house gathered to watch him....Nothing.

He moaned, thrust his hips forward, but she held him expertly in her maddening rhythmic vice. Not even if there were a gun to his head could he stop himself now.

His free hand dropped to the top of her head, gripping her wet hair, as his control deserted and he exploded in her mouth.

He slumped backwards against the wall, then down to the floor of the shower as the water rained down.

"Fallon," he said.

She straddled him, pressed her lips against his and passed him a mouthful of his warm semen. He spluttered in surprise, rolled on his side as he spat it out, splashed water into his mouth to rinse away the salty taste.

Then a moment of light as the door opened and closed—and she was gone.

FLOATER

The gardener spotted the partly submerged body among the bullrushes at the bottom of his employer's property in Marina De Gama.

He removed his dirty floral sun hat and stared into the rushes for some time. It made sense to him. The previous week he'd found a large leopard toad in the garden; he'd been expecting something bad to happen.

His employers' house stretched down to the marina. He knew they'd be very upset by this, but wasn't sure what the best course of action was. He could have reached out with the rake and dragged the body to the bank, but he resisted and instead notified the maid. She screamed in shock when he pointed out the body among the vegetation, and ran to the house to make the necessary phone calls.

The maid told the gardener that the *amaphoyisa* were coming. This concerned him for some time because he didn't have papers. Not many Malawians in Cape Town did.

While waiting for the arrival of the police, the gardener kept watch on the embankment. The tide was coming in and rocking the body gently back and forth. He didn't want the body to disappear before they arrived. He'd be blamed for wasting everyone's time.

Three men arrived. All were fat, two wore uniforms; the other was in blue jeans and a short-sleeved shirt with a Toyota logo on the pocket. He spoke on his cellphone, seemed to be in charge. The uniformed men had nice boots. They declined his offer to use the rake; instead one of them stepped into the mud and waded over to the corpse. The gardener was surprised that he would ruin his boots like that. He would have taken them off first. His own broken takkies were bound together with tape.

The policeman in the water slowly guided the corpse to the bank; his partner dragged it under the armpits onto the grass.

"Hayi!" exclaimed the maid, clutching the gardener's arm. The body was a white woman, entirely naked. Bloated and greying.

The maid had had enough; she returned to the house with her hands to her face. But the gardener watched with interest as they laid the body face up on the grass. He'd never seen a naked white woman before; he thought she looked underfed.

The man in charge pulled a hand-sized digital camera from his pocket and started taking photographs. "Lekker sexy this, boys," he said with a snort.

"As jy's mal vir 'n shaven haven, né detective!" said the policeman with

the wet boots, pointing at the woman's crotch.

"Should I check her pockets?" joked the one with dry boots.

The gardener understood very little English or Afrikaans. He'd learned a few local words that got him by. Like *amaphoyisa*. He was saddened that they laughed in the presence of a dead person. The girl looked to be in her early twenties, her face translucent, blotched with blue and grey.

The detective whistled. He looked up and down the waterline and then crouched onto his haunches, lifted the girl's eyelids with a thumb. "Bruises on her neck. Strangled maybe," he surmised.

"Hoe lank?"

"At least a day. Could be a re-floater?" He bent down and touched the edge of the girl's ripped eyebrow. "You see this?"

The constables leaned forward, shrugged in unison. The detective took a close-up.

A car hooted outside the house and the gardener hurried to open the gate. A stout white woman marched past him without greeting. Behind her an ambulance had arrived; two men pulled a stretcher from the back.

The gardener returned to his vantage point.

Presently the white woman approached the embankment, with the maid in tow. She was dressed in uniform. A badge on her breast said "Vermaak." He couldn't read but he thought the three shiny stars on her shoulders meant she must be important.

"What time did you notice the body?" Vermaak said, tucking the loose tail of her shirt into her pants. She eyed the three policemen on the grass below.

He didn't understand. The maid interpreted and he shrugged and tapped his bare wrist.

"He doesn't have the time," the maid replied.

Vermaak looked at him strangely. "How does he know when to go home?" she asked, snapping her book shut.

The maid started to tell Vermaak that she'd been told about it an hour before, but the policewoman had already turned her back on them.

The gardener was glad. He didn't want anything to do with this business. He needed to mow the lawn and dig out the beds.

Vermaak was thinking about her outstanding workload. Dozens of fat files lay on her desk. It was too early to tell, but she had a hunch about this one. Runaway girl, possibly prostitute, murdered by her boyfriend or pimp. There was no family back home worrying about where she was. And if there was, they'd be in some remote town a thousand kilometers away and the link would never be made. The body would lie on a cold mortuary slab for a regulation three weeks before receiving a pauper's burial at state expense.

"Anyone organize a boat?" Vermaak said, without making eye contact with the others.

Someone sniggered.

"What the *fok* for?" asked the detective. He'd lit a cigarette.

Vermaak's mouth tightened. The detective yawned out a mouthful of smoke.

"See if there's any more bloody things floating around," Vermaak barked.

The detective smiled and tapped the wet cop on his shoulder. "This here's our boat, *kaptein*!" he said.

The men all laughed.

"Should he drain the lake while's he's at it?" the detective added. Even Vermaak smiled. The detective reminded her of her late husband. A joker. He'd been facing suspension at the time he was killed. She didn't get paid out his death benefits. Fat joke.

The detective offered her a cigarette. She ignored him, removed a pack of Marlboros from her top pocket.

"Bloody children, all of you," she said, staring at the men. Sometimes she got mad; mostly she felt sorry for them. She didn't miss that part of marriage; the crude jokes and childish camaraderie. Men were definitely from Mars.

A new arrival with a crime-scene bib marked out the area with orange traffic cones. The dry, fat policeman rolled the body over and stepped back.

"Jiss!"

On the embankment, the maid grabbed the gardener's arm again.

Purple lines were striped in thick welts across the dead girl's back. The policeman followed the direction of the lines to a large white flower tattooed in the small of her back.

"Wat die fok?"

Vermaak knelt closer, exhaled smoke through her nose. First the ripped eyebrow, now this.

She wasn't too happy about this development, was glad there was no press around. They'd catch wind of it in due course, of course. The story might even make front page because of the respectable neighborhood. But it would disappear soon enough.

A gentle wind rattled the branches on a row of silver trees, the sheen on the leaves reflecting like small mirrors. The gardener rubbed his hand across the speckled stubble on his face. It didn't make sense that so beautiful a flower, so colorful and alive, could be on the drab body of the dead white girl.

SUGAR AND SPICE

Korn, Slipknot, Linkin Park....A playlist of hard rock pumped out at high volume, music being generated by Tony Beacon's laptop and operated by remote control. Speakers blared from the walls throughout the living area, including two on the veranda.

"Shotgun!"

Tony Beacon used a screwdriver to gouge a hole at the bottom of a closed can of Amstel beer. He wore a Panama hat and striped boxers. Satisfied with his handiwork, he lifted the can to face level, placed his mouth over the opening and cracked open the can; its contents rushed out unhindered and were consumed in seconds.

"Come on!"

Tony crushed the can and threw it across the room. Vuka moved in like a seagull, removed the offending object.

The Beacon lounge came straight out of a décor magazine: couches covered by hopsack linen with floral throws, faded red lanterns, vanilla- and rose-scented candles in starfish holders, rosewood coffee tables, wax-like cymbidium orchids poised like swan figurines.

Robbie finished a gold can of Castle in the more traditional manner, and fetched himself another from a silver ice bucket on the mahogany cabinet. The dinner table was decked with platters of snacks, fresh bread from town, cheeses and cold meats. The transparent cover of a Salton hot tray revealed a row of readied plates.

Robbie scanned the room, eyeing out each girl in turn. He felt... he couldn't say. Conflicted? He thought about Melanie and what they had meant to each other. Stupid feeling; he hoped it would pass.

Pull yourself together, man! You can't be acting like a loser after receiving the most unforgettable knee-trembler of your life!

He had to admit it: a part of him did feel rather proud. Like he'd got a monkey off his back. His mother may have warned him about casual relationships when he was still at school—"A moment of pleasure for a lifetime of hardship"—but at least there couldn't be any comebacks on a blow job, he figured.

Callie lifted her head out of the latest *Heat* magazine and looked around the room sleepily. She was definitely Callie; Robbie had checked with Tony. She wore a frilly cotton top over her bikini. He wondered how she could read with all the noise.

"You had some awesome waves," she called to him, chewing gum vigorously. "I watched you."

"Thanks," he smiled back and raised his can to her. Her hair was damp. But she couldn't have been the one, Robbie thought to himself. Those little boobs. And probably couldn't stop chewing for long enough...

Chinese Eyes and Sinead were playing backgammon at the table. Chinese Eyes had dry hair and Sinead— well, it definitely wasn't her.

Pearls was swapping saliva with some guy on the couch. Fast mover if it was her.

Robbie swallowed hard and cracked the Castle. The volume of the music was killing him. He fiddled with the amplifier, turned down the sound.

"You had some cooking waves earlier, man." This time it was Tony Beacon throwing the compliment. He ran a hand over his spiky head and grinned at Robbie.

"Thanks, man."

"Way to go, Rob." Beacon gave him a fist-bump.

Robbie stared blankly at Beacon. Could this be one of Tony's tricks?

Fallon slipped in through the veranda doors. Wet hair, towel draped around her shoulders, a pair of lamé shorts hugging like clingwrap to her behind. She brushed past Robbie. Even in the dim light, he could see that her pupils were constricted, mere pinpricks.

Hardhead followed, flushed in the face from exercise, with sandy feet and red Ferrari cap. Sweat ran down his ripped torso, soaking his white vest.

The color faded from Robbie's face. He looked away quickly.

"Been running, uh, Ferdi?" Tony said after them.

"Ja. Twenty kays along the beach."

He had an accent that Tony liked to call American-Boksburg. Tony elbowed Robbie. "Twenty kays? Nice one, bru."

Ferdi stayed close to Fallon, who was collecting a blue margarita from Vuka, the rim of the glass crusted with salt. She took a sip, silver bracelets jangling on her left wrist, and blew a kiss towards the smiling Vuka.

"Real lime! I love you, Vuka." She held one hand to her heart.

"Twenty kilometers on sand, he reckons?" Tony whispered to Robbie. "The oke must've run to fucking Knysna."

Robbie ignored him, kept an eye on Fallon while sipping his beer.

Margarita in one hand, she loaded a shot glass with tequila, tilted her head back and drained it. Light reflected off her forehead, her eyebrows like swooshes painted on with a black pen.

"What's the matter with you, Robbie?" laughed Tony. "You look totally random, man!"

Robbie shrugged, took another sip of beer.

Ferdi departed via the stairs, and Tony put his arm around Fallon, whispered in her ear.

"Wanna go do it?" he teased.

She slapped him playfully, made eye contact with Robbie as she did.

Robbie turned away and strolled out onto the veranda, leaned against the wooden balustrade, ran his hand along the yachting cabling that linked each beam. A thick piece of rope, reclaimed from the sea, wound around the balcony like a coiled snake. A canvas hammock swayed in the sea breeze.

Someone came up behind him and ran her fingers over his shoulders, triggering gooseflesh on his arms and knotting his stomach.

It was Callie.

"Help me," she said. He secured the brightly colored hammock and she climbed on.

"Heaven," she said, falling into the canvas.

Robbie found himself a deck chair and settled in with his beer. He'd had enough excitement for the day; time to take it easy.

Robbie lay on the balcony under a fluffy blanket and stared out into the mist. It was early morning, still dark, but he couldn't sleep. The Beacon Isle glowed like a giant moon marooned on the beach. He'd pulled on a jersey and tracksuit pants, socks damp from walking across the cement. The house was quiet.

He replayed the shower scene in his head.

Do you like fun?

He couldn't summon up that bravado any more. It seemed dirty now.

Robbie's feet rested on a side table. The balcony was strewn with last night's excess.

He ran through it one more time.

Chronology. She must have watched him come up the steps from the beach. Timing. Hardhead was on his marathon run. Was the shower light on or off when she walked in? He'd felt her breasts against his chest.

It was definitely wrong.

Not even if there was a gun to his head...

He slapped his hand on his leg, memory of the eroticism passing over like a hot flush.

What about Fallon's silver bracelets? Surely he would have felt them? He tried to remember whether she was wearing them on the beach.

He imagined her sleeping downstairs. Which room was she in? What if she came to him now?

Was this her proposition? The second favor? Having fun? Release for the criminal lawyer?

He clenched his jaw and pulled the blanket tight around his body.

Crystal glasses with residue of Bombay Sapphire gin and half-finished bottles of Bramon, the local champagne, littered the patio. Robbie wondered what this weekend would cost.

This world required money, Robbie knew. It was their privilege.

Money.

Money and fun.

Robbie stared into the inky darkness of the sea in front. Yesterday, he'd been surfing in that sea. It was in his vision, but he couldn't see it. He imagined his feet on the ocean floor, slimy creatures touching him.

He shivered, hours before the morning sun would burn off his unease.

Breakfast of smoked salmon, cream-cheese bagels, scrambled eggs with chopped chives and peppered mackerel greeted bleary Sunday-morning guests at the Beacon mansion.

The wind was up, a howling southeaster pounding sea-facing windows and doors. Callie drizzled chocolate sauce on an ice-cream bombe. She lived in her bikini, gum on a side plate alongside.

"Awesome breakfast," said Chinese Eyes. She was wedged between Fallon and Sinead at a table set for sixteen. Beacon presided over the first shift, his eyes hidden behind dark aviator Ray-Bans.

"Totally awesome," agreed Amber.

"Awesome, awesome," said Tony. "What's with you girls and awesome? Everything's freaking awesome these days."

"Or hectic," Robbie added. He looked across the table at Fallon. He wondered where Ferdi was.

"Morning, everyone." Sylvana arrived at the table in a nightie, slid her hand lightly across Robbie's bare shoulder and slipped into a vacant seat at the breakfast table. Robbie glanced up from his breakfast: she looked like the French girl from that movie *Swimming Pool*, he thought to himself.

"What's that taste?" Callie asked Fallon, licking her lips.

"*Moskonfyt.* Hanepoort grapes." Fallon held up a jar of amber syrup.

"Awesome," said Callie. "Your mother teach you?"

"Not likely," Fallon replied, brushing the hair out of her face. "From the farm stall." She was the only girl at the table wearing make-up.

"My God, what a fucking night," Sylvana said. She claimed a pancake, caught Robbie's eye and winked at him.

"The honey, please," she said, reaching toward him. Her nightie dropped open for a moment and he caught an eyeful of breast before she covered herself. Robbie pushed the honey in her direction, looked away as he did.

"We went *so* huge," Beacon chipped in. He lowered the Ray-Bans, eyes bloodshot.

"Can't remember a thing," Sylvana admitted, spreading honey onto the pancake on her plate.

"Amnesia, Sylvana?" The guy called Pete said, sitting to her right, nudging Tony in the ribs. "Tony been at it again?"

"How's your mind?" said Tony, testy, head down, scooping All Bran furiously.

Pete coughed out the name Angie Dean; Callie giggled.

"Ask Robbie," said Tony. "He's the one with the connections at the Blue Venus."

Robbie's face reddened, all eyes on him. Fallon leaned forward.

"Come on, Tony," Robbie protested. "Look what you've started."

Tony raised his hands and laughed. "Nobody drugged Angie Dean, dude. Believe me!"

"Well, I definitely felt drugged last night," Sylvana said, her voice hoarse. Robbie felt a shiver up his spine and the table fell silent.

"Jesus," said Tony, eyes wide, dropping his spoon in his plate of cereal.

"By a dozen Screwdrivers and glasses of champagne!" Sylvana shouted, and everyone burst into laughter.

Robbie eyed Fallon; she laughed along with the others, but her face was inscrutable.

The moment past, Sylvana passed Robbie a jar of spice. "Try some of this," she said.

"What is it?" Robbie examined the label on the jar.

"It's cinnamon," Sylvana answered. She lowered her voice. "It improves the taste of your cum."

Robbie swallowed, blushed. No one else had heard. He pushed the cinnamon container back toward her.

Sylvana squeezed lemon juice, rolled her pancake into a mop and took a bite.

"Mmmm."

JACKER

Carlos spell-checked a letter he'd penned to Senator Marriott of Washington State.

```
Dear Senator,

I refer to my letters dated 17 March and 22 June
as well as complaints lodged with the Internet
Crime Complaint Center (IC3). I demand that action
be taken to address my concerns. The Internet is
the Wild West, an unregulated cesspool of
pornography, violence, and deprivation. Search
engines enable immediate access to material that
should never be presented for public consumption,
let alone made freely available to the children
of our fine country. My concerns have been raised
with Senators Davidson and Leckie, and were mooted
for discussion at the last Senate Forum. I would
like to urge that immediate action is now required.

I refer to the following four examples:

www.watchit.com/yt/clip4156:
drunk human having sex with a horse.

www.wrstviolence.de/bbfths/mrdchina.wwf:
stabbing murder of a Chinese gangster.

www.underagechicks.jp:
underage girls engaged in lesbian activity.

www.watchit.com/albums/norwayjoachinchench.html:
public boasting of Joachin Chenche prior
to the Norwegian massacre.

There is no possible argument for allowing this
type of material into the public domain.
In our country, where the slip of Janet Jackson's
```

nipple can create a massive uproar with stiff
repercussions, the same people viewing that
innocent clip could, at an accidental click
of the mouse, be subjected to deplorable filth.

I call for immediate censorship and control of
Internet material, namely:

All new sites should be registered and regulated
by a central authority.
Sites should be classified according to the
material they distribute.
Stiff penalties should apply to any site
broadcasting unsuitable material.
Search engines should be prevented from creating
links to forbidden sites. (See China's Green Dam
initiative)

Yours Sincerely,
Colin Palmer

Carlos pressed send and then leafed through his investment accounts.

Of his database of 475 clients, fewer than ten had ordered new material in the last month. About fifty were sporadically working the Mickey Finn network, but operative fees were exorbitant and he was aware that clients had started shopping around their business for the best rates. He had no control of the Mickey Finn Club, so was powerless to prevent their disloyalty.

Earlier in the day, he'd received word from Jacker that the *Polisen* in Sweden had arrested a key patron. That brought to three the number of recently busted Dark Video clients. They had been released from custody, but the damage was done: private lives devastated by the humiliation and suspicion, their Dark Video relationships terminated. For now, at least.

He Skyped Jacker.

"What's the status?" Carlos asked. Video was disabled. Jacker's user profile was a picture of Eric Cartman; Carlos displayed an anonymous identity.

In creating Dark Video control software, Carlos had originally used a variety of developers to create independent components. He specified each component, the functionality sufficiently generic to shroud the overall goal of the code. And he'd had the skill to unite them into one program. With this approach, Carlos had protected himself from a rogue developer.

Jacker was one of the sharpest of the lot, and he was necessary for business maintenance to ease Carlos's workload. Without him, he'd be chained to his desk. Carlos considered his dependency on Jacker a manageable risk.

"I'm working on it, boss. Round the clock," Jacker replied.

Carlos suspected Jacker resided in the Washington area, a bit close for comfort. Certain clues he'd picked up in their countless Skype conversations.

"What news?"

"Same as the last one. Police arrived unannounced. Media were informed."

Carlos believed in hedging. If Jacker was his most important technical-support man, he was also a security threat. Every bet must be covered by a counter bet. It diluted the size of the immediate gain, but the security benefits were essential. So Carlos had developed an independent custom-made tracking system to identify any attempt by Jacker—or anyone—to trace him. The software continually monitored the floating Dark Video site for attempts to follow any of its thousand of pseudo connection tentacles, one of which led back to Carlos.

"That all we know? This intelligence is costing me a tidy sum."

"I know that, Carlos. I'm working on it. What about a list?"

A list. Jacker was a software programmer, a bits and bytes man. Carlos resented such presumptuous thinking from him. Jacker's job was to monitor malware and botnets and other cyber threats, and to hack information for him. Sometimes he thought that if he knew Jacker's abode, he'd send the Chestwound round to remind him of his place.

"Impossible!" retorted Carlos.

"But you said that..."

The rogue Gorillas mule had supposedly tried to trace Carlos's identity three years previously—before he'd been lain to rest by his trusted hitman, Samuel Chester.

"I know what you're thinking. But that danger was extinguished. The mule is dead. And he didn't have a list. He lured a handful of clients to a website called Mangle, that's it."

Passwords protected Dark Video products, the client had both a safe and a panic password. The panic password would disable the video immediately.

Besides the income lost, Carlos was confident that police busts could never directly threaten his business. He had too many fail-safes. And besides, clients of Dark Video were likely to be involved in other dubious activities—drug use, gambling, sexual deviancy. Much easier to pin down. The respective police forces would be too easily distracted to even bother with Dark Video.

For now, Carlos's primary fear was of a panic that might spread among his clients if word got out about a possible leak of their confidentiality. They'd drop and run for the hills.

He had other issues to contend with as well.

In January, his Russian contractor had managed to acquire footage of the Moscow airport terrorist blast from a traveler's camcorder; the guy had been filming his wife checking in when the explosion went off. But the mule had sold the images to CNN instead. It was a sign of things to come. More recently, a prison gang rape he'd purchased appeared on Watchit before he could approach a single client. And despite their premier Wen Jiabao's Green Dam initiative to filter Google, even his Chinese clients were finding what they wanted.

Carlos heard an engine idling outside. He flicked on the monitor of his security cameras. A large red sedan cruised past. Something triggered a lurch in Carlos's gut. He recognized the same feeling he'd had in London during the meltdown of the original Dark Video business twelve years ago, after his partner committed suicide and Scotland Yard descended on his Chelsea flat. He'd escaped out the back way with the clothes on his back, picked up his emergency bag from his safety deposit box and headed straight to Dover to catch the ferry to Calais. He'd eventually flown to the United States from Portugal. And that was before 9/11. He didn't want a repeat of that process. Ever.

His wife had left a file of cutouts on his desk. It contained pictures of Bermuda and Barbados. On the front she'd written. "Please, please, please!"

I thought I said Belgium!

It occurred to Carlos that she could be luring him into a trap.

That flight from Lisbon was the last time Carlos had taken an international flight. Could he risk it? He was older, of course, but he didn't look that different from when he first arrived in the States.

He was aware that the Feds were looking for him, as was Interpol. Probably PSIA in Japan and FSB in Russia....But what were they looking for? Air? As far as he knew, his name—his new name, that is—was still clean.

In a sense, Carlos regretted that he could not enjoy his notoriety in a more public forum. When he died, they would not screen documentaries about his life or write books about his business acumen. He was anonymous. It was a beauty and a curse.

Carlos placed his palms flat on his desk. Taped to a narrow recess between the top drawer and the panel at the back of his desk was a leather wallet stuffed with eighty hundred-dollar bills. An emergency fund.

He unlocked the top drawer of his bureau and removed a burgundy-colored passport. Colin Palmer. Would it work? Perhaps if he picked some lowlife destination....South Africa was Third World. They could barely run their own country, let alone pick up an obscure Internet criminal, surely? *I could slip in and out without anyone knowing. Like a snake in the grass.*

A GOOD FIND

Sunday afternoon.

Lynch bit down repetitively on the skin of his forefinger, trying to console himself with the notion that no news was good news. He'd endured a nervous few days since Thursday morning, made a hash of his golf at Steenberg, but surely he would have heard from Kryff if there had been a problem with the girl he'd abused? Still, he couldn't shake the anxiety. The lurching feeling in his stomach wasn't remorse; more like physical concern in the wake of a critical mistake.

The beating he'd dealt the girl shocked him. He'd broken a behavior code of the Mickey Finn Club. *Do not damage the goods.* The penalty could be expulsion or exposure.

And yet it felt so right at the time.

He wondered what Kryff had done. Maybe dropped her outside a public hospital?

The weekend had come quickly. He'd gone to watch his beloved Holly play netball at her school the day before to help calm his nerves; had decided to watch from a distance rather than risk running into her mother. He knew there would be a scene; there always was. The witch didn't even have the decency to let them take it in turns; always had to be there. She refused to let him know where and when Holly was playing. He'd had to phone the school directly to get her fixtures list.

He shook his head, fingered the phial of scopolamine that Kryff had given him at The Pump. Devil's Breath. Undetectable.

If the operators refused to work for him, he'd go it alone.

Exposure was an altogether different proposition and his awareness of this danger was sobering. *No risk.* No comebacks. That is how the Mickey Finn Club had been sold to him.

A reminder popped up on his Motorola:

```
Holly birthday tomorrow
```

During the divorce, Sandy had written to him. It was years ago now, but Lynch remembered her words. She'd described him as "emotionally dead." He was "a vacant soul who smiled and said the right things, but without the remotest expression of true feeling." She felt it had gone wrong for Julian during his boarding school days because he had been deprived of parental affection.

What Sandy didn't know was that Julian had been banished from Cape Town for an "incident" with Estelle, his sister. He was sixteen. A most impressionable age.

Lynch shook his head.

He added another reminder to his phone, to call Holly.

On the Friday night, he had attended the fiftieth birthday party of a golfing partner's wife. A lavish affair in a marquee in Constantia with sushi, a band, dancers and cases of expensive wine. It had struck him how little people really knew about one another. He had watched the social dynamics of the party guests with bemusement—free flowing alcohol, loud voices competing for airtime, flirty wives longing for attention.

He wished he could grab the microphone and tell everyone his secret; how he got his kicks, how he'd beaten the shit out of a drugged girl with a riding crop. Shake them out of their boring existence.

It's not appropriate behavior.

He remembered his mother's words, the day before he was sent to boarding school in Kimberley.

Not appropriate.

How was he to know? He just loved his sister.

At boarding school, he learned appropriate behavior: how to masturbate quickly among a group of peers, how to fuck the foam mattresses in the gym hall, how to finger a girl after the school social.

Except the girls never let him.

The night before, he'd stayed up until midnight finishing the Patty Hearst paperback. He didn't learn anything he didn't already know. The kidnapped heiress had formed a relationship with one of her captors, Willie Wolfe, who had raped her. Yet she refused to be rescued, and later called Wolfe the "gentlest, most beautiful man." That morning he'd ordered *The Short Life of Willie Wolfe* by Jean Kinney.

He opened his journal and thumbed the pages, pausing at a line he'd written: *Desire: The powerful monster.*

He wished he could name his desire openly. Talk about it. Share his feelings with others.

After the netball game, having successfully avoided Holly's mother, he had slipped off home to Bishopscourt. He'd passed the time listlessly, sorting through the cellar and separating old wine bottles from the new ones he had purchased more recently. Now he suddenly wondered what would become of the house if something happened to him. He imagined estate agents stamping around with their clipboards poised, amoral rodents, noting the neglect with lament.

What a shame. Such valuable property to let go to waste.

Someone would buy his family home and their brats would dig up the bones of his boyhood pets. Then an investigative reporter would look up the previous owners and disgorge the sordid history of his family.

A suicidal family....People who couldn't make it...

Bobby Lynch. Did he really?

In a small cardboard box in the top drawer of his desk, tucked beneath a wad of cotton wool, Julian kept newspaper cuttings of his father's death announcement. And his mother's.

His father had received twenty-four obituaries, four that ran for three days, one from his father's brother who lived in Glasgow, two from old work colleagues and one from Julian's mother. His mother's contribution read:

```
Bobby Lynch. Passed away 19 July. Sadly missed by
his wife Margaret, son Julian and daughter Estelle.
```

Passed away! Sadly missed!

Lynch recalled how he felt at the time: as though he were living on a different planet. When his mother died a year later, his was the only obituary. He ran it for three days in both the *Cape Times* and *Argus*. He copied his mother's words:

```
Margaret Lynch. Passed away November 15.
Sadly missed by her son Julian.
```

Back in his study, Lynch fetched his black-framed reading glasses and turned to the latest entry in the journal. He'd called the beaten girl Lotus Flower.

Although there had been little to record regarding her clothing or possessions, he had made a few remarks in his sloping handwriting.

> 12 strokes: one for each strike of the clock.
> Afterwards I sat and stared into the fire.
> I remember my father doing the same, as if
> communicating with the leaping flames.
> In a world of his own. It took all the
> persuasion of my inner self not to take the
> poker from the fire and impale her with it.

He had cut a lock of her hair and pasted it with sticky tape underneath his inscription. Next to the hair, he'd attached the bloodied ring from her left eyebrow.

Below it he wrote.

Of course I could have taken it off in
a number of ways. I could have opened the clasp.
I could have cut it open with pliers. I chose
to rip it off because the scar she will have
will be my mark on her forever.

Lynch closed the journal and booted his workstation. He had fifty-six outstanding emails in his inbox. He was finding it harder to concentrate at work. The thrill of his mid-week obsession was infiltrating his daily thoughts.

He logged into his bank account and checked the balance. Overdrawn again. He cursed at the deduction from Protection & Surveillance; they hadn't cancelled the debit order.

The maid had left a list of issues on his desk: the pool was green; there was no detergent; the washing machine was leaking; a missed phone call—no name; there were rats in the house—Rattex required; no space left in the garage for storing newspapers and bottles.

He stared into space and pondered his financial situation. He'd mortgaged the house three years ago and borrowed heavily from the bank to invest his last piece of decent capital in a Ponzi scheme that had gone belly up the previous year. He'd been struggling ever since. Hadn't told anyone.

He was thankful now that Sandy's stubbornness meant she'd refused his offers over the years to pay Holly's private-tuition fees. He'd always felt it his paternal duty, but Sandy wouldn't even give him that satisfaction. The last time he'd brought it up, she had simply passed the phone to Greg, the new husband.

"Look Lynch, enough is enough," he'd said coolly. "She wants you out of her life. Don't call this number again or we'll get a restraining order, you understand me?"

In retrospect, that turned out to be one of the more fortuitous calls he'd made. Minimized their conflict and left him without the crippling school fees he couldn't dream of paying now. But what about his other bills?

Lynch clapped his hands together and smiled.

"Jules. You can do it. You always have," he encouraged himself.

He'd found a way to get by. He logged out of online banking and returned to his inbox. One of the emails was titled "Golden Ratio."

The previous week at the office, he had downloaded software that assigned a scientific value to facial beauty, an algorithm called the golden ratio. He applied the software to the photograph taken of the girl in the Newlands Forest video. The mathematics behind her beauty was an impressive 7.2. As good as Charlize Theron.

He thought of running it against his own photograph, laughed at the idea.

It reminded him. He'd asked Kryff to find the girl. He needed a name, something to call her, to open a new page in his journal and enter her details.

He flicked open his Motorola and tried to contact Kryff again. No reply.

Lynch blinked his eyes. The big clock showed 8:15 pm. He had nothing to do.

Diva, the Dark Video operative, only answered his phone calls on a Wednesday.

ENNUI

Lynch dimmed the lights and pulled the drawstring on his toweling gown. An open bottle of Château Libertas sloshed in one hand as he approached the master bed and slapped the blonde hard across her backside with the palm of his hand.

"Mmm, I like it," she hissed at him, a red handprint forming on her buttock.

The blonde was on her hands and elbows, squirming like an adder, sharp pointy breasts, tongue darting into a redhead's lap. The redhead lay unmoving, eyes closed.

"I said eat her!" Lynch commanded.

He raised the bottle by the neck and swigged, a dribble running down his chin and ending as a maroon blemish on his white gown.

Monday night and the urge had tormented him like a drug addict. He hadn't been able to get hold of Kryff or Diva so he'd ordered two strippers for a private display, hoping it would lead to something interesting.

"You like this?" the blonde said, gyrating her ass without conviction.

Lynch's mind was all over the place. On the girls, on work, on the week ahead. The auditors would keep him busy ticking boxes until Wednesday afternoon. Then golf. He planned to take money off his fourball after two lean weeks. Friday would be board reports, office administration, and meetings with the landlord. No time for a massage at the club.

Lynch tried to focus on the girls. "To you, Bobby! Dad!" he shouted, raising the bottle in tribute to his late father, his mouth stained red. The Libertas was thin and corked, but he didn't care.

The blonde continued half-heartedly, her motivations transparent: let's get done, get paid, and get the fuck out of here.

Lynch adjusted the rim of his reading spectacles and parted his greasy fringe. Some time in the not-too-distant past, this room had hosted the sanctity of his marriage; his parents' marriage for many years before that. He pictured his ex-wife Sandy beneath the creased duvet. Even back then as a woman in her twenties—what was it, fourteen, fifteen years now?—she'd been overweight and self-conscious; her podgy white body swathed in pajamas, pretending to be asleep when he came up from his study. All those nights, he lay silently beside her, the sweat from his body soaking the sheets, his desire under control.

"Jesus," Lynch swore, shaking his head, his good karma evaporating like spit in the desert.

Sex for money had limited appeal to him. His morbid thoughts were not alleviated by the strippers' soulless efforts. He resented their tired eyes, minds like clocks continually ticking, enduring him. Sure, he enjoyed being in charge. But it wasn't the same when there was a financial transaction involved. The power was reversed, he knew; vested in the stripper, who could coerce money from him for a few cheap tricks.

Without the knowledge that he was taking something from the girl, that she was powerless, where was the pleasure? These were strippers—hookers!—nothing more.

The two girls, performing for him on the white linen, held their own sex in low regard. Two thousand rand each.

If it's so cheap for you, why would it be any value to me?

Bobby Lynch had liked hookers. Julian remembered watching them from the window of his upstairs bedroom as they left the house in the early hours of the morning in their bright shiny clothing: high heels, dangling earrings, red lipstick. Julian hated the stereotype. He wondered why his mother had never complained. Assumed she'd just preferred to live in her own world; preferred to not know.

Desire. The powerful monster.

After his divorce, Lynch had trawled the Southern Suburbs bar circuit. On Friday nights, he'd encountered scores of desperate women; had even bumped into Sandy a few times. But the women who did intrigue him were always uninterested in him. He would give them his business card, J LYNCH, FINANCIAL DIRECTOR, and finger his BMW key fob. He'd even mention his big house in Bishopscourt when he recognized the familiar onset of rejection. So many nights, he'd returned home hot, frustrated, and empty-handed.

Lynch lifted the wine and gulped from the bottle. "What's with you Russians?" he said.

The blonde had thin, black eyebrows that looked as if they'd been drawn on with eyeliner. The redhead was virtually asleep. Lynch gripped the bronze poster of the Victorian bed. He imagined ripping it out and smashing it over the girls' heads.

"We're not Russians," scowled the blonde. "We're Romanians."

Eastern Europeans dominated the local strip-club scene. Russians, Latvians, Romanians...Lynch faked a smile. "Who gives a fuck?" he said.

He was done with prostitutes. He'd tried them on and off over the years—when the rejection got too much. Never developed his father's attraction for them, though. After Sandy, they were a release, something he could do; even discuss with his golf buddies on occasion, an acceptable social norm. Each time he fucked one, he felt better about the time he'd wasted on that bitch of an ex-wife.

Maybe that's what his father was doing: punishing his mother for something.

But in time, they'd come to bore him. He'd only continued to dabble for want of a better option—so that he had something to sustain him. Then Dark Video and Mickey Finn had come into his life, and Lynch had realized what it was he was searching for.

Now the idea of paying a woman for sex was common and ugly. The drugged girls that arrived at his house every Wednesday were pure and compliant, unhindered by motive. Their eyes showed him no masked scorn.

He lifted the bottle again; wine splashed onto his robe and dripped down his chest. In the dim light, he looked disheveled, hair hanging over his face, his jaw slack, a gullet of flesh hanging below his chin, his Adam's apple prominent with every swallow.

"Fuck this," Lynch slurred. His limp penis poked through the gap in his gown. There'd be no entry in his journal for this; he wanted to keep nothing from these vulgar whores.

He lashed out again, landing a flat hand on the blonde's back.

"Hey! That is sore!" she said, straightening up, a thin dribble of saliva running down her chin.

Lynch ignored her; picked up her G-string and stretched it between his hands.

Sex offender. He'd first heard the term when he was sixteen. His mother had uttered it. *"I can't believe I've raised him to be a sex offender. He's just like you."* She had been talking to his father.

Lynch didn't feel any less of a sex offender because the prostitutes consented. Sex as a transaction was rape, he rationalized. Both ways. They were raping him too, taking advantage of his urges in exchange for money. When he no longer had money, their willingness would evaporate.

"Let's have some fun," Lynch said, lunging at the blonde.

He lassoed the G-string over her head, wrenched her off the bed and fell on top of her.

"What the fuck're you doing?" she screamed, legs scissoring around his torso. "Get the fuck off me!"

Lynch wrenched the underwear tightly, the material cutting into the blonde's neck. The redhead roused herself into a sitting position.

"Help! I can't breathe!" the blonde screamed again. She tried to reach a discarded stiletto.

The redhead leaped off the bed onto Lynch's back, her long red nails digging into his shoulder as she tried to free her partner.

"Fucking asshole!"

Lynch seized the redhead's arm in one hand while maintaining his grip on the blonde with the other. Her neck felt like Plasticine beneath his fingers. Both girls were now clawing at him with extended nails, hacking at his face and neck. Lynch elbowed the redhead off him, but lost his hold on the blonde in the same movement. The redhead fell backwards, hitting her head against the edge of the door. He refocused his attention on the blonde, clutching for the G-string at her chafed neck.

The redhead recovered and charged at Lynch.

"Let her go, bastard!" she screamed, wrapping her arm around his neck and pulling him backwards. He lost balance and released the G-string. The two hookers ended up on top of him in a tangle of naked bodies.

"What the fuck!" screamed the blonde, slapping him repeatedly in the face.

Lynch started to laugh. Finally, he had a hard-on.

Lynch's empty house echoed the hollow feeling in the pit of his stomach. The hookers were gone. He'd had to dispense with the last few hundred-rand notes in his wallet to appease them. They'd left in a clamor of foreign epithets and hand gestures as they stomped down the drive to the waiting car. Lynch had ensured the front door was locked, just in case their handler had any funny ideas.

He sat at his desk. He'd just watched *Forest Frolic* again, his favorite video. Amazing how an innocent girl in the woods could arouse him so much more efficiently than two naked prostitutes on his bed.

He dialed a number. This time Kryff answered his call.

"Mr. Lynch," Kryff said. The voice was impassive.

"Finally you answer. I really did not appreciate what you delivered to me last week," Lynch said.

"I noticed," Kryff replied. "You left me with damaged goods."

Lynch swallowed.

"Well, what did you expect? It was a waste of my week."

"A waste?"

"I couldn't do anything with her. She was...tacky." Lynch's anger had subsided somewhat. As an afterthought, he asked. "What did you do with her?"

"You shouldn't concern yourself with that," Kryff said coolly.

"Well, what happened to the waitress? Kim?"

After a pause, Kryff replied, "It's not an exact science, Mr. Lynch, as I'm sure you can appreciate. I tried. There was no adequate opportunity. I apologize for the...the problem. I sincerely hope that a similar incident doesn't happen again, and I strongly advise against it, if you get my meaning. But I think I understand your needs better. It won't happen again."

Lynch was encouraged. Kryff was not about to expel or expose him.

"I hope not," he said calmly. "I can always go back to Dark Video, you know?"

"Of course," said Kryff.

"Now, I called to ask about..." Lynch began.

"The photograph you showed me?"

"Yes," said Lynch, squeezing his cellphone in anticipation.

"I have news."

"Yes," Lynch was impatient. When Kryff did not continue: "Get on with it."

"A good find. We haven't discussed the costs for this project, Mr. Lynch," said Kryff. "I think ten thousand is a fair price. I have incurred expenses."

"Yes, of course," said Lynch. Ten thousand. It was steep. But he'd carried the dream for so long that it seemed inevitable.

"Thank you. I have her name and address."

Lynch felt his heart pound. *A good find.*

"How would you like me to proceed?" Kryff asked.

THE STRIP JOINT

Robbie cursed, pulled his head from beneath the bonnet of the Mazda and looked up to the heavens. A sheet of high clouds looked like cracked ice in the sky.

An annoying start to the afternoon. His car battery was dead and he'd just dropped his Nokia, sending the battery and plastic case in different directions. When he reassembled the phone and entered his pin, there was a text message:

gorky park 8pm meet me for business deal Sylvana

Sylvana. What did she want?

The sight of her name caused Robbie's face to redden as he cast his mind back to that darkened shower. Was it her? That cinnamon comment...

And why did she want to meet at Gorky Park, a "revue bar" in town? Surely she wasn't a stripper? With that body of hers, though, she could easily qualify.

Robbie was intrigued. He imagined Fallon might have something to do with it. He called Tony Beacon but got no answer, decided against leaving a message. No one checked voicemail these days anyway.

"Damn it," Robbie muttered, as the plastic face of the phone came loose again. His car was a dud, so was his phone.

A new model Ford Focus with six surfboards on the racks raced down the hill. The driver hooted when he saw Robbie struggling to get his car going.

Robbie wiped his hands and shut the bonnet. He'd give it a try a bit later; otherwise he'd have to roll start down the hill.

A few hours later, Robbie parked in Buitengracht Street, on a corner so he could get a car guard to push him, just in case. His wallet contained two R200 notes from the envelope. He'd spent less than a thousand on the Plett weekend, most of it on petrol. Tony's largesse had kept the costs down.

He pocketed his keys and slammed the Mazda door.

Any night at Gorky Park was busy. Wednesday was no exception. The bouncer blocked his progress, pointed at the ticket booth.

"Uh," Robbie hesitated. "I'm here to meet someone. On business."

"Everyone's here to meet someone," the bouncer replied. "On business."

"No. I mean. I've been invited," Robbie explained.

"Yeah. Who?"

"Sylvana," Robbie said.

The bouncer chuckled. "Sorry, mate. You still got to pay at the counter."

R150 entry fee. Robbie swallowed and paid up. He was glad he'd worn a collared shirt.

Gorky Park was one of Cape Town's premier strip clubs: a house of illicit glamour, sexy girls, and expensive drinks. The clientele was predictable. Men with power, men with Porsches and yachts and villas, men wanted in overseas countries.

Robbie felt the hackles rise on the back of his neck.

The room was filled with seated men looking like punters at an auction; topless girls primping on chairs or hustling between the tables; nude girls performing air dances on tables, writhing elastically on shiny poles to Kelis singing *Milkshake*.

Robbie bowed his head and maintained focus, stopped a waitress, clothed.

"I'm looking for Sylvana."

The waitress pointed to the stairs. A sign above indicated that it led to the VIP Section.

He made for the stairs, where a hostess stopped him. "You VIP?" she asked.

Robbie shook his head. In the back yard of student-land, Rondebosch, he would have spun a story. Here he was out of his comfort zone.

"I'm here to see Sylvana."

The hostess asked his name and left him waiting at the VIP entrance. She returned presently and opened the gate.

"Up this flight of stairs, then another."

A thick aroma of cigar smoke, perfume, and body odor choked the building; the scent was deeply ingrained into the walls and the couches, hinting at danger and mystery. The VIP lounge contained low drinks tables and chairs, couched booths with open curtains, more clients, more girls, the décor plush and velvety. Robbie watched a girl in six-inch clear-plastic heels lead a man behind a curtain.

He ascended a second flight of stairs to the top floor, an area ten meters by ten: the Platinum Zone. A handful of patrons were outnumbered by dancers. Heads turned as Robbie entered.

Robbie looked at his shoes. Navy Polo shirt, khaki pants, and sockless tennis shoes. He doubted he topped the shortlist of house desirables.

He scanned the room for Sylvana, half expecting Fallon to emerge. He hoped she would.

Curtained cubicles surrounded the room, some closed, some open. In the center, a solitary girl with her back to him swayed on a small circular dance floor enclosed by chrome railings. She was tall and slim, with a perfect pert ass. Like she'd come out of a machine.

Robbie entered a cubicle, curtains open, and eased himself along the cushioned couch to face the dance floor.

The girl on the dance floor swiveled in his direction. Robbie's heart jumped as he recognized her: Sylvana. She was a stripper after all. She spotted him, winked, and twisted away to the rhythm of the music.

A clothed waitress arrived to take his drinks order.

"One Castle."

"And for your lady."

Robbie hesitated. My lady. He hoped this wasn't going to be a waste of his time. "What do you recommend?"

The waitress smiled and laid down starry place mats on the table. She was early thirties, looked older; he imagined she'd once been attractive. He wondered what she thought of Gorky Park, whether she envied the young girls and their tight bodies and fistfuls of easy cash. Or pitied them.

"Bubbles," she said with a smile.

"Good to go," he said, giving her a thumbs-up. She returned shortly with a silver ice bucket, an unopened bottle of Moët et Chandon, and a single Castle. Robbie fingered the label on the bottle. He'd never ordered champagne before.

What the hell am I getting myself into?

He leaned back and tried to make himself comfortable. He was intrigued, as he watched topless girls parading past the booths. He could see them assessing each client: clothes, looks, state of intoxication. Relentless predators, trained to pounce. Masters of self-exploitation and the up-sell. In the limited time they had to recover their nightly investment in the place, they strutted their stuff hard upon the strip-club real estate.

A dark-haired girl with a glittery bra and tassels slid in beside him without invite. So much for formalities, Robbie thought. He wondered what his ex-girlfriend would think of her lingerie. He could see her red nipples through the sheer of her bra.

"I'm, uh, with someone," Robbie said, sipping his beer. He kept his eyes straight in front.

"You like it here, honey?" she asked in foreign accent, ignoring his attempted barrier.

"Awesome," Robbie replied without enthusiasm.

"Yes, it's awesome. I think so." Marketing and Communication 101. Lesson one: reflect the client's language. "What your name?"

Robbie smiled. He didn't want to appear rude. He was suddenly wondering why he was here. Because he thought he was going to get lucky? Because he thought he had another blow job on the cards?

"I'm Robbie."

"Robbie. I'm Nadia. Please to meet you, Robbie." She said it as if she'd been waiting all day for this moment to meet him. Great technique, thought Robbie.

She offered her hand, soft and feminine, made eye contact. Robbie was starting to appreciate the allure. Unfortunately, he wasn't planning to regale her with stories of sports cars and speedboats so she could demonstrate her listening skills then analyze his prospects and maximize the spend.

"Would you like to buy me drink?" she said. The bottle of Moët floated untouched in its ice bucket.

"I really am here with someone," he said. He felt awkward for her, imagining the pressure she was under to sell herself over and over again. "I am sure there are lots of people requiring your company. You are very beautiful."

Two men entered the lounge pursued by five eager dancers.

"Thank you, Robbie." Gracious. "What do you do?"

Robbie sighed. Poor student. He doubted she'd show him her underarms for what he was willing to pay.

"I'm a systems engineer." A white lie. But he'd hopefully be one in a few years' time. He resisted asking questions about her. Checked the time instead.

"Oh, engineer? That's really good." Gratuitous praise. "I love engineer." Flattery. She smiled broadly.

Robbie glanced at her. The tassels came from inside her quarter-cup bra. She crossed her legs. Robbie wondered whether she got formal training on the art of seduction, or was it just dressing-room secrets passed down from veteran to rookie?

"I love your country." More praise. And a positive attitude. Robbie was considering applauding her soft-sell technique when Sylvana appeared at the table. He hadn't noticed her set finish. He looked up to see a dark-skinned girl in a leather jacket and knee-high boots in her place on the stage. Portishead's haunting *Glory Box* now played over the club speakers as she swayed from side to side. "Give me a reason to love you," sang Beth

Gibbons sexily, as the girl unzipped the jacket and let her well-crafted breasts reveal themselves.

Sylvana muttered some words to Nadia in a language that sounded to Robbie like Russian, and the girls exchanged places in the booth. Nadia disappeared into the darkness of the room without a word.

"And I love yours," Robbie muttered as she left.

"You having a nice time?" Sylvana raised her eyebrows at him as she made herself comfortable.

"Awesome," said Robbie, watching Nadia gather herself and scan the room for another target. He felt as though he knew her. A moment shared.

"No really, Robbie, how are you?" asked Sylvana more forcefully, capturing his attention.

It dawned on him that perhaps he'd misread the text message. He was the business. He'd better break the news soon.

The waitress appeared. Sylvana gestured at the bottle of champagne, and she removed it dripping from the bucket, gently popping the cork. She filled Sylvana's glass and disappeared.

Robbie wondered where Tony Beacon had found Sylvana. Here? Had he paid her to spend the weekend in Plett with him? It seemed a plausible notion.

A suited, grey-haired man emerged from a booth in conversation with a young stripper. Their faces were red. She had her hand on his arm, was whispering into his ear. Robbie saw him hesitate, then reach into his pocket and extract several hundred-rand notes. The girl smiled and led him back into the booth, closing the curtain behind them.

Fantasy costs.

"This isn't my scene." Robbie turned his attention back to Sylvana.

Sylvana nodded and smiled, removed an HP Palmtop from her handbag and placed in on the table. "Let's get down to business." She fiddled with the Palmtop.

Business, thought Robbie, lifting his glass. *This should be interesting.* Not quite what he'd expected, though. At a table across the room, he watched a credit card being swiped. He didn't even own a credit card.

A girl mounted a table between two men.

Robbie's grain of doubt suddenly seemed to grow. This was not his place. These were not his people.

The girl squatted against one of the men's face. Robbie tore his eyes from the stripper, guilty for intruding on her privacy, and his eyes fell on the dark-skinned dancer on the stage. She was entirely naked, entwined around the center pole.

"So Robbie," Sylvana said, grabbing his attention. "You need some cash."

Robbie was surprised.

"Who told you that?"

"Never mind. You'll take four thousand?"

"For what?" Robbie stared at her in amazement.

"For the weekend in Plettenberg Bay."

Robbie screwed up his eyes, scratched behind his head. He didn't have a clue what she was talking about.

"I'll show you. You'll like," she said, her eyes dancing. Sylvana dragged the stylus across the Palmtop, opening up Windows Media Player.

Robbie heard the sound of running water before he saw a picture. He realized immediately what was coming.

"I get six thousand," said Sylvana. "It's fair. For wet hair and mouth of cum. Watch!"

Robbie stared in disbelief. On screen, he kicked off his shorts and stepped beneath a torrent of water. The shot changed: another camera panned down his naked body. There were at least two cameras, professionally edited. Robbie leaned forward, appalled, mesmerized.

"Whoosh." Sylvana mimicked the sound of the water. "I love special effect. You got good body, Robbie."

On the Palmtop screen, the lighting changed, a door closed, a girl entered. Sylvana. A wink and big smile for the camera.

"Jesus, it *was* you!" Robbie whispered in acceptance. *Those* tits should have given it away. Like ski jumps. He looked away from the screen. The dancing girl was swaying like a serpent. He looked back; Sylvana was between his legs, her head bobbing back and forth. By now the shot was in night vision. The camera zoomed in. Robbie recalled how dark it had been, couldn't believe the clarity of detail. Where were the cameras hidden?

The shot panned to his face, lingered on his pleasure.

"Why?" he asked. He tore his eyes away, thought he looked ridiculous.

Sylvana rubbed her fingers together. "We all need bucks, Robbie."

"But who pays for something like this?" His stomach swirled with horror and revulsion.

She waved her arms extravagantly. "Look at these people. Take your pick. If they're not here in club, maybe they're at home with computer and Internet."

On screen, Robbie's moans were audible above the sound of running water. He looked back at the screen, cringed.

"Fuck this!" He snapped and slammed the screen down. "Turn it off!"

Sylvana raised both hands in fright, knocking over her glass of champagne. "What you doing, Robbie?" she said.

He stood up, rage rising in his throat, and stuck his index finger in her face.

"This is flipping outrageous," he spluttered. "This is illegal. It's a fucking invasion of my privacy."

Sylvana's shoulders narrowed. "Robbie. I know you need money. I..."

He pointed to the Palmtop, interrupting her: "I'm not that desperate. I swear. Get rid of it! Nobody is going to see that."

Sylvana reached into her handbag, removed her purse. "Robbie, I..."

Robbie grabbed the purse, stuffed it back in her handbag and pushed the handbag into her lap. "What don't you understand?" he shouted.

Sylvana looked around, concerned that Robbie would attract the attention of the bouncers. Every inch of the building was under 24-hour surveillance; she didn't want the manager asking questions.

"That video was taken without my consent," he said. "I could get you thrown in jail."

Sylvana shrugged and removed a packet of cigarettes from her handbag, her lips tight as tweezers.

He stood up.

"I want nothing to do with this."

"Be my guest," she said, lighting a cigarette with a BIC lighter. "But first you must pay for these drinks."

Robbie took out R50 from his pocket, threw it on the table. "That's for my beer."

"It costs lot more than that," Sylvana said. She inhaled deeply then blew smoke though her nose. "Careful you haven't drunk what you can't afford, Robbie."

Robbie stared at her. "Get fucked." He turned in the direction of the stairs.

A MATTER OF WHEN

Lynch floored his red, old-model BMW 525i along De Waal Drive. He veered into the left lane to overtake a Nissan bakkie advertising plumbing services, then pulled in front of it. The driver flashed him a middle finger out the window.

Not appropriate behavior.

Waiting nine years before having a second child—now that was not appropriate, Lynch thought. He'd been an only child for nearly a decade, his father taking him shooting, riding and fishing. The special child. Then she'd arrived, the pink bundle. Estelle! He had instantly hated her. And yet he'd loved her, too. Such conflicting emotions.

Lynch flicked on the CD player and tried to ease the black, angry thoughts that filled his head.

Let's change the subject, his mother always said. He'd wanted to know why Estelle was always getting presents.

Change the subject. Golf.

His golf bag was in the boot of his car. His lousy round at Steenberg had been expensive: drinks and a few hundred bucks taken off him with relish. He didn't know what was wrong; he seemed to hit from one sand bunker to the next. At the bar afterwards, Vic Masoni had quizzed him relentlessly about his love life.

"Come on, Jules," he'd said, with the others as audience. "You're lucky, you can take them home, no problem."

In the past, he'd accompanied his married golf partners on nights out in town, which invariably ended up under the soft lights of a strip club.

Neither Vic nor his other golfing buddies, Steve van der Westhuizen and Mike Turnkey, had ever visited his house in Bishopscourt. Not that he'd ever dream of having them around. Vic drove a Ferrari Modena Spyder, owned houses in Hermanus and Fancourt. Mike had been married three times. Steve had two mistresses. Why would he want them at his house? It's not like they had much to talk about.

But Julian wanted so badly to tell them about the Mickey Finn Club.

He'd thought about it. After all, he justified, it wasn't as if he'd killed anyone. But he'd held his tongue.

At the Rondebosch turnoff, Lynch looped under the highway and up the hill into the UCT campus. Fresh shoots of cling ivy gripped the knobby wall fronting from the university onto De Waal Drive. Some wag had graffitied the road sign: "Upper Campussy," it read. After two aimless circles of the campus, he drove down Woolsack Drive and turned left onto the narrow roadway passing between two orange blocks, the Leo Marquard and Tugwell residences. He pulled his car into a parking bay and turned off the engine.

Lying on the passenger seat was an A4 print-out of the *Forest Frolic* girl and a parcel wrapped in brown paper. His girl. On the back, printed in black ink, were details provided by Kryff: "Terri Phillips. Tugwell Hall." Beneath the name and residence was her identity number.

Lynch turned the photograph upside down and stared up at the concrete paneled building. A thin line of cloud, like the vapor trail from a jet, seemed to streak downwards toward its rooftop.

Terri Phillips lived here.

Angie Dean was also from Tugwell. It had been on her student card. It was more than coincidence, Lynch decided. A sign. Angie Dean was a message. That he was close. He should never have discarded her, never let her go. He was going to keep Terri Phillips. Just like Willie Wolfe kept Patty Hearst.

He opened his window and allowed the heat to mingle with the cool conditioned air inside the car.

Terri Phillips would be his; he knew it with utter certainty as he gazed up at the vast tubular building. Perhaps she was upstairs getting dressed. Or showering.

He imagined bringing her to drinks at Peddlers in Constantia to meet Vic and the others.

That morning Lynch had written Terri's name in bold print across the top of a new page in his journal. He'd printed another image taken from the *Forest Frolic* clip, and pasted it in the center of the first page. He planned to dedicate a number of pages in the journal to her. She'd be number ten. On Wednesday night, number nine had been a second consecutive disappointment. Delivered by Diva, the Dark Video operative, she'd been so heavily sedated he may as well have been making love to a dead person.

Lynch opened his eyes, adjusted his dark glasses and leaned back in his seat. He could watch the girls come and go via his rear-view mirror.

Earlier in the day, Lynch had logged on to Premier Marque's company website and tampered with the instructions in the company's banking interface, diverting half of the following week's bimonthly VAT payment to his own account. Lynch had tried this twice before; both times the fraud had gone undetected, by his company and the South African Revenue Service.

The payment would cover his overdraft and allow him to settle some of the outstanding bills. He'd pay Kryff and Dark Video first.

Without the engine running, the temperature in the BMW spiked rapidly. His shirt felt damp. He decided he needed to get a feel of the place on foot; stepped out of his car and crossed the road, parcel in hand.

The embankment outside Tugwell was interspersed with fast-growing clumps of winter grass. He entered the building and approached the reception desk. "Terri Phillips, please," he said. He wiped his forehead with the sleeve of his shirt.

The receptionist skimmed a list of students then buzzed on the switchboard. It rang five times.

"She's probably at lectures," the receptionist said, smiling politely.

Lynch smiled back.

"I'm her father," he said. He put the parcel on the counter. "I'm meant to pick up a letter from her room." He checked his Rolex. "She said she'd be back by now."

"You want to wait for her?" the receptionist suggested.

Lynch checked the time again.

"I would, but I'm late for a board meeting." He tapped on the counter in a show of impatience. The receptionist smiled sympathetically.

"No way I can shoot up and collect it?" he said.

The receptionist's expression changed. "Unfortunately not. Rules. Plus I don't have a key."

"OK," said Lynch. "Understandable. I'm glad security is solid. Can I leave this parcel for her?"

The receptionist took the parcel from him and slotted it into a pigeonhole. Room 515.

Lynch flashed a toothy smile.

A girl sauntered in, clutching books to her chest, shapely legs extending from a short skirt. She walked past Lynch without a glance.

"Is there anything else?" the receptionist asked. She'd been watching him admiring the girl.

Lynch cleared his throat. His cellphone beeped: a message from his secretary checking whether he would be returning to the office. He held the phone up. "My meeting," he said.

Lynch returned to his BMW and drove back to the office. He'd gone in hope more than expectation; knew that seeing Terri was unlikely, but he'd wanted to breathe in the atmosphere of her surroundings.

The glimpse of the girl in the short skirt had aroused him. He wished it were Wednesday again already.

He phoned Kryff and suggested he put a tag on Terri Phillips.

He wouldn't rush this one.

It was simply a matter of when.

Lynch stripped naked, chuckled at the message in the changing room: MASSAGES FOR THERAPEUTIC PURPOSES ONLY.

The masseuse was new, a humorless woman with huge hands. She scrubbed him down with salt, sprayed him with jets of water.

"Do you mind if I do your front?" she asked. He picked her accent as German.

Lynch's weight was a constant 100 kilograms, not bad considering his height, but his sagging gut was causing him to stoop.

"Mind?" Lynch replied. He rolled over, the masseur holding the towel out before her. "Be my guest."

He wished the masseuse could see the type of girls he was fucking. Young and beautiful.

He wondered what Terri Phillips would make of the parcel in her pigeonhole: a folded newspaper from 1990, the year of her birth, wrapped in brown paper. He knew her room number: 515; wished the receptionist had allowed him in to see it.

The masseuse worked up from his feet, his upper leg, drilled into his groin. Her fists pressed lightly against his scrotum. Nothing moved.

"You like doing this?" he asked her as she moved up, took his right arm and stretched it.

"Ya." She looked German too. "What do you do?"

"Never mind," he answered and closed his eyes.

He pictured Terri Phillips's room. It would be pink, with teddy bears resting on the pillows of her bed.

The masseuse pressed her thumbs against his temple.

He pictured a maturing bottle of wine, his body the bottle, his head the vagueness of its cork. Lynch felt the pressure against his scalp, the sensation echoing throughout his body. He had a mental image of his head in her hands, as her thumbs rotated slowly and firmly in clockwise circles.

He thought about Kryff. *Death was a remedy.* His father had obviously realized that. When the world got too big for him, he checked out.

He imagined his own interment, his brain a block of butter. The masseuse's fingers seemed to be grinding deeper and deeper into his head.

Deeper and deeper.

He felt himself disconnecting, fracturing; he wanted to move, to sit up, but couldn't. She was anointing his face in oil. He could feel it drying on his skin, his face a pale-grey color. Shiny. Her fingers broke through to the place where the damage was set and his brain collapsed like a rotten cork.

He jarred, sat upright.

"Get the fuck away from me!" He retched forward, a foul-smelling odor in his nostrils.

Lynch composed himself on the pine planks of the sauna, visualized toxins seeping from his pores, staining the flooring.

It wasn't good form to abuse the club's staff, he knew. Like shitting on one's own doorstep. He'd apologized to the masseuse, offered her a tip.

The scent of eucalyptus oil filled the narrow room as he ladled water from a wooden pail onto the furnace.

What had happened on the massage table scared him. He pressed his thumbs lightly against his temples.

The masseuse had triggered some forgotten memories, he reckoned, their recall smothered by years and years of practiced amnesia. The smell had unlocked the flashback; the memory of his previous life.

The intrusion scared him.

He pictured a tarred playground at junior school, little girls in grey skirts running along the edge of the tennis-court fence. He stood alone, socks down, knees bent, staring through the fence. When he saw the teacher, his expression changed from thrill to fear. He ran away.

No, thought Lynch. He didn't want to think about it.

He was an adult now, a director of a listed company and a member of a golf club with successful friends. The boy was gone; those desires were not his.

How long ago was it? Thirty plus years. Where in his subconscious had these thoughts been residing—in the far recess of his brain, under a cluttered warehouse full of other memories? He needed a fire in his head to get rid of it.

He remembered his father's car, an old Ford Cortina, powder-blue like the sky, the humiliated boy sitting in the back in silence. His father never said a word to him. On the seat next to him was his little sister.

Not appropriate behavior.

Lynch's stomach turned.

The incident with his sister had been an act of revenge and love at the same time. *Do unto others.*...She belonged, he didn't. His mother loved her more than him. He loved her more than himself.

"For fuck's sake." Lynch clapped his hands together and forced out his wide grin. It didn't matter.

He was Julian Lynch, a director, a successful businessman, with his choice of beautiful women.

He tried to picture one of his conquests, stood up suddenly. Sweat dripped from his body like a tap, the planks below wet and greasy with impurity.

The heat was overwhelming. He closed his eyes and pictured his father in the coffin, face grey and elongated.

When the torment ends, he concluded, there is death.

ROBBIE'S PUZZLE

Milton Cullen owned a cellphone, but it was never turned on. Robbie knew to call his father on the Albany farm line.

"Dad," he said. He normally spoke to his mother. She spoke for them both.

"Yep."

Always the gruff old man.

"I..."

He wondered what his father would say about the video. *Stupid fool.*

In the background, he could hear a tractor. He could picture his father in short khaki pants, green Wellingtons, skin brown as berries. Robbie had three elder brothers, all farmers. They'd all end up looking the same.

"You busy?" Robbie asked.

"Always. Chicory doesn't farm itself, you know, boy?"

The same old line. Sometimes chicory, sometimes pineapples.

Robbie was worried. He wanted to talk, needed advice. It wasn't only the video. It was the incident at the Blue Venus and the money he'd received from Fallon.

"How's university?" Milton Cullen asked. A rare question. He'd ask a few more if Robbie got him onto the subject of rugby.

"Fine."

Robbie could hear the slow rasp of his father's breathing. He imagined he'd come into the farmhouse to make some coffee, wanted to get back to the lands.

"Is Mom around?" Robbie asked.

"She's gone into town to buy groceries."

"OK then. Will chat soon."

"Sure, Rob. You go well, boy."

"A most disturbing tale."

Denny attempted some sympathy, but his glinting eyes told another story. He dragged on a stick of skunkweed, looking like an old man in the furry light. Words came out as he exhaled, sounding like he was talking underwater.

Robbie's bottom lip was swollen, a purple bruise below the left eye. Strip-club bouncers don't appreciate it when you forget to pay the bill. After upsetting one of their girls.

He knew he'd behaved stupidly, but it was the guilt that was killing him.

Guilt. Like a slow worm eating your brain. You have to tell someone: the employee his colleague, the husband his buddy, the criminal his cellmate, the pervert his diary.

"Happens all the time," Denny continued. "Meet a chick at a club, next minute she's giving you massive head butts in the shower. Except it turns out to be some Russian stripper and they want to swallow your DNA and then pay big cash for high-def footage!"

The walls of Denny's room were papered with beer adverts and unframed posters depicting half-naked women, their corners frayed and torn. There was one of Marilyn Monroe above the desk that the previous resident had left behind. A papsak of Drostdyhof semi-sweet wine perched on an adjacent shelf, the silver bag reflecting the sun through the window, a long transparent straw trailing down from the bag to Denny's desk. Drinking gadgets were one of the bonuses of studying engineering.

"Footage!" Denny exploded in a fit of dagga-induced giggles. He was running the iChalky application on a new iPhone.

Robbie shook his head and rotated the elephant-hair bracelet.

Flashbacks from the shower scene repeated on him like a bad meal. He'd been played for a sucker.

Robbie dragged on the cheroot, the smoke biting his throat. He coughed.

Denny's room was pristine for a change: bed made, no dirty coffee cups, the counter and desk wiped, no mushroom cultivars. He was turning over a new leaf, he claimed. Denny would do anything to avoid studying.

"You get any good shots in?" Denny asked, sparring with a few air punches, as he stepped forward to eye out Robbie's wounds.

He appeared to move toward Robbie, his face too close, a complete disrespect of spatial boundaries. He reclaimed the wet joint from Robbie and attempted a final drag, then stashed it in a perlemoen-shell ashtray.

Robbie ran his sleeve across his face and shook his head.

"They were fucking bouncers, man. What could I do?"

The single Castle and bottle of champagne had cost him more than the weekend in Plett. He clenched his fists at the thought.

Denny wore a pair of blue baggy underpants and an athletics vest, hadn't shaved for three days. Two plastic bank bags contained his stash of marijuana. Swaziland's finest.

"What we really need is some cheese," he said, referring to a supply of hydroponic marijuana doing the rounds in Cape Town. "That stuff really gets you flying."

"Yeah, this is putting me to sleep," said Robbie. He seldom smoked with Denny. It just sent him to bed early.

But the weed wouldn't dull the edges of his agitation. He had a bad feeling about Sylvana, told Denny as much.

"Hey, stop being so...paranoid, dude," Denny chided. He paused, appeared pleased with his choice of word. "Paranoia, paranoia, everybody's coming to get me!" he sang. Then he snapped back to the matter in question. "Look, Robbie, dude, you've got to suck it up, man! Are you kidding me? You got a free blow job from a Russian stripper and now she wants to pay you for it? Most guys would give their left nut for that story. And you don't even have a freaking girlfriend!"

"It's not that simple, man," Robbie responded, gesturing to his black eye. "The reality is..."

What was the reality? What did Sylvana have planned for the video? He imagined the kind of people who would watch it, watch him. It made him feel sick, violated. Some people might not care about other people watching their most intimate moments, but he wasn't one of them.

There was some truth in Denny's fatalistic advice, though. Robbie couldn't get his head around it. He didn't have a girlfriend. He needed money. Was there a problem?

"Reality is gravity, bru!" Denny professed. "Jump out a fucking window and see what happens. Reality is, there's terabytes of that shit. No one's going to notice. Take the cash, ask questions later, fly free like an untamed wildcat."

Robbie knew Denny was high as a kite, but some of what he said made sense.

Incense burned in a modified candlestick holder, a scent of sandalwood blending in with the smell of weed. Robbie squeezed his eyes shut, trying to focus. Nothing. Just gravity.

"I have a feeling," he said eventually. "Something she said. 'Careful you don't drink what you can't afford.' Something like that."

"So don't drink it."

"It was past tense."

"No, you said, 'Don't drink.' That's present, my friend." Robbie tried to interject, correct himself, but Denny continued: "Doesn't matter either way. It's too late then. So you're out of the cash and now some crazy bitch has a video of you bare-assed in the shower and who knows what she's gonna do with it." Denny curled his arms above his head. "Whoa! Whoa! Now that's big news, bru." He pushed his face into Robbie's. "Whoa!"

Robbie grinned and pushed Denny away.

"You can't be serious about anything," Denny said before Robbie could get it out.

Robbie's smile disappeared. He couldn't explain how he felt. Melanie had been his only girlfriend. And they were broke up. So it wasn't a big deal getting a blow job in the shower. And he could have stopped it but he didn't.

Denny shrugged, pulled a packet from his pocket, and extracted a bent cigarette. He struck a match on his shoe and lit it, drew, blew the smoke at Robbie. His expression softened.

"I'm serious about this," he said. "'Don't drink what you can't afford.' She's foreign. It was literal. Why'd you order fucking Moët?"

He waved his hands about then let rip with a canister of Glade.

Robbie nodded, stared toward the window, as Denny quietly giggled to himself.

"This wouldn't have happened if..." Robbie started then tailed off. He didn't respect self-pity.

Denny cleared his throat and drew on his cigarette, long and slow.

"You thinking about your ex? Whoa! The chick who dumped you? Stole your youth then ran off with some douchebag artist wanker freak? What's she got to do with fucking anything?"

Robbie stared at the wall. He'd been thinking about Fallon. If he hadn't been hoping it was her in the shower, maybe it wouldn't have happened.

"Listen. Best thing that ever happened to you. You gotta see the world, son. Variation. Love the one you're with."

Robbie stood up gingerly. Melancholy was a waste of time. He felt exposed, couldn't think straight. And, like Denny, he was very, very high.

Robbie was thirsty. He poured water from his kettle into a glass and downed it.

He opened the cash envelope received from Fallon and counted out nine two-hundred-rand notes. *Bloody Moët.* "Bubbles"—he didn't know the difference between champagne and sparkling wine; how was he to know they'd charge him nearly two grand for a bottle of booze?

Robbie sat down at his desk, brought his laptop out of hibernation. It reported the delivery of an email, a message from Tony Beacon to say he'd posted photos from the weekend in Plettenberg Bay on Facebook.

Shit, Robbie thought. He needed to chat to Tony. He checked his watch. A bit late.

Robbie clicked on the link, scanned through them. Tony in most of them, lots of girls in bikinis, then Sylvana's big red lips....Robbie felt ill.

Why was Sylvana in Plett in the first place? he wondered. A random invite by Tony? Perhaps a similar incident had happened to him.

Fallon wasn't in any of the pics.

I'm very serious. This is life and death. You must never refer to what happened.

He eyed the envelope. First he'd received money for aiding Fallon at the Blue Venus. An undercover job, she'd said. Now he'd been offered money for acting in a porn clip. Was there a connection?

Fallon had asked him for discretion. But if her organization was involved in investigations into drink spiking, maybe it was best to tell her about this.

What if she asked him why he didn't stop Sylvana in the shower? It wasn't like he was incapable. Would he admit that he'd thought it was her?

He clicked through to his home page on Facebook. He had friend requests from six people. Three he recognized from Plett: Chewing Gum, Chinese Eyes and Pearls.

He searched the site for Sylvana. Several options, but not his Sylvana. Not the girl who'd sucked him off in a shower and filmed it...

Robbie clicked on Fallon Trafford's profile. They weren't friends so he had limited access; wished he could see a list of her friends.

Fallon Trafford

Fallon   is unavailable

Studied   BA LLB University of Johannesburg
Lives in   Cape Town, Western Cape

From   Joburg
Born on   19 December

You and Fallon No mutual friends

Education and work

Employers
Grad school   UJ

Philosophy

Religious Views   Capitalism

Favorite Quotations

> *"Whoever said money can't buy happiness*
> *simply didn't know where to go shopping"*
> *—Bo Derek*

Arts and Entertainment

Music	Black Eyed Peas
TV	South Park

Activities

Other	Travel

Basic Information

Interested in	Men
Relationship Status	Single
Sex	Female
Looking for	Friendship

Rather bland, Robbie concluded. Except for that missing employer. Why leave that off? He thought about Fallon's flat in Rosebank, the cheap rental furniture, the stark decor, no TV or electronics. Something was missing. Like she didn't really live there; like her real life was somewhere else.

He felt uncomfortable viewing her information without her knowledge. He hardly knew her.

His Nokia rang: the caller ID stated Tony Beacon. When Robbie answered, the alarm in Tony's voice was palpable.

KING CARLOS

Carlos dimmed the overhead lights in his study. Rain was forecast for Yarrow Point but outside the sky was clear, a full moon presiding.

He opened a bottle of sparkling Perrier and returned to his desk, connecting a spanking new MacBook Air to one of the big screens mounted on the walls of his studio office. He'd bought it with cash the day before, the latest ultra-thin model with some extra RAM tacked on, and then reloaded a clean configuration from a flash drive.

The continual loading and reloading of software did not irritate Carlos. Rather, he found it therapeutic. He enjoyed wiping his system and creating a fresh instance; enjoyed the predictable progression of the laptop cycle— from all-powerful communications node to spent carcass. Sometimes within just a few days. He didn't trust a re-format. Jacker had created a reload process, which would, in case of emergency, allow Carlos to escape with a single flash drive and effortlessly resume his practice in another location.

The study was silent. His wife had been absent the whole day, returned laden with parcels from Gymboree and Carmilias, and sporting a spray tan. He had tracked her on GPS and kept track of her calls; she hadn't made any. Shopping was a good sign.

Carlos tapped in a URL address and entered a password. Besides the bottle of sparkling water and the MacBook Air, the surface of his desk was clear.

He clicked on a Flash Video format download and saved the URL in his Favorites folder. Once the download was complete, he disconnected from the Net to make certain the video did not contain any synchronization features. It was a standard trick of the trade. While this particular version of the video could play on a standard flash video player, Dark Video productions were shipped with a proprietary viewer; the application contained a cipher that synced back to the master host and enabled Carlos to track clients' usage of his works. So he knew their habits better than they did themselves.

Satisfied that his system was secure, Carlos reached for his handgrips in the lower drawer of his desk and settled back in the Aeron to evaluate a client's private moments.

Carlos lay flat in contemplation on top of the covers of his king-sized bed. As his thoughts turned over, his gaze drifted from the solid ebony head with bronze metal casing above him to the ceiling-wide mirror overhead. He found himself staring thoughtlessly at his wife beside him; she wore a frilly black nightie, cut low over her enhanced breasts. Looked like an actress from *Desperate Housewives*.

Having finished in his office for the day, Carlos had spent an hour in the downstairs gym, moving randomly between equipment, ending up with a speed session on the bicycle. He'd then showered, trimmed his moustache and prepared for a cleansing night's sleep.

His wife had other ideas, tried a saucy cleavage reveal as she turned to him. "You in the mood?" she asked, and slipped her hand into his silk shorts. Squeezed.

He wasn't.

She nuzzled her face against his armpit, breathed him in. Carlos used neutral scent deodorant. Fragrance was a distinguishing identifier he preferred to avoid.

She gave up, rolled back to her side. "When are you going to take me away, Carl?" she asked to his image on the ceiling.

Carlos was thinking about security. Jacker had shed no new light on the mystery of the arrested Dark Video clients. Whenever Carlos vented, Jacker got surly.

"Just fucking get to the bottom of it!" Carlos had blazed. "Stop giving me your techno-babble excuses."

Carlos liked Jacker to think he was technically limited.

Jacker had thought the list was the most viable explanation. What if someone with access to a Dark Video client list was leaking details to the authorities? Carlos knew it was impossible. He didn't keep a list; had no need for addresses and middle names because he knew his clients by heart.

He'd advised Jacker to stop thinking and start following instructions.

That, he mused, was the difference between Jacker and Samuel Chester, his paid muscle. Chester was an artisan. He followed instructions. He wasn't paid to think or have emotions. He was like a rocket bomb sent to travel silently through the night. But he was a rocket with no power of his own. He stood cold and dormant until Carlos programmed the destination and pulled the pin.

"Carl. For heaven sake!" His wife squeezed again; no interest, pulled her hand out, looked at it. "Are you with me? Why are you so distracted?"

He pulled her hand back into his shorts, tried to focus for a moment. Her fake tan smelled odd. She had also dyed her hair again. Even darker this time. He hadn't noticed until now.

Jacker had eventually been placated, but it riled Carlos that it was necessary to accommodate other people's egos. And he was concerned about the lack of explanation, had to conclude that anyone close to him was a risk—as they'd always been.

She pulled her hand out of his trunks, sighed. "Why aren't you interested in me, honey?"

Carlos got up, walked to the bedroom window. "Is your passport up to date?" he asked, looking out, scanning the floodlit perimeter. He would carry out a physical check on the fencing tomorrow. Sometimes in the virtual world, one neglected the obvious threats in the physical one.

"Passport?" She was sitting upright on the bed now, picking her nails and chewing gum with an open mouth.

Carlos knew that all the hi-tech security technology in the universe could not guarantee his safety. Breaches came from innocuous sources. A conversation overheard in a restaurant, a password carelessly written down, a boastful associate.

"If you're going to travel, you'll need some fucking papers."

"Carl!"

The way she said his name grated him. *Carl!* In a nasal cat-like twang. He had hit her before. That was why she left him. She had been nagging him about the amount of time he spent with his kid. Which was zero. She hadn't nagged again.

Her voice softened. "I don't like it when you swear, honey."

There was something wrong, he thought to himself. This wasn't the spoiled little princess he'd married. This was some gum-chewing skank. What was her game?

Top of Carlos's watchlist was the FBI. Their recent partnership with the National White Collar Crime Center and the Bureau of Justice Assistance was filtering cyber-crime leads to a crack team of law-enforcement agents.

"Where will we go?" she asked. He barely registered the question.

Dark Video had suffered a previous intrusion that had almost cost him dearly. Most worryingly, it had gone undetected by either himself or Jacker until the last moment. The breach had come from Cape Town—the same place giving Dark Video hassles right now....Was there a link?

Carlos had concluded that the offending mules in that case had used skill, perspiration, and a healthy dose of luck to come close to tracking him down. He wasn't sure what skills exactly, but he'd adjusted his procedures accordingly, including eliminating the ambient noise levels on his Skype calls and limiting the duration of calls.

But luck was difficult to defend against.

Tomorrow, he would schedule a fresh set of tests on the Dark Video website. Without Jacker's assistance.

Eliminate risk. Reduce dependency.

Carlos mused for a moment on his original Cape Town team, the Gorillas. What a treasure trove they'd delivered to him with their *Men In Grey Suits* masterpiece. And what a pity that he'd been forced to dispatch Chester, his silent rocket, to put an end to that silliness.

"Carl?"

Carlos ignored his wife, walked through to the bathroom. It was 10:30 pm. Soon he would go to sleep and another day would be lost to him forever. He picked up a set of red-handled handgrips and pumped obsessively.

So many little deaths...

It was a concept few people understood. The day that started when he awoke would end in sleep and nothing would ever be the same again. When his eyes closed and his brain relapsed into slumber, that day, with all its concerns, would be over forever and a new day would beckon.

The daily reincarnation gave Carlos optimism that all challenges could be overcome.

He leaned forward and splashed his face with cold water, gazed intently into the mirror. He understood the aspirations of the person who stared back at him. In his last breaths of the day, he always enjoyed the sight of that person's face.

VIRAL

"Give me the link," Robbie said weakly through his high, trying to focus on the words he was hearing. Tony Beacon was on the line, rapidly bringing him back to earth. Clothes were strewn about on the floor of his room; the munchies were kicking in.

"I don't know, it's long. Just go to YouTube. Search for 'blow job' and 'shower.'"

Keeping Tony on the line, Robbie logged on to the Internet using his Dell laptop. He typed in a few options, eventually located the clip, his face clearly discernible on the thumbnail. The full title was SUCKERED IN SHOWER: A VIRGIN BLOWJOB. 110 views, 5 likes. Posted one hour ago, by someone called Neveragain.

Robbie pressed play then stopped it immediately. No need; he'd seen it already.

"You got it?" Tony asked.

"Yeah."

"You're a star, man!"

Robbie was at a complete loss, his mind scrambled. "Listen, Tony. I had no idea I..." The counter clicked to 111. Somewhere someone had just watched him being sucked off by a stripper. He felt light-headed, like he was caught in a moment of unreality—as though he was watching himself watching himself.

There were two comments listed below the posting. From MustarD:

    WAY TO GO ROB!

And a second, five minutes ago, from someone called sKankY cHicK:

    OMG! I cant believe it. This Robbie Cullen!

He clicked Video Statistics. Most of the accesses were coming from mobile phones.

"How did you hear about it?" Robbie eventually managed.

"Got a text, dunno who from. Hey, I frigging paid that chick a couple a grand for the weekend—got some good poke but no shower blow job! Why didn't you tell me, dude?"

"I didn't know," Robbie answered, instantly aware that his answer sounded ridiculous. "I mean, I thought it was someone else." Even worse.

"What the fuck! Who?"

Robbie refreshed the window. The counter had increased to 112. Another person at his computer, or hunched over his cellphone, watching him.

"You make a good porn star, man," said Tony. He was obviously watching the video again.

"Look, Tony, I didn't know it was Sylvana. Serious."

Robbie's thoughts raced, a bead of sweat ran down his chest. How could he stop this? He couldn't just grab a cable and pull it out. And why had Sylvana posted the video on YouTube? Revenge for the scene in Gorky Park? For not going along with her? There was no cash to be made this way.

"Jesus, Rob. Hardcore. This is like a buy one, get one free!" The counter clicked to 113.

"Listen to me, Tony," Robbie implored. "I swear to God. It..." He was about to say: *It wasn't me.* "I mean....I didn't know it was Sylvana. I flipping didn't know it was being filmed!"

"That's your story and you're sticking to it!" Tony laughed. "Cool bananas, dude."

Robbie's email pinged:

Robbie! What you thinking?

The sender was an old schoolmate from St. Andrews; Robbie hadn't talked to him in a year.

Robbie clenched his jaw. He could see himself becoming the fail story of the year on FMyLife:

"Today a video taken secretly of my sexual
ecstasy—my 1st indulgence after three months
of abstentia—was posted on YouTube for all
my friends to watch. FML"
I agree your life sucks—you totally deserve it.

"So no idea who sent you that text you say?" asked Robbie wearily.

"No idea, man. No caller ID."

Shit, thought Robbie. How many teaser messages had been sent out?

"Look, Tony, send me the original text you got and I'll call you back."

Robbie toggled to YouTube's privacy tab and read the instructions for reporting a violation. An ominous message advised: "Contact your local police for further assistance if you feel you are in physical danger." He completed the six steps of the Privacy Complaint Process. His submission gave the uploader of the video forty-eight hours to remove the video. *Forty-eight hours?* I can't wait that long! Robbie checked his watch, wondering what time Gorky Park opened.

In step 3, the complaint process advised him to contact the uploader via YouTube's private messaging facility. He tried to get hold of Neveragain. She—or he—hadn't posted any other videos.

The video counter refreshed: 115.

Robbie picked up a dart and hurled it at the back of his door. He took a deep breath, imagining students on campus hunched over their laptops pressing play. He had to catch it before it went viral.

Tick, tick, tick.

He could almost hear the view counter ticking over. Once a video was online and viral, there was no way of halting the spread. If they killed it on one site, it would reappear on five others. Like the heads of the Hydra.

Robbie's cellphone beeped, another text:

> If you want to get a-head,
> you've got to give it. Nice!

Robbie slammed his palm on the desk. These were friends of his. The way they perceived him would change forever.

At 3 pm, Robbie was waiting on the street outside Gorky Park when the night manager arrived to open the club.

"I remember you," said the manager, wagging his finger. He wore a tight black T-shirt, Popeye on the front, "Beefcake" printed beneath.

Robbie explained. The Moët. The unpaid R1,800. He hadn't had the money on him.

"Oh dear," said the manager, adjusting his tight black jeans and exaggerating his facial expression. He pointed to Robbie's black eye. "Such bullies," he sympathized. "I'm Deon, by the way."

Robbie followed Deon into the glass-walled office and handed over an envelope containing the outstanding debt. The stale scent of smoke and perfume reminded Robbie of his previous visit. In the sterile light of day, it was hard to imagine the writhing girls and eager punters; the empty floor was devoid of energy.

"Hmm. R200 notes. Gonna have to check them."

Robbie shrugged.

Deon counted the notes deliberately, then took each one and cracked it, held it up to the light, checking the watermarks, coat of arms, latent image and security thread.

"We get some colorful customers—nothing against you," Deon said, looking up with a smile. "Such a pain," he continued, now scrutinizing the notes under a portable UV light. "They can even beat this thing nowadays. These look fine."

"Debt settled then, right?" Robbie asked, arms folded.

"Sure, buddy. You're welcome again in Gorky Park."

"That's not why I paid it. I need to speak to Sylvana."

"Sylvana?" The manager gave Robbie a once-over, checked his watch. "The girls come on at six. That's if she's working tonight. Whatever arrangements you make after hours..."

"So you have her number?" Robbie cut in. "I urgently need to speak to her."

"Whoa, cowboy." Deon opened the cash register and deposited the notes, shook his head. "Sorry to disappoint."

Robbie grabbed his arm. "It's very important I get hold of her."

"Look, darling, you look like a nice boy," said Deon, slowly removing Robbie's hand from his arm. "It's always important. But it's against club policy, so I don't have her number."

Robbie stared at him, sizing up his man. "Do you have an Internet connection?" he eventually asked.

Deon gestured to a flickering Compaq workstation.

"I want to show you something."

Robbie linked to the YouTube video. 188 views. *Fuck!* A message now accompanied the clip: "This content may contain material flagged by YouTube's user community that may be inappropriate for some users."

It then invited users to verify they were eighteen and sign in to view. Robbie did so, then pressed play.

"This is me," Robbie said.

Deon stared. "Didn't take you as a skin man."

"And that's Sylvana," said Robbie, as Sylvana entered the shower.

"Yes, yes. I can see." Deon straightened up, patted Robbie on the back. "I'm honored, but I'm afraid this isn't my scene—"

"That video was made and uploaded without my knowledge," Robbie cut in.

Deon frowned. "Hmmm. Strictly speaking she's not supposed to be—"

"Look, man, I need her number. Or an address."

Deon leaned forward and pressed play again.

Robbie moved in between him and the screen.

"Deon. You look like a decent guy. This was filmed without my consent. I'm not cool about it. I need her number."

The manager straightened up, nodded primly.

"I only want her to remove it," said Robbie, looking from Deon to the screen and back.

"Sure. I'll get her number for you. We don't keep addresses here but I can get hold of her." Deon flicked through his cellphone for a number, pressed dial. "Hey," he said, looking up at Robbie. "How do I know you're not going to try something with her?"

BEST-LAID PLANS

Saturday evening. The call from Kryff came at 9:30 pm.

Lynch was dining with three Johannesburg-based company directors at the V&A Waterfront. They had been discussing the offshore structure he'd been setting up for the Premier Marque directors to channel funds out of the country.

The call was unexpected; Lynch held up an apologetic finger as he answered his phone.

"She's at Elevation," Kryff said tersely. He sniffed loudly, waited for instruction.

Lynch excused himself from the table, stepped away, holding his glass of Merlot.

"You want me to get her?" Kryff asked.

Lynch wiped his mouth and cupped a hand over his Motorola. He eyed the table, figured he could get away; no one wanted to talk business on a Saturday night. He wondered what Kryff would charge to drug and deliver Terri Phillips to his doorstep.

"No," he said. She was too important. His face contorted as he checked his Rolex. He cursed the inconvenience. Normally he was at home alone on a Saturday night, just in case Holly's mother would let her spend the night. Of all the nights...

"No?"

Lynch took a sip of wine and ran some calculations. It was his third glass. He felt mildly intoxicated. Elevation was a five-minute drive from the Waterfront. But he'd have to go home first and collect the vial of scopolamine. He'd also want to change clothes, ready himself.

"No," he repeated. He looked up and scanned the table. The directors were locked in conversation. About how they would shaft the shareholders and streamline their exit plans.

Kryff's loud sniff signalled disapproval.

"Thank you," Lynch said and ended the call. He returned to the table and folded his serviette.

"Family crisis," Lynch explained. His colleagues knew about his troubled family background, didn't ask questions. "My daughter can't stand her mother any longer." He smiled knowingly, both upper and lower gums visible, and the table nodded politely.

Terri Phillips and her friend Katie danced together, hands touching, the beat grinding out through dry ice, the Elevation nightclub floor alive with writhing bodies.

Euphoric revellers looked the part in the high-end club: *No T-shirts, no shorts, no tennis shoes, boots or hats.*

"Oh my god! I've missed this so much!" Terri shouted over the music. She'd been overseas for nearly two years, living with her lawyer boyfriend, had returned to Cape Town earlier in the year to complete her degree. The long-distance relationship thing wasn't working—he wasn't that kind of guy.

A couple slow-danced alongside them, oblivious to the thumping music and the sea of people. Thirty-five floors below, Cape Town's city lights dazzled through wall-sized glass windows.

"Woohoo!" shouted Katie, body wet with perspiration, hands raised above her head. Earlier they'd sipped cocktails on the stuffed couches in the VIP lounge. *No baggy jeans, tank tops, sandals or athletic wear.* Now it was time to let loose.

Terri flicked her hair back and shook with laughter, rotated full circle. She was thinking about Katie pulling the bouncer's ponytail an hour or two earlier—before they'd been drinking. Over Katie's shoulder, a guy dressed in blue dungarees motioned to them with a bent finger. Terri shook her head, mirrored his gesture with an enticing finger of her own.

Terri closed her eyes and surrendered control to the beat.

"What's the matter, baby?" The dungaree guy was alongside, boozy breath like an assault in her face. His hand slipped down across her hip.

"Let's move," Katie said into her friend's ear.

Terri smiled and they danced away, melting into a throng of dance-floor addicts.

The drunken dungarees wouldn't be put off that easily, appeared again, lifted his hands in the air and wiggled his hips in front of Terri.

"How about a hug, huh, baby?"

His hand slid down Terri's thigh, teased the hem of her shimmering green dress. Katie pushed him away. "Fuck off!"

"Come sit on my face, huh baby," he slurred.

"Why, is your nose bigger than your dick?" Katie countered.

Katie grabbed Terri by the wrist and led her deeper into the throb of bodies, bending at the knees and running her hands from Terri's shoulders, down her sides, to her hips. Terri smiled, raised her hands in the air, and was consumed by the music.

$\otimes$

Midnight. Lynch parked his BMW in the basement amid a showcase of Porsche, Lamborghini, and Ferrari.

He'd raced home, showered, shaved, discarded the suit, and pulled on a pair of jeans. He wore a collared shirt, hanging loose.

Terri Phillips.

Before he left, he'd fired up his desktop and watched his favorite video, *Forest Frolic*, again for inspiration. Now he played the video over in his head. Twice he'd made to leave his car and head up to Elevation; each time he'd lost confidence. He'd been on the brink of calling for Kryff's assistance.

A car stopped behind his, angling for his spot, waited then hooted. Lynch gestured for the driver to move on.

Armed with the paperback, *The Strange Case of Patty Hearst*, he settled back and skimmed a few pages to calm his nerves.

When the Symbionese Liberation Army kidnapped the heiress Patty Hearst, they kept her blindfolded and imprisoned in a narrow closet. This was a crucial part of the process, Lynch knew. And he knew just the place for breaking Terri.

He wondered how long he would have to keep her before she "turned." Patty had become Tania; Terri would become...Polly. Or Estelle. Yes, Estelle would be appropriate.

Seated in the airless BMW, Lynch considered whether he was doing the right thing in attempting the abduction without Kryff. Kryff would hit him for at least twenty thousand to deliver the girl. He could do it for free, all on his own. And anyway, he didn't want that shifty mongrel touching her.

Perhaps he could simply approach her, he mused—she might be interested in a relationship with him. Angie Dean had liked him, he was certain. Memories swirled in his head. Angie was his current favorite. So willing.

Lynch fiddled with the CD shuttle, scanning for music to soothe his nerves. He stopped on *Californication*. Chili Peppers again. He turned it up loud, closed the paperback, and set it down on the passenger seat. Terri Phillips might soon be in this car, her tight ass on the cool leather seat. The prospect ignited a rush of excitement. How could he get her to the car?

Serendipity. He hated the word, a favorite in the vocabulary of his late mother.

"It's just serendipity, Julian," she'd say when he complained how unfair it was that he was at boarding school while his sister Estelle was spoiled at home. But possibly it was serendipity at play. Serendipity that he had watched the Newlands Forest video and been so turned on. Again when he realized that it was filmed in Cape Town; that its star must live here. And then Kryff locating her and identifying her...

He was resolved. He would walk into Elevation and drug her, offer her a lift home. It would be easy.

Lynch shivered. He felt powerful, excited to be upping the ante. Canned deliveries were a thrill, but choosing and securing your own date raised the bar to another level altogether.

"Come on, girls!" The sexy barman rolled a small white tablet between his thumb and index finger. "E for your pleasure?"

Elevation was packed to its maximum: five hundred bodies.

Terri and Katie exchanged glances. Terri shook her head with a smile. "I can't."

"She's had, like, a bad experience," Katie interjected.

"You only live once," the barman said, flushed cheeks alive with temptation. "Any more drinks?"

Katie checked her wristwatch and tapped it. "Curfew," she said.

Terri stuck out her tongue in playful defiance.

Someone tapped Terri on her shoulder; she spun around to find a young man next to her smiling a toothy smile. "Can I buy you girls a drink?" he said.

Terri smiled shyly. She was conscious of his stare, his chin jutting forward, sun-bleached eyebrows. He had broad shoulders, a face that suggested arrogance and pride were hard to separate. She thought of her boyfriend in London, the exact opposite visually—but a similar manner about him.

"Fake eyelashes!" said Terri's admirer. "How '80s!"

"They're not fake!" giggled Terri, looking to Katie for support.

"Really? Let's take a closer look."

Terri closed her eyes. He leaned forward and licked her lips. She opened her eyes immediately, blushed.

"Sorry, my mistake," he laughed. Terri wiped her mouth.

"That's an old one," said Katie. Behind his back, she whispered to Terri: "He's an asshole!"

He caught the barman's eye. "Three tequilas."

"Not for me," said Katie.

"OK, two."

Salt, lemon, José Cuervo.

Katie whispered to Terri, left for the bathroom. Terri's new admirer shook salt onto his forearm, turned to her. "Here! Lick it off my arm."

"I'm not leaving you here," Katie said. She pulled Terri away to one side, stood with arms on her hips.

"I'm fine, Katie. Honest. I'll get a ride home."

Terri spoke clearly, but Katie didn't like where this was going. Tequila guy couldn't take a hint and leave them be. She looked over at the bar where they'd been sitting; three new tequilas were waiting. Time they headed home, she argued.

"Excuse me."

An older man in blue denim jeans passed between Terri and Katie, brushed against Terri and then looked back expectantly. The girls ignored him, continued their argument.

"No!" Katie shook her head.

"He seems nice," Terri tried.

"Listen, Terri! You don't know who that guy is. He's a creep!"

"We're drinking tequila, not fucking," Terri laughed.

Katie narrowed her eyes. "Terri! What happened to you in London?" She was laughing too. She pointed at the bar. "Look at him!"

The kid with the jutting jaw threw back his head and downed a shot.

"He's so funny," Terri giggled.

Katie looked away. "Let's go!"

"Oh, Katie, come on!" Terri tried to pull her back.

"Terri, we came here together. We'll leave together."

"Well, stay then," pleaded Terri. "Come on. We're having so much fun."

SYLVANA'S CALL

Thud, thud, thud.

Robbie hurled three darts in quick succession into the board behind his door. At 11 pm, when he'd last accessed the Web, the shower video counter reflected 317 views and 15 comments received—including one from someone in Brazil. Melanie, his ex, hadn't been in touch, but he was convinced she would have seen it by now.

Earlier, unable to raise Sylvana on the cell number coerced from Deon, the Gorky Park manager, he'd left a terse message: "Sylvana. The police are involved. Call me back immediately. If you don't, you will face the consequences. I will find you. It's Robbie."

Face the consequences? He sounded like his headmaster at school. *Everything has consequences!*

He regretted the message now, but it was how he felt at the time. Indignant. Outraged. And desperate.

The electronic hum from his bar fridge was working at his nerves. He threw open the window to his room. The residence was alive, lights blazing, students awake and engaged in a wide spectrum of late-night weekend activities; the diligent few working on assignments or studying for tests, the rest getting drunk or high or laid.

Robbie turned off his bedside light and checked his cellphone in hope of a response from Sylvana. She was probably working; her phone could be off all night.

He wondered how to handle her. Clearly, the current approach wasn't working.

After his encounter with Deon at Gorky Park, he'd driven to the Mowbray Police Station, opposite the Shoprite Checkers on Main Road, to lay a charge. Of what, he wasn't sure. Extortion? Defamation? The cops weren't either.

He'd waited half an hour amid a gathering of hard-done-by rabble before receiving attention. The bewildered charge officer, not knowing what to make of his problem, had referred Robbie to a senior detective in a private office. The network was down, so Robbie couldn't demonstrate the evidence. The detective sent Robbie back to the charge office.

"Just fill in the charge."

Another half an hour, the charge officer attempted to retake his statement, crossing out and starting a new sheet, then finally asking if Robbie could fill it in himself. Robbie declined and left. "Don't worry," he told the charge officer, "I'll sort it out myself."

"Contact your local police." Clearly, YouTube didn't have Mowbray in mind when they issued their advice.

Lying on his bed in the darkness, Robbie felt claustrophobic, muddled. He opened his door to allow the through draft to cool his room. Snatches of music and voices were audible down the corridors.

He needed to think clearly.

Is this bad? Really bad?

Denny hadn't thought so. But Denny wouldn't care; would probably relish the attention.

He still had no idea why Sylvana had loaded the video on YouTube. It would surely have ruined any financial arrangement she had. If she was after money, she gained no benefit from embarrassing him.

Robbie's inbox was choked with messages, his cellphone regularly beeping the arrival of new text messages, reactions ranging from shock to hilarity. Already in the corridors of Kopano house, fellow students were pretending to brush their teeth when they saw him. He imagined what his rugby team would have to say at Tuesday's practice. High-fives all round, or silence and shame?

Robbie looked over details of the original text flyer, which Tony Beacon had forwarded to him.

        Robbie Cullen gets suckered in shower.

The message contained a URL link to the video.

Robbie's head throbbed. He could make no sense of it.

Why send Tony the message? And who else did she send it to? Did she think that he and Tony would fall out over the video?

Robbie concluded he was unlikely to make a decent detective.

He flipped his laptop back open, typed a message on his Facebook page:

        Someone made a video of me (bad)—I didn't know—
        and stuck it on youtube. Some people were sent
        a text directing them to the link. If u did
        could u snd me a note. Thanks.

Before pressing SHARE, he decided against sending it. The status update would simply stimulate more intrigue.

Despite the cool draft, Robbie was hot and clammy. He pushed his chair back, picked absent-mindedly at the elephant-hair bracelet. A thought occurred to him; he Googled for other instances of the video, was relieved when he found none. Spoiled it by checking the YouTube link again and seeing the hits had jumped above 350.

Nearly 40 hits in under an hour!

His mind was a confusion of questions.

What would his parents think of him?

Should he phone Melanie and explain?

What about Fallon? He couldn't think of an obvious connection between her and Sylvana. Except that Fallon was in Plettenberg Bay in the *same house* at the *same time.*

He took a deep breath.

Never trust coincidence. Where had he read that again? Stephen King? Roald Dahl?

Fallon. First the chance meeting at Blue Venus, then the rescue. And then she just happens to be in Plett at Tony Beacon's house the weekend he gets set up in the shower. He'd avoided asking Tony Beacon for the lowdown on her. Discretion.

He tried dialing Sylvana's number again, received the same telecom message: *The subscriber you have called is not available. Please try again later.*

Laying a charge and taking Sylvana to court would be costly and time-consuming. He just wanted it all to go away. Right now.

Beating the shit out of her would be his father's way. Not his.

He pictured Sylvana in the strip cage at Gorky Park: her slim, twisting body; her greedy red lips. Greed. The packs of hungry strippers, the flicking credit cards, the relentless trade of flesh for cash.

Maybe he had it wrong, he thought. Maybe he *should* make her pay him—her share and his, the full amount. Ten thousand. Another fat envelope; this one to ease his humiliation. Robbie sighed. He knew what his father would say. Next time someone joined him in a shower, he wouldn't be so naïve.

At 1:05 am, a beep from his cellphone woke him.

You have one new voice message.

He dialed 121. The voice was female, a thick foreign accent. Sylvana. She sounded frantic. "Robbie. I....It's....I have to talk. Please, Robbie.

I didn't know. Robbie....It's Sylvana. Phone me. Please phone me."

Didn't know? Didn't know what? That the video was posted?

Robbie sat upright, instantly awake, alarmed by the fear in her voice. He checked the time of the call. Four hours ago. Why had the message only come through now? He phoned back immediately. It rang eight times then reverted to message. Her voice message echoed the message left on his phone.

"Robbie. I....It's....I have to talk. Please, Robbie. I didn't know. Robbie....It's Sylvana. Phone me. Please phone me."

Robbie clenched his jaw. How could the voice message he'd received be the same as the message on her answering service?

His phone beeped again. A text:

> Robbie. 56 Lendell Road, Rondebosch.
> Please come!!! Now!! Please.

LYNCH'S FRUSTRATION

Lynch ordered an Appletiser then cruised the nightclub. Brown shoes matched a thick leather belt wound loosely around his waist, his jeans too short, white socks visible. He walked a practiced executive stroll, upright, core muscles tense.

In the smoky light of Elevation, he'd battled to distinguish one girl from another, but returning from the Gents, he'd spotted his prize. There she was, in earnest conversation with a friend in the corridor. He'd brushed past, continued walking, looked around expectantly, imagined that she'd seen him too and wondered what someone of his stature might be doing in a place like this. How to progress from here, though? Perhaps he could talk to her, see if he might tempt her without any narcotic assistance.

Lynch rejected the plan, made his way back to the bar.

"I'm looking for a girl," he said once he had the barman's attention. His voice was steady, belying the trembling in his body, an all-consuming cocktail of lust and desire.

He described Terri Phillips: clinging green lycra dress, Alice band, white lace-up sandals. He wished he could explain what was underneath.

"Yeah," the barman frowned. "So?"

"I would like to, uh, avail myself of the service."

Lynch removed his wallet, placed it on the counter and leaned forward conspiratorially. The noise of the music made it impossible for anyone to overhear.

"Mickey Finn," Lynch said. He smiled showing both sets of teeth then flashed the vial of scopolamine. "You can use this."

The barman looked around, his expression morphing from interest to disdain. "What you on about, buddy?"

Lynch hesitated. The barman waved his hand towards another barman. "Hey!" he called to his colleague.

Lynch pocketed his wallet and closed his hand around the vial. He laughed and leaned back on his stool. "Only kidding, only kidding," he said, holding up a hand. But it was too late. The barman spun away and strode toward the other end of the counter, engaged the colleague, turned and pointed towards Lynch.

Lynch felt the rise of panic in his chest, the overwhelming thud of his racing heart. He abandoned his drink, stepped back from the bar into the crowd, knocked into a patron. He hurried back to the Gents and locked himself in a stall.

What was he thinking? Saving money, taking a huge risk...

I've blown it!

He opened the vial of scopolamine and poured the transparent liquid into the toilet bowl. A complete waste.

And now he had to get away. If they stopped him at the exit, he would explain that the barman had misunderstood him. That he'd only wanted a drink.

He waited five minutes before opening the stall door. The men's room was busy, a queue for the urinals. Lynch steadied up before the mirror over the row of basins; his face was hot, perspiration on his brow and upper lip. Removing a strip of paper towel from the dispenser, he wiped his hands and surreptitiously folded the towel around the empty vial, depositing it in the bin.

With a deep breath, Lynch pushed open the swinging door of the Gents and strolled out, crossed the floor with head bowed and took a seat at the bar opposite to the one where he'd propositioned the barman.

Plan B, he decided: leave it to the experts. He flicked open his Motorola to call Kryff. The music was too loud. He twisted around and looked across the room, spotted a woman speaking with the barman he had propositioned.

Lynch sensed trouble. *Shit.* He had to make a run for it.

In the parking garage below Elevation, Lynch seethed with frustration.

He punched his fist against the dashboard of his BMW.

Fucking asshole barman. Mickey Finn? Mickey fucking Mouse! What was their problem?

He had been so close. Had actually *touched* her. The barman ruined everything.

He turned on the CD shuttle in an attempt to distract himself, caught the tail end of *Californication* fading to nothing...

That's when he saw them.

Giggling and unsteady, Terri Phillips in green lycra and the friend with blonde curly hair.

His heart thumped.

Serendipity. It's just serendipity, Julian.

You were right, mother.

Serendipity was the explanation his mother used to pass off every accidental occurrence. It allowed Julian to explain away his dark desires. They were not his fault, just the fulfilment of destiny.

Buoyed by his good fortune, Lynch watched the two girls in the rear-view mirror until they disappeared from sight. He started the BMW and reversed, followed the exit arrows up a ramp and into the street.

Terri and her friend would have to exit via the same gate.

Lynch pulled to the side of the road and waited, engine running. He skipped the next few songs, kicked off Nirvana's *Polly*. A few moments later, a red Citi Golf exited the parking lot and drove past, the curly-haired girl he'd seen talking to Terri at the wheel, Terri the passenger. Lynch smiled.

What did he need Kryff for? The SLA hadn't needed scopolamine or any other substance when they burst into Patty Hearst's fiancé's apartment and dragged her out.

Lynch pulled away from the curb and followed Terri Philips into Strand Street. At the first robot, he overtook and accelerated onto the Eastern Boulevard. He knew where they'd be going. Rather lie in wait than risk being spotted on their tail.

CUTTING TIME

With a nagging sense of unease, Robbie turned into Lendell Road, tried to make out the numbers on the gates and walls. When he realized he was headed into the lower numbers, he U-turned and drove slowly back in the direction he'd come.

Number 56 was dark, no outside lights. He parked on the verge, immediately checked his phone.

After Sylvana's frantic text, he'd tried to get hold of Denny, felt he needed a wingman. No sign of Denny in his room. He'd considered calling Tony, even the cops. But what would he have said? And he couldn't waste any more time.

Please come!!! Now!! Please.

Robbie buttoned his shirt and slipped his bare feet into a pair of Adidas cross-trainers. He fingered the canister of Bulldog pepper spray in the pocket of his jeans, steeled himself, eyeing out the surroundings. He'd spent many a night camping out under the stars with no lights; he wasn't about to let a dark house scare him.

He opened the car door and wished for a moment that he'd avoided watching all those horror flick DVDs: *The Hills Have Eyes, Wrong Turn, Texas Chainsaw Massacre.*

Why the hell would Sylvana be living here? he wondered. The place looked deserted. He'd expected her to live in Green Point or Camps Bay, somewhere chic and trendy. Rondebosch was for families with schoolkids. Most of the houses hid behind electric fences, infrared laser beams and internal alarms. This one was an exception.

The low gate to the property was chained with a heavy padlock. Robbie could hop over easily enough, but the house lay dark and ominous behind. He hesitated, unsure, afraid.

No ways! Who knows what's in there?

Robbie mentally calculated the distance back to his car, ready to make a run for it. Fear and adrenaline enhanced his senses. At the Blue Venus, the contact had been immediate; there'd been no time to think about what he was doing—but this brought back memories of a terrifying night five years ago. Alone on the Cullen farm in Albany, he'd woken to hear the dogs going crazy, a window breaking. He remembered each agonizing moment, wondering how many there were, praying the burglar bars would hold. He'd crept quietly through the house and punched the panic alarm in his parents' room, setting the intruders to flight. Afterwards, he'd sat in the dark for half an hour, shaking quietly, waiting for the armed response to make their way out to the farm.

Anticipation created a different type of fear. This was right in front of him.

Robbie stood still and listened, constantly looking down to check his cell for a new message. It was an eerie contradiction of localized silence punctuated by distant noises: howls from a cat fight, the dull whirr of a late-night car on Sandown Road, an unheeded alarm whining pointlessly several blocks away. Under it all, the pulse of blood throbbing through his body.

Taking a deep breath, Robbie scanned left and right, trying to work out potential scenarios. An ambush, perhaps. He didn't fancy a rematch against the blonde surfer from Blue Venus, or the Sharks rugby guy and his baseball-wielding accomplice.

"Come on, Sylvana," he whispered to his phone, pressing redial. Eight rings then the same desperate message from Sylvana.

"Robbie. I....It's....I have to talk. Please Robbie. I didn't know. Robbie....It's Sylvana. Phone me. Please phone me."

I didn't know. What did that mean?

A car appeared several blocks away, eased along Lendell Road and slowed. Robbie looked away to avoid being blinded by its headlights, wondered if this could be Sylvana. Or the Blue Venus attackers. He gripped the Bulldog pepper spray; it felt cold in his pocket.

False alarm. The car drove on and turned at the stop street.

"Sylvana!" Robbie called, leaning up against the gate, instincts on high alert.

A streetlight illuminated the driveway of number 56 and an alleyway on the mountain side of the house. Robbie's eyes were becoming accustomed to the light. He noticed an open window.

"Sylvana!"

He rattled the chain on the gate, instincts telling him to get out while he could.

"Sylvana?" he called once more, hands gripping the driveway gate.

No reply.

Fuck it.

He leaped the gate easily, crouched like a cat on a garden path, listened. Silence.

No dogs. No beams. He straightened up and crept up the path, ascended three red-painted steps. He took a deep breath and banged on the front door.

Brainless to come here, he thought. He visually retraced his steps back to the gate. Could make it in five steps, hands on the gate, jump and out.

Brainless.

He turned his back to the door, spray held low in his right hand, cell in his left, muscles tensed.

If someone came at him from behind, he'd kick back using the front door as stabilizer. If they came from inside, he'd nail them with the spray.

No reply.

Shit.

The door had a wooden frame and frosted glass-panel center. No way to see in.

He redialed Sylvana's number one more time, listened.

There it was: a noise from inside the house. The ringtone of a phone.... He killed the call and the sound died.

"Sylvana?" Robbie inquired. He turned the brass handle of the front door; it was open.

Warm air smelling of damp wood wafted from the house. Robbie pushed the door wide open with his foot, stood back, tensed in anticipation of an ambush. He pointed his Nokia into the inky blackness, the thin beam of light from the screen casting a spectral glow inside the entrance hall.

"Hello? Anyone?"

Every muscle in his body was rigid.

He inched forward, the house silent, only his rank breathing, alternating between mouth and nose, and the creak of his footstep audible.

"Hello, hello. Sylvana?"

He fumbled on the wall for a light switch—couldn't locate one—pressed redial and froze, braced, hoping the nozzle of the Bulldog canister was pointing forward.

"Come on Robbie," he muttered to himself, trying to control his fear, brain urging him to turn and flee. He checked that his escape route was unobstructed.

The ring came from the first room on his right, sounded like banjos playing.

He tightened his finger on the nozzle and tested the door with the toe of his shoe, felt it creak ajar. He kicked it open and entered the room in one quick movement, keeping low, almost crouched.

A pulsing light on a coffee table identified the source of the ringtone. A trap? Robbie spun around, anticipation in overdrive: a gang with baseball bats, the Sharks guy, the blond surfer with the cold smile, the freaking hillbilly cannibal mutants from Wrong Turn.

No one.

Covering the door with the Bulldog canister, he shone his Nokia around the room. He was in a lounge. The phone on the coffee table stopped ringing.

"Hey! Sylvana!" He spoke loudly, emboldened by the depth of his own voice.

The cellphone on the coffee table beeped. Robbie picked it up, fiddled with the keys.

You have one new message:

    smile!

"Fuck this!" Robbie dropped Sylvana's phone on the table. "Tony?"
Another flipping prank? Are they filming me?

"OK, come on, what's your story?" he shouted, mustering up as much bravado as he could.

He relaxed a little. If he was being punked in some joke video, best he look a little less like Horatio Caine.

Still on guard, he groped for a light switch next to the fireplace, flicked it up and down. No light. He scanned the room slowly from one end to the other, his pupils dilating as they adjusted to the dark.

"Guys. If someone gives me a fright they're going to be flipping sorry," he tried. "This isn't funny."

It was starting to make sense. A setup. Forlorn house, weird phone messages. This smelled like Denny's handiwork.

"Denny!" Robbie shouted.

A noise from down the corridor startled him—a heavy sound, not glass. Something falling over? A door slamming?

The floorboards creaked as Robbie exited the lounge and tiptoed down the passageway, his back pinned against the wall, pausing after each step to listen. A narrow corridor led from the entrance hall, reached a T-junction, and then continued left and right.

Robbie spoke into darkness: "Hey Denny. Bru, I know it's you. Look, I've lost my sense of humor about this, 'kay?"

A door banged shut.

Robbie shuffled noiselessly down the corridor, toed open the first door and fumbled around the corner, flicking the light switch. Nothing. The light from his Nokia projected a dull beam towards the center of the room. Empty.

"I'm going to give you such a *klap*, Denny, I swear."

Robbie edged to the next door, peered around the corner, pointing with the Nokia light. He struggled to discern anything in the gloom: a window was open; the curtains half drawn, rustling gently; the outlines of a bed perhaps. Robbie's breath stopped in an instant and he felt cold tendrils of fear creeping down his neck—he could sense the presence of another human being.

Someone was in the bed.

He held his position for a moment that seemed to stretch out of reality; felt the surge of his heart rate and the pounding of blood in his head.

"Sylvana?" he whispered. "Is that you?"

No response.

He edged closer, into the room. The beam of his Nokia settled and illuminated a figure with long blonde hair stretched across the pillow.

"Sylvana? You OK?"

He took another tentative step. Stared. Something was wrong: the angle of her head on the pillow, the duvet halfway across her face. One more step. There was something plastic underfoot, sheeting, then something sticky.

Robbie heard his own scream as he touched the lifeless head on the pillow.

The head rolled back. By the dull light of his phone, Robbie could see Sylvana's throat was sliced from one end to the other.

"Jesus!"

Robbie staggered backwards, suppressing his nausea, legs stuck in an invisible web. He tripped, head bashing against the edge of the open door, Nokia almost lost. Bounced to his feet in panic, expecting someone, something, to grab him. Staggered from the room, stumbled blindly down the passageway.

He heard a noise, then the ringtone of *Dueling Banjos* emanated from the lounge.

Someone was calling Sylvana's cellphone.

The killer knew where he was.

INTERRUPTUS

Lynch sped down Woolsack Drive, followed the off-ramp past the Tugwell residence and parked in a bay outside Baxter Hall. It was early morning, getting on for 3 am. The area was deserted.

His head was perfectly clear; he was aware that his moment had come, that destiny was about to deliver. He looked up at the ugly tower of Tugwell Hall, now a thing of beauty to him in the night light, and counted five floors, imagining the room of Terri Phillips.

Tonight, he had been close enough to feel her.

He focused on a bus stop outside the residence and judged the distance from his car to be less than a hundred meters. Tapping the wheel of his BMW, he looked about, alert for security guards then. Figuring he may attract attention lurking in his car, he stepped out into the night. He checked the time on his Rolex and waited for the Golf to arrive.

A blue Mazda screeched to a halt and a young man jumped out, sprinted across to the entrance and banged against the glass doors of Tugwell Hall.

Julian Lynch shrank into the shadows of an oak tree and watched. The young man stepped back from the door, ran around to the side of the building, shouting loudly. He wore blue jeans, takkies, looked very agitated. Lynch strained his ears as the yelling continued. Lights were popping angrily, heads appearing at windows.

"Fuck off, you mullet!" shouted a student from the male residence in the adjoining tower. Toilet rolls and other missiles started raining down.

Lynch looked on as a security guard sauntered across the mezzanine toward the young man. Presumably they dealt with this type of commotion on a frequent basis: spurned lovers inflamed with alcohol.

Lynch withdrew instinctively as a second torch shone briefly in his direction. He pressed his body against the tree, wondering what he'd say if discovered.

The anxiety triggered forbidden memories: hiding from his parents, knowing that when they found him, the consequences would be severe. His little sister had had angry red welts around her neck and wrists. And on other parts of her body....The gardener had found her tied up in the shed.

The second security guard spoke on the radio, continued past Lynch toward his partner and the young man.

Sixteen, he'd been at the time. *A most impressionable age.* It was an act of revenge. He'd hidden in the loft of the stables, watching the jagged path of his father's torchlight across the grounds. He knew he'd be found in the end. That he'd have to deal with what he had done.

Waiting for the red Citi Golf to appear, Lynch knew that once he'd kidnapped Terri Phillips, there would be no turning back. He wouldn't be able to simply return her to the street like the rest of his girls. They'd catch him if he did. And he didn't want to face those consequences.

His parents had sent him away to boarding school. He remembered the astonishment on his father's puffy face. "Why, Julian?" No one explained to him why. He remembered overhearing his mother: "We shouldn't have waited so long."

So long? Before coughing up the stupid sister? Before sending him away?

His sister had died anyway. At twenty-one, in a car crash in Manchester. Estelle. He hadn't seen her since the fateful day in the garden shed, had opposed her body being shipped back to South Africa. She didn't belong with them.

Lynch watched the security guards escort the young man to his car. He didn't appear drunk.

At the bottom of the hill, Lynch waited another hour for the red Citi Golf. Then he masturbated beneath the oak tree, returned to his car, and drove home.

A BIT OF A PROBLEM

"Speak," said Carlos, adjusting his Bose headphones and plugging in an encryptor. He closed his study door with a remote, and rubbed his smooth upper lip. The moustache was gone, shaved off that morning. He thought it made him look like Freddie Mercury.

It was his Cape Town operator. "A bit of a problem," the woman said.

This wasn't a Skype conversation. Carlos offered cellphone contact to very important associates only. Which was to say, those who brought in the good money.

His number connected to an automatic answering system on a site called AutoDial. AutoDial forwarded the call to Dark Video's website which tested the incoming number against a database of numbers that Carlos religiously updated. If the call ID could not be validated, the caller received an out-of-order message. If validated, the Dark Video site patched the call through to the last SIM card registered to the administrator of the site. He changed his card every week. The encryptor was Carlos's last line of defence.

"A problem at..." Carlos checked his watch, avoided giving away his time zone—"...whatever time this is. It better be good. What shall I call you today? Diva?"

Carlos monitored every attempted contact with Dark Video, tracking the calls and emails, verifying the users. He was scrupulous about keeping up to date with the ongoing investigations into his activities. Various law-enforcement agents had posed as clients in the past, but he'd identified them easily enough. He always took great satisfaction in leading them on wild goose chases.

"Are problems ever good?" asked Diva.

Carlos had faith in his latest Cape Town operative. Jacker had run her details through his entire bag of online tricks; Samuel Chester had checked her over in person. She was doing important business with big clients and she understood the chain of command.

"It's a client," she said. "Lynch."

Carlos flicked through a series of photographs of the operative in action, most of them stills captured from CCTV footage. He zoomed in. She had a standard disguise: grey hair and a scarf. Smart operator, he acknowledged with a nod. And a lot more sophisticated than his average mule. There were other women operatives in his employ, but none as savvy.

"Yes," said Carlos with a sinking feeling. Lynch, an active Dark Video customer, had become a regular user of the Mickey Finn Club. Was graduating up the chain. Becoming more prone to taking risks, more dangerous. Carlos recognized the signs.

But Lynch was a regular and a good payer. A client worth keeping.

"Arrested?" Carlos did his best to mask his concern. The issue of the arrested clients was disturbing. Clients got arrested; it was not unusual. But three in one month, each potentially bleating about Dark Video.

"No, Carlos. Seems he's found a new agent."

Carlos clicked his teeth. His first reaction: *So fucking what!* Poaching in Mickey Finn territory was widespread, uncontrollable. Like the Web. Sometimes Carlos likened his clients to unprotected computers on the Internet: so badly infected that only a disk reformat could purge their collective contamination.

A loud bang distracted him.

Over twenty years, Carlos had developed an almost instinctive sense of danger. Because his daily routine was so consistent, any deviation was treated with suspicion. If an electrician or plumber was needed at the house, Carlos made sure to watch them like a hawk on the internal security cameras. Every room of Carlos's house was wired, cameras housed in innocuous looking smoke detectors or behind one-way glass. He even kept an eye on telephone repairmen and municipal workers outside his property. Caution was his watchword.

He flicked through the cameras. The garbage truck from Allied Waste was outside collecting the refuse—which pleased him. A homeless person in the area had been shitting in packets and dropping them in his waste bins. He'd hired a "pest" control company to dispose of the vagrant.

"Carlos, you there?" Diva asked from across the world.

"Yes. I'm here," Carlos answered. He wondered how the rival agency had cottoned onto Lynch. He recalled that Lynch had complained about an unfulfilled order. Could his operator have been negligent?

"How?" asked Carlos.

"I have no idea," she replied.

Carlos remembered Jacker's warning, the lingering concern about a client list.

"And another small issue," Diva continued. "A fetcher was working on your golden girl tonight at a club in town."

It was standard procedure for operators of the Mickey Finn Club to use a fetcher to collect victims. The fetchers posed as patrons of the establishment, distracted the intended victim, lured them away from places of safety.

"Who? Terri Phillips?" The star of one of his videos!

"Yes. Don't worry. Nothing happened."

"How the fuck!" Carlos shouted, temper immediately boiling over. "That can't happen. When did she get back from London?"

"I don't know," the woman replied.

"Jesus Christ!" Carlos ranted. He wasn't too worried about Lynch shopping around within the Mickey Finn space, but this was far more serious.

"Do we know who it was? Was Lynch involved?"

"Possibly. The fetcher works for the same operator that is sniffing at Lynch. I've run into him before."

"What's the operator's name?"

"Kryff."

Carlos noted down the name.

"What do you want to do?" Diva asked calmly.

"I'll come up with something, talk to the big man if necessary," said Carlos. He was infuriated. *He* cultivated the clients. Nobody was going to reap his harvest. It would be worthwhile having Samuel Chester sort this out, he thought.

"I can handle it," Diva offered.

"But you quite clearly can't," Carlos replied with bite. "Is that all?" He sensed other issues in her hesitation.

"On the other matter, the shower video. It's been resolved."

"Yes?" Carlos was intrigued. Cape Town was white-hot at the moment. "Are both parties...resolved?"

"One," she said.

Carlos waited for more.

"We've terminated one of the parties. But there won't be any more problems," she added.

"You know the rules," he said, the words delivered as a warning, with no change in tone. Mickey Finn was a new and evolving venture and he allowed some leeway there, but when it came to Dark Video business, he never compromised on the protocol.

Carlos ended the call.

He flicked to his security cameras. The front camera panned down to the lake, a misty blue line at the end of the rolling lawn.

If they come for me from the water, what's my best escape route?

A FOKKEN MESS

The morning after discovering Sylvana's lifeless body in Rondebosch, Robbie presented himself at the Rondebosch Police Station, the clothes and shoes he'd worn the previous night in a plastic Checkers bag. After taking a brief statement, filing a nine-page handwritten explanation of events and inserting his cellphone and wallet into a Ziploc bag, Rondebosch CID transferred him in an unmarked white Toyota to the Wynberg Police Station. They didn't handcuff him. A constable showed him up a flight of stairs and into a windowless office.

"The *kaptein* will be here shortly," the constable said, closing the door behind him. Robbie didn't hear the door lock.

He checked the time. 8:45 am. The grey-painted room contained a wooden table with metal legs and two plastic chairs positioned opposite one another. A government-regulation light fitting hung from the center of the ceiling.

Robbie was desolate, unable to comprehend his predicament. Sylvana was dead and he had found her. His bloody footprints were all over the house. His fingerprints were on her cellphone, the door handle, all over the house. After contacting Crime Watch, anonymously reporting the murder and giving the street address, he had fled the scene of the crime. In a moment of blind panic, he'd tried to track down Melanie, his ex, the one person in the city he felt he could still trust. He'd driven to her residence when she didn't answer her phone, been escorted away by security.

The evidence against him was overwhelming. A manager from Sylvana's place of employment could testify he'd made threatening comments about her. His menacing message would be found on her cellphone.

He had called no one else. Not his parents, not Denny. Besides his desperate attempt to locate Melanie, he hadn't said a word to a soul until he'd reached the Rondebosch Police Station.

A stocky policewoman shuffled into the room. She was carrying a briefcase. Robbie stood up immediately.

"Mr. Cullen," she said, "I'm Captain Vermaak. You can sit."

Robbie sat down, clasped his hands together.

The policewoman dumped the briefcase on the floor and removed her blue jacket, hung it behind the door. She sat down opposite and stared at him.

"Ja, well," she eventually managed. "Quite a story, *né?*"

Captain Vermaak opened her leather briefcase and extracted some files, arranged them in order. Robbie noticed his handwritten statement—his *confession*—among the documents.

"OK. You called Crime Watch at 3:05 am yesterday, *jammer*, this morning to report a woman murdered in Rondebosch."

Robbie nodded.

"What did you do after that?" Vermaak scanned the documents as if searching for the answer.

"I drove back to my residence at UCT. I..." Robbie faltered. "I stopped briefly outside Tugwell. It's a..."

"I know Tugwell. Why did you do that?" Vermaak's voice was firm but calming, not intimidating.

"Melanie. Uh, my ex-girlfriend. I wanted to talk to her."

Vermaak pulled more paperwork from her briefcase. Robbie paused.

"Ja. Carry on," she said.

"I went back to Kopano."

"Another residence?"

"In Rondebosch, yes. It's a UCT men's residence. Where I stay."

"OK."

"I couldn't sleep. I knew I shouldn't have left the house. My thinking was uh...jumbled. I was awake all night. I phoned the Rondebosch Police Station early this morning then turned myself in."

"Jumbled?" Vermaak was puzzled.

"I mean, confused."

Vermaak pursed her lips.

"You phoned them at 6 am?"

"Uhh...yes, that sounds right. It was early."

"And you weren't, what you call, jumbled?"

"Uh. No."

The constable who had led Robbie to the room knocked and opened the door. He looked inside then backed out quickly, tried to close the door.

"Hey!" yelled Vermaak. "Where's my fokken coffee?"

The constable pushed the door open.

"You want some?" she asked Robbie.

"No thank you."

She turned back to the constable.

"Net een."

"Uh, Kaptein," the constable said. *"Ganit lank vat? Du Preez soek 'n lift terug Bellville toe."*

Vermaak glared at the constable. "Not long," she said. The constable departed and she turned her attention to Robbie.

"Mr. Cullen. This is your statement." Vermaak held up his signed statement.

"Well. That's what I wrote down last night. But they took my statement again in Rondebosch."

"It's, like you say, a bit jumbled. Well, for my head..."

"I tried to put down everything," Robbie explained.

"I'll skip the introduction because, well, it makes no sense," she said, waving the handwritten statement then beginning to read from it. "'She left message on my cellphone. Please help me. I drove to house, phoned again. Her cellphone on table. Message said smile.'"

Vermaak looked up at Robbie briefly then back at the statement.

"But this bit I understand: 'Sylvia in second bedroom down the corridor.'" Vermaak screwed up her face and held the statement closer to her eyes. "'Her throat was cut.'"

"Sylvana," said Robbie quietly.

Vermaak looked up curiously.

"You wrote all this when?" she said.

"Last night, I..."

Vermaak raised her hand. She returned her attention to the statement.

"You thought it was an ambush. Barmen from a club in Claremont. The Blue Venus." Vermaak shook her head.

Robbie cleared his throat. He hadn't mentioned anything about Fallon and the envelope full of money. He'd sworn to be discreet. But he had to explain somehow.

"Yes, er, the barmen at the Blue Venus spiked a drink of....Uh, you've heard about Angie Dean?"

"Ja, ja. The UCT girl. What's she got to do with this?"

Robbie rubbed his eyes. He couldn't think straight.

"I'm....I'm not sure. I..."

"You jumbled? Can I ask you a question?" she interrupted. "Are you on any medication?"

Robbie shook his head.

"You seeing a shrink? Been using any recreational narcotics?"

Robbie had a flashback to his last reefer session with Denny, how high they'd got. "No. I had nothing to do with Sylvana's murder," he said.

Vermaak stared at him, trying to work him out. She shuffled on the plastic chair. Breakfast had been two boerewors sausages and scrambled egg. Her pants felt tight around her waist. Last week had been quiet, a rare opportunity to ease the backlog, attend a feedback session from the

Anti Drug/Tik Youth Seminar.

The constable delivered her coffee in a polystyrene cup.

"Ek...er, Kaptein," the constable stammered. "Du Preez het gevra–"

"Tell Du Preez to go pull his wire. I'll be ready when I'm ready."

The constable grinned and departed.

She tested the coffee. "Tastes like fokken chlorine," she muttered, contorting her face.

"Sylvana," she said, consulting her papers. She pronounced it with her top teeth sliding over her lower lip. Sylfana. "Nice name. You said her cellphone was in the house you went to."

"Yes," Robbie replied. "I picked it up. It rang when I entered. It will have my fingerprints. Did they recover the phone last night?"

Vermaak pointed to the phone in the zip-lock bag. "Whose is that?" she asked.

"That's mine."

She opened the packet and removed the phone, fiddled with the keys then showed the face to Robbie.

"That's not Sylvana's phone. It's mine," he repeated.

"This the last number you called last night?" Vermaak said, ignoring him.

"Uh, no. Go back. I called Crime Stop and then Melanie."

Vermaak continued to fiddle with Robbie's Nokia. "This is her number? This..."

"Sylvana. Yes."

"Where's speaker phone?"

Robbie showed her. Vermaak pressed the green phone icon. After three rings, somebody picked up. A woman.

"Hello, who is this?" Vermaak asked, placing the Nokia in the center of the table.

"Sylvana Natlova."

Robbie's jaw dropped.

"I have someone who wants to say hello to you."

"Sylvana?" said Robbie.

"Yes, who is this?"

Robbie was speechless.

"Miss uh....Ja," Vermaak leaned forward and addressed the Nokia. "This is Captain Vermaak of the South African Police. I have a young man here who is concerned about your safety."

"Oh."

"Where are you?" Vermaak asked.

"My safety? I am sorry, I don't understand. I'm at OR Tambo Airport."

"Where are you going?" asked Vermaak.

"To the Ukraine."

"Is there anything you want to ask her?" Vermaak asked Robbie.

"Sylvana. It's Robbie."

"Yes," she answered.

Robbie looked at the screen of his cellphone.

"I don't think this is Sylvana," he told Vermaak.

"It's me, Robbie," the voice said. "It's Sylvana. What's the problem?"

"You phoned me yesterday on my cellphone. I..."

"Robbie. Yes. I think I know you. From Plettenberg Bay. I didn't phone you. Well, I can't remember."

An airport announcement sounded in the background.

Robbie was confounded; he couldn't think straight. *I'm going mad. Stark raving fucking crazy.*

"Anything else?" Vermaak said. Robbie was too shocked to answer. "Thank you."

"I....I..." Robbie began.

"So tell me now, Mr. Cullen, what exactly is the problem?" Vermaak's voice remained neutral, calm, as though she dealt with nutcases every day.

"I don't understand," Robbie placed both hands over his face and rubbed. "I *did* get a message from Sylvana. Check my phone." He toggled through his inbox, showed her the text.

Vermaak did not check his phone.

"This is it. Look!" Robbie pressed the phone forward.

Vermaak shook her head slowly.

Robbie's face flushed. "If it wasn't Sylvana, then who was it?" he said.

"Who's who?" Vermaak said, her lips curling into a funnel, slurping the coffee.

"The girl in the house."

"Well, that's just my problem, Mr. Cullen. Where exactly is this girl you're talking about, because we didn't find no one."

Robbie felt tears running down his cheeks, shame burning from his skin. He wiped his face. Couldn't think of anything to say.

"Tell me, son, what you on?" Vermaak was bemused. This kid had come to deny his involvement in a murder that never happened. Nearly thirty years, she'd never heard anything like it. Like trying to break *into* jail, she'd said to a colleague earlier. "Come now, I've seen it all, don't be *skaam*. Is it tik? Sugars? *Nee*. I can see you're not some junkie. But maybe you've tried some bad hash? Or acid? Acid can throw your head into a *groot fokken gemors, né*. Make you crazy for a bit, make you—"

"I'm not *on* anything," Robbie interrupted. "There *was* a dead girl. I saw her with my own eyes. Number 56 Lendell Road."

She stared into his eyes. He didn't look like a crazy but she'd been around long enough that nothing surprised her. She had a good mind to send him for a drug test and then throw him in jail for wasting her time. Forty-five minutes drive from Bellville for this shit.

"I thought it was Sylvana," he said shaking his head. "She phoned me."

Vermaak checked her documents.

"Number 56. Ja. There was a bit of a problem there. Looks like the officer first went to 65 on the other side." Vermaak spoke slowly, interpreting the scrawl. She chuckled. "Jissis. An Alsatian fokken bit him. Why's he writing this stuff up?"

She looked up briefly then back at the report. "Then he went to 56. Looked in all windows. No sign forced entry. Had to break the glass at front door because it was a potential emergency. No occupants."

Vermaak looked up. "The owners are overseas. No alarm." She whistled and shook her head. "We had to guard the house all night, then get the window fixed. Do you know what I—"

Robbie interrupted again, more forcefully, anger rising above the confusion. "You seriously think I'd make this up? I'd waste my day to come down here and—what?—suck a story out of my thumb?"

Vermaak looked up in irritation.

"What time did he get there? Your officer?" Robbie asked.

The big policewoman scanned the document.

"4:50 am."

"That's nearly two hours after I phoned in. Someone must have cleaned up, removed the body. Look at my shoes. Hey, why don't you look here." Robbie rummaged in the packet of evidence, showed her the soles of his black Adidas takkies. "What's this then? What's this?"

He stood up. Vermaak raised her hands. "Sit down, Mr. Cullen," she said firmly.

He sat down, tried to pass her his shoes.

"Put them back," she said.

"Why won't you look at them?"

"Look. I'm sorry. I don't have the time for this fokken mess. I have no idea why you want to do this." Vermaak retrieved his handwritten statement and tapped it on the desk. "There's sex video stuff in here. Strip clubs. But you're wasting my time and yours."

Robbie's frustration boiled over.

"What's this on my shoes?" he half-shouted. "Come on! Test it."

"Mr. Cullen!" Vermaak held up her hands, nodded for calm. Recognized that she needed to refine her approach. "That looks like mud maybe. Or dirt or maybe ash. Could be many things."

"It's blood," insisted Robbie. "It's Sylvana's blood. And what about the house? The room. There must be....Can't you do that check for blood?"

"*Kom nou*, Mr. Cullen, we just phoned this—Sylvana—and she sounded very alive to me. Try seeing this from my point of view. What's more likely: that this woman who was talking to me is dead, or that you have maybe become confused about what's going on? Maybe it's drugs, maybe you've got—how do they say it?—an obsession about her. Maybe you had a bad dream." She looked down and reread a phrase from his statement. "'Oral sex in the shower.' Maybe a nice dream."

"I can't believe this," Robbie said. "I know what I saw. I—"

Vermaak banged both hands on the table in unison. Nothing was working on this kid. Didn't he realize she wasn't about to order a Luminall spray on some crazy whim when there were real crimes that needed solving? "Hey!" she said. "You saw nobody. *Fokall.*"

Vermaak was done here. She had bodies to attend to. All the violence-on-women cases. An elderly woman in Bellville only a kilometer from her own flat, then two prostitutes apparently murdered by their Nigerian pimp in a residential hotel in Sea Point. She had organized a meeting with the Nigerian "building committee." She expected some bribes to be offered. Plus she had bloody Du Preez on her case whining for a lift.

"OK. Last chance," she said, laying down the cards. "Where can I see this video you talked about? On the Internet, right?"

Robbie put his head in his hands. "You can't. It's gone." He'd checked YouTube earlier that morning before leaving for the cop station. YouTube admin had granted his request. The video was erased.

He heard the sound of Vermaak folding the papers, felt the irony burning through his body, the conspiracy overwhelming him.

"When you find a body then we're talking? OK, Mr. Cullen?" She was already thinking about the Nigerians.

Vermaak did not take bribes and she did not report those that did. She knew a traffic officer who worked a stretch of road between Green Point and the CBD who regularly took a thousand rand a shot off drunk drivers. It wasn't her problem. She couldn't fix it if she tried.

That was the problem with the public. They actually believed the police could stop the shit. Stop them farming dagga, kick out the Nigerians, stop the murders. It was all cause and effect. Closing down one channel simply opened other windows of opportunity. Often more dangerous.

Strategy. That was what her boss Joseph Zoli advocated. Control and regulate. For example, stopping the export of dagga because the income was used to import harder drugs.

After decades on the force, Vermaak had her methods, knew when to stop chasing up a blind alley.

But the kid had said something that interested her. The barmen at the Blue Venus, She was looking for the weak link in that chain. Whether or not the Angie Dean case had any merits, she was aware that the narcotics division's undercover team was focused on barmen involved in drink spiking in Cape Town bars. Problem was, the last time they hit the nightclub scene and bust a dozen bouncers selling ecstasy to clubbers, Nigerian dealers working through white female associates filled the vacuum. With them came discounts and harder drugs. Just putting the barmen away wouldn't stop the demand. Vermaak wanted to get behind the racket.

"Are we clear, Mr. Cullen?" she repeated more forcefully.

Robbie shook his head. Oddly, he felt a wave of relief surge through his bones. Maybe he was mad. He needed to sleep. To forget everything.

Vermaak stared at him. Robbie got the feeling she was trying to decide what to do with him.

THE BOMB

"Yeah, Carlos?"

"Samuel. Good day to you too. You sound grumpy."

No answer. Carlos opened the front page of his fake passport, examined the unsmiling face.

"I have some good news for you, Samuel," Carlos continued

No reply.

"Samuel, are you there?"

"I'm here, Carlos."

"I said, I had some good news for you."

Samuel Chester sighed and shifted his weight painfully off the couch in the dank living room of his apartment. Crushed pizza boxes were scattered around the room, an empty two-liter Coke bottle on the table. He'd just returned from a trip to Boston, shaking down another Dark Video client who'd been less than timely with payments. The expenses incurred almost accounted for the shortfall, but Carlos had gone on about principle and all that again. Was all about principle at the moment. Principle, Samuel thought, was a rich man's prerogative.

The client had been surprised. Very surprised. So much so he'd let Chester have a round from a Colt Cobra. A snubbie. The bullet grazed his right shoulder, but it could have been worse. He'd snapped the shooter's wrist then smashed in his nose with the heel of his hand. The guy had fallen back, cracked his head against the sharp corner of a drinks cabinet, blood everywhere. All for a couple of grand.

Chester was getting tired of the dry work, the small-fry jobs. Making stupid mistakes.

"You don't sound very enthusiastic," Carlos said.

"Well. You know the score, boss. Sometimes your good news is my bad news."

Chester examined his fingers. He wouldn't eat anything until lunch. His diet was wreaking havoc with his nails, white spots everywhere. But he was down to a more manageable three hundred pounds.

"Not this time, old friend. Fancy another cruise?" Carlos laughed. So the guy was into pirates. Everyone had a fetish. He pictured the big black shape of Samuel Chester in a room full of pirate cutlasses, dreaming about the sparkling waters of the Caribbean, a skinny little island girl in the bow beneath the sailing ship, maybe two of them, him at the wheel, the mast in full flight.

"I'm listening."

As with all his other work contacts, Carlos had never met Chester in person. But he'd looked after him well for the eight years they'd worked together. And he'd seen him through the bouts of drinking and gambling. When Chester was in a bad place, Carlos's patronage had pulled him through. The apartment he lived in, for example: paid for. Carlos knew he was owed.

"Africa," Carlos said.

"Not that motherfucker place," Chester hissed out of clenched teeth.

"What's wrong with Africa, big boy? Is it 'cos grandpapa is down on his knees every evening thanking the Lord for delivering him to America?"

Chester didn't bite.

"Anyhow. I've got a job for you in Cape Town."

"What job?" Samuel Chester's voice was flat. His shoulder ached and his apartment smelled of stale food and disinfectant. He might have gone to a doctor, but bullet wounds attracted the wrong kind of attention. He kicked at an empty box of Scooters Pizza. Pasta and Coke were OK for his diet as long as he consumed them after lunch time.

Carlos outlined the objective of the assignment.

"I'll need some cash," said Chester.

"Of course. The usual rate," Carlos confirmed.

"I'll need some upfront," Chester insisted. He was overdrawn everywhere, had a sick sister, bills to pay. Atlantic City bills.

"Oh." Carlos let his reply sit. "How much?"

"All of it."

Carlos cackled down the line.

"Samuel. Not like you to haggle about money, my friend. Is this a 'you need me more than I need you?' Because I have to warn you, I'd just as soon go over and sort things out myself. I'm in that kind of mood." Carlos tapped the passport against the desk.

"Nothing like that, boss. Just short, is all."

"I'm serious, Samuel. I've been thinking about getting a bit more hands on."

Like Ralph Fiennes's character Harry from his *In Bruges*. Harry may have been the boss, but he got stuck in at all levels.

"Maybe half?" Chester said.

Carlos let him stew. Checked his watch. He hadn't exercised today.

"We have a deal. I'll be in touch."

Carlos smiled. With Chester, when you dropped the bomb, you knew it would go off like a motherfucker.

THE INEXORABLE TRUTH

In his study, Lynch twisted the brass dial of a two-hundred-kilogram antique safe, once property of Standard Bank in Adderley Street, and pulled the lever. The heavy door opened smoothly. He unlocked an inside drawer and removed an 1864 Remington revolver.

The trap door down to the cellar was open. Nirvana played through the lounge speakers, Kurt Cobain agonizing over *Pennyroyal Tea*. Funny how he loved his old grunge, Lynch thought to himself. Music triggered memories.

Lynch gathered a handful of loose ammunition, swept aside clutter on his desk and sat down. He held up the revolver and pointed it toward the door.

Lynch was glad he'd kept it and resisted the pressure to surrender his unlicensed firearms. He ran his hand along the weapon, admiring the shiny bluish barrel and the impression of the faded cartouche on the butt.

He turned the barrel and held it against his temple.

Just as his father must have done.

"Pow," he mouthed and curled his finger around the trigger. How much pressure would be too much? He closed his eyes and squeezed gently, imagined the percussion of the hammer, the resonation through the room, through the house. Through his brain.

He wondered what his father was thinking when he shot himself. Probably not about his children or his wife; probably focused on his miserable self and his charmed life that had mutated into a cesspool of shame and debt.

Death's a remedy.

He lowered the Remington and placed it on top of his journal. The weapon looked dark and evil, out of place amid the debris of books and papers.

The Dark Video woman had phoned. He'd declined her offer of a Mickey Finn delivery and she'd sounded annoyed. *Fuck her and her commission. I'm the client.*

Kryff hadn't been in touch yet but that was no surprise. He generally waited for instruction.

Lynch tapped his fingers on the desk and tried to concentrate on the task ahead. He wore only a pair of cotton underpants. An empty bottle of Libertas perched on the desk. He'd allowed the maid a day off.

The track changed; Lynch had queued one of his favorite albums, *Unplugged*, an early '90s classic. The next track was *Dumb*. He stared into space and listened to the lyrics. *I'm* not like them, but I can pretend.

His thoughts wandered to Saturday night at Elevation. Why had the barman reacted in the manner that he did? Kryff had clearly specified the venue as a place affiliated to the Mickey Finn Club. And after the club, what *had* he been thinking? Lying in wait outside Tugwell, what was his plan? Why hadn't he been more careful?

Lynch took a deep breath. He was losing control; his plan had been lunacy.

A mist of perspiration enveloped his body.

Nothing wrong, he told himself. *I've* done nothing wrong.

He took stock. The scopolamine was gone. He'd have to procure another vial from Kryff. But he hadn't scared off Terri. His muse. And there were other methods to acquire a date. The Remington might suffice, for example; or another drug to induce submission.

Lynch pulled a finger through the crease made by his gut and blinked his eyes.

At the outset, the Dark Video woman had explained that the guiding principle of their interaction was based on an event that never took place. If the girl couldn't remember anything, then nothing had happened. Like a tree falling in a forest. If no one is around to hear it, then the sound does not exist.

Kidnapping was a different story altogether. If he used the Remington, he would never be able to erase the trauma of a public kidnapping from the victim's head.

In which case, he would have to keep her.

In Patty Hearst's case, it had taken four weeks for her to break. Lynch grinned and slipped the journal out from under the Remington, opened at a page headed "Terri Phillips." He'd already pasted in two still shots captured from the Newlands Forest video. He'd also sketched the iconic photograph taken of Patty Hearst in the Sunset District branch of Hibernia Bank, brandishing an M1 carbine. He wondered where he might buy a jacket like the one Patty was wearing.

A bullet fell off the desk and rolled across the floor. He watched it slip under a filing cupboard, left it.

Under a picture of Terri he'd written: *I am the most beautiful and gentle man you'll ever meet. You'll see.* Patty Hearst had described her abductor this way. Willie Wolfe, also known as Cujo.

Lynch twirled his Parker in his fingers, then jotted from memory under his inscription: *cannot escape, isolated, threatened, token kindness.*

Lynch froze as the track ended. He knew what was coming next: *Polly.*

One of his favorites, perfect for Terri. Cobain was singing about a fourteen-year-old girl, abducted after attending a punk-rock show. He closed his eyes and mouthed the words. The girl had been tortured with whips and a blowtorch. He'd thought Polly was the name Terri could assume after she accepted him.

Lynch stood up, leaving the Remington, journal and bullets on the desk, and walked though the lounge to the hallway. Earlier he'd phoned in sick to the office. His secretary had mentioned the MD was looking for him, something about a call from the Receiver of Revenue. He had three missed calls on his cell.

A neat stack of envelopes lay unopened in a pile on the entrance-hall table. Lynch assessed the volume, at least a month's worth of correspondence. Normally he'd sift through them and extract the important ones, the utilities bills, services that would be discontinued if he failed to act on time. The rest of the mail he simply filed without opening.

His landline telephone rang. Lynch frowned and retraced his steps back to the office. He seldom got calls on that line. Chose to let it ring. Probably another fucking call-center agent offering him a new Cell C contract special.

The ringing stopped.

Then started again.

Lynch lifted the receiver. "Yes?"

"Julian?"

"Speaking." He recognized his ex-wife's voice; one of the missed calls on his cell had been from her number.

"It's Sandy."

"Hello," he replied, picking up a loose bullet and holding it up to the desk lamp. He pictured her wearing a floral skirt and creased T-shirt, overweight, unkempt hair; wished she could see the last woman he'd had in this house.

"You're not at work?" she stated.

"No. Day off."

Lynch dropped the bullet on his desk, looked toward the windows, the curtains drawn. He wondered what time it was; hadn't put on his watch earlier, couldn't tell if it was morning or afternoon.

"Oh," said Sandy, after a pause.

Lynch said nothing, stroked the Remington, fingers picking at the nipples and fine screws. He lifted it off the desk. "Pow," he mouthed silently. He could end it now, with her on the phone. How traumatized she'd be! But he would never show such weakness to her. Even in the last act.

"Is everything OK?"

"Absolutely, Sandy. Absolutely."

He turned the Remington toward his face, sucked on the end of the muzzle, pressed the sight against the roof of his mouth. The maid would find him, blood pooled on his bureau, dried to a black sticky mess.

"Julian?"

"Yes, Sandy, what do you want?" He had no time for her any more. After all her anger toward him, all her years of hiding Holly from him, all her threats. All her bullshit.

"Klaus phoned me."

Lynch said nothing.

"Klaus Simmonds."

"I know who the fuck Klaus is," he snapped. Klaus Simmonds was the managing director of Premier Marque Asset Management. His boss.

"I just thought I'd let you know," she said, her voice locked in a narrow emotionless tone range. "God knows why he called me. I mean, how should I know where you are? But he was very apologetic. Appeared rather concerned. Says they've been trying to get hold of you and that it's urgent."

"Urgent?" Lynch had a flashback to married life. Sandy had always been so melodramatic. Such a drama queen. Reading her true-life tales about husbands who murder their families in the night. She'd once told him she thought him capable of such an act. *Pow.* He mouthed the word while aiming the Remington at the portrait of his father that hung on the study wall.

"Look, Julian. I know it's been years since we were civil to each other. But is everything OK? Is there something I should know?"

"No. Everything is fine. Thank you," he said. Then, suddenly realizing the opportunity: "But I do think it's about time you let me see Holly."

"Jesus, Julian, I've told you before, I refuse to discuss Holly with you."

Lynch sucked in the rebuff.

The same selfish bitch. Nothing's changed.

"Sandy..."

He knew she was waiting for him to say something more; would think it a question, something he was going to tell her. He put the phone down.

The room was silent. Lynch twirled the muzzle of the gun on the tip of his tongue. His computer beeped quietly, signaling its switch into hibernation. The wallpaper on the monitor revealed an image of Terri Phillips, cross-legged, blindfolded with red material, her lips moving slowly.

Lynch put down the Remington and moved to the curtains, pulled them open.

I refuse to discuss her with you.

Another rejection.

Let Kryff bring me another girl and see who rejects me then.

Outside the clouds were like smoke swirling around a light, relentless in their motion.

Everything was moving so fast.

The observation was his first lucid thought the entire day.

You haven't done anything wrong. There's still the chance to walk away, restore sanity, slow down the rush.

He wondered if that's how his father had felt? Settling one loan with another more punishing one, then again and again until he was sucked into the vortex of his hopelessness.

He stared at his father's portrait, a bald-headed man with grey moustache, black suit and red tie, gold braiding around the frame of the canvas.

Thirty years ago, Lynch reflected, he was an innocent young boy living a privileged life. A little more than ten years ago he was married to Sandy, maintaining a position of compliance. Then came Holly. How times changed. And after that he was on his own, alone to seek out what he really desired.

He eyed the Remington. Now he was poised to enter the never-never.

At least his mother and father were dead. They'd never know.

ESCALATION

Carlos stretched, clicked his neck from side to side to release the tension of an uncomfortable night. An alarm, false, triggered at 2:30 am, had desecrated his sleep.

He pumped repetitively on his handgrips, commanded himself to relax. *There's no list of Dark Video clients. Nobody can find me.*

He'd run his latest laptop reformat the day before, loading another fresh operating system. He'd swapped Internet service providers and changed a number of access hops, bypassing the UK and French legs and rerouting via Turkey and Portugal.

Carlos rolled out his shoulders, breathed deeply, the paranoia quieted for now.

Connecting through the wireless network, he traversed a number of proxy servers to receive his latest messages from a remote server. No messages to or from his account remained on any server for longer than twelve hours. He avoided Gmail or Hotmail or any similar services that stored information on a user's behalf. May as well leave your wallet with a stranger, he figured.

He checked his email.

First thing: no message from Samuel Chester—a good sign. He didn't expect to hear from him except in case of emergency. The big man had arrived two days earlier in Cape Town with clear instructions; he wouldn't need babysitting.

A text from his wife interrupted his thoughts. What did he want for lunch? Easy. Something cleansing. Sushi. He texted back, just the one word, from a pay-as-you-go cellphone he'd purchased at a store in neighboring Bellevue.

She called back on the same number. "Wanna meet me here rather?" She was shopping in downtown Seattle, a ten-minute drive away at this time.

"Honey. Go ahead and enjoy yourself," he told her.

He worked his thumb into a knot in his shoulder while she squealed on about their kid's shitting habits. He didn't feel in the mood to get out. And he had work to do. So much for sushi.

A new email caught his eye; he digested a terse message from an agent of the Mickey Finn Club complaining that his operatives in Cape Town were abusing the service. Sounded like a fishing expedition. The only Dark Video operator in Cape Town was the woman. Diva. Carlos chuckled. It was a good name. He typed back asking for details.

The response came immediately. It included a date and reference number of the incident.

"Shit," thought Carlos. "Automated response system. Not bad." He logged the reference number and perused the detail on the screen, wondered if there was anything to it.

He ended the call and drafted a text to Diva in Cape Town.

```
MF causing problems. Complaints that we are
hijacking other agents' merchandise.
Confirm: did you pay for MF services ref
20111710/BV71?
Confirm: are you in position to terminate
MF rival(s)?
```

Satisfied, he turned his mind back to his security measures. Time for another scan, he decided. The paranoia was making noises again.

"You can't!" Carlos declared into his phone. Diva in Cape Town.

When his wife had failed to return home by 4 pm, Carlos had gone downstairs and made himself a glass of fresh orange juice. Though hungry, he'd chosen not to eat. Two hours later, sitting on the edge of his bed, he was ravenous—and testy. Diva was only making things worse.

He'd decided to make the call on his pay-as-you-go phone because the Mickey Finn hijacking message had bugged him and he wanted answers now—even though he realized he'd have to bin the SIM card afterwards. But Diva was flying way off target now, hadn't answered any of the questions he'd sent; was now trying to negotiate access to Terri Phillips, the star of his *Forest Frolic* video.

"Out of bounds," he emphasized.

"But you said only while she was involved with the Morgan boy. He's in London, they're not together any more. We could earn a lot from this."

"Someone pays me a lot more to keep her safe," he replied, getting up and walking through to the bathroom. He picked up a handgrip on the basin, squeezed twice, put it down.

Carlos had no special feelings for the girl either way. But she was valuable enough to be emphatic on this point.

Terri Phillips had been in Dark Video's firing line before. Two years previously, she'd suffered at the hands of the Gorillas gang; had unwittingly starred in one of their projects and been caught up in the killing spree that had decimated the gang. But it turned out her boyfriend's father was a Dark Video client based in Johannesburg and had intervened. He was a valuable client and Carlos was happy to keep his end of the bargain.

"Lynch is really insistent, Carlos," the woman persisted. "The other operator, Kryff, has offered to get her."

Carlos looked around the bathroom, considered whether he should do another sweep with the video intercepter. He'd already meticulously checked the house that afternoon.

"Really?" Carlos smirked. "I thought you told me you were handling this Kryff."

"You don't understand, Carlos. If I get rid of him, another Kryff will come along. It's a service industry. Lynch is desperate for Terri Phillips. He'll get her one way or the other. We must give the client what he wants."

Carlos smiled. *Give the client what he wants.* He had trained her well.

"Or just stop the fucking competition giving it to him," Carlos responded.

"I don't understand," she replied. "Are we—"

"You don't understand! *I* don't understand." Carlos took a deep breath, tried to remain calm. He'd always felt it unbecoming to shout, but Diva was testing him. "I would like to know how Kryff got *our* client's contact in the first place," he said pointedly.

At daybreak that morning, Carlos had spent an hour on Skype with Jacker. A client in Portugal was being harassed after someone sent his boss an incriminating email. Jacker had again suggested the possibility of a list.

Carlos had the handgrips in his grasp again, pumped repeatedly as he strode from the bathroom, pacing the bedroom back and forth. Before Diva could reply, he shot another question at her: "Who is this bloody Kryff anyway?"

"He's some small-bit operator," she replied. "I don't—"

"Some small-bit operator who's fucking with our big rollers!" Carlos exploded. "Jesus, woman, I want to know how in the fuck he got to Lynch. Tell me!"

Diva was silent.

"I'll take that as an 'I don't know.' But you can find this out, yes?"

"Yes," she replied quietly.

"Are you sure?" he pressed. "Really goddamned sure?"

"I can do it."

"Bloody hell you can. Burn his fucking face off if you have to. It's time to start sending out some very clear messages."

Carlos breathed through his nose, long inhalations. He was calmer now, quieter. The outburst had helped. But his concerns remained. Four clients now outed by random tip-offs: in Japan, South Africa, Sweden, Portugal. The threat to his base was escalating. As if someone were playing games with him.

What if someone has been able to build a list?

"Look, Diva," Carlos said. "I'm getting static on my lines. My sources have mentioned a possible list. Do you know anything about this? Could this Kryff—could he somehow have got his hands on a list of Dark Video clients?"

"I know nothing about a list," Diva replied. "How would he—"

"Never mind," Carlos interrupted, catching his paranoia. "Are you staying close to the Russians?"

"That particular threat has been closed down," she answered immediately.

"I didn't ask that, Diva. Are you testing me? Are you seeking a reaction from me? Must I remind you that my most trusted fixer is in your city this very evening and looking right over your shoulder this very instant?"

"No, Carlos."

"So I said, are you keeping close to the Russians?"

"Yes, Carlos."

"How close?" He wished he could see her face. Wished Chester really was right there right now staring over her shoulder.

"Close enough."

"Yeah, close enough," Carlos said. "But not fucking close enough. That's another gang cutting in on our business. Just because you stopped one girl, doesn't make the problem go away. *Another Kryff will come along.* Your words, no?"

Carlos had got the full report from Jacker: a band of Eastern European strippers were recreating their own version of the Mickey Finn Club at Cape Town strip joints. Clients were being drugged, robbed, and blackmailed. Or set up. The girl in question had even tried selling a Dark Video-style production to a local businesswoman.

"I told you, Carlos," the operative replied calmly. "It was nothing. Some kid got blown in a shower without knowing he was on camera. We got hold of the clip, stuck it on YouTube before they could cut a deal. Exclusivity compromised, problem solved. It was peanuts anyway."

"Who's the kid?" Carlos laughed—even in this mood he could see the humor in that.

"Nobody," she replied.

"But you've taken care of him?"

Diva paused a moment, measured her answer: "We gave him the biggest fright of his life. Don't you worry, he's not an issue."

Carlos sat down in front of the monitor at his bedroom desk, linked to the office mainframe. He tabbed through the latest video clips from Jacker, pressed play. He was looking at Robbie Cullen in the shower.

"He looks like an actor. What's he fucking do?"

"A student. But there's no need to worry about him. He's completely compromised. After our operation…well, we've got his fingerprints on her phone, his footprint at the scene."

Carlos wasn't convinced; wasn't taking any chances. "I don't care. Check him out. Thoroughly. Hard drives, cellphones, everything. Understand?"

"I understand."

Carlos sighed. He'd given Diva a chance to raise the email from Mickey Finn regarding the hijacking of another operator's target. She hadn't. It frustrated him when a star operator disappointed him. Disappointed herself. She had so much to offer, but Carlos could read the signs.

He ended the call and looked out his window. A fat pigeon sat like an ornament on the telephone wire. Carlos wished he had a pellet gun.

LOGIC 101

Robbie had spent two days in his room, leaving only for meals. He'd arranged for a classmate to drop off lecture notes, claiming illness. Not that he could concentrate on them for more than a minute.

Melanie had sent him a message:

```
Rob. Whats going on with u?
```

It was a response to the desperate message he'd left her on the night of Sylvana's murder. He regretted trying to get hold of her, felt a fool. Had followed it up the next day with an abrupt response:

```
Never mind
```

He was relieved that Melanie had made no reference to the shower video.

Returning from dinner, Robbie found a note from Denny pushed under his door. "Suggest you keep low profile at Blue Venus," it read. The bar gang must have worked out who he was.

Robbie crumpled the note and threw it in the bin. His washing bag contained a batch of clean and ironed garments. On his desk was a plastic bank bag into which he'd scraped clotted blood from his takkies with an old toothbrush. He tidied his room and threw out all his first and second year notes. Then he punched holes in the new lecture notes and inserted them into lever-arch files. He was looking for order, anything to stop his mind racing.

The image of Sylvana's gaping throat tormented him; he'd need liters of bleach to fade the flashbulb memories that clawed at his guts. He couldn't bring himself to phone her cellphone again; instead, he called Deon from Gorky Park and asked if he'd seen her. The manager confirmed Sylvana was overseas, but didn't know if her trip had been planned or not.

Robbie also called Tony Beacon to check if he'd heard from her. Negative.

Robbie knew one way to order: logic 101, the cornerstone of an information technology degree. He tried using the basics to create system from his muddled thinking; tried the logical approach.

He'd seen a dead body—if not Sylvana's then whose?
He'd been called to the house—why?

The body had been removed—why?

Three questions, no answers. His inner monologue skidded to a standstill.

I need a theory.

The discipline of writing, his professor would always say. Put your thoughts on paper and they crystalize. He pulled out an A4 pad and attempted to follow the advice.

Sylvana made a shower video. I am in it.
She planned to sell it and give me a cut. (She must have a client—who?)
I rejected her offer.
The video was posted on YouTube.
She was killed.
I witnessed her body.
Her body was removed.
She—or someone claiming to be her—is alive and has gone home.

Shit! Robbie thought. One and one makes zero. He searched the web for a copy of the shower video: no luck. No video, no body. His life didn't exist. It was like something from *The Twilight Zone*.

He thought about the message on Sylvana's cellphone: "Smile!"

Smile for what? A photograph?

If the Blue Venus gang had killed Sylvana, they had proof of his presence in the house. That's what he'd thought the night of the murder.

But no body?

Whoever killed the girl had access to Sylvana's cellphone, had deliberately lured him to the house.

Why?

Barring the barmen at the Blue Venus, Robbie could think of no other enemies. He wondered what Denny had heard, what was behind his warning to stay away from Blue Venus, and why it had come now. The Blue Venus gang was a bad bunch, he knew. Killers?

Fallon said: life and death.

But why kill Sylvana, if they wanted him?

Robbie's stomach was a tumult of knots as the questions and what-if scenarios turned over and over in his head.

He considered his options. Involving the police was out for now. The policewoman he'd spoken to had thought him on drugs, was more likely to arrest him than help him.

But there was no second option.

Fuck!

Robbie stood up and stretched, turned on the kettle. He dropped his last Five Roses tea bag into a mug, claimed from his bar fridge a fresh glass of milk that he'd taken from the dining hall. At least he was thinking clearly enough to get his tea right.

He returned to his desk and delved further back in his memory, scribbling down notes, trying to apply logic.

Melanie breaks up with me.

I meet Fallon.

Fallon is attacked at Blue Venus.

I save her.

She is investigating something or someone at Blue Venus.

She turns up at Plett where Sylvana punks me in shower.

The kettle boiled and Robbie filled the mug with hot water. He added milk and sugar from a Wimpy sachet, removed the spent teabag, and stirred.

He reviewed what he'd written. "Melanie breaks up with me." No relevance except to signify the start of his problems. He wondered if Melanie was taking Picasso home to Albany for the midyear break. That would be awkward.

He looked at the second line: *I meet Fallon.* It was hard not to consider a link. His life up to four weeks ago had been so ordinary.

He redrafted his notes.

Angie Dean is drugged at Blue Venus.

Fallon is attacked at Blue Venus.

I save Fallon.

Fallon is involved in a covert operation ("life and death").

Down the passage a door banged. Robbie looked up, spotted the bank bag with the blood from the takkies.

Blood from takkies. Could get Doc Louwtjie to check it out.

Doc Louwtjie was a med student on his floor. Robbie shook his head, wondered if he'd been watching too much *CSI.* But it would prove there was a body, and he wasn't crazy.

What other angles were there? He recalled Sylvana's message. It was still on his voicemail. "Robbie. I....It's....I have to talk to you. Please, Robbie. I didn't know. Robbie....It's Sylvana. Phone me. Please phone me."

"I didn't know." I didn't know what?

Could it be that Sylvana thought he was linked to Fallon's operation?

Robbie sipped his tea, felt it warming his chest. He felt better for having written down his thoughts.

He figured he had to return to class the next day, had to do his best to keep up appearances. And besides, he couldn't afford to bomb out in his final year.

He scanned his notes. If he screwed up the page and threw it away, would the nightmare be over?

The blow-job video had disappeared from cyberspace, the furore it caused on campus already easing into urban-legend territory. Would be long forgotten in a few months' time.

And Sylvana was out the country. Or dead?

Besides being strung out, embarrassed, and nearly terrified to death, Robbie realized he was OK. The envelope with Fallon's money caught his eye. He had two thousand rand remaining, enough to tide him over quite comfortably for a while.

Fallon.

This is life and death.

But was she legit? he wondered. Was it normal for the police to reward a citizen for helping someone within their organization? And if she was on-side, then didn't he owe it to Fallon to warn her? She might be in danger.

Robbie fingered his Nokia, scrolled through the contacts list. One call to Fallon, he thought. She may know nothing. She may be able to answer everything.

She'd paid him to be discreet, not to acknowledge her.

He put the phone down.

Logic made no sense.

He placed his head in his hands. This wasn't going to go away.

Like sliding doors, he had two courses of action. He could go to it, or it could come to him.

Robbie swallowed the last gulp of tea from his mug.

DISPOSAL

Kryff watched from a table near the entrance of the Poseidon Bar and Grill. To the young and the hungry with eyes only for their desires, Kryff was invisible, a nonentity.

He'd scanned the room, evaluating the different pockets of patrons. The date tables, quiet and involved, oblivious to the loud bass driving the music; the bawdy students at one end of the bar getting drunk mid-week; the lone woman waiting opposite, embarrassed to be on her own, sipping from her wine glass behind dark glasses.

He'd found what he was looking for; was watching five teenagers, kitted uniformly in bouncy miniskirts and black stockings. The lively one with a blonde bob and cheeky smile couldn't have been older than fifteen. Probably fake student IDs in their bags—though nobody asked.

First Wednesday of the month, hardly his busiest time, but he had an order. Kryff was always on the lookout for clients to add to his list of regulars. He employed a fetcher from time to time but mostly he operated as a one-man band, tapping into the Mickey Finn Club network when necessary.

A waiter stopped at his table, blocking Kryff's view of the teenagers, asked if sir would like another drink. Kryff hadn't touched his vodka, lime and soda. Never did. The drinks order was just for show.

The waiter had a toothpaste-white smile, bleached hair, and sharp blue eyes. A student, thought Kryff. Paying his way.

"Which one?" the waiter asked without breaking his smile.

Eeny, meeny, miney, mo.

Young and fresh, any one of them would be perfect.

"Your choice," said Kryff.

The waiter left him; Kryff's eyes followed, watched him duck under the bar counter, engage the barman quietly in conversation, slap him on the back as he moved on. Across the room, the girls were giggling.

Kryff checked the time: 10 pm. Still early for a place like this. He looked back at the girls. Schoolchildren with rich parents, no doubt. They'd have told them they were going to a movie or a shopping center. Or a school function or another girl's house....Pick one. They'd have come by a taxi diverted from its intended destination, organized cheap liquor, which they kept in their purses to avoid the high costs of the bar.

The lively one was doing a pirouette, arms curling in the air. The buttons of her blouse were undone to her midriff, large breasts bouncing above.

Possibly already augmented, Kryff judged. *Kids these days.*

"Whee!" He heard her girlish pleasure.

Kryff was glad he didn't have kids. He had no respect for parents. Bringing up children came with obligations, and yet modern parents were monsters. They wanted the world for their precious angels, would give and promise them the best of everything—and, as a result, gave them the worst.

He caught the eye of the woman across the bar. She smiled at him.

Kryff licked his lips, looked away quickly.

On occasion, Kryff felt guilty about the nature of his work. He realized he wasn't a psychopath because his actions registered in some faint vestige of his conscience. At these times he would rationalize that his occupation was no different from other businesses. He was just a man doing what he did best to get by. Most importantly, he simply filled a need. If he didn't do it, someone else would. Yes, competitors got eliminated, staff exploited. And young women were taken advantage of. But it all went on with or without him. And besides, how was it any different to the sex trade? Prostitution may be illegal, but it was as old as time and widely accepted as a part of life. There was no difference between a whore on the streets and one of these girls; neither of them had a choice. Perhaps this was fairer, in fact; more random. And the girl wouldn't know any different.

The lively one tripped on her high-heeled shoes, fell on her ass, her friends guffawing. She got unsteadily to her feet. The barman placed a round of Jägermeisters on the counter. Kryff approved. The color and the taste would mask any evidence.

Tonight one of the little darlings would be going home very late. It was like shooting deer in a zoo with a tranquilizer gun. Her friends would panic and probably say nothing, too concerned about their parents' reactions. Kryff would drop her off close by in the early hours of the morning, and tomorrow no one would be sure what had happened. Young girls drinking too much without adult supervision. What a shame. The parents would worry the school would find out, that people would talk; they'd say nothing. Maybe she'd be grounded for a few days. Everyone would just be happy she'd come to no harm.

And his client would be satisfied.

When he looked back at the woman in the dark glasses, she raised her wine in greeting, allowed him half a smile. Poor thing, he thought, stood up like that. *What the hell.* He returned the smile and raised his drink to her, took a slow sip. It had been a while since he'd consumed alcohol.

The lively one mounted the bar counter. She unbuttoned her blouse, revealed a turquoise bra beneath. Her friends giggled below, passed her a shooter which she downed, balanced the glass upside-down on her head.

"Woohoo!" She held out her arms like balancing poles, jiggled her breasts from side to side.

So many years of sobriety yet the vodka settled so nicely inside him. Kryff took another sip and checked his appearance in the adjacent mirror. He thought he looked presentable, wondered if she might like some company once business here was done.

Kryff swallowed the remainder of his drink in one long gulp, felt the warmth of the vodka penetrate his blood stream. He waved to the barman, requesting another. The woman raised her empty glass, offered him a wider smile. To his surprise, she stood up from the bar and approached his table, a Gothic black handbag slung over her shoulder.

"Good evening, Mr. Kryff," Fallon said, offering her hand in greeting.

Mr. Kryff?

He frowned as he stood and reached forward to shake her hand, but his legs buckled underneath him. She hooked her arm into his.

"Come with me, Mr. Kryff. I have a car waiting outside."

Kryff screamed, gripped with fear.

A bald man with a head like a bullet struck a match and held it to Kryff's petrol-soaked moustache. It ignited with a burst, singeing his face to his eyebrows. Kryff screamed again, this time in agony, rolled onto his side on the concrete floor attempting to suppress the pain. His hands were bound behind his back.

Fallon waited a moment, let the pain bring him to his senses, then threw a bucket of water over Kryff's head.

"Ferdi, be so kind." Fallon indicated to her bald accomplice to roll Kryff over so she could talk to him face to face.

"How did you get Lynch's details?" she probed, leaning forward to inspect Ferdi's handiwork. The stench of burnt hair pervaded the deserted parking lot.

Kryff knew she was the woman from Dark Video, though he hadn't expected her to be so young. Through his pain, he flashed back to the chain of events that had brought about his downfall, starting with the girl outside the Blue Venus. Angie Dean had been *his* target, a delivery for a wealthy client in Plattekloof Glen. He'd acted by the book: created an online requisition to the Mickey Finn Club at Blue Venus, then dispatched his fetcher to collect the order while he waited around the corner in his white Polo. When the breathless fetcher had returned with details of her theft at gunpoint, he'd immediately suspected one of the bigger players. They had spotted the silver X5 glide past and followed it to its Bishopscourt destination. It had been a piece of cake getting in touch with Julian Lynch after that.

"I've already told you," Kryff managed through gasps of pain. "I followed you after you…you snatched…the girl from me."

"You know your man was trying to fuck the girl in the carpark?" Fallon snarled, realizing Kryff was telling the truth. "What kind of Mickey Mouse operation were you running?" But she was furious at her oversight. It wasn't what she wanted to hear. She'd been wrong to break the rules, steal another operator's target without paying. Now Carlos suspected a conspiracy, that the competition had somehow accessed a list of Dark Video clients. Kryff's explanation was simpler: she'd fucked up. She glared at Ferdi; he'd been the driver that night.

Kryff mumbled something under his breath; Fallon kicked him in the gut, venting her anger. "What did you say? Did you call me a bitch, Mr. Kryff?"

"I said an X5 is not hard to follow."

Fallon glared at Ferdi again. It had been his idea to acquire the jacked X5 via one of his contacts. Previously they'd used a discreet sedan as transport. She was furious with herself. Why had she listened to him? Why had she let the details slip?

"Where's the list?" she tried again.

"I told you, I don't know about a list."

Fallon kicked Kryff again, flush between the legs with the sharp point of her stiletto. He sucked in the hurt, felt the nausea rising from his gut and overwhelming the pain of the burn.

They were two floors up, the parking lot a stand-alone unit; packed with cars by day, empty and unguarded at night. The scene was illuminated by the headlights of Ferdi's Opel Astra. Kryff rested his head on the concrete, kept his eyes closed, felt his mind returning to that place of darkness, so familiar to him years ago in prison. How stupid, he thought. An hour ago he'd been in control of his world, of everything, of other people's destinies. Vanity, the ultimate downfall. How could he have believed the woman at the bar would be interested in him?

She was certainly a smart operator, though. Whatever she'd used was fast working, efficient enough to make him compliant without knocking him out completely.

"What do you know about the Russian girl? Sylvana? Was she working for you?" Fallon tried another line of questioning.

Kryff mumbled truthfully that he didn't know anyone with that name.

She kicked him again, aiming once more for his groin. The contact wasn't flush this time; she stamped down on his stomach with frustration. Kryff rolled onto his side, then his front, wheezing. The heels of Fallon's stiletto had drawn blood.

"You're lying. You worked with her. We have photographs of her at Lynch's house. Did she tell you about Lynch?"

"No," Kryff rasped.

"Where's the fucking list?" she screamed, lifting her leg again and stabbing her stiletto into his back.

"She's got it!" Kryff shouted, playing for time. "The Russian."

Fallon looked at Ferdi. He shook his head.

"Bullshit!" The stiletto crashed down again.

Fallon reached out to Ferdi with an open palm; he pushed off from the concrete pillar he was leaning against and placed a 9mm handgun in her hand, cocked and locked. Her gun: a Sig Sauer P238 Lady.

A ringtone emanated from the car. Ferdi retrieved Kryff's cellphone, held it up to Fallon. She nodded at him to answer.

"Where the fuck are you?" said the voice.

Ferdi winked at Fallon. "Is this Mr. Lynch?" he asked gruffly.

"Who's this?" The tone on the line shifted abruptly from irritation to suspicion.

"Plans have changed," Ferdi replied.

"I am looking for Mr. Kryff. Who's this?"

"It's Ferdi," he said. "There's been a buyout, Mr. Lynch. Kryff works for us now."

Kryff groaned on the cement. Lynch. He shouldn't have touched him. He'd known Lynch was a Dark Video client. Taking on Lynch had been payback for their stealing Angie Dean from under his nose. Kryff knew he should never have offered Lynch the waitress from The Pump or accepted the brief on Terri Phillips. The man's needs were too rich, too unrealistic. When Kryff had failed to coax Kim from The Pump, he'd fallen back on the territory he knew well and found a callgirl from Bellville. He hadn't expected Lynch to abuse her as he did.

On the phone, Lynch was silent, obviously pondering developments. He cleared his throat.

"I had an, uh...deal with Kryff. And..." Again Lynch hesitated. "Tell me, will the price tag be the same?"

Kryff groaned. An image of the girl with the tattooed lotus flower replaced that of Lynch in his mind. There was no way he could have put her back on the street without comebacks, so he'd suffocated her in his car and dumped her body in the marina. As the pain washed over him, he felt a faint sense of regret for the killing. There had been too many.

"The price?" said Ferdi, shrugging his shoulders.

Fallon grabbed the phone from Ferdi.

"Dark Video rates," Fallon said firmly.

"Is that you, Diva?"

"Yes, Mr. Lynch. Unfortunately we can't fulfill any orders tonight because we're finalizing details of the..."—she raised the gun in the air as she found the word—"merger."

Lynch hesitated. "Will Mr. Kryff be getting back to me?" he asked.

Fallon glanced at Ferdi with a grin.

"I'm afraid he'll be a little late," she said, terminating the call and tossing the phone back to Ferdi, who slouched back against the pillar, chewing gum like a bovine.

Fallon crouched down besides Kryff, grabbed his hair, and lifted his head up.

"What do you know about Terri Phillips?" she asked.

Kryff opened an eye. Fallon's short black miniskirt was bunched around her thighs: through the numbing pain of his torture, he had a perfect view of her shaved sex. Fallon noticed; intended it.

"A bit late for that now, Mr. Kryff. Time to answer the question." He felt the cold muzzle of the gun against his ear.

"Lynch wanted her."

Another big mistake, thought Kryff. After Lynch had rejected his offer of sourcing Terri Phillips from Elevation, he'd dispatched his fetcher to get her anyway; figured Lynch wouldn't be able to resist if he had her drugged up and good to go. The fetcher said he'd got close, but the girl's friend had coaxed her away.

"You didn't get her name from a list?"

Fallon motioned to Ferdi who lifted a plastic jerry can, stepped forward, and doused petrol over Kryff's body.

"Last chance," Fallon said, maintaining her hold on Kryff's thin hair, the gun in his ear.

Kryff sniffed and spluttered blood from his burnt mouth. He ran his tongue over his upper lip but there was no sensation. Kryff did not fear death; it was a remedy. On one occasion he'd watched Van Rooyen dispose of a body at the crematorium. Air, water, and guts—and, when it's all over, just whitewashed bones.

"Speak, motherfucker," Fallon said, jabbing the point of her stiletto against his ear and clicking the safety off the Sig Sauer.

Kryff opened his palm on the cold cement. He didn't want to die here; he wanted to die in the open, rotting until the smell brought the animals.

Fallon looked quickly across at Ferdi. Then she tensed her hold on the Rosewood grip and shot Kryff without looking down, the sharp crack echoing in the concrete building, the bullet exiting Kryff's skull and ricocheting off the cement floor.

"Fuck's sake!" shouted Ferdi, jumping backwards and raising his free hand to the side of his head.

"He didn't have the list," Fallon said, dropping Kryff's head and standing up straight.

Ferdi grinned, a mixture of scowl and malice. The gaps between his teeth were too wide; they didn't do orthodontics in Rustenburg where he grew up.

"Come here." Fallon gestured to Ferdi. She'd marked the edges of her permanent eyebrows with a black pen, the upward arc giving her a demonic appearance. Ferdi emerged from the shadows and gripped her around the waist. She placed her free hand on the top of his dome and pressed downwards.

"Yeah, baby!" said Ferdi, running his hands down the front of Fallon's top, feeling the hardness of her nipples as he sunk to his knees. This was one crazy bitch, he thought to himself. He wasn't sure whether they had a relationship or not, but he'd fucked her a few times, even been away with her on a long weekend in Plett, and she'd been wilder than anything he'd ever had before. A flashback to a quickie in the back of the X5 gave him an instant erection.

With Ferdi where she wanted him, Fallon threw her leg over his shoulder. Her skirt was so short the position gave him perfect access; her lack of underwear even more so. He leaned forward and plunged his tongue into her.

"Oh yes!"

She moaned and twisted savagely, spreading her heat over his face, his stubble like the rasping tongue of a cat. He cupped his hands under her buttocks and flicked his tongue back and forth over her cleanly shaved lips, savored the scent of her sex.

"Let me!" Fallon groaned.

She dug her nails into his greasy pate and fought off his attempt to limit her movement, thrusting back and forth, faster and faster, the friction igniting her tinder of lust and danger. She still held the Sig Sauer in one hand; rubbed it against her chest, then under her mesh top and across her breasts.

"Hold still!" Ferdi gripped her ass tighter and tried to slow her gyrations.

"Oh my god!" she groaned, drawing blood as she bit her lip. The contrast of pleasure and pain intensified as her body began to tremble.

"Sweet Jesus!" she uttered, her orgasm a violent explosion of relief.

"That's it, baby! That's it!" Ferdi massaged his hands on her ass, maintaining his kneeling position as Fallon fell back against the concrete pillar. His cock throbbed rock hard in his pants. His turn was next.

"That was fucking amazing!" panted Fallon, an irrepressible grin spreading across her face. She laughed out loud in triumph, then she placed the gun barrel on the top of Ferdi's skull and fired, the bullet exiting through the back of his head and pinging off the cement with an explosion of dust. She kicked him backwards and he slumped on top of Kryff, convulsing drunkenly as the life exited his body.

"You always loved a bit of head," Fallon said, before emptying the remains of the jerry can over the two bodies.

HERE KITTY

Captain Vermaak stopped off on the way home to pick up a bottle of Klipdrift from the local Picardi Rebel. She'd come from a national conference run by the Family Violence, Child Protection, and Sexual Offenses Unit, and she figured she'd earned a drink. The conference focus had been on drug-stock theft from state hospitals and it made for dire analysis. Chris Hani Baragwanath Hospital in Soweto was reporting losses of up to fifty percent of stock, and it was the same story around the country: drugs pilfered by doctors, pillaged by nurses and, on occasion, cleaned out by brazen gangs who were tipped off when major deliveries had been made. Most concerning for her, Vermaak knew these were smart drugs that subsequently found their way onto the Cape club circuit in any number of guises.

She trudged up the back steps of her seventh-floor flat and opened the kitchen door, threw her jacket on the plastic table.

A white cat miaowed its greeting.

"Ag voetsek," Vermaak said back. She set the brown paper packet of booze on the table.

The cat kept two paces ahead as Vermaak completed her homecoming rituals, shuffling through the kitchen into the lounge.

She turned on the television and scanned the on-screen menu for the night's movies. Something with Sandra Bullock.

Returning to the kitchen with a tumbler, she broke the seal on the Klipdrift and filled the glass to a quarter without removing the bottle from the packet.

The cat miaowed again.

"Ja?" Vermaak replied and gulped from the glass. One, two, three. She banged it down on the table and filled another quarter. Klipdrift had been her man's favorite. She'd never touched alcohol before she met him.

She returned to the lounge and slumped onto the couch. The cat watched her with thin yellow eyes, didn't join her.

"Ja?" Vermaak said again.

The cat had been with her for three years. She didn't know where it came from. One evening it was hiding behind the curtain in the kitchen, no left ear and half a tail. Old injuries, but the fear remained. She'd put down a small bowl of milk. Next day it was gone, milk too, but it returned the following evening. And then it kept returning.

Another miaow.

Three years later and it still wouldn't let her pet it.

Vermaak ignored the cat and rested her boots on the low glass coffee table.

The theft of nearly a thousand boxes of prescription drugs from the Salt River warehouse of one of the Cape's leading pharmaceutical companies had been a discussion point at the conference. Robbing a pharma company was more profitable than robbing a bank these days.

And there'd been news of another case of drinks spiking involving a student from the University of Cape Town. This time the victim had provided a urine sample and undergone an internal examination. The doctor's report was inconclusive because the girl had showered, but the toxicology report showed traces of a nervous-system suppressant called GHB. Gamma hydroxybutyrate.

The following day Vermaak was due to see an assembly of wardens and counselors at UCT to explain there was nothing going down. She thought about the other girl. Angie Dean. She'd told her audience at UCT that the girls all just drank too much. That wasn't up for debate. But...

Vermaak swallowed a mouthful of brandy, felt the bite.

"En wat sê jy?" she said to the cat.

Vermaak scrolled through the movie options again, then flicked up to the food and entertainment channels. DSTV was one of the few luxuries she permitted in her life. But she didn't feel like Sandra Bullock tonight.

Five years in this flat in Bellville, time seemed to be standing still. She'd hung on to a little semi in Durbanville until the rusty window frames and leaking pipes and geezers had driven her crazy. When she left, she'd boxed all the memories she'd brought with her from Vereeniging—her wedding photographs, her man's marathon medals, his old vests that she'd slept in—and thrown them away.

The food channel reminded her to feed her friend. She headed back to the kitchen, cat following this time. She spooned out a serving of Tuna Feast into a bowl, placed it at her foot. The cat waited until she moved away before approaching.

"A pleasure, Kitty."

Vermaak sipped her glass as she watched the cat eating. Sometimes she wished it would let her touch it. She'd called it Kitty; couldn't think of anything better.

Vermaak returned to the lounge with her glass and the bottle still in the packet.

Watch your drinking. It was the right advice. If the kids didn't drink, they wouldn't be targets.

But that wasn't the whole story. The new intelligence was disturbing. Ten incidents in the last month, mostly female but two males as well, two resulting in hospitalization, all claiming drinks were spiked.

If barmen were drugging girls as had been suggested, who was their market? Surely it wasn't kids.

The cat padded quickly through from the kitchen in a burst of post-prandial energy, jumped onto the counter and then on top of the television, where it started to clean itself, paws first.

Vermaak flipped stations, had another look hoping she'd missed something first time round. MK Hoordosis played Jack Parow. She changed quickly. *Meet The Fokkers* came on at 8 pm on MM2. She'd watched it twice already.

She lifted her eyes to the cat above the screen, its cleaning ritual a lure, hypnotic. One-eared, half-tail. Wouldn't let her near, though it relied on her for life.

And it gave her reason to come home each night.

She closed her eyes, tried to relax, but the names of the suspect clubs kept ticking over in her head. One rang a bell. The Blue Venus Nightclub and Bar.

That crazy kid, the one who claimed he'd been secretly filmed in a shower and then reported a nonexistent murder, had mentioned the place.

She couldn't quite remember what he'd said.

INSANITY RISIN'

In his study, Julian Lynch removed the portrait of his father and rested it at an angle between the wall and wooden floor. A rooikrans fire raged in the fireplace, the orange flames like ethereal dancers.

The cluttered room was littered with empty coffee mugs and plates. On the desk a resignation letter from the maid, no notice. She was returning to family in the Transkei. She thanked him for his employ.

Lynch gazed at his father's stony-faced image, then let out a guttural cry as he raised his foot and kicked straight through the canvas with the heel of his shoe. He picked up the pieces of broken frame, cracked them in half across his knee—once, twice, three times—and tossed them into the fireplace.

"The urge," he said aloud. "It is the urge!"

Desire. The powerful monster...

His isolation was now complete. Parents, wife, family, gardener and guard were all gone. Losing the maid signaled the end of the last vestige of normality and order. Now he could allow chaos to descend.

Twenty-five years before in this same room, Bobby Lynch, unable to deal with the humiliation of his failure and bankruptcy, had shot himself with the 1864 Remmington. He'd preserved the house in a trust for his only son, the disappointment, Julian.

Your behavior is very disappointing to me, Julian.

Julian, who his mother had hoped would restore family respectability. And then went on to destroy it in its entirety, he thought wryly.

The dry canvas crackled with flame. Lynch watched mesmerized, concerned his father's portrait would not burn.

A year after his father's suicide, his mother, tanked up on anti-depressants and vodka, had stepped out of a window and onto the roof in her high heels—and plummeted two stories to her death.

Death was their secret family remedy.

His younger sister had been taken away to live with his mother's family in England. Someone wanted her. No one had felt the same about him.

Lynch removed his glasses and watched the flames engulf the painting.

He'd been on summer holiday from boarding school in his post-matric year when his mother killed herself. He'd moved her body into the house and kept it there for three days before the servants alerted the neighbors. There'd been police, but eventually they'd left him alone. The actions of a traumatized son, they'd said.

Lynch fetched his journal and flicked through the pages. The first few were dedicated to his sister, Estelle. There was a picture of a young girl in school uniform followed by lines of his sloping handwriting.

He had wanted to love Estelle, but he'd found he could only hate her.

His mother had said that the age gap was too vast, that Julian had spent too long as an only child, spoiled and pampered, before his sister's arrival.

Perhaps.

He turned the pages irritably.

I didn't go and die in a car crash. I didn't shoot myself, or jump off a roof. Big fucking disappointment.

He flicked through the rest of the journal.

Angie Dean had been his favorite to date. He looked at a picture of her naked body, arm stretched upwards. She looked dead.

It didn't really matter whether she was dead or not, thought Lynch.

The trap door to the cellar was ajar. He'd fetched a bottle of Château Libertas. There were only six left.

The grandfather clock chimed ten times.

Lynch banged the journal on his desk. *Fuck Kryff! Fuck Dark Video! It's Wednesday night. My night.*

Neither Kryff nor Diva were returning his calls; their phones on message. Lynch grabbed his Motorola and scanned through his contacts list until he reached SARS. After an interlude of lift music, the call diverted to a cellphone.

"Sonya?"

"Yes." The voice was tight. Sonya worked for the South African Revenue Services.

"It's Julian Lynch."

"Yes."

She couldn't talk. He'd probably woken her up.

"I hear there's some shit with the VAT. Make it go away. There'll be ten thousand in your account tonight."

"I..."

"Sonya. I don't want to hear it. Make it go away. Otherwise there'll be big shit."

He put the phone down, texted his MD.

```
Sick as dog, back next week. sorted out
VAT with receiver, payments went wrong account
Julian
```

Lynch pocketed the Remington and left via the back door. He removed a toolkit from the boot of the BMW, placed it in the passenger footwell, then drove out past the vacant guard's hut and through the main gates. He flicked on the CD shuttle, skipping disks to load a Rolling Stones compilation.

His car smelled damp from being parked out in the rain—but he couldn't help it. When the stables were full he'd started to pack the garage; now even that was overflowing.

Lynch gunned along the M3. Passing Newlands Forest, he felt his blood rushing as he gazed for a moment into the darkened trees, site of his beloved *Forest Frolic*, before they were gone, replaced by the ivy-covered walls of UCT. He slid off the Rondebosch off-ramp, decelerated down Woolsack Drive—from the site of his favorite video to the residence of its star performer within a minute. He could almost hear his pulse now, the thud of excitement in his head as he stared up at the lights in the turreted Tugwell block—up to the fifth floor, where Terri Philips was waiting for him, longing for him, in her room.

Focus!

Lynch hung a left into Main Road, continued toward Mowbray, calming himself, applying his mind to the job at hand.

Mick Jagger spewed out the words to *Midnight Rambler*.

A sex worker with a purple blouse lifted her matching skirt as he passed by.

Inappropriate behavior.

A tabloid headline fastened to a streetlamp blazed: *Die Hacker en die Hooker?*

He crossed the bridge over Settlers Way, cruising the streets until he located a quiet cul-de-sac in Observatory. A bohemian suburb of students and hippies, cars parked on the road outside the houses, no space for garages or off-street parking. Lynch spotted a white Hyundai, an older model.

Perfect.

He found a place to park, pulled in, waited. Watching for activity, he knew that patience and caution were critical. *Do this right. Don't get ahead of yourself. Don't make a mistake.*

Satisfied there was no one about, no nosy neighbors peering out of windows, he reached into the toolkit, locating a screwdriver. He alighted from his car, crossed to the Hyundai, bent down and removed the rear number plate without missing a beat. He was back in the BMW within forty-five seconds.

Heading back to Main Road, the Hyundai plate on the back seat, Lynch felt satisfied. He'd needed the older style of plate for his car; they were easier to remove than the new plates with double-sided tape.

He loaded a new CD: a mix of tracks he'd downloaded using Pillage. The first step of his plan accomplished, he continued in the direction of the city, into Salt River where he repeated a similar exercise, this time with a number plate removed from a blue Fiat. As smooth as before.

Lynch U-turned and headed back down Main Road, upped the volume on his CD player and wound down the window. *Scar Tissue* by the Red Hot Chili Peppers. Appropriate music. He felt the song could be about him and Terri Phillips.

He slowed as he passed the prostitute in the purple suit.

NAB

Thursday morning. An unfulfilled Wednesday evening was now in the past, but Lynch was not entirely displeased—his plan was in motion.

As early as he dared, he contacted the Registrar at UCT, introducing himself as John Phillips, in town from London and unable to get hold of his daughter Terri due to the theft of his cellphone. A mugging, within hours of his flight landing the day before. Very traumatic. Any assistance in locating his daughter's timetable for the day was gratefully appreciated. A sympathetic assistant in the Registrar's office located Terri's student record on the computer and referred him to the English department with some kind words. He repeated the ruse and established the pattern of her lectures for the week.

At 10:30 am, Lynch entered the university's upper campus in his BMW, fake plates attached, signed in using his father's name, and parked in the visitor's bay, where he checked the timetable which he'd neatly recorded in his own script. English literary studies concluded at 11 am.

He was excited that Terri was an English student. He imagined she'd speak beautifully. Later, he decided, he would transcribe the course details into his journal.

Lynch positioned himself outside the lecture theatre in the Arts Block, waited until the doors opened and the students spilled out of the packed auditorium. He held his suit jacket over his arm. So many young girls, all looked so similar.

But he couldn't mistake Terri.

He stepped closer to observe as the students filed past him, clutching files, dragging satchels.

Terri wore faded blue jeans and a loose-fitting white jersey. The strap of a light-blue bra was visible on one shoulder. If he reached out his hand, he could have touched her. But he was focused again, needed to make his move at the right moment. He headed out the center behind Terri, watching intently, careful not to get in anyone's way. The invisible man.

She walked in a group of three girls, a slow wander, chatting, making plans, in the direction of Jammie Stairs. Lynch hung back, watched. If he guessed right, they would chat for another few minutes before going their separate ways—the other girls to another lecture, hopefully, and Terri back to Tugwell, her residence.

It was time to make his move. Slipping into the bustle of student traffic, he swiftly made his way past the girls, taking a right down the stairs toward the Smuts and Fuller residence parking lot. Halfway down, he halted to one side, pretending to check his phone, checking surreptitiously to see if anyone had noticed him. He pulled on his jacket, slipped on the dark glasses he'd kept in his pocket, and took a deep breath, composing himself.

Now's your time to shine, Julian.

Lynch turned back up the stairs, purposefully, skipping the last few steps. At the top he looked ahead, taking in the grand sight of Jameson Hall, as if for the first time, then left and right. He consulted a piece of paper in his hand, hesitated. Clearly, he was lost.

"Hello," Lynch approached a small group of students congregated at the bottom of Jammie stairs. "You wouldn't happen to know where's Tugwell Hall?"

"Terri's in Tugwell," said a girl in pink pants, pointing to her friend to one side, tapping on her BlackBerry.

Terri stopped, looked up, squinting into the sun.

"My lucky day!" said Lynch. "Are you in Tugwell?" He fiddled with his tinted glasses.

"Yes," said Terri, looking down to press SEND.

"I'm meeting my daughter there," said Lynch. "Her name is Holly. They're having an open day at the UCT residences. She's set her heart on Tugwell."

"Oh. Is she still at school?" said Terri. One of her friends squeezed her hand and waved goodbye, heading off with the other girls.

Lynch had her to himself.

"Erm, yes," said Lynch. "I'm afraid I'm terribly lost." He checked his watch. "And I'm late."

Terri pointed down the hill. Below them the suburbs simmered in a grey haze. Their view stretched from the university's vantage point on Devil's Peak out over the Cape Flats toward Somerset West and Stellenbosch.

"It's just down there." Terri pointed left along the road exiting Upper Campus.

"Follow the road, then down the hill and then left at the off-ramp. Tugwell's the—"

Lynch touched her arm. "Would you mind terribly? I mean, showing me. Are you on your way down there? I can give you a lift."

Terri looked at Lynch. He wiped a bead of perspiration from his upper lip and smiled.

"I would be so grateful." He looked at his watch again.

Terri flicked the hair from her face. "I, uh, would really love to," she began and paused. His hair was longish, she noticed. Grey suit jacket over a shirt tucked into jeans. No belt. Cowboy type boots. Unfashionable glasses. "But I, uh, I'm not going back to Tugwell right now. Look, it's easy. Did you come in from Rondebosch?"

He held her wrist gently.

"No, please," he said. "I'll bring you right back."

Terri looked down at the hand on her wrist. He released his grip, smiled again.

"I've got to go," she said, taking a step backwards, pointing toward the library. "Got to get some books. Down the hill. First left. It's the second building." She waved, moved away, the distance between them five steps, six, seven.

"OK," said Lynch. He waved back. "Thank you. Thank you."

He watched her walk away and disappear into the library entrance.

"Thank you, Terri," he said.

Fifteen minutes later, Lynch waited in the BMW in the parking lot between the Smuts and Fuller Hall residences, one level down from his conversation with Terri Philips. He'd fetched the car and positioned himself to intercept her on her way back to Tugwell.

His body trembled with pleasure. The meeting had left him with an undeniable sense of certainty. When he'd first spotted her in Elevation, he had still been unsure. Now he knew that she was meant for him. Her soft voice, the sheen on her cheeks, the hint of woman in her stance....There would be no need to drug her.

Before leaving Bishopscourt for UCT that morning, Lynch had tidied up Holly's room—it had also been Estelle's room. He'd removed the magazines and picture frames, the childish posters on the wall. Then he'd boarded up the window with solid planks of pine purchased from a hardware store in Wynberg. He'd tested the key in the door and placed an empty bucket behind it. He'd be keeping her for longer than one night.

The house was in a terrible state, clothes strewn around his room, the stench of a dead rat in the kitchen. He decided he would blindfold her, just like she was in the *Forest Frolic* video, before leading her up the stairs to his daughter's room.

Lynch started the engine to allow the air conditioner to cool the car. He fixed his gaze on Jammie Stairs, down which she was sure to come shortly.

He knew she would come because he could sense his plan reaching fruition.

His heart jumped.

There she was.

Terri Phillips descended the stairs with two books clutched against her chest. She skipped past him through the parking lot and down the next set of stairs toward the rugby fields. Lynch knew the exact path she would follow.

He slipped the BMW into gear and sped down Residence Road, turned right and descended into the parking area behind the university's sports center—the footpath to the lower residences edged past the lot.

The area was filled with cars. Lynch double parked in the shade near the path, removed the Remington from the cubbyhole, and opened the door. He left the engine running, scanned for trouble. The coast looked clear.

Terri reached the sports center entrance and continued downwards along the arcing path.

Lynch strode across the car park, looking left and right, Remington in his right hand, guarded by the left forearm.

Terri was moving quickly; Lynch accelerated into a loping run.

Ten meters, nine...

A male student with Rasta hair and brightly colored T-shirt appeared, heading up the hill in the opposite direction. Lynch pulled up, turning away, dropped the Remington to his side, watched as Terri Phillips walked unwittingly past.

"Fuck's sake!" he cursed under his breath, turning around and hurrying back to the BMW. He reversed hard, wheels squealing as he roared out the lot and down the hill toward the Tugwell off-ramp.

He pulled to the side of Woolsack Drive, below the pedestrian bridge.

There was no sign of Terri Phillips.

THE LIST

Carlos had checked into the Grand Hyatt under an assumed name, using one of several flawless fake passports. He'd taken his room as one Christopher Davidson. The passport was stored safely in his briefcase, along with two others in different names and a variety of business cards. His emergency fund was also included: eighty one-hundred dollar bills. The briefcase didn't leave his sight.

Something had worried him the day before, got his warning receptors going.

His wife had planned to come home with sushi for lunch; then she'd brushed him off to shop, and ended up visiting her parents for the night. She'd left a message to say as much, hadn't even bothered following it up.

Without calling her, Carlos had packed a bag and left the house in the early hours of the morning, catching a cab across the 520 Bridge and into the city. He'd been dropped off a couple of blocks from the hotel and walked the rest of the way. Just to be careful. From his room, he'd engaged the same private detective he'd used to follow his wife previously.

By the time the detective reported back that all was in order—his wife *was* at her parents, in Tacoma—Carlos was enjoying a hot tub in the marble bathroom of his Tony Chi-inspired ambassador suite.

Carlos lifted one arm, noticed the damp perspiration patches underneath. Out of habit he felt for his handgrips, but he hadn't brought a set with him. He wondered if there was a sports shop nearby.

He pocketed his phone and rose from the seat, strolled through the glass sliding doors into the foyer. The staff behind the reception desk greeted him when he passed.

Back in his room, Carlos went online and checked the home-security cameras at his house via a remote connection. It looked like a glorious day. The cameras panned back and forth, the grass recently mowed. Inside the house, all was quiet. He closed the connection.

Time for a quick business check. He ran through the latest messages from operatives across the globe. There was one from Cape Town: a scanned PDF of an article in *The Cape Times*, a single column insert reporting two charred bodies found in a railway-station car park, close range bullet wounds. No identification, no eyewitness. A presumed gang hit.

Carlos was impressed with Diva. She'd tidied up the problem. Even got rid of her accomplice, whom she'd suspected of collaborating with certain Mickey Finn barmen.

A blip on the screen signaled a contact request from Jacker. Carlos's mood changed abruptly. He enabled his voice distortion software and contacted Jacker on Skype over the hotel network.

On Carlos's screen, Jacker's face appeared as an Abraham Lincoln avatar.

Jacker had spent the last twenty-four hours investigating the arrested Dark Video clients, checking for patterns or connections. Importantly, did they know one another? He ran Carlos through the steps he'd followed: hacking the Swedish police network and searching for the email that had shopped the client. Same thing in South Africa for similar information.

"I've been thinking about a list," Carlos butted in.

"I thought you said there wasn't one," Jacker replied flatly.

Carlos memorized all his clients' details. He had no need for a physical list. In any case, his private files were never available on an Internet-connected network, nor accessible physically to anyone except Carlos.

"I set myself a challenge, Jacker. How would *I* get it?" Carlos explained. "If I couldn't steal a physical list…" He picked up his Hyatt Gold Passport card and twirled it in his fingers. "Well, how could I create one?"

"The Dark Video website moves too quickly for someone to hack it," Jacker said.

"So you assure me," said Carlos. "But clients synchronize with the Dark Video website before every screening. If a hacker were sophisticated enough, he could listen to the codes that are sent down and create a search string. Then he could use this search string to *listen* for other Dark Video conversations. Every time a client synced, he'd pick up the address and use it as a reference for tracing the client."

Jacker was silent in contemplation.

"Is this possible?" asked Carlos. He squeezed the gold card in his hand, felt the sharp edges cut into his palm.

"Theoretically, I suppose."

"Then why the fuck haven't we blocked it!" Carlos yelled. The card snapped.

"Hey, listen up, Carlos. I only said it may be possible. In reality, it would take a technical expert of immense skill. Not some kids from college, not some random hacker. We're talking a dedicated bunch of professionals."

Carlos hurled the gold card across the room and banged his fist on the table. He wasn't thinking varsity kids; he was thinking FBI.

"Carlos?" Jacker said.

It still didn't make sense to Carlos. If the FBI were building a list of his clients by tracking accesses to his floating website, why were they randomly targeting them in foreign countries? But it was the only plausible explanation.

"I don't like this," he muttered. "I don't like this at all."

TERROR

Jacqui Simpson had had a fight with her boyfriend, was regretting storming out of the Panthers pub in Rondebosch in a huff—the walk back to her digs just off Main Road, near the Baxter Theatre, was longer than she'd realized. And darker. The strap of her handbag dug into her left shoulder and she had to hold on to the hem of her skirt with her right hand to keep it from blowing up as she walked.

So stupid, she thought. A bit to drink, a silly argument and look what happens. She couldn't even remember what they were arguing about.

She was making her way toward the theatre when a man in a BMW stopped and offered her a lift.

"No thank you."

She declined without looking at the driver and continued on her way, brushing her long blonde hair off her face, wondering about her boyfriend. He'd better call her or else. Or maybe she should just call him. The BMW sped away.

She trudged on, turned left, up into Burg Road, the oak-lined avenue behind the administration building. Almost there. Her feet were sore; she hadn't expected to be trekking home in high-heeled shoes.

The sound of an acorn crunching on the pavement surprised her.

She didn't know what hit her.

Jacqui Simpson felt a hand touch her hair, then firmer at the back of her head as the blindfold was removed. She screamed. It wasn't a nightmare.

"Get away from me," she said, shaking her head manically, eyes adjusting to the light from a naked bulb hanging in the center of the room.

Her head throbbed and her vision was blurred, but the realization of fear was as clear as a bell. She was in a wine cellar, her hands behind her back, bound with duct tape to the back of a steel chair. Her ankles were fastened with cable ties to the front legs of the chair. She squeezed her knees together, was still wearing her high heels.

"Help! Someone help me," she screamed as loudly as she could.

Julian Lynch smiled with both sets of teeth.

"Terri, Terri, don't you see? Whatever has happened before, it's different now. We'll be together. And I have as much time as you need."

"Oh my god," she said, pulling at her trussing, looking about frantically.

"Relax, Terri," Lynch soothed her, stroking her cheek. Her handbag hung across his shoulder.

"Listen here. Please. I'm not Terri. My name's Jacqui, I swear." Tears rolled down her cheeks.

Lynch laughed. "You're not meant to choose a new name so soon, my sweet." Besides, Jacqui wouldn't do, he thought. He really was taken by the idea of Polly.

"Look at my ID document," she implored. "I don't know anyone called Terri."

Lynch tipped the contents of the girl's handbag onto the floor. He wore a long-sleeved collared shirt tucked into blue jeans, bare feet.

"Can I touch you?" Lynch said, ignoring her. She had a red welt against her temple running along her cheekbone, the makings of a nasty bruise. Her tartan miniskirt was hiked up, revealing sheer black stockings beneath.

She screamed as his hand snaked forward, fingers between her thighs, thumb against her crotch. She threw her weight to one side. The chair toppled over.

"Get away, get away!"

She wriggled helplessly on the cement floor of the cellar.

Lynch bent down and righted the chair. Jacqui sobbed. Behind her back, she struggled desperately to free her hands. Lynch picked up a fresh roll of tape from inside a wine rack and walked behind her, looped another coil of tape around her hands.

"I do hope we can work together, Terri," Lynch said. He cupped her breasts from behind; she could hear his breathing in her ear.

"Please don't do this," she sobbed.

"Should I take my shirt off?" he asked, perfectly pleasant, releasing her and walking to the far end of the cellar.

"Please, please," she begged, unable to look at him. "Help!" she screamed again, looking up to the trap door.

Lynch removed his shirt. Underneath he wore a white vest; his arms were hairy.

"There." He offered her his shirt. "Do you want it?" He dropped it into her lap. "Terri, there's no rush. I have all day. All month! Perhaps you want to give me something in return?" He scrutinized her for a moment. "The tights?"

A wave of adrenaline shot through the girl. "I'm not fucking Terri!" she screamed at him, wriggling in her bonds. "Now fucking let me out of here!"

Lynch's expression changed in an instant, his smiling visage exchanged for a blank façade without emotion.

She regretted swearing. "I'm sorry. Please. You have the wrong person. Look at my ID book."

Lynch retrieved her green ID book from among the debris on the floor, ripped out the front page and put it in his mouth. He started to chew.

Jacqui stared at him.

"I'm going to eat you, Terri," he told her.

THE CHECK-OUT

Robbie Cullen wore a pair of blue shorts and a blue-and-white athletics vest.
Salt streaked his face, the sweat drying rapidly on his body. An hour of touch rugby had swirled the blood through his veins.

He jogged barefoot down the corridor of Brown Block and opened the door to his room.

"Whoa!" Robbie stepped back, startled.

Fallon wore a white vest and black miniskirt, velvet gloves and black stiletto heels laced above her ankle. She sat on his bed, the vanilla essence of her perfume permeating the room.

"Come in, close the door," she said.

He did as he was told. The key was in the lock on the inside of the door.

"Dangerous to leave it open," she added, standing up. "Please lock it."

He turned the key.

"You surprised?" she asked.

Robbie shook his head.

"You were expecting me?"

"Sooner or later," he said, finding a voice.

Fallon smiled and looked down at his muddy feet, then directly at him. Like he owed her money. Her lips glistened with ruby lip gloss.

"The big blue swimming-pool eyes," she said with a flashing smile, moving toward him. She held her sexy black Gothic handbag with silver chains and safety pins on the outside.

"I wanted to call you," he said, self-conscious, aware of her proximity.

She leaned forward, reached up and kissed him lightly on the lips, Robbie reacting like he'd received an electric jolt.

"Glad you dressed up for me," she joked.

Robbie tried to pull himself together, picked up an open Valpré bottle from his desk, downed the contents. Fallon flicked her hair from side to side and placed her bag on his desk.

"You don't want to know what my week's been like," he said. He ripped a towel off the rack and wiped his face, threw it on the floor.

She was a head shorter than him. His eyes dropped; she wore no bra, her breasts visible beneath the skimpy vest. Her emerald eyes sparkled as his eyes returned to hers. She dropped her hands to her sides.

"I have some idea," she said.

"You do?" Robbie sat down on the counter.

"Put on some music," she said. She touched her ear with a gloved hand

and walked to the window, looked out. She ran a hand down the curtain but left it open.

"What do you like?" Robbie asked, bringing his computer out of hibernation and selecting iTunes.

"Anything."

He kicked off a local playlist, started with The Dirty Skirts.

"Do you like rock or blues?" he asked, searching for conversation, feeling the return of that stomach-lurching desire he'd experienced for Fallon in her apartment.

What is it about her?

She shrugged. "As long as they don't scream."

Robbie opened the fridge and removed another bottle of Valpré, twisted off the cap. "Just tap water," he explained. "Tastes better in a bottle." He offered it to her; she declined.

"Last week, I received an email with an attachment," she explained. "The sender was Sylvana. You know? That lovely girl from Plett? But of course you do. Because the attachment was a video you made with her in Tony's house." Her eyelashes fluttered as she spoke.

"No ways!" said Robbie, choking on his water.

Fallon turned her back, fiddled with her BlackBerry, then read: "Hi Fallon. Attached is picture from video at Plett. Me and Robbie in shower. What you think? I think it very sexy. I looking to sell video. Love Sylvana."

"She offered the video to you?" Robbie rubbed his face in disbelief, the nightmare reappearing. He imagined Sylvana, twisting and turning inside the chrome arena of Gorky Park; Sylvana with a slashed throat.

Fallon watched him closely. "I was in Plettenberg Bay under cover," she said. "Of course you know Tony Beacon is a suspect in the Angie Dean drug rape. But it's Sylvana we're after. She's part of a Russian stripper syndicate that is infiltrating Cape Town revue bars."

"But why would she send the video to you?"

"There's a market for 'reality' videos like this overseas. The US, Europe, a few other places. They pay good money. Lots of young people, students, do it for extra cash. It's linked to the rise in drink spiking we're seeing. Often the girls"—Fallon paused—"or the guys, as may be the case, are drugged first. I approached Sylvana as if I were a buyer."

Robbie took a deep breath.

"Got to say, you didn't look drugged, Robbie," Fallon continued. "Looked like you were having a good time, if I had to guess. I figured you were involved in her scam. You know your friend Denny le Roux does this kind of thing through The Blue Venus."

"No way." Robbie shook his head. He couldn't believe that Denny was spiking drinks. "Listen. That whole story about Tony Beacon is such bullshit. He didn't even go to Blue Venus."

"He'd arranged to meet her there."

"Maybe. But he didn't go. I know the guy. I believe him one hundred percent."

"And you, Robbie?" she asked, tilting her head to the side. "What's your involvement?"

He opened his arms.

"Nothing! I swear. I don't know what the fuck's going on. My life has turned upside down. Do you know about Sylvana?"

Fallon shook her head.

"She's dead."

Fallon looked at him with disbelief.

"How do you know this?" she asked.

"I..." Robbie began but stopped. No way he was going to humiliate himself twice.

"My people tell me she is out the country," Fallon said, her eyes wide.

Robbie picked up the plastic money packet off his desk. "Her blood," he said, pointing, then showing Fallon an accompanying note: "Hey Robbie. Pink, drumsticks, No agglutinogen. Human blood, female, O positive. See the attached results. Wassitallabout? Yours in medicine, Doc Louw."

"I took it to the police. No-one believed me."

Fallon stared into space, as if considering the consequences and course of action.

"You can't believe the shit I've been through," Robbie reiterated. He described his horrific fortnight. The meeting with Sylvana at Gorky Park, her subsequent phone calls, what he saw at the Lendell Road house, how the police refused to believe his story.

She rubbed his arm gently as he spoke.

"Well, I'm relieved you're not involved, Robbie," she said when he was done. "To tell you the truth, I was disappointed when I saw you in the video. You didn't seem like someone who would..." Her voice trailed off.

"Fallon. When we first met, you spoke about a proposition..."

"It was a test," Fallon explained. "Your friend Denny from Blue Venus... I asked him if he wanted to make some quick cash. He gave me your name, said you were looking for opportunities."

Robbie stood up, walked to the window. She followed him.

"Everyone's a suspect, Robbie. You were friends with a barman who we knew was slipping customers drugs. And with Tony, who was potentially involved with Angie Dean's abduction."

Robbie shook his head.

"You know this for sure? About Denny?"

Fallon touched his hand. "We don't have all the proof. Yet. Listen, Robbie, you cannot breathe a word about this."

"You thought I was…"

She rubbed her hand up and down his arm. "I can only try and appreciate what you've gone through," she said, looking him in the eye.

Silence. A moment's hesitation.

She dropped her hands and spun around, looking about his room, eyes halting on the bar fridge. "Jesus, I'd kill for a drink."

"Sorry. I didn't think."

She pointed to a bottle on an upper bookshelf. "Whiskey?"

Robbie stood up and reached for the bottle of Single Barrel Jack Daniel's, a gift from a bottle-store owner whose IT systems he'd installed.

"You got ice?" she checked.

He crouched down, removed a tray of ice from the small freezer section of the fridge. "I even have a glass or two."

He filled two glasses, cracked the ice tray and added two cubes to each. Passed her a glass. She took a sip, nodded. "Something was different about her. Something on her face. Her eyes. He hadn't noticed they were green. He had thought they were brown."

"I'm hesitant to suggest a toast," she said.

Robbie sipped the amber liquid, feeling the warmth migrate through his chest. He placed his glass on the desk, retrieved a blue Hang Ten cardigan from his cupboard, pulled it on and zipped it up to the neck.

"How's your boyfriend?" Robbie asked her.

"Oh." Fallon seemed taken off guard. "I got shot of him," she said eventually, rummaging in her black Gothic handbag for her cellphone.

"Got to go?" Robbie asked.

She checked the screen, replaced the phone. "Actually, no. Only later." For a moment, Fallon seemed to look right through him. Then a change of demeanor with a change in topic: "The shower scene in that video— it seemed so real. So much passion. So much…" She patted her cheeks dramatically, smiled at Robbie.

He felt embarrassed, grabbed his drink off the desk for a big gulp.

"It didn't belong on some sordid teenage fantasy site," Fallon continued.

Robbie blushed. He remembered her words at the Blue Venus. *Do you like fun?*

Late afternoon sunlight was now streaming through the open window, shining directly into Fallon's eyes. Robbie closed the curtain, took another big sip.

Fallon nodded her appreciation as she removed her right-hand glove, scooped a handful of ice from the tray and added it to her drink. "More ice?" she asked.

Robbie nodded.

She slid the remaining ice in her hand into his glass.

"I keep thinking back to something Sylvana said," Robbie said. "'I didn't know.' What didn't she know?"

Before Fallon could respond, Robbie continued. "Fallon. Can't you talk to the cops? The one I was dealing with, a captain, I think, her name's Vermaak."

Fallon patted his hand. "I'll take it up with her. Don't you worry."

She returned to her seat at the edge of the bed while Robbie sat down on the ledge below the window. He chinked the ice in his glass and sipped slowly.

Robbie couldn't focus, his vision a simultaneous perception of Fallon and her double, two bodies swaying backwards and forwards. He closed his eyes and pressed a hand against the wall, tried to maintain balance.

"Shit," he said, falling backwards. The bottle of Jack was nearly empty.

"Robbie."

He heard his name spoken. Fallon's voice. But it came to him as if it was inside his head. He couldn't be sure she'd even said it.

"I'm so flipping drunk," he said.

She helped him up. Her vanilla scent was in his face. He nuzzled into her neck, felt the warmth of her skin against his mouth.

"Oh, shit," he said again.

"Lie down," Fallon said. "You'll feel better."

Robbie collapsed onto the bed. Fallon stood up and turned off the music, checked the door was still locked, removed the key and dropped it in her purse.

"Robbie, look at me." Fallon sat down on the edge of the bed, turned toward him. She rubbed her index finger into the remnants of a sachet of white powder then ran it across his lips, discarding the empty sachet into her handbag.

He licked his lips, eyes rolling back in his head.

"You've got to be kidding," he giggled. The world seemed to be spinning.

"I can't believe I'm so wasted."

She slipped her right hand under his cardigan and T-shirt, up over the muscles of his stomach, then dragged her fingers slowly downwards. Robbie tried to sit up.

"Robbie. Did Sylvana tell you about how she was getting her clients? Did she mention a list?"

Her fingers reached the top of his shorts, proceeded further, rubbed gently up and down.

"I don't think..." he began and flopped back, the effort to raise himself too great.

She continued to rub through the fabric of his pants, now with the palm of her hand.

"Come on Robbie. I'll help you," she said. She dragged her nails along his bare inner thighs, returning the palm of her hand to his crotch, squeezing. "Did Sylvana say how she found a buyer for the video?"

He grabbed her wrist. "Fallon," he slurred. "What's happening to me? I'm too drunk."

"Sylvana. Did she mention a list?"

"Sylvana is dead."

Fallon tried to free her hand. "Let go," she said firmly. "Let go of my hand."

His grip eased. She pulled her hand away, massaging her wrist. Change of plan. She retrieved her phone again, enabled an application on her BlackBerry and tested for video reception at a variety of frequencies.

Robbie was oblivious, eyes closed, the room turning uncontrollably. He'd never felt this drunk before.

Application set up, Fallon scanned Robbie's room looking for hiding places. She got up and quickly went through his cupboard, rifling through each drawer and running her hands under his clothes. Then his desk, where she was more careful, opening documents and files, flicking through books. She placed the plastic money bag containing the blood from Robbie's tackies and the note from Doc Louw in her bag.

Footsteps at the door. A knock.

Fallon sat motionless.

Another knock.

"Boom-Boom-Boom. Let me in your room!"

The visitor waited, knocked a third time. Fallon heard the sound of retreating footsteps. No key in the inside lock meant the occupant was out.

Fallon continued to examine Robbie's drawers, intermittently checking on Robbie. She opened the manila envelope containing the remaining

R200 notes in his top drawer.

Robbie was breathing heavily. Fallon checked his pulse then drained her glass of Jack.

She returned her attention to his cupboard, lifting up his carelessly folded clothes, fingering through the pockets of his pants and shirts.

Robbie's Nokia beeped—an online advertisement. Fallon flicked through his saved and sent messages before connecting with Bluetooth and downloading the content of his SIM card and memory to her phone. She removed his battery and replaced it with a new one from her handbag, fitted with a geo-tag.

Next she sat down at his desk and took control of his laptop. From her purse, she removed a USB flash disk and pressed it into a slot at the back. She worked for several minutes on the keyboard before removing the flash drive and returning it to her purse.

"OK," she said.

She filled Robbie's empty glass with water from the kettle and swirled it around, shifted the curtain and tossed the dregs out the window, cleaning both glasses with a towel. Next, she used Robbie's computer to connect to a proxy server in Austria and direct a message to an address in Atlanta, Georgia. The message read: "Checked out BJ boy. Clean. Will upload content of harddrive to secure server for evaluation."

Fallon removed the room key from her purse. She looked back at Robbie, hesitated.

She returned to the bedside and knelt next to him, running a gloved hand under his vest, up his corrugated stomach to his chest.

"Pity," she said softly. "I think we could have put on quite a performance." She sighed deeply, eyes settling on his elephant-hair bracelet. "I suppose that will have to do."

CAPTIVE

In the darkness, Jacqui no longer had any sense of time. Her kidnapper had switched the light off when he left, and no natural light permeated the dank room. She'd worked out she was being held underground, probably in a cellar; recalled the sound of the deranged man exiting up wooden steps. But how long had she been held captive? Hours, presumably. It felt like days. She had screamed herself hoarse and was desperately thirsty.

Jacqui struggled with the duct tape to no avail. With some effort, she could shift her chair on the cold floor by extending the points of her toes—but in the darkness there seemed little point. The terror was a slow dread. So far he had hardly touched her, but she was under no illusions. The vacant eyes, the disconnected smile—she knew there had to be worse to come. She had never been in such a situation before, but wits and common sense had always been her strength. If she angered him, he would harm her; of that she had no doubt. She closed her eyes and squeezed out the tears then sniffed and composed herself.

Presently, she heard footsteps above her head. The bulb above her head clicked on and the trap door shifted across. Blinking in the light, she looked up to see the studied face of her kidnapper peering down at her.

"Behaving yourself, my dear?" he checked.

Convinced she was secure and not waiting to ambush him, Lynch lowered himself onto the ladder and descended the six steps to the cement floor of the cellar.

"It's quite musty in here, don't you think, Terri?"

He was carrying a bowl and a glass of water, wearing just the vest and jeans.

"What's your name?" Jacqui asked, hoarsely.

He smiled with both sets of teeth. "I'm Julian, thank you for asking. I've brought you lunch."

Lunch, she thought. People would be looking for her. Her boyfriend would have phoned the residence. Or would he have after their argument?

Lynch held the glass of water to her mouth and she drank from it thirstily. He put it to one side and peeled off the plastic film from the bowl.

"I'm not very hungry," she said. It concerned her that he was making no attempt to disguise his identity. It could only mean he had no intention of letting her go. She fought back the panic.

Lynch ignored her lack of appetite. He pulled up a chair alongside, scooped a mouthful and held it to her face. It looked like cottage pie.

She accepted and ate, nodding. "Mmm. Tasty," she said. "Did you make it?"

Through her fear, she knew she had to keep it together to stay alive; knew she couldn't allow herself to disintegrate. Right now, he was showing her kindness. She had to capitalize and use the opportunity to win his trust.

Lynch chuckled. "Woolworths."

He fed her another spoonful. She swallowed quickly, smacking her lips again. "Julian," she said. "Where am I?"

"Oh, you're at my house," he replied.

"And where's that?"

He smiled. "Bishopscourt. Do you know where that is, Terri?"

"I've heard of it," she replied, accepting another spoon of mince. She grew up in Durban, had barely ventured beyond Rondebosch and Mowbray. "Is it a nice house?"

"Spectacular," Julian replied. Then after a pause: "It needs some work."

She declined another spoon.

"I'm quite full. I don't have much of an appetite."

"I can appreciate that," Julian said. He checked the time on his Rolex, then scooped the remaining food from the bowl into his mouth and placed it under her chair. "You can use the bowl as a toilet," he said, smiling.

She stared at him in disbelief. "How am I going to do that? I'm tied up!" she blurted. Then, more composed: "Julian, surely I can use the bathroom like any normal person." She needed to pee.

"Normal," he replied. Lynch felt a savage intent surging through his blood, fought to keep it at bay. He breathed deeply, busied himself cleaning up the contents of the girl's handbag, which he'd upended earlier. She was lucky he didn't have his crop with him. Or a blowtorch. "You think I'm not normal?"

"No, of course not," she replied, watching him closely. She tried to spot her cellphone; it would be in a side pocket of her bag. If she could somehow get it... "But you're not treating me normally."

Lynch smiled with both sets of teeth exposed.

"Listen to me, Terri. I know what you're doing," said Lynch, smiling with both sets of teeth as he hitched the bag over his shoulder. "This is mine now, not yours, so don't get any ideas."

"Julian–"

"Listen!" He leaned forward so his face was in hers. "Let me tell you how it's going to be. You're with me now. This is where you're going to live for four weeks. Until you are ready."

Jacqui gasped. *Four weeks. Until you are ready.*

"So get used to it. I have prepared a room upstairs. If you are good, very good, I may shorten your initiation."

As the nausea rose in her gullet, Jacqui bit her lip to suppress the terror.

Jacqui had given up screaming, had concluded no one could hear her cries beneath a house in the suburbs. And besides, she had no voice any more.

Though she could not hear or see anything in the pitch blackness, she had noticed during Lynch's visit that the cellar was filled with empty wine bottles. Potential weapons. She was going to fight him with everything she had.

Her bladder was bursting but she refused to pee in her pants, refused to be degraded. Either she had to break the frame of the chair or rip out of the bind.

Option two.

She hadn't only noticed the wine bottles while the light was on; she had also spotted vertical metal struts in the cellar wall, which formed the framework of the wine racks. If she could locate one of the struts in the darkness and maneuver her wrists against a sharp surface, she may be able to make inroads into the duct tape binding her hands. Energized by the fear of what lay in store for her if she remained captive, she rotated the chair in the direction of where she thought the nearest strut was, then slowly, painstakingly, edged herself backwards, standing on her toes to leverage the legs of the chair, first one, then the other. Inch by inch, the chair moved, her calves straining, toes in agony against the hard floor.

With every passing minute, Jacqui's fear of discovery escalated. What would the madman do if he caught her trying to escape?

Finally, she felt something with the tip of a finger: a wine bottle. *Careful.* A mistake now and she could break several bottles in one go. She didn't know if he might hear the sound of shattering glass through the cellar door.

Fingertips wriggling, she searched left and right, felt another bottle, and another. *Got it!*

She could feel the cold metal of the strut—more importantly, a sharp edge. Quickly, she set about working her duct-taped wrists against it, picking away slowly and persistently until eventually she managed to create a small tear. As she gradually increased the length of the tear, she wrenched apart her hands as vigorously as she could, finally creating some wiggle room.

At last, Jacqui broke her hands free, rubbing the raw skin of her wrists as she clutched them to her chest. The intense concentration on the task evaporated in the darkness and in an instant the accumulated pain of her efforts—what seemed like an hour's work or more—coursed through her muscles: her neck, back, and arms ached, her calves burst with cramp. Her bladder was bursting. She wrenched at the cable ties cutting into her ankles, securing them to the legs of the chair, but knew she was out of time, was beyond desperate.

"Legs still fixed to the chair, she lifted her ass, shimmied down her stockings and panties and let go. The stream poured from the chair seat and pooled beneath her. The relief was exquisite, seemed to go on forever. She pulled up her panties and tights. She'd won; she hadn't wet herself."

The small victory galvanized her, steeled her to fight on. How could she escape?

Lynch could look down on her when he opened the trap door. If he saw her out of the chair, he would be alerted to her escape. Either she needed to surprise him as he opened the door or pretend to be bound and wait until he descended the stairs.

But first she had to free her legs. And then she needed a weapon.

Her heart pounded. She had one chance, a bottle. If he came back now...

She bent forward and ripped at the cable ties. Too tight. She couldn't even edge them down the chair leg. Falling forward onto her knees away from the puddle, she crawled to her right, dragging the chair behind her. All but blind, she groped into the blackness until her hand touched a wine rack. She removed a bottle; it was empty.

She held it in her hands, wondering how to break it. Would he hear it? What if there was a monitor in the room she wasn't aware of?

She didn't have a choice. She had to free her legs, had to be armed.

Gripping the empty bottle by its neck, she knocked it against the cement floor. Once. Twice. On the third attempt, the back of the bottle shattered, the noise a virtual explosion in the tiny space.

She listened for footsteps, her heart thumping in her ears.

Nothing.

She carefully tested the jagged edge, got to work on the cable ties, inserting the longest piece into the small gap beside her Achilles heel. No joy; the tie wouldn't give. Again, nothing. The glass wasn't cutting, not enough room for leverage. The tears rolled, dripping to the floor, as she struggled, getting nowhere. *Come on!*

In an act of desperation, she tried to leverage the glass against the hard bone of her leg, pushed the neck of the bottle with the palm of her hand as hard as she could.

"Fuck, fuck, fuck!" she cried, as the bottle slipped and she felt the glass slice her flesh. She clutched her leg, felt the warmth of her blood running down her leg as a new pain took hold, fell back on the cold floor, hands to her face as the sobs came.

But one cable tie was gone!

As the realization hit her, she clenched her fists with elation, felt a new rush of adrenaline. With more room to maneuver, she stood up and wrenched the chair around her leg as hard as she could, turning and opening a gap between her skin and the unbroken cable tie. Gritting her teeth, she slid the glass in the space and cracked off her bond.

She was free.

She righted the chair and listened. No noise.

CLUELESS

Captain Vermaak returned to the Wynberg Police Station, her ears ringing from an *uitkak* session delivered by her superior, Joseph Zoli, commander of the Peninsula Narcotics and Sexual Offences Squad. On a Saturday, nogal.

A UCT student, Jacqui Simpson, had disappeared somewhere between Thursday night and Friday morning after an argument with her boyfriend at a Rondebosch establishment called Panthers. The girl's mother had reported her daughter missing on the Friday afternoon after her housemate had called her. The worried woman had been palmed off with the usual "Give it twenty-four hours and I'm sure she'll appear" one-two, but she hadn't been deterred. By that evening, she'd stirred up a nest of university warders and counselors.

Simpson was a star student, on the Dean's list. The press caught wind of the story and the *Saturday Argus* ran a story headlined: STUDENT FEARED MISSING IN RONDEBOSCH.

A chronological diary of recent drink-spiking allegations appeared in a sidebar to the article. In an interview, Mrs. Elizabeth Euchus, the warden of Tugwell Hall, stated that drink spiking had become an unchecked crisis on campus yet the SA police refused to take their concerns seriously.

"Fokken spike this, spike that," Vermaak muttered.

Typical. It couldn't have happened at a worse time. On the same night as Simpson's disappearance, detectives from her unit had staked out the Blue Venus Nightclub and Bar, caught a barman in the act of adding an illicit substance to a patron's drink. The barman was in custody.

Also typical was Zoli's outburst after picking up flack in the press. He hadn't reacted positively to one single announcement of the unit's successes in the last year, but on the first whiff of a bad smell in a head-line, he had the baseball bat out and was looking for heads.

Another weekend ruined.

Vermaak balled her fist, looked malevolently across her desk at a young man at the other end of the table: Jacqui Simpson's boyfriend, the bugger who had let his girlfriend walk home on her own in the middle of the night. Hadn't even known she was missing until the cops came knocking. Vermaak couldn't decide what she detested more: the piercing in his nose or the black T-shirt with skulls and crossbones that he wore.

"She wasn't pissed," the boyfriend told Vermaak. When they'd picked him up at his house, they'd searched his house.

"So you just let her walk home, then? Alleen. What kind of *man* behaves like this?" she accused. She'd almost said *poes*—by the tone of her voice may as well have.

He glared back at her defensively, feeling her contempt.

"It wasn't, like, far. And I didn't *make* her to go, hey. When Jacqui wants to do something, you can't stop her, you know."

"What was the argument about?"

Vermaak had a meeting at the university scheduled for 3 pm. During the flipping rugby. She was dreading it. She'd already spoken to the barmen on duty at Panthers, but there didn't seem to be a connection. She had no intelligence to suggest that the Panthers barmen were linked to the activities at the Blue Venus in any way, and the CCTV camera footage that recorded Jacqui Simpson arguing with her boyfriend outside the entrance to the pub a little after midnight seemed to show her angry, determined, and fully functional; not the actions of someone under the influence of roofies or GHB.

"Go after that fucking boyfriend," Joseph Zoli had advised Vermaak. "Whatever it takes. Nine times out of ten, the boyfriend knows."

The boyfriend didn't have a car, drove a Vuka scooter. Quite difficult to cart a reluctant victim or a body around on one of those, Vermaak mused sourly while considering Zoli's advice.

She had dealt with enough kidnappings in her time. First thing to establish was whether it was a genuine kidnapping, not just someone wanting to disappear for a while. Maybe the girl was trying to give the boyfriend a scare? Maybe she got hit by a car and was in hospital somewhere, a Jane Doe?

Unlikely. Vermaak's officers had made enough calls to rule out both options. The big policewoman knew this was the real deal.

Next was to establish whether the victim was alive or dead. Harder to work out with the facts at hand, so Vermaak listened for that little voice from somewhere, perhaps the victim's, whispering in her ear. From what she could work out, the girl was smart, had her head screwed on—the boyfriend was obviously just a phase—and her cop's intuition was telling her Jacqui Simpson was alive.

Somewhere deep inside her, the passion of the job was stirring. She *had* to find her. Zoli may be a first-class asshole, but Vermaak knew he'd been right to call her in.

"She was fucking acting up," the boyfriend hissed.

He had a sneering face; Vermaak wanted to stick her fist in it. She wanted to ask Mrs. Simpson what type of mother lets her daughter go out with a sniveling shit like this.

Earlier, after Vermaak had left the other officers at Panthers and traced the missing girl's likely route toward Tugwell residence, she'd spotted three security cameras along the way that should have filmed her. Turned out, one was non-operational—just for show—and they couldn't yet access the premises of the shop guarded by another; the manager was out of town for the weekend. But they'd got lucky at the third, outside the Baxter Theatre.

"You know anyone with a red BMW?" Vermaak asked the boyfriend.

His mouth curled. "Fucking maybe," he replied defiantly, stared back at her.

"We think she got picked up by a red BMW."

Baxter security had reacted swiftly to locate the relevant backup, and Vermaak had been able to view footage from a camera covering the intersection of Main and Burg roads. Twenty-five minutes after midnight on Thursday night, a red BMW had slowed and turned that corner. A couple of minutes later, a girl matching Jacqui Simpson's description followed the same path. The BMW's plates were not immediately distinguishable, but they got a reasonable impression of one. Vermaak was hoping for immediate feedback from the digital lab in Pretoria. Zoli had pulled some strings to get them moving.

She'd faxed the impression to a motor-head at the Bellville office, who'd identified the model as a mid-nineties 525i.

"I don't know anyone with a red BMW," said the boyfriend.

"Would she have hitched a ride?"

"No way," the boyfriend replied. Emphatic. "Sides, she was almost at her place anyway."

Vermaak looked at her watch. It was more than thirty-six hours since the abduction. The voice in Vermaak's head was getting softer.

AMBUSH

Julian Lynch returned from Cavendish Square. He'd bought three days' worth of provisions: ready-made cottage pie—*Terri* loved it—milk, cheese, eggs, bread, tea and washing powder. In the clothing section, he'd bought a red silk nightie. He would ask Terri to wear the nightie while he washed her clothes.

He unpacked the groceries, made a sandwich with cheese, and settled into his study, kicking off his loafers and thumping on the trap door with his bare foot.

"I'm home," he said, but he knew she couldn't hear.

He sat down at his desk and opened his journal. He'd wanted to listen to the original version of the Nirvana track *Polly* off *Bleach*, but his zone controller was on the blink. Either way, he couldn't pipe the music into the cellar, which was something of a disappointment.

Staring at the first page of his journal, a picture of his sister Estelle framed in the center, he considered that it was time he moved on from it. He tore out the page and then screwed it up.

I'm with Terri now.

Next was Holly. Beloved Holly—the picture an official school photo from a couple of years before. When had he last been allowed to speak to her? he wondered. It seemed like years. Of course he followed her progress so closely, still went to her recitals and her netball games when he could, watching from a distance, but as he stared at her beautiful face, he acknowledged within himself that his bitch of an ex-wife had managed to cut her off from him completely. Would she even recognize him if she saw him?

He wrenched the page and crumpled it furiously into a ball. Then another page, and another, until no written pages remained in his journal. All his favorite girls cleansed. He gathered the balls of screwed-up paper and dumped them into the fireplace, lifted a fire starter from the mantelpiece and lit the remnants of his journal.

Watching the orange flames, he felt satisfied. He had eradicated his past in one swift motion. There was only the future to look forward to.

Jacqui tensed as she heard the trap door unlock and a thin shaft of light enter the cellar. Lynch looked down on her.

"Sorry to have kept you waiting so long," he said. "Is everything OK?"

He didn't turn on the light.

Jacqui remained motionless, mentally charging herself, the jagged bottleneck gripped tightly behind her back. She'd left the broken cable ties around her ankles and loosened the straps on her high-heeled shoes, ready to kick them off in a hurry.

"I'm taking orders for dinner," he said.

She stared straight ahead. Prayed she was aligned in the exact spot he'd left her, prayed he wouldn't notice anything amiss. Her heart was pounding so loudly she was scared he could hear it.

"Would you like some more cottage pie?"

"That would be nice, Julian," she replied. She glanced up briefly. His black eyes stared down at her.

"It smells like you used the bowl," he said.

"I couldn't. I had to just go. I'm tied up, remember?"

"Of course. Would you like me to...help you clean up?"

"Yes. Please."

She heard the trap door slide across, the creak of the ladder. The flick of the switch as the naked bulb illuminated the cellar. Jacqui sucked in her breath.

You can't see anything unusual, you can't see anything unusual.

Six steps. She heard each creaking footfall on the ladder, then his bare feet appeared on the concrete. She kept her eyes on the floor.

He paused. *What's he doing?*

"How did the bowl get over here?" he asked.

Fuck! The bowl.

In the darkness, she'd tried to rearrange the room as best she could; had forgotten about the damned bowl.

She looked up and flicked her fringe out of her eyes.

"I must have kicked it," she said.

Lynch took a step forward, bent to pick up the bowl.

"I'll need to take off your—"

Gripping the broken bottle as tightly as she could in her right hand, she lunged at him, aiming at his eye. He reacted late, taken aback, and the glass gorged into the flesh of his cheek. Lynch cried out, dropping the bowl with a clatter and staggering backwards in shock.

"What the fuck!" he bellowed, holding a hand to his face. The sharp spear of glass had pierced into his gum, dislodging two teeth; blood filled his mouth and seeped down his chin.

Summoning all her aggression, Jacqui kicked out of her shoes and rushed at him, feinting with the broken bottle. Lynch stepped back smartly, one hand on his cheek, the other palm forward, open and defensive.

"Move back," she commanded, her voice shrill. She wanted him away from the steps. Lynch stepped back, face aghast, glancing from the girl to his bloodied hands and back.

"Terri, how could you?"

"Move! Away from the steps!" she screamed, thrusting back and forth with the bottle neck.

Lynch took another step backwards, skidded on the glass shards from the broken bottles, bellowed again as the sole of his foot was sliced open.

Jacqui dashed for the ladder. One step, two steps, three steps.

Lynch lunged at her through the slats of the ladder, grabbed the stockings on her inner thigh. She jabbed down with the bottleneck as he ripped through the gauzy fabric. He had a grip on her leg, his heavy weight too much for her; she felt herself being pulled downwards. A second wild thrust of the bottle caught him in the fleshy side of his arm, breaking his grip.

Four steps, five steps, six steps—she lifted herself through the trap door and into the study.

"Help me!" she screamed. "Someone please help me!"

Lynch came clattering up behind her, too late to shut the trap door. She bolted, slipped on the wooden floor as she raced through the study and into the lounge.

"Help me!"

Lynch hauled himself through the trap door.

She sprinted to the front door, her injured leg crying out in agony. Tried to open it.

Locked. No key.

"Shit, shit, shit!"

She rattled at the door as hard as she could.

Lynch moved surprisingly quickly for his size. As she turned, he was on her, leading with his right fist; he turned it away at the last moment and knocked the girl clean off her feet with the edge of his elbow.

HANGOVER

Robbie Cullen opened one gummed eye, then the other. For several seconds he didn't know where he was. A dim grey light filtered through the curtains of his room.

"Whoa," he moaned. "My head."

He was fully clothed. When he tried to sit up, the room spun uncontrollably; he thought he would vomit. He closed his eyes and fell back on the pillow, tried to ignore the nausea.

His radio clock blinked the time at him: 8:15 am. *What the hell?* The last thing he recalled was being with Fallon in his room the previous afternoon. *Shit!* He must have been asleep for fourteen or fifteen hours.

Fallon. Through the haze of hangover, he could smell her vanilla perfume in his room. He slipped back into unconsciousness, wondering what had happened.

He woke a moment later—except the clock now said 9:40 am—with pins and needles in his left arm, head still throbbing. The bed sheets were on the floor. Never again, he swore, reaching for his pack of KGB hangover pills; the pain would take more than a greasy breakfast to resolve.

Before he could pop the pills, though, he felt the wave of clammy nausea return. He scrambled out of bed in a rush to get to the communal bathroom, fumbled with the key to his door, realized it was unlocked, sprinted down the corridor and made it into an empty stall just as the vomit spilled from his mouth.

A minute later, as he sat on the stall floor, leaning on the toilet seat and spitting yellow oysters of bile into the cistern, it occurred to Robbie that he hadn't puked since first year. He'd never really been that guy.

What the hell happened to me yesterday?

The question ran through his mind as he cleaned up as best he could, then as he undressed and as he sat forlornly under the good shower head, water gushing down. Returning wet and naked to his room, clothes under his arm, he still couldn't work it out.

He scanned his desk for an explanatory note, spotted the cause of his cranial damage: the empty bottle of Single Barrel.

Got to be kidding!

He couldn't believe he'd blown his evening with Fallon by getting pissed. Or that he'd managed to get so drunk on half a bottle of whiskey.

And yet Robbie couldn't even remember Fallon leaving. Jesus, he must have passed out right in front of her. She must think him a complete child.

After dumping his clothes into the wash bag behind the door, Robbie's phone rang: his mother. She launched into a monologue of news from the Albany district. Robbie half listened, still trying to work out what had happened the night before. With his mother prattling on, he noticed his elephant-hair bracelet was missing.

"Uh, mom," Robbie tried to temper the download of information.

"Darling?"

"How's Dad?" he asked. He lifted the sheets that had fallen onto the floor.

"Oh. He's fine. You know your father. But how are *you*, Robbie? You doing well?"

Well?

Robbie could still taste the bile in the back of his throat. Besides the nausea, there was another creeping feeling nagging at him. He couldn't quite put his finger on it.

"You're not still missing Melanie, are you?"

Robbie rubbed his wrist, the sunless stripe a reminder of the bracelet's absence.

"It's important to enjoy your student years," his mother went on. "I love Melanie, of course, you know. But I think it is good for you to experience life. To have fun."

Fun? Let me see.

Robbie shook out the sheets, looking for his missing bracelet.

I got paid five grand for saving some CIA-type chick in a bar. That was fun. But the barmen want to break my head with baseball bats.

And I got a surprise blow job in the shower. Which was sure fun at the time, but I didn't know the lips belonged to a stripper. Oh, and that it was filmed and posted on YouTube for all my friends to laugh at.

"Yeah, I'm fine," Robbie replied.

"Are you, Robbie. Really?" His mother was always the amateur psychologist.

I'm so fine I can barely stand up. I don't really want to share this, Mom, but my body feels strange and I have no idea whether I had sex with the CIA-type chick last night or not. Good enough?

"Yes, mother. I'm good. No problems."

Well, maybe a few small ones. When I close my eyes, I see the slashed throat of a Russian stripper called Sylvana. And let's not forget that the local police captain wants me certified.

"Well, I'm glad, Robbie," his mother replied. She didn't sound convinced. "Your father and I are very proud of you, you know?"

Wait til you see my starring role on the Net.

"Sure, mom. Let's wait and see," Robbie replied.

"For what, Robert?"

Uh, whether I get arrested for murder. Or expelled from varsity for being a porn star. Or beaten to death by the barman mafia of Claremont. Take your pick.

"Er, whether I pass at the end of the year, graduate, you know."

"Of course you will, Robert. I have no doubt. You take after your father in that regard. You're a finisher!"

Robbie was relieved to end the call. Felt a moment's regret that he couldn't talk honestly with his mother, but he'd never had that kind of relationship with his parents.

Coming slowly to his senses, he noticed a folded envelope on the floor next to his door. He frowned. Had it been there when he went to the bathroom? he wondered. Must have missed it in the rush to hurl.

Robbie tore open the envelope; inside was a black-and-white CCTV photograph printed on computer paper. It showed a car entering a gate. The date stamp in the corner indicated the picture had been taken in the early hours of Friday morning. He turned the piece of paper over; on the reverse side, a message.

Robbie thumped his fist on the desk and then grabbed the keys to his Mazda.

NEGLIGENCE

This time Jacker woke Carlos, the beeps of consecutive incoming text messages stirring him from sleep. It was nearly midnight. He logged on to his laptop, followed his security procedures and made the Skype linkup. This time Jacker appeared on screen as a laughing clown.

Carlos yawned audibly as they made the connection. He looked down at his fist; it was curled around a red flash drive.

"Took a while. I didn't know you slept," were Jacker's first words. Fishing. Time was a clue. Carlos had often used it himself to narrow down locations.

"I don't," he replied with irritation, slipping the flash drive into his pocket and immediately opening another window on his laptop to check his remote cameras at the Yarrow Point house.

Following their previous discussion, during which Carlos had shared his theory about how an experienced hacker might go about creating a Dark Video client list, Carlos had invoked a persistent cookie that had been custom developed for him two years before by a German IT guru. As he'd run it, he'd smiled grimly at his foresight. He hadn't got to the top of his game by luck.

The German cookie generated trace activities from logs stored on the Dark Video Trojan. He'd never needed to run it before because this was a function Jacker performed with his own software. But, having explained his theory, Carlos needed to be sure that Jacker had not been creating a list in the very manner he had explained. He needed to run security on his security.

The statistics showed zero intrusion attempts over the previous two years, no viral cookies.

Carlos felt satisfied. He'd not only formed the theory of how the generation of a list may be achieved, he'd also now proved that no one had done it. He waited to hear Jacker's latest update.

"You were right about the list, Carlos."

"Oh really?"

Carlos pulled on a white Hyatt toweling robe, scanned the room as he settled in for the conversation. The duvet was on the floor next to the bed. Unusual, Carlos thought. He never moved in his sleep. His warning senses were definitely on edge.

Despite his wife and kid returning from their overnight stay in Tacoma, Carlos had chosen to stay on at the hotel. Something still didn't feel right. Even now, flipping through the different camera views, he could see the two of them fast asleep in his king-sized bed. The house and grounds were otherwise empty and devoid of activity. And yet...

"Yeah. Good news and bad," explained Jacker. "The bad news: it can be done. With the right know-how a hacker could ostensibly build a list of all clients who access a particular video or site."

"Isn't that what I told you?" Carlos asked calmly.

"But it's near fucking impossible, Carlos. More importantly, no one's tried it. I checked. And—"

"And that's the good news, I take it?"

Carlos already knew this, didn't feel like wasting time.

Jacker started to explain the tests he'd performed, but Carlos cut him short.

"So we agree there is no physical list, yes?"

Jacker agreed.

"But we're still losing fucking clients, yes?" Carlos licked his lips. He felt exposed. Was annoyed by the sleeping anomaly.

There may be other ways to build a list. Ways he hadn't considered. And yet it seemed unfathomable that the FBI or anyone else would invest the number of man-hours required to perform such an exercise. There were bigger fish to fry. Even if they caught him, the case would be difficult to pin down. The Internet was an unchartered hive of activities. So few legal precedents, so many international laws and regulations to consider. What had he done wrong? Distributed some porn? Who could prove he solicited the actual manufacture of illegal material?

Carlos looked around the room again. He had no cameras to observe what was going on within the Hyatt. If agents were congregating in the foyer ready to swarm up the stairs, he would have no prior warning. They could be outside his door this very moment.

"I think it's random negligence on behalf of the operators," Jacker stated.

"We all want to believe that," Carlos replied blankly. That was a manageable problem, at least. The fix was cheap and nasty: terminate the operator and get a new one.

"Especially this freaking Mickey Finn," Jacker said. "It's way too messy, Carlos. I think we should put surveillance on all operators in the affected regions, and we should consider not using the service, at least for the time being."

"I think we should too," echoed Carlos. *We.* He hated it when Jacker made assumptions.

The concept of a list still swirled through Carlos's mind.

The dead mule from the Gorillas gang had been building a list. How did he do it? What if he were still operating?

Prior to Diva's appointment in Cape Town, the mule had murdered two Dark Video clients. But he was dead. Fish food, as verified by Samuel Chester, who'd carried out the hit. Chester had found an air ticket among the dead mule's belongings, via Johannesburg to Washington DC. Was he planning on making a connecting flight to Seattle? Could the mule have discovered his lair? Could he have passed on the information?

Carlos shivered, pulled the robe tight around him. His thoughts wouldn't stop.

Messages from the dead. Messages triggered off by some time-controlled mechanism, sourcing addresses, gathering details of law-enforcement agencies in different countries.

It was all so random. He could discern no connection between the busted clients; not by geography, not by taste, not by operating systems.

How were his clients being selected for exposure?

Carlos stood up, carried his laptop through to the living room of his suite. The room was well-equipped, functional, but entirely without charm; Carlos neither noticed nor cared. The tan colored curtains were drawn back, blinds open, light streaming in. He was surprised he'd slept so long.

"Carlos, you there?" Jacker had been trying to expand on the security checks he'd run. Carlos wasn't interested.

"Yes, I'm here. Ever thought about a timing device?" Timing devices were programs set to run at specific intervals and perform automated tasks, such as the FutureMe site that enabled users to send emails at a given date in the future. "Say the list was created a long time ago. From before we were monitoring. A website has a list and the timer device kicks in each month and sends off the tip."

"That Cape Town mule. Devon? No ways, Carlos, it can't be."

"And what makes you so sure?" Carlos asked testily. Jacker's cockiness had always annoyed him.

"One important point," Jacker replied.

"Yes?" said Carlos. He tapped irritably on his keyboard, running through the Yarrow Point cameras yet again.

"Wasn't the Swedish client a recent signing?"

Carlos cleared his throat; closed his eyes and opened them. He wasn't feeling himself. Jacker was right: the Swedish client was recent. Less than a year. In which case, a list with a timing device implemented several years previously didn't make sense.

"Yes," Carlos conceded. Stupid not to think of that. He brought up his bedroom camera. His wife was still sleeping, the kid tucked in next to her. He stared at her, wondered what she was up to.

Carlos's unease annoyed him further. Why had he slept so badly? Why was he picking up warning signals? He patted his pocket, subconsciously checking on the red flash drive.

Using the remote control, Carlos enabled the sound system and selected a background of contemporary music. Perhaps he just needed to relax.

Carlos stretched. Outside his window, 8th Avenue bustled, the drone kept out by thick soundproofed glass.

"I want to show you something, Carlos. Maybe this will shed some light on the problem," Jacker said. "You asked me to investigate Lynch, that weirdo in Cape Town. Remember? About how our competitor got his details."

Carlos leaned forward, interested.

"I accessed Lynch's home network," Jacker began. "Easy as pie, seeing how his Dark Video password enables the whole network." Not that that would make much difference, Carlos knew. Firewalls were no more than a plastic fence to cut through with shears for a hacker with Jacker's skill. If a client's computer connected to the Internet, he could infiltrate it.

Jacker went on to explain how he'd infected Lynch's systems with a bogus video application that enabled him to control the security cameras around his house. "The app's so smart, I can see what his cameras are seeing live. It's beautiful. Better than a webcam."

Carlos bit down on his lip, allowed Jacker his moment.

"I've been through gigs of stored footage from his cameras, specifically the days when Dark Video supplied him Mickey Finn packages. Check this out. I've streamed backups from one night in particular. Watch the screen."

Hazy black and white footage appeared on Carlos's laptop showing a silver BMW X5 entering the black sliding gates of Lynch's property. Carlos noted the date and time on the bottom right-hand corner of the screen.

"That's the operator," Jacker said. "Nice car. Bit flash, mind you."

The screen split: one camera through the gate, the other on the car. The door opened, two women climbed out the BMW X5, one clutching drunkenly onto the other. Carlos recognized Diva under the scarf with grey hair.

"Check the second screen."

A white VW Polo drove slowly past the gate.

"Now watch again when it's magnified."

Jacker rewound the footage, froze it to produce a still shot of the passing car, the driver blurred but visible. While Carlos watched, the screen divided again, in the top picture, the frozen still, in the second a shot from a CCTV camera showing Diva and Kryff beneath the flashing sign of the Poseidon Bar and Grill.

Kryff, thought Carlos. He rubbed his hands, felt unclean that his organization was subject to competition from such inner-city scum. He wondered if Jacker knew Kryff was dead.

"Naughty girl," Jacker said. "She was followed."

Stupid bitch, Carlos thought. That was the problem—too many untrustworthy sources in the chain. He'd seen enough, but Jacker wasn't finished.

"I've said all along, Carlos, the Mickey Finn problem is not about a list. It's negligence. Straightforward. And that's not all."

It wasn't just Jacker's cockiness that annoyed Carlos; it was his overconfidence. If Jacker managed Dark Video, he'd probably double profits in his first year and end up in jail in his second, he thought.

"Go on, Jacker."

"I made contact with our Mickey Finn connection. Diva didn't engage their services on the night of this video. She must have arranged the mark on her own."

Angie Dean. Carlos recalled the name of the girl. Was obsessed with details like that. But how had he made such a critical oversight in not knowing about Diva's activities?

"You certain?"

"Of course," said Jacker with irritating confidence. "She's scamming you, Carlos. Claiming her fee but saving on the expenses. If I were you—"

Jacker had halted the replay of footage from Lynch's camera. LIVE appeared in bold wording in the top right-hand corner of the screen. Jacker's advice to Carlos was halted in mid sentence.

"Jesus!" said Jacker.

"What the fuck!" Carlos barked.

LYNCHED

A dirty gale rattled the windows of Lynch's Bishopscourt home. In summer, the house was sheltered from the prevailing Cape Doctor, but the winter northwesterlies that brought with them ominous mid-latitude cyclones from the cold southern oceans hammered through the valley, tearing out tree stumps and ripping off roofs.

It was the same wind that used to make his mother irritable.

Standing naked except for a loose Lacoste shirt, Lynch used his thumb and forefinger to press together the loose flaps of skin on his cheek, tentatively feeling the mangled flesh of his gum with his tongue. His damaged jaw throbbed; he had no medication to dull the pain. This was serious, he knew, not some trifle injury he could explain away. Even if he'd had the faintest inkling of returning to work, there was no chance of it now.

Lynch hobbled down the stairs, his cut foot swathed in old bandages that he'd managed to dig out from under the bathroom sink. He barely noticed the putrid smell that pervaded the kitchen. Opening the back door, he stepped out into the wind, still half naked. Outside the sky was heavy with purple cloud, rain imminent.

Damp cardboard boxes filled with wine bottles were packed up against the wall. Tall grass and weeds spewed from the cracks separating the concrete slabs of the back patio. The grass reached above his knees as he traced a path across the back lawn and picked up a rusty spade leaning against a vibracrete wall.

The girl was back in the cellar and bleeding. She'd proved problematic, to say the least.

Lynch plunged the spade into the ground, biting into the hard clay-like earth, then stopped as if distracted, tossed it against the wall with a clatter.

What could he do?

He imagined what he would tell his secretary: "I tripped against a window and went straight through it. God, it was lucky I didn't cut my jugular. Then, to make matters worse, I stood on the broken glass."

He had to get to a hospital to get his face stitched. And a dentist to look at his teeth.

Lynch leaned against a dying pine tree, cones littered at its base. He looked to the heavens as if summoning inspiration. How had his meticulous plans gone so wrong? Why did no one else see the world as he did?

He checked the time. His father had been wearing the Rolex when *his* time stopped. He removed it from his wrist and dangled it in his right hand. Time. Once upon, his father would have stood in the very place where he was standing. Underneath the pine tree when it was still strong and green.

What's the fucking use? A fucking tree has more worth than us. Outlives us, mocks us.

He put the watch back on and took a deep breath, eyed the spade. Perhaps there was a way out. Kryff could help. Could get rid of the girl. If he could get hold of him. He'd tried calling a number of times now, but his phone kept going straight to message. Had he really joined forces with Dark Video?

He'd also tried to contact Diva, but she wasn't taking his calls either. He crouched and scratched his fingernails into the ground where the spade had turned the earth.

He couldn't bury the girl here.

Or could he?

Lynch placed his hands on his hips and sniffed the air.

Unwashed dishes clogged the sink, loose vinyl tiles were scattered across the floor.

"Fuck's sake," Lynch cursed. He'd touched the wound on his face; it was still seeping.

And the music system was still on the blink, and he couldn't get the damn network to work. Everything was conspiring against him.

He opened the pantry door and scanned the shelves for coffee. Fish moths slid along the shelf, buried themselves beneath a packet of open rice.

Lynch cried out in rage, sweeping the shelf clear with his arm, packets, tins and glass jars smashing onto the floor.

Patty Hearst's abductor, Willie Wolfe, had been incinerated in a burning house. The real-life kidnapper of Nirvana's Polly was in jail for life.

Lynch raised his fists in the air in anger and then sank down to the floor.

Did they feel this way, too?

It occurred to him that he had been in this situation before. When his mother had jumped from the roof to her death, he had collected her broken body and carried it to her room. The feelings of desperation had worsened as the days went past—before the cops and psychiatrists had intervened. But this time he'd gone too far; there was no turning back.

Is it too late?

The question cleared his thoughts. He had recovered from that horrific day so many years ago when his mother had chosen to leave him, and he could do so again. Back then the investigating officers had felt sorry for him.

Surely they'll feel the same way this time?

Sonya from SARS had sent him a text:

all clear

He could get his face stitched up and return to work next week as planned. People were too embarrassed to ask questions when someone had been in hospital.

It wasn't too late, after all, he concluded, making his way back into the house.

Whatever happens, it will be on my terms. Just like Father.

Upstairs in the master bathroom, Lynch peeled off the ineffective bandage and examined the jagged wound in the mirror.

He hadn't expected the girl in the cellar to fight back; thought she was aware of the process she had to undergo. Turned out she was right. She wasn't Terri Philips. She was just some little bitch unworthy of his attention. She would never submit like Patty Hearst; would never be his willing lover.

He took a deep breath, pondered his options.

He would kill the girl. Shoot her. Maybe bash her around for good measure. She deserves it! And then he'd remove all evidence of her presence in the house. He was a smart man; he could do that easily enough.

After that, what had he done wrong anyway? He'd had sex with a few girls of consenting age. Consent. That was not his problem. Dark Video delivered the escorts to his front door, for which he paid hard cash. It was not for him to question how their services had been procured.

He left the bathroom and turned into Holly's empty room. Holly, his beautiful girl. Her smiling face beamed from a framed photograph on the side table, alongside a grey-haired teddy bear. Was she as disappointed as him that they never saw each other? he wondered. Of course she was.

Lynch sat down on her bed and stroked the fresh sheets he'd laid down. He'd brought the girl here after her attempted escape to clean her up. The pillow was still covered in blood; he must have broken her nose.

The Remington lay on the side table, next to the photograph and the teddy bear, where he'd left it after returning the unconscious girl to the cellar.

Stupid! I should have shot her right there in the hall, when the rage was on me. It would have felt so good.

Lynch smiled at the idea.

The old house creaked and groaned in the wind. Lost in his thoughts, he only registered the intercom bell on its third ring.

Lynch looked at his watch, stood up, and pressed his face against the boarded window. Through a gap between the pine slats, there was an unobstructed view to the front gate. He couldn't see anyone, assumed it was a vagrant asking for money or looking for work.

He stepped away from the window, staring abstractly at his daughter's bed, lost in contemplation.

Options were available, he reasoned.

Get rid of the girl. Get my face fixed. Go back to work. Slow things down and gain control again.

Sonya had made the tax problems disappear. That was very good news.

Problem solved. I can get my life back because I'm too smart for the cops, for Kryff, for Dark Video—for anyone!

He could be golfing with the boys in a couple of days' time if he played it right. They would understand, this was a man's world, pleasure was a right, men deserved to fulfil their urges.

The outside bell rang again. Downstairs the big clock chimed. He compared the time to his Rolex: 10 am on Sunday morning.

He stroked his crotch and thought about the girl in the cellar. Maybe he should have a little fun before he got rid of her.

A grinding metallic clamor interrupted the beginnings of his fantasy. Lynch sat upright and listened. A loud crash ensued.

He stood and strode to the loft window, looked out to pandemonium.

His wrought-iron front gate had been ripped off its rail and lay on its side in the driveway. A swarm of policemen entered the property, armed, urgent.

The blood drained from Lynch's face; he felt faint, his head swimming. The unwashed scent of his body filled his nostrils, his skin suddenly sticky with fear.

Sonya said it was all clear. Why are they coming to stop my fun?

He counted eight men, some in uniform, some in plain clothes. Vehicles were parked at odd angles across the front entrance. One policeman pointed at Lynch's BMW, parked in front of the house, noted the number plate. Lynch went cold.

How could they have found him? he thought frantically. He'd swapped the plates with the originals immediately after kidnapping the girl. The stolen plates were hidden in the garage.

Two officers in plain clothes covered a third in uniform who approached the front door cautiously, weapon drawn.

"No!" Lynch shouted. "You didn't get the message!"

He spotted more policemen creeping around the side of the house, peering into windows.

Sonya had said it was all clear. It didn't compute.

He heard hammering on the door, then a loudspeaker and a woman's voice with an Afrikaans accent. "Julian Lynch. We know you're inside. We know you have the girl. Come out of the house now with your hands raised."

The announcement shattered Lynch's final false delusions. They were here because of the girl, because of Dark Video, because of his lust, his sin.

They were here to get him.

"No!" he cried out again, scrambling for the Remington. "This is *my* house! I'm in charge here!"

Lynch furiously weighed up his options, wondered if he could get downstairs to Terri in the cellar. Perhaps she might convince them she was here to be with him, of her own free will.

Simultaneously, he heard breaking glass, violent thumping as the back kitchen door shuddered then broke open.

But it's not Terri.

Lynch raised the Remington, stood up, and returned to the window.

Like his father, he could still choose his destiny. He could still win. No one would draw any satisfaction out of his dead corpse. And he would be free.

All he had to do was let go of life.

Death is a remedy.

Footsteps thumped across the wooden flooring. Outside the two covering policemen were tense, firearms pointed at the door.

The loudhailer barked again.

It was over, he realized. The real Terri would be so upset. Would be shattered. He wouldn't be able to explain to her. But once he was dead, nothing would matter. It would be instant clemency.

He opened his mouth and inserted the muzzle of the gun, closed his eyes. His father had shot himself in the temple; he would be different.

"For you, my darling Terri," he whispered. Images from *Forest Frolic* filled his head. The night in the club, the day on campus....Her voice. "Is she at school?"

"Gaan bo!" a guttural voice urged. Go up!

The staircase groaned under boots thundering with impending retribution.

Lynch cocked the weapon. His father and mother were right. And Kryff. *Death is a remedy.*

A door smashed open. Lynch recognized it as the door to his bedroom. A temporary lull. He visualized the policemen in his room, boots on the Saxony carpet, shuffling the curtains, throwing open the cupboard doors, looking in the bathroom.

"I'm sorry, Terri," he whispered.

Thump, thump! Boots back on the wooden passageway. Then the door to Holly's room smashing open, hitting the wall with the force of the policeman's entry.

"And to you, my sweet daughter." Lynch gazed longingly at the framed photograph of Holly as he pulled the trigger.

Nothing.

The policeman crashed into Lynch, knocking him against the wall with the initial blow.

Lynch clung to the gun, held it to his head this time, and pulled the trigger again. The hammer clicked uselessly.

The cop came at him again with a grunt, shoulder-charged Lynch against the wall, knocking the energy out of him, grabbed his gun hand and rapped it against the wall, the weapon clattering to the floor.

Lynch felt the crack of his clavicle, the policeman's arm locked around his neck, forcing him in turn to the floor.

"It wasn't loaded!" Lynch shouted. "It was never loaded."

A second policeman charged in. Lynch felt a knee ram into his back, before his face was slammed against the wooden floor.

"Ons het hom!" the second cop shouted.

They had him.

THE PRESENTATION

Jacker hooked up with Carlos on Skype at 12 pm GMT. Carlos's screen filled with the title page of a presentation, headed: CAPE TOWN INVESTIGATION.

"Evidence proves it was another tip-off," Jacker began.

The previous night, Carlos had not slept. He'd mentally scrolled through lists of clients, grouping them geographically, by age, profession, taste, turnover, looking for some commonality that would link the six busted clients: now two in South Africa, and one each in Mexico, Japan, Portugal, and Sweden. Carlos couldn't work out how, if someone was working from a list, the busted clients had been selected?

"You watching, Carlos?" Jacker enquired.

The arrested clients were regulars who paid their accounts but dabbled with rival operators, and were occasionally in trouble with the authorities for other misdemeanors. And they'd all played the Mickey Finn game.

"Go ahead," Carlos said. Lynch's bust the night before had happened like reality TV; he'd watched it live through Jacker's feed. The ultimate coincidence to ruin his day. He was still in shock. Still cooped up in the Hyatt, the paranoia running rampant.

All the arrested clients had been problematic; at various times, he'd had cause to check up on them.

Someone was getting rid of his problems.

"You said focus on Cape Town," Jacker spoke through his encoded voice, the Mickey Mouse avatar on Carlos's screen. "Suddenly when I collate it, everything falls into place."

A black and white photograph showed Robbie Cullen at a bar with a young woman.

"That's Diva," said Jacker. Carlos nodded but didn't respond. "And that's the kid. The cyborg. It was taken in a bar called Blue Venus, evidently the first time they'd met."

"Cyborg?" Carlos queried.

"Studies computer science."

"Very good," said Carlos, scrutinizing the picture and recounting intelligence gathered by Diva, also known as Fallon. She'd said the kid was dim, definitely not the type to be decoding digital data streams. But the picture on his screen was definitely the young man he'd watched in a shower sex video. Regular surveillance had been enabled on all new operators; Fallon was no exception. "Is this standard surveillance or part of the special project?" He was thinking about how he'd recruited Diva. There'd been no possible connection between her and the previous Cape Town operators; he'd made sure of that.

"This was standard," Jacker admitted before continuing as a new image filled the screen, a still from a CCTV camera.

"Then this is Cullen at Diva's flat."

A series of stills showed the operator stepping out of a car, Robbie Cullen helping her toward the gate of her Rosebank flat.

"Let's not get carried away," Carlos reasoned. "This was after Diva was attacked by personnel at the Blue Venus if I'm not mistaken."

"Correct. Retribution for illegally hijacking a Mickey Finn club victim for another operator."

"Angie Dean," Carlos muttered. "So much trouble for just one girl."

Jacker continued: "This video was taken in Plettenberg Bay. It's a holiday resort on the south coast of South Africa. It's the video the Russian girl tried to sell our client."

Carlos watched the opening sequence of the shower video.

"Yes, yes," he said impatiently. "I've seen this. After discovery, our operative sourced the video, loaded it on YouTube, and got rid of the Russian girl."

"But Diva was in Plettenberg Bay. With the kid. At the same time," Jacker added, allowing the video to run.

"She was," Carlos agreed.

"See the quality. The lighting, the headshots, the expressions."

"You think I didn't notice that?" Carlos replied, irritated. He was the supreme expert in video evaluation. It was his job. His art.

"The kid was acting," Jacker said.

"I don't agree. But I know what you're getting at," replied Carlos.

"The video was shot using expensive remote-controllable micro cameras with top-of-the-grade light sensor. No way the Russian girl put that together on her own."

"I repeat," said Carlos. "Your point is taken, Jacker. Move along."

More shots from Plettenberg Bay flicked over his screen, date stamped.

"Where did you get these?" Carlos enquired.

"Acquired from the kid's hard drive."

"Ah yes, which Diva procured for us. What's this one?"

A still shot showed two kids talking outside a building.

"That's Cullen with a barman from the Blue Venus. His name is Denny le Roux. Obviously that creates the link between Cullen and Mickey Finn and..."

"Jacker," Carlos interrupted. "Just show me the evidence. I don't need anyone to connect the dots." Carlos patted his pocket to reassure himself that his red flash drive was in place. Everything he had was stored on it.

"OK, boss. Now here's an important one."

Robbie Cullen stepping out of an unmarked police car.

"This is outside a police station in a suburb called Wynberg. The day after the Russian was put to bed."

Another photograph showed Cullen walking into the same building.

"Yes, yes, hurry it along," Carlos muttered.

"No. Look at the date."

The photographs were from two separate occasions. The second was two days previously, the day before Lynch's bust. The day *after* Diva was supposed to have checked out everything about the kid and came back with an all-clear verdict.

Carlos picked up a handgrip that he'd arranged to be delivered to the hotel, and started to work his right arm. What was Cullen doing seeing the cops the day before Lynch's bust? he wondered.

"Can I continue?"

"No, wait."

Carlos pumped with his right hands until blue veins bulged in his forearm. He changed hands, pumped as hard as he could, as his mind ran through the evidence.

Who was this kid? *Checked out BJ boy. Clean.* Was Diva lying to him?

Cullen was studying computers.

He resided at a residence at the University of Cape Town. The same residence where one of the gang members from Gorillas had stayed.

No, thought Carlos and rubbed his face.

Cullen's friend was a barman at Blue Venus, a Mickey Finn institution.

Cullen had made contact with his operator.

He had acted in a high-def production, which was offered to a Dark Video customer.

He was in contact with the South African police.

No, no, no. None of this was possible. Carlos tried to regain his concentration.

Could Cullen be a mastermind student following in the footsteps of the previous rogue Dark Video operatives? Perhaps a friend of theirs? Or even a member of their gang who'd managed to stay below the radar until now? Possibly in cahoots with Diva now and out to undermine his business?

Carlos felt a sudden surge of overwhelming tiredness. He longed to take a walk, visit a café, chat to a pretty barista.

"OK," Carlos said. "I've seen enough."

"But I..."

"Good job, Jacker. You'll be paid."

Jacker had quoted him $18,000 for the report. Over and above his monthly retainer. The cost of combating client losses was mounting.

Carlos closed the Skype session without further interaction.

Jacker's presentation was irrelevant. Carlos had already decided on a course of action.

Cheap and nasty.

WARNING

"Very good work, Maryka," said Joseph Zoli. The commander stood in the doorway of Vermaak's cramped office, a big man with a big stomach.

Vermaak shuffled her boots on the wooden floor beneath her desk in embarrassed acknowledgment. He liked using her name. Maryka. She hated being called that. Her man had called her Ryk—"rich" in Afrikaans—said she was his treasure. But for all his crap, Zoli was good to her, and she treated all authority with obedience. Besides, Maryka was better than Tannie.

Zoli had just returned from a press conference. Turns out it was most satisfactory to be given a public blasting session and then respond with an immediate arrest.

News of Jacqui Simpson's abduction in Rondebosch had made the weekend papers; now, at the start of the week, the arrest was on the front pages. BISHOPSCOURT PERVERT NABBED.

"There's always complaining about us. A year or two ago they'd have said, 'This shit is not good for the soccer,'" Zoli said without bitterness. "Now they say, 'After the soccer the police don't care any more.' But when we, wham!"—he slammed his right fist in his left hand— "strike, then the bad news is good news for us."

Vermaak nodded. "But then sometimes the good news is bad news, hey boss?"

The wardens and counselors from the university, as well as two head-mistresses from private girls' schools, were all over her department now, demanding that their drink-spiking concerns be taken seriously. Vermaak's name had been mentioned at least twice in the *Cape Times* that morning and they were asking for her personally.

Still, the big policewoman was happy to give Zoli his triumph. And she felt the satisfaction of a job well done. At the end of the day it's why she was a cop. Jacqui Simpson was traumatized, certainly, but at least she was alive—a lot better off than the victims in so many of her other cases.

She had over two hundred open dockets. Would be more if a few hadn't gone "missing." So opening and closing one in seventy-two hours was satisfying. The follow-up workload would be gruelling. Lynch, it turned out, had been a serial offender. "A proper nutcase," as one of the officers had said when they'd pulled the injured girl from the cellar. They'd found a box of goodies he'd acquired from victims. They'd do their best to track them down, perhaps close a few more dockets.

"It's 'cuz you keep your eyes open, Maryka," Zoli said. "That's what I tell the others. Because you still care."

Vermaak shuffled uncomfortably on her hard plastic chair. Her eyes had been closed for years, she'd tell people. You can't care about them all.

She was like her cat, she thought. Reliably she arrived each day. Received her supper. As long as no one tried to touch her…

The number plate on the red BMW trawling past the Baxter Theatre on the night of the girl's abduction had not been visible to the naked eye, but the digital lab technician in Pretoria had worked his magic. To Vermaak's disappointment, the discernible number was registered to a Hyundai. They'd tracked the owner, whose vehicle was minus a rear number plate, and given him a grilling. A dead end.

Then she'd returned to the Wynberg station and found a surprise waiting. Robbie Cullen.

"*Ag, nee wat!* Not you," she'd greeted him, shaking her head. "Had any more fun in the shower lately?"

She remembered the kid's eyes: clear and blue, they seemed to look right into her. He hadn't smiled. Just handed her an envelope; in it, a picture taken from what seemed to be a home-security camera. Front-on view of a car, single occupant, male, driving into the gates of a house. A street sign captured in the background served as visible identification of the location.

"What's this?" she'd asked. Despite the black-and-white image, Vermaak's interest was instantly piqued by the old-model BMW in the picture. Except the number plate was wrong, different to the one recorded by the Baxter Theatre's CCTV.

"I don't know," Cullen had said. "All I know is that the other night I saw a real dead body and whoever was involved wanted me to give you this picture. Look on the other side."

Vermaak flipped the page, read: "Tell Vermaak to check the date stamp."

Friday morning. Forty-five minutes after midnight.

It was only then that Vermaak had considered that the front and back number plates might be different, that the Cullen boy might not be off his rocker.

"So what's his case? This bloody umlungu with the girl under his house?" Zoli asked, genuinely intrigued. Cases like this were rare in this part of the world. "A psycho or what?"

"Ag, you know, boss. Psychopath. Sociopath. Antisocial personality disorder. Whatever you want to call it. They've got a shrink talking to him, but basically he was out of his fokken tree," Vermaak said, spinning her index finger in circles around her ear. She'd personally coordinated the raid, taken a good look around the house afterwards. The overflowing garage had attracted a lot of attention. "Turns out he was a collector."

"Ja? Of what?"

"Junk. Magazines, newspapers, wine bottles, deodorant cans. Everything. You should see his place. Tons of the stuff. A whole stable filled with it. From years ago."

Zoli frowned and stroked his moustache. "So he keeps all his stuff. But what for?"

His moustache intrigued Vermaak; it seemed out of place on Zoli's wide-smiling face.

"Maybe he doesn't like to let anything out," Zoli suggested. The commander walked around behind her desk. Too close for Vermaak's liking; her shoulders instinctively narrowed. He inspected an organizational diagram on the wall behind her chair. "Is the girl OK?" he asked, gripping the edge of her chair.

Vermaak breathed deeply, relaxed as he let go and sauntered around to the front of her desk.

"She's at the Kingsbury. Said he *moered* her a couple of times. Once when he grabbed her off the street and also when she tried to get away. Broken nose, some bruises."

"Was she...?" Zoli inverted his palm and wiggled his fingers.

Fokkenmen.

"No," she said. "Doesn't look like it. He seems to have had some kind of fantasy in store for her. A day or two more and who knows what would have happened?"

Zoli took a seat opposite Vermaak, the plastic visitor's chair buckling under his weight. He thumped his boots on Vermaak's desk.

"And the connection to these other student cases?"

"Yes. We're looking into a link with the drink-spiking gang," she said. "Very likely there's something there."

"She was drugged?"

"No, not that we can tell. But we found plenty of evidence at Lynch's home linked to other cases." She described the box that Lynch had filled with keepsakes from earlier victims. A blood crusted gold ring, an inscribed gold bangle, locks of hair, an Alice band. "And, quite convenient, ID books. The boys are tracing them all as we speak."

Zoli widened his eyes and stroked his moustache.

"Sick shit," he said. "This oke was not well."

"We don't know half of it yet," Vermaak agreed, shaking her head in disbelief. "We've got his computer, but it looks like he might have wiped it."

Vermaak had no computer in her office, could barely turn one on.

"Really?" said Zoli. He twirled the edges of his moustache down. "You know, my son-in-law's an IT specialist. He can find anything."

Vermaak shuffled a file of papers and averted her gaze. She'd heard about Zoli's son-in-law and all his money and whatnot. Zoli's wife did the catering; his brother serviced the vehicles. She was glad her husband was dead and didn't have to deal with this shit.

"Let me know if you want his number," Zoli said. Vermaak nodded discreetly.

It's 'cuz you keep your eyes open, Maryka.

Zoli's cellphone rang. He removed his boots off the desk, fumbled in his pocket and answered. Vermaak opened a folder and pretended to peruse the contents, listened carefully to Zoli's conversation: Yes, yes, I understand, yes, yes.

The call ended. Zoli held his phone up and stared at the screen.

"We must let the boy go, Maryka," Zoli said, replacing his phone. "The barman." He was referring to the barman from the Blue Venus. The boy's parents were phoning around calling in favors; someone had contacted a minister.

Vermaak didn't look up. *No fokken way the little bastard's getting away with this.* This was what she hated the most about the job.

"But, sir, we caught that little....We caught him slipping GHB into a drink. Two plain-clothes eyeballed it, and got the drink for analysis."

"You've identified the substance?" Zoli asked, serious, official, sitting up straight.

"Yes, sir. GHB. It's like sleeping pills, but really bad with alcohol."

"What's the link? With the kidnapped girl?"

"Like I was saying, sir. We found IDs and stuff at the house in Bishopscourt. At least three of them belonging to girls who said they'd been spiked at the Blue Venus."

Zoli whistled through his teeth. "What's with these people?" he grimaced, shaking his head.

These people.

"Not everyone's interested in stealing laptops and big-screen TVs," she remarked, eyes down.

"How long we holding him? The barman?" Zoli asked, ignoring the comment.

This was the irony, thought Vermaak. The barman was son of a wealthy businessman from Johannesburg. Now she was getting heat from the same type of people who'd been pushing her to bust him. These people had one rule for themselves and one for everyone else. These people.

"We want to find out who pays him," Vermaak said. "And who else is involved."

"Pays him? So it's not the Lynch person?"

Vermaak shook her head. "Don't think so. There's a middle man. A facilitator. There could be a lot more Lynches out there."

"What's the barman say?"

"Says he was working alone. But we've got information about a fight at the bar. Like a turf war. Some woman and an accomplice. We're checking CCTV, talking to people. We think they may be the operators."

Zoli stood up and smiled at her. "I like you Afrikaners," he said.

She looked up and narrowed her eyes. *You Afrikaners.*

Just feed me, she thought.

"Don't take too long, Maryka," said Zoli as he departed. "The barman's parents are kicking up a stink, making my life difficult. You know what the conditions are like."

Vermaak said nothing. They could stink it up to high heaven, she countered silently. If the barman had been doing what was alleged, she hoped he was already some prison gangster's *wyfie.*

A KILLER'S PREPARATION

Samuel Chester washed his hands at the basin in his hotel room at the Woodstock Holiday Inn. After drying with a regulation hotel towel, he removed a tube of Cherry Blossom handcream from his toilet bag and squeezed it into his palms. Rubbing his palms together, he ducked under the door of the bathroom, humming along to a tune playing on MTV.

"Baby, baby, baby, oh…"

The view from his window stretched over buildings and houses then over scaffolding and harbor cranes into Table Bay. The water was glass; hard to believe this was the Cape of Storms.

Laid out on a solitary table was a short-barreled Rossi revolver, a cleaning kit, a shoulder holster, two boxes of .38 Special ammunition, a car-rental agreement, a travel itinerary and a BlackBerry running an application targeting mobile phones over a continuous frequency range of 400MHz to 2,000MHz. He'd acquired the hardware items yesterday. Uncharacteristically, Chester fixed a small key ring with an American flag to the trigger guard. Normally he'd have sawed the trigger guard off the 26 ounce gun to accommodate his sausage-like fingers. But he wasn't planning a shootout.

Chester stared at the kid on TV.

"Baby, baby, baby, oh…" Chester's honey-pitched voice was incongruous with his appearance.

He liked the song, though he'd never seen or heard of the singer before; didn't keep up to date with pop music. But the boy's pudding-styled hair was a bit much.

Chester patted his hands dry. He took great care of them. They were soft and sensitive. They were also large enough to close around a man's head.

But modern operations relied more on guile and expertise than brute strength.

Chester cracked his knuckles, lifted the Rossi and examined the silver barrel. The weapon had a history, a straw purchase on behalf of a notorious Cape Flats gangster. The gangster had been killed in a roadblock the previous week. Chester bought it off the street as he always did; the seller had assured him it was no longer hot. Made no difference either way. It was fitted with a contoured mother-of-pearl grip, which felt smooth in his hand.

Chester stretched. His lower back ached, the result of an inadequate bed.

He picked up a wristwatch from the bedside table and strapped it on, briefly held it to his ear. A luxe Cartier Pasha, well worn. It had been a very special purchase; he'd used the upfront payment from Carlos before leaving the States.

He should have been back in the States already, but Carlos had extended his contract. Though not technically complicated, the additional assignments were terminal.

He was forced to reschedule his flights and postpone that Caribbean yacht charter with Heaven and Earth.

Typically he got into a very black mood before executing capital projects. But, as always, he could do with the extra cash.

He was looking forward to getting away from this place.

Chester had little time for so-called kinship with his fellow black brothers of Africa. His passion was sailing: passive sailing, a harem of girls with creamy skin and wind in his sails. He found Cape Town unfriendly. He didn't overly regret that his great-grandfather had been prised from this continent and dumped in America.

Chester pulled on a baggy pair of khaki pants, buckled the leather belt and pondered the choice of shirt. A jagged scar ravaged the length of his chest and the bullet he'd recently taken formed an angry red welt on his right shoulder. He settled on a cream short-sleeved shirt with a cougar monogram.

He rigged up the shoulder holster, inserted the Rossi, and stood before a mirror on the back of the cupboard. He pulled on a beige overcoat and wiggled his hips.

No. Not comfortable.

He adjusted the straps and posed again.

Better.

Then he opened the chamber of the stainless-steel Rossi and loaded six bullets. He wondered how many he'd need to kill the two.

NOWHERE TO RUN

The accent was American, the caller female, and the unnatural delivery of words indicative of a text message translated to voice.

Someone's going to kill you.

Robbie pulled his cellphone away from his ear like a hot coal. He checked the number: Caller Withheld.

The nausea returned and Robbie keeled forward to retch in the Kopano car park. He hadn't been right since the night Fallon visited.

"Shit sake," Robbie cursed, wiping the dribble from his lips, a sour taste in his mouth. He figured he must have caught something. No way he could be that sick on half a bottle of Jack Daniel's.

He tried to call Fallon again. No answer, subscriber unavailable. Same message for three days.

He didn't seem to be able to get hold of anybody. Denny le Roux hadn't been in his room since the weekend, his cellphone off. That wasn't unusual; he'd often head off up the West Coast for a few days' surfing.

Robbie wore a thin jersey, though it was a clear and warm winter's day. He tried to recall his conversation with Fallon, remembered moments: that Tony and Denny were suspects in Angie Dean's abduction; that Angie had been raped; that they were investigating a Russian link. How could he have passed out like that?

Tony and Denny? Robbie had spoken to Tony. Carefully. Robbie wasn't certain whether Fallon had actually told him that Tony was a suspect or that he'd dreamed it.

Strange sensations intruded. The vanilla scent. He could still smell it on the sleeve of the sweater he'd worn that night. He felt a connection to Fallon that he couldn't explain.

He wanted to see her.

It was three days since he'd delivered the message to Captain Vermaak. Hadn't heard back from her. Wondered if there was any point in pursuing it. Robbie had no reason to suspect a link between the information he'd passed on and the snippets of news he'd heard about a UCT student's abduction. The more he thought about his meetings with Vermaak, the less he wanted to deal with cops. Another concern: he couldn't find the plastic moneybag with Sylvana's blood sample. Fallon must have taken it. Or perhaps he'd thrown it away in his stupor on Saturday.

His shadow lengthened against the cobbled wall surrounding the Astroturf hockey field; his cellphone looked like a gun against his head.

Silhouetted against the cars in the parking lot, Robbie spotted Denny on the rise, one strap of a grey satchel hoisted over his shoulder.

"Hey!" Robbie called out, hurried up the stairs to speak to him. "Hey Denny, where've you been?"

Denny was jumpy. "Robbie, hey man. I need a ride," he said, meeting Robbie at the edge of the Astro.

"Where?" Robbie replied, out of breath, wondering if he could trust his stomach.

"The airport."

"Why? What's going on?"

"Cops busted a guy at Blue Venus," Denny said. "Can you take me?"

"What guy? What happened?"

"A barman. You don't know him. He was spiking drinks."

"Shit! You serious? That surfer dude?" Robbie asked.

A vacant expression passed over Denny's face, as if his screensaver had just been engaged.

"Hey, Denny!"

"What?"

"Was it the surfer?"

Denny shook his head, nervous energy catapulting him back to the present.

"Where's your car, dude? Can you take me?"

"Wait," said Robbie. "Who was he?"

Denny spotted the Mazda, pulled on Robbie's sleeve. "Please, dude. I'll pay petrol."

Robbie was bemused. "OK, whatever."

He followed Denny down the hill.

"Why the airport? What's this got to do with you?"

Denny looked about nervously. "They suspect me of ratting on him. They're out to get me. I phoned my folks and they said I should come home."

Denny's parents lived in Durban.

"Who's they?"

Denny didn't reply. Screensaver mode again. Robbie grabbed his shoulder and spun him round.

"Denny, what the hell's going on, man?"

"Robbie. For fuck's sake, I have to get to the airport."

"Who's they?" Robbie insisted.

"I don't know! I got a fucking message. That they're going to kill me!"

"A message?" Robbie almost choked. He stopped and reached for his

Nokia and grabbed Denny's shoulder with the other hand. "American voice? Automated? 'Someone's going to kill you.'"

Denny's eyes were wild.

"How do you know?"

"I got one too."

"What the fuck," said Denny. "Let's get out of here."

"It's bullshit," Robbie didn't move. "It's that surfer prick, isn't it?"

Denny shook loose and pulled up Robbie's wrist, checked the time. 3:30 pm. Soon the N2 would be clogged with traffic.

"Robbie. This is big shit! We've been taking money. Please. I need to get to the airport. These are serious people." He pointed to the Mazda and patted Robbie's pockets. "You got keys?"

"Taking money? What do you mean?" Robbie grabbed Denny by the collar, jaw set, starting to realize that maybe Fallon was right about Denny; something very bad was at play.

"Rob, it was nothing, just needed some extra cash."

"You've been taking money," Robbie interrupted. His voice quivered. "For what? For drugging girls? Angie Dean?"

"No. I swear Robbie. Not me. But I..."

Robbie let go of Denny's collar.

"You what? Fuck you, Denny. What type are you?"

"Robbie, please!" Denny implored. "You've got to help me."

Fifteen minutes later, the drive completed in silent accusation and guilt, Robbie pulled into the drop-off zone at Cape Town International.

Denny drew out two twenties and a ten.

"Will fifty do?"

Mickey Finn. Mickey Fun. Picked the front pocket. Robbie remembered Denny joking in the shower.

"I don't want your flipping money," he said.

Denny tried to push the cash into his lap, Robbie lashed out with his fist.

"OK, OK," said Denny.

Robbie was short of cash, needed petrol—but he was damned if he was going to accept money from Denny.

"Tell me one thing. Did you know about Angie Dean?" Robbie boiled over at last.

Denny tried to open the door but Robbie reached across and slammed down the lock.

"I didn't. I swear it, Rob. You know I wasn't working that night." Denny was near tears, his voice cracking.

Quiet rage consumed Robbie. He'd entered a zone where his anger would fuel his action. He could feel the imaginary taps on his shoulder. *Cool it, Rob. Let it go.* He was past that point.

"What fucking lowlife does something like that? I want names, Denny. If you want to get out of this car, I want names!"

Denny looked about desperately. Robbie gripped him by the front of his shirt.

"Tell me!" he shouted.

Denny's nostrils flared. He didn't try to break Robbie's hold. "It's a system, Rob. The Mickey Finn Club. Most of the barmen at the Venus are doing it. And some other bars too. Don't get involved. Those guys are mad. They'll hurt you." His eyes darted about. "I'm warning you. You don't want to be involved."

"I'm not scared of that surfer prick," Robbie said, spittle spraying.

"They'll kill you, man. The message was no joke."

Robbie thought about Fallon, the danger she'd been in the night he'd rescued her at the Blue Venus. What would they have done to him if he hadn't got the drop on them? And to her if he hadn't arrived? They'd cut her; would they have killed her? Either way, now he had proof for her about what was going down.

Denny reached for the lock but Robbie restrained him once more.

"Who do they work for?" he asked.

"They'll kill me," said Denny.

Robbie maintained his grip on Denny's shirt.

"I don't know. Please, Robbie. Fuck. The time."

Their eyes locked; Denny looked like a terrified animal.

"We're done," Robbie said, releasing him. He thought about all the good times he'd shared with Denny over the years. It was all a farce. He wanted to bash Denny into the concrete.

Denny opened the passenger door, swung his satchel over the back seat. He slammed the door and looked left and right, took a step forward then stopped, spun around and tapped on the window. Robbie leaned across and rolled it down.

Denny's mouth quivered. "Shit, Robbie!"

Robbie's jaw was set. "I said we're done," he repeated.

"What're you going to do?" Denny asked, lip quivering.

Robbie ignored him.

"You don't have a clue," Denny said, shaking his head slowly. "You don't even know who's for you and who's against."

Robbie turned the keys and pulled away from the curb.

SIXTH SENSE

In Seattle, Carlos once again scanned the live video feed from the surveillance cameras at his house in Yarrow Point. He'd changed hotels, moved across town to the Marriot on the Waterfront. His corner suite had a view north to the Space Needle a mile away, and west across Puget Sound to Bainbridge Island. Carlos barely noticed.

He was listless; hadn't slept in twenty-four hours. There'd been a gym at the Hyatt but he hadn't used it. Couldn't be bothered to even check if there was one here.

His wife was at home. She'd called him twice already. He'd told her he was at an Apple conference in San Francisco.

The previous day she'd left the house at 9 am, kid in tow, and returned before lunch. According to his PI, she'd dropped the kid at preschool, visited the mall at Bellevue, and picked up the kid again on the way home. All seemingly normal.

Using the fast-forward and then freeze-control buttons, Carlos had noted every car driving past his house, recording their number plates. He figured he needed something to do if he couldn't sleep.

One in particular intrigued him. A truck marked Telecom & Data was parked in sight of one of his street-view cameras.

Carlos's senses had immediately prickled.

He'd phoned in a complaint to the T&D hotline, making up a story about a faulty Lucent PR1 phone connection. The agent had repeatedly asked him for his account number, but he'd had a line ready. "First thing I want to know is what's the quickest you can get here?" He'd given an address two blocks down from his house.

"Sorry, sir. There are no technicians in the area. The soonest we'll be able to get there..."

It was all he needed to hear. So what was the T&D truck doing down the road from his house?

Watching the South African police swarm across Lynch's property had horrified and fascinated him. The cops were like army ants. He imagined uniformed men climbing over his walls in Yarrow Point, breaking down his doors. He was in a state—and, for the first time since he escaped from England to the States fifteen years before, he wasn't sleeping.

He was in contact with Jacker three to four times a day.

Even as Lynch was being cuffed and hauled to the police van, Jacker was erasing the electronic fingerprints of Dark Video from his computer.

Complete systems crash.

Carlos flicked to a live feed from his cameras. The T&D truck was still parked down the road.

Without sleep to rejuvenate a new instance of his life, Carlos was unable to clear his mind and focus his thoughts. Fragments of uncertainty were scattered around his consciousness, continually interrupting his deliberations. He wondered whether he would ever sleep again; perhaps only in final death would sleep come to him. It would be terrifying: he imagined his own corpse, hands and legs bound, plagued by an eternity of nightmares.

For in that sleep of death, what dreams may come? He shivered at the thought, recalling Hamlet's immortal line from school days.

Get a grip, man!

Another Skype meeting. Jacker's avatar was Ronnie Reagan.

"Bad news," he greeted Carlos. "Looks like they're about to pick up our guy in Mexico." He was referring to a Dark Video client who had been complaining to Carlos of police harassment.

Carlos was listening to Jacker but his eyes followed the relay feed from his surveillance cameras. The maid was putting out the washing on the line, the garden-service company had arrived to mow the lawn. He watched his wife walk out to the gate. Normally she'd just buzz them in from the lounge. Carlos paused the stream.

"I've run checks," said Jacker. "Mr. Bernardino is an Argentinean living in Mexico. Prior convictions back home. They're gonna deport him."

"That'll be a first," said Carlos. It reminded him of the joke about why Mexicans didn't have an Olympic team. Because every Mexican who could run, jump, or swim was across the border.

The frozen frame on his screen showed Carlos's wife. He rolled forward a single frame. Then another. He let the stream run again. She opened the gate and talked to a man in overalls. Carlos recognized the garden-services manager. She stood at the gate as he entered. Carlos froze the footage again. Slow forward. His wife closed the gate. As she did, Carlos thought he spotted her glance quickly down the road toward the Telecom & Data van.

"Domestic violence, interference with a minor," Jacker was saying. "A real scumbag."

"Another coincidence?" Carlos asked. He replayed the sequence in extra slow motion, stopped again to make sure of his wife's furtive glance down the road. He slapped his hand on the desk.

"Or operator error," said Jacker. "What should we do?"

Another job for Samuel Chester, Carlos decided. Or another fixer. He may have to tap his LA contact again; he'd done some good work in the past. It was going to be costly; eliminating operators and training new ones was a meticulous job.

He wondered how Chester was doing in Cape Town, hadn't heard back from him yet. He removed the red flash drive from his pocket, peeled open a condom he'd had in his toilet bag and wrapped the flash drive inside.

"We gotta expect shit from shit," Jacker was saying. "Don't panic, Carlos. Is it raining there too?"

Don't panic? Cheeky motherfucker.

Carlos swallowed hard. He checked that his voice filter was engaged.

"Raining? Where?"

KILL TIME

The suburb of Rosebank shimmered under the distorted light of a gibbous moon.

Someone's going to kill you.

Robbie had been to the Blue Venus. The place was a morgue, the blond surfer gone. The solitary barman on duty couldn't place an employee with a Sharks rugby jersey either.

"Only just started, dude," he'd explained.

Robbie believed him, had left a note to give to the surfer—his name, number and address—and a message: "Tell him I'm waiting."

Robbie would have fought the entire staff; he was in that kind of mood.

He'd then phoned the Wynberg Police Station and tried to contact Captain Vermaak. She wasn't available; gone for the day.

"Fuck them," Robbie declared, gunning his Mazda down Liesbeek Parkway.

Just after 8 pm, Robbie pressed the buzzer of Fallon's flat. Number 15.

The time for discretion was over. Fallon and her flipping special forces people needed to know the truth.

No response on the intercom.

Pressing the buzzer again, Robbie pulled down his striped beanie then checked his phone for messages. Before leaving res, he'd sent Fallon a text saying he was on his way to her flat. But she hadn't answered or returned a call or message since the night he'd passed out. Come to think of it, Robbie thought, she'd never answered a call or message from him, full stop.

How would he find her if she wasn't at home?

He buzzed the intercom again, a full thirty seconds, hoped the thing worked.

Light from the streetlamp was partly obscured by overhanging branches of an oak tree. Cars lined both sides of the road. Robbie's Mazda was parked down the road on a yellow line.

"Hello?" Fallon's voice sounded on the intercom. Robbie's heart jumped; he leaned forward.

Then he heard a metallic click.

From the shadows behind the wall, Robbie glimpsed the danger as it struck. In an instant the assailant was behind him, arm like a python around his neck, cold steel thrust against his temple.

Bang.

A bright spurt of light flashed in his eyes as the world went silent, just a ringing in his head. Robbie knew he'd been shot.

Instinctively, he sunk his teeth down, deep into the arm of his assailant and twisted viciously.

"Motherfucker!" the assailant shouted.

A momentary relaxation of his attacker's grip allowed Robbie to duck out of the headlock. He fell to the ground and rolled into the gutter of the road. His car keys clattered on the cement.

A sharp jolt bit into his side. A second gunshot, he assumed—because he couldn't hear a thing.

Robbie jumped up and ran blindly. His body was functioning. He glanced once over his shoulder, a gap opening, ten meters, fifteen. His assailant was stationary, bent over his weapon.

"Fallon!" Robbie stopped and screamed, aware he wasn't being chased. He ducked behind a stationary Land Rover. Lights were flicking on in the neighboring flats. Robbie had picture, but no sound—just the accelerating tinnitus in his ear, an alien signal from another planet. He probed the wound in his flank, felt faint at the sight of blood on his hands. Rubbing his head, he couldn't work out if the blood came from his side or his hair. If he'd been shot in the head, why was he still alive?

"Fa—" he started to shout again then suppressed the call.

Breathing raggedly, Robbie stared across the road at his assailant. An enormous black man in a beige overcoat, he seemed to be reloading his weapon. The man looked at him and called out; Robbie couldn't hear what he said.

He looked up at the face-brick building, scrutinizing the different apartments. Which floor was Fallon's flat? He regretted shouting out her name. What if the man were after her too?

He knew he must try to lead the assailant away.

"Help me!" Robbie yelled out. "Phone the police!"

He was sure someone would be calling neighborhood watch.

At that moment, the man lifted his weapon and swiveled in Robbie's direction. Robbie turned and sprinted up the road.

Samuel Chester pointed the Rossi in the direction of the fleeing kid and fired.

Click.

"Motherfucker!" Chester roared in frustration. He considered hurling the Rossi into the gutter. This was the problem with rush jobs. He'd serviced the Rossi, but hadn't had a chance to shoot with it.

No two firearms were alike.

At the strike, the first joint of his oversized index finger had slipped slightly in the trigger guard getting off the first shot before he'd intended it. He'd missed at point blank range, the bullet just skimming the kid's hair. It wouldn't have happened if he hadn't first cocked it.

He'd fired a second shot, but not clean, just grazed the kid.

Then a fucking lockup!

Malfunctions had happened to him before; more so with pistols, but sometimes with revolvers.

Twice, he recalled. A loose ejector rod that backed out under recoil. He couldn't remember the weapon. He'd also had a cylinder malfunction on a cheap Taurus. This was the last job he'd be using a Rossi, that's for sure.

Chester stared malevolently at his errant firearm, the American-flag key ring flapping below.

He opened the cylinder and examined the rounds inside.

Fucking cheap ammunition.

He removed the bullets and closed the cylinder, took aim toward the flat on his right.

A woman screamed and the lights were extinguished.

Six clicks.

Satisfied, Chester fed the four remaining bullets into the chamber then holstered the Rossi in the harness beneath his jacket.

A Smith & Wesson, Chester remembered—the first time a revolver jammed on him it was a Smith & Wesson. It was in the mouth of his victim, a lawyer from Miami.

He picked up Robbie's keys as well as the two spent casings.

The Miami lawyer thought he'd been spared. Chester had slit his throat with a kitchen knife. Not his chosen method of execution, but effective enough.

"One deaf mouse, one deaf mouse," Chester recited quietly. He considered briefly going into the block of flats, but the cacophony of whining alarms convinced him otherwise. He crossed the road and ambled towards his rental, a white Ford Fiesta courtesy of Tempest Car Hire in Sea Point.

"Have ever you seen such a thing in your..."

Chester looked leisurely about. Most of the lights that had initially gone on in the surrounding block of flats were now off, residents watching from darkened rooms.

"Have ever you seen such a thing in your house..."

Chester started the Fiesta and disappeared in the direction in which Robbie had departed.

Robbie scaled the Metrorail fence and crossed the southern-route railway line that connected Cape Town and Simonstown. He mounted the fence on the other side of the line, then jumped down.

Above the line, hugging the fence, he ran in the direction of Claremont, clutching his side. The pain refused to subside.

He crouched down against the fence and lifted his T-shirt. A cylindrical gash on his left side hurt like hell. He wiped his bloody hands on his jeans.

Fuck! I'm shot. I'm in trouble.

A memory of his first hunting experience flashed to mind, with his father and three older brothers on a game farm in Albany. Robbie was twelve. *Come on, Robbie, shoot it, shoot it.* He'd lain in the long grass and watched the kudu, its helix horns and unmistakable face paint. He'd squeezed the trigger, afraid of missing.

Kill time.

Now he was the hunted.

He tried to absorb the shock. If the attacker came after him, he'd need all his instincts to escape.

His hearing was slowly returning. The ringing in his head remained, but at least he could make out sounds from his right ear. His left ear was deaf.

Removing his beanie, Robbie tried to pinpoint the wound on his head, couldn't find one.

Another memory flashback: the twelve-year-old boy hunter, a faded photograph, his face smeared in blood.

Focus on the present!

This was no mugging. This was no barman with a baseball bat.

This was the reason for the warning.

Someone's going to kill you.

Very nearly did.

He checked his cellphone. Two missed calls from Fallon.

A Ford Fiesta cruised slowly along the road on the opposite side of the railway line.

Robbie sucked in his breath. Was it his attacker, or some random car?

The car passed Robbie's crouched position, continued up the road for another two hundred meters.

Red brake lights flashed.

Robbie silenced his Nokia and watched the car from the cover of scraggly grass growing against the fence. A row of low-walled cottages stretched the length of his view. He could either flee along the road then up to Main Road or find refuge in one of the cottages.

He looked back along the road to see if he was leaving a trail of blood. *Shit sake.*

White reverse lights lit up, the Fiesta reversing in Robbie's direction. *Stand or run?*

He still had the fence and the line between them.

The Fiesta stopped just twenty meters away. The enormous man emerged, Robbie shuddering as he recognized the gunman. Unmistakable.

"See how it runs, see how it runs."

Robbie picked up the frightening pitch of his hunter's voice. His body readied for flight. But if he made a break for it now, the man would have several free shots at him through the fence.

The man fiddled with an object in his hand, looked about. Up the road. Down the road. Back at the houses on the Rosebank side.

What was he looking for? Robbie wondered. The point where Robbie had climbed the fence and crossed the line was at least a kilometer back.

The man stepped onto the narrow pavement and pressed up against the railway fence. He seemed to be looking for a way to the other side.

Robbie kept his head down, barely breathing. If he heard the fence take the man's weight, he'd make a dash for it.

His assailant consulted the object in his hand again, sang out once more: "Never have seen such a thing in his life."

The sound of approaching sirens disturbed his rhyme. Chester looked about and cursed. Should be called the country of sirens, he muttered. He buttoned his overcoat and returned to the Fiesta, drove off down the road.

Not to worry. The mouse couldn't go anywhere.

Robbie reached the intersection of Main Road and hailed a minibus taxi heading north towards the city. The loose arm of the marshal swung out of the passenger window and the taxi halted immediately. A tailing tow-truck veered into the right lane, hooting as the taxi's door slid open and Robbie hopped in, drawing gasps from the passengers.

"Can you take me to Groote Schuur?" he said.

"Shap, babba," said the driver calmly and accelerated. The marshal reached back and slammed the door like a guillotine.

Robbie shuffled to the back, slouched down next to a dodgy looking character with flashy sunglasses. Kwaito blared from the speakers, seemed to flex the vehicle like a plastic packet.

Robbie pulled R50 from the back pocket of his jeans and passed the note forward. He watched it go from hand to hand and reach the marshal, who pocketed it and returned two twenty rand notes. The change followed the same hand-to-hand route back.

Robbie leaned back and clutched his side. The blood on his hand had dried a crusty brown. He bit his lip and tried to stay calm. He had no idea how bad his injuries were, was scared he'd bleed to death.

The taxi jerked to a halt, two people got out and one in. The departing passengers looked back at Robbie through the window. Robbie closed his eyes momentarily. He knew he mustn't lose consciousness. The man in the Fiesta had been waiting for him outside Fallon's flat.

How did he know?

Robbie pulled out his Nokia. No more missed calls from Fallon. He thought to call her, decided not to. She'd heard his voice on the intercom, the gunshots; she must know the danger.

The man had been able to follow him along the railway line. But he hadn't seemed rushed or urgent. Seemed to know where he was.

How did he know?

The taxi came to a stop below Groote Schuur Hospital. Robbie clambered out and dragged himself off toward the emergency room.

As the taxi pulled away down Main Road, a passenger in the back seat noticed that the injured whiteboy had forgotten his cellphone on the seat.

THE SILENCE OF DEATH

Chester turned on the rental car radio, pressed the first auto select button.

First button. A language he didn't understand. He listened to a rapid barrage of strange clicks then tried the next one.

The second and third buttons were static.

The fourth tuned to Heart Radio 104.9FM, a silky woman playing soul on the community station. Chester liked her accent. He figured he might like to take her on his next Caribbean cruise.

His BlackBerry rested on the passenger seat. He crossed the Belmont Road bridge and turned right at Fountain Circle into Main Road, checking his position against the moving coordinates of his target.

Chester patted the top pocket of his overcoat. Before setting off from the Woodstock Holiday Inn, he'd removed his Cartier and placed it in the top pocket of his beige jacket. He'd damaged expensive watches before on jobs. No need to be careless.

The song ended and DJ Shafika announced: "It's eight-thirty and the night is opening up to the sisters and brothers of soul. But not everyone shares our trust and love. I had a call from a mournful Marney. He says the end of the world is nigh. What do you think?"

Chester rolled up a sleeve and examined the bite marks on his arm.

Animal, he thought. The kid had broken his skin. Chester knew a dark bruise would form around the imprints of the teeth. He'd need a shot probably. But he didn't harbor any thoughts of vengeance; expected nothing less from a target. He would simply carry out the hit as intended. It seemed petty to take revenge on someone about to die.

"I'm taking a call from Faizel," DJ Shafika said.

Chester turned off the radio.

"Course there's an end of the world, you morons," Chester reflected. "The crust of the earth's gonna peel off and hot lava's gonna run red all over."

He followed Main Road, stopping at each traffic light.

"Problem is everyone talking about dates. Armageddon. But the grim reaper don't know that shit. He don't know nobody's dates."

Parallel to the old Mowbray Hotel, he checked his BlackBerry and noticed that the target had turned and was moving in another direction altogether.

Night came to Khayelitsha with no respite.

The wooden door of the corrugated iron-shack smashed open and a huge shape ducked under the metal frame.

Lying in bed with his three brothers, Kwela was woken by the noise, watched the shadow, and beyond that the gaping hole in their house. The terror gripped the children simultaneously, Kwela pinched his closest sibling and the warning of silence was passed along, not a sound uttered, each remembering the last time the door was broken down.

"Hello there," a honey-toned voice called out into the darkness.

The enormous man coughed, surprised at the open fire smoldering on the floor.

Kwela fingered the Nokia. Somehow he sensed it was connected to this evil. It was the fat pig, Mxenxe, his mother's boyfriend, with his greasy head and gangster sunglasses, who'd given Kwela the phone. A bribe in return for absolution: the beating given to Kwela's mother on Saturday after the football. Why was his mother, so fearless, prepared to accept that scumbag's temper? Kwela would never forgive. He would wait and wait. One day Mxenxe would expose his belly.

The Nokia still had contact names from the previous owner. It had rung twice. If his mother knew, she'd never have let him keep it. He hoped it didn't ring now.

Chester removed his BlackBerry and checked the global positioning coordinates. It was exact. He was very close. He replaced the phone and removed the Rossi from his shoulder holster. He tested the grip, his fat index finger now accustomed to the trigger guard.

He was mad as hell. Getting into this labyrinth of metal shacks in a motorcar required falcon-like skills. It had taken nearly two hours to locate the GPS coordinates broadcast from his BlackBerry application. He'd dropped the Fiesta in a massive pothole and dinged the fender; rental people were going to argue about that.

The poor roads and dead ends had exhausted his patience. He felt as if he'd left the planet and entered another world.

The kid sure had guts to run as hard as he did. Wouldn't expect to be found in here. A great hideout. But nothing stopped Chester on a hunt.

Carlos had called, twice, but Chester wouldn't respond until the assignment was complete.

He cursed his own incompetence. He should have got it right the first time.

Getting old, man. Getting old.

Now he had a damaged rental and his mood was blacker than anthracite. He nearly tripped over a steel bath in the room.

"Fuck this toxic hole to death!" he bellowed as the rim whacked against his shin. Another bruise. He patted his top pocket, checked on his watch.

The iron walls creaked.

Chester spun about and listened, Rossi aimed toward the sound.

"Have ever you seen such a thing in your life?" Chester recited.

He checked the coordinates again. Spot on.

"Come out, my friend. Time for the reckoning."

Silence.

Chester coughed loudly, cursed his lack of torch light. He placed both hands on the Rossi and wiggled his finger inside trigger guard. Last time he'd ever use a Rossi, he reminded himself.

The room remained silent but, as Chester knew, silence is not stillness. Some primal instinct prickled the hair on the back of his neck. Then he felt it. Like a sting....A thin, hot spike stabbing into his spine, ending with the thump of the fist against his back, a second blow directly into his heart through his back.

He sucked in his air. Didn't bother to turn or fire.

He slipped down to his knees.

Kwela pulled out the sharpened screwdriver and screamed to his neighbor for help.

SOMETHING

"Hello, honey," his wife said. "When you coming home?"

Carlos watched her like a hawk on the screen of his laptop as he held the phone to his ear. The camera mounted in the foyer showed her on the house phone, back to him; he could see the line of her G-string through her silky white pants.

He closed his eyes. A dark beard covered his face from three days without shaving. When they opened, she was still standing in the same place.

"Soon," he said. A tray of breakfast was untouched on the carpet beside his bed. "What have you been up to?"

"Oh, the usual. Being a mommy."

She twisted around and looked up toward the camera. She looked confident and relaxed.

Carlos clicked next and panned through the seven internal zooms.

A flicker on the TV screen distracted him. A shooting in a Seattle coffee shop. Four dead. Carlos looked away. Nothing was safe. Nothing was like it should be.

He had worked throughout the night, without sleep, to restore his internal operating system. His thinking was muddled, as if someone had dragged an eraser randomly across his brain. Strange thoughts and memories were triggered. He couldn't concentrate on one thing.

He clicked back to the foyer camera. His wife stood before the mirror, adjusting her breasts.

"Seriously," she said. "When can we expect you?"

Carlos tabbed to the camera posted outside the front of his house. The T&D van was still outside.

He clicked next.

The front garden camera panned across the front lawn down to the water's edge. He could see the jetty. Wondered if he'd ever sit on it again.

The rainfall measure cylinder was visible in the flowerbed to the left. He zoomed in. No further rain since he'd checked it last night.

Jacker had found him, he was sure.

He cut his wife off as his screen filled with the last usage statistics from the Dark Video Trojan site.

Carlos closed his eyes and tried to concentrate. He recognized that paranoia was a dangerous affliction, that he must remain rational and make decisions without emotion. Numerous incidents had raised his suspicions in the past; none had turned out to be consequential. Of course, the telecom van could be a coincidence. And Jacker could have been taking a flyer about the weather in Yarrow Point.

He drew the blinds and stretched out on his bed. He tried to imagine that the room was a tomb and when his eyes closed he would never awaken.

No.

He wasn't imagining it.

He tried to phone Chester in Africa but got no response. More paranoia. What if Chester was involved? No, not possible. But he wished Chester was available. It would be comforting just to be aware of his presence. Though he had no way of deploying him against a virtual enemy.

The scent of danger burned like cordite in his nostrils. The thought of another flight from danger, another reinvention of his life, seemed more daunting than before. He'd been younger then, more elastic.

Maybe I'm wrong, he thought, his judgment troubled.

No. There was no doubt.

After the call to Jacker the previous night, he'd rerun the German's persistent cookie. No attempted breaches. Which surely proved Jacker wasn't looking for him. But something still didn't seem right.

He flicked through his Yarrow Point cameras again. He couldn't see his wife. He bit down on his lower lip. *Fuck her!*

She must be in with the FBI.

Carlos lowered his head and squeezed his forehead between his thumb and index finger. The shooting in Seattle, the telecom truck, Chester's unanswered calls, his wife's G-string, Jacker's laughing avatars.

"No!" he shouted to the empty room.

Carlos rebooted the laptop and function keyed into the BIOS before Windows booted. He started a reformat of the drive and then walked to the bathroom and flushed his face under the taps.

Time was crucial. Every second would count.

He returned to the bedroom and checked his passport. Christopher Davidson. Pocketed the wallet stuffed with hundred dollar bills. It would have to do. The flash drive he slipped down the front of his jeans.

Then he packed his toilet bag and clothing and left the laptop reformatting on the top of the unmade bed.

HOW IT WORKS

Early morning in Khayelitsha, commuters already bustling toward the taxi rank, a crowd gathered outside the shanty home of Kwela's mother.

Constables Mgwena and Rykens from the Lingulethu West Police Station returned to the police car to await the arrival of the detective from the Western Cape Organized Crime Unit. This was the third murder radioed in last night, but the first site attended. Something very odd about this one.

Rykens had five hundred US dollars in his pocket; likewise Mgwena. They counted themselves very fortunate. Although the call had been received at the station last night, they'd pretended no patrol cars were available. A midnight murder call in Mandela Park was no one's idea of a good time. The body had lain in the shack for hours; the money could have easily gone missing.

Mgwena dug his hands deeper into the pockets of his blue pants. He kicked at a stone with his boot, fingering the worn Cartier he'd found in the victim's pocket. He hadn't told Rykens about that.

Rykens leaned against the police car and fiddled with the cellphone found on the body. He pulled out the SIM card and tossed it on the ground. The GPS-enabled BlackBerry would make a great replacement for his rickety Siemens. Mgwena was eyeing it too, but possession was ten tenths of the law in these parts. The Rossi .38 and shoulder holster were long gone.

"What you make of this shit?" Rykens asked his partner.

Mgwena shrugged.

"I thought they were joking, man. A fucking American!" Rykens snorted through a thick handlebar moustache. The car-rental papers gave the victim's name as Sylvester Chambers, an American citizen.

Mgwena shifted his feet back and forth in the dust.

"It's got the Twitter going on the Flats, hey!" Rykens commented. Last count there were 60,000 gang members in the Cape alone, the Americans and the Mongrels key rivals for the lucrative tik and mandrax markets. He eyed out the gathering crowd. "Why these blackies not in gangs, huh?"

Mgwena remained silent.

"Maybe they don't like Guccis and Ray-Bans," laughed Rykens.

"They've got gangs," Mgwena said gruffly.

The police radio crackled and Rykens answered. The detective was lost. Rykens provided rudimentary directions. He looked up at the knot of illegally connected wires.

"No burning tires for landmarks," Rykens joked. He pointed to a stream of sewerage running down the hill. "Told him to follow the shit."

Mgwena was worried about the watch. It wasn't right.

"What's a larney like him looking for in a place like this?" Rykens persisted.

Mgwena lowered his chin into the collar of his jacket.

"Probably pussy." Rykens answered his own question and laughed.

"Here? How's your mind, man?" Mgwena scowled.

A young kwedien came forward and stopped in front of Constable Rykens.

"Ja, what you want, snotnose?" Rykens said. He winked at his partner.

Kwela, looking at his feet, opened his palms and passed Rykens the Nokia. Behind him, Kwela's mother stood at the mouth of the shack, hands on her hips.

Rykens tossed the phone to Mgwena.

"One for you, huh, buddy."

DON'T STEP BACK

"Your mother's been worried." Milton Cullen's rough voice sounded tired, far away.

"I'm OK," Robbie replied.

There was a long silence. The father who never asked questions, slept with one eye open.

"I made some bad choices, that's all," Robbie said eventually. He adjusted the bandage around his waist.

"We all do that," Cullen replied and cleared his throat. Robbie could picture his father's calloused hands on the receiver. Tanned skin with deep veins bulging from the back; hands you'd like on your shoulder.

"Dad, I..."

Robbie swallowed. He remembered rugby matches played in places like Queenstown and King William's Town, his father driving him and three other players from St. Andrews in the family's Toyota Hilux. He'd sit in the passenger seat, leaning over the back of the headrest to chat with his friends. Milton Cullen just drove. After the match, Cullen would stop at the Engen and buy Cokes. Win or lose, he didn't say anything.

After a long pause, Cullen senior spoke. "It's real dry here."

The Cullen farm was losing money. Transport costs were mounting. The new factory in Bathurst was taking time.

"Mom told me," Robbie answered.

Then there were labor problems, government regulations, new production equipment required, security issues.

"The dam's near empty. We're going to be irrigating with sand one of these days."

Cullen senior was preoccupied with the weather. It was something he could do nothing about.

"Mom says she's going to open a guesthouse."

"The auditor's been on at me," Cullen said, ignoring Robbie's distraction. "I might need one of those machines of yours soon." He spoke of a computer like it was a harvester.

"I'll help you," Robbie replied after a long pause. "I have a little unfinished business, then I'll be home for the holidays."

The farm line crackled.

Unfinished business. No going back.

But Milton Cullen was silent.

Robbie had got his hair cut at last, looked like a soldier.

The last few days had been impossible. It was now three weeks before midyear exams and he hadn't caught up with his lecture notes yet.

Three days after he'd been shot, agents from the Federal Bureau of Investigation, no less, had interviewed him by telephone. Specialists in Global Internet Crime on a conference call from Washington DC.

He learned that his assailant, an American citizen called Samuel Chester, who'd entered South Africa on a false passport and was on the Feds' wanted list, was killed in Khayelitsha, hours after the attack in Rosebank. The license plates on the Ford Fiesta abandoned in Khayelitsha linked Chester to the attack in Rosebank.

The Feds were obviously keen to find out why Robbie thought Chester attacked him, though they already knew. They had viewed the shower video and questioned him relentlessly about the details of its creation.

Were you aware that you were being filmed in the shower video?

No.

Were you paid for participating in the shower video?

No.

Has anyone ever approached you to spike someone's drink?

No.

Have you ever heard of Dark Video?

No.

Robbie stretched and opened the door to his room. His perforated eardrum was on the mend. Strolling down the corridor, he pushed open the door of Denny le Roux's empty room.

Have you ever heard of the Mickey Finn Club?

Yes.

Four barmen from Blue Venus, blond surfer included, were in custody. The initial barman caught by the Narcotics Squad for drink spiking had spilled the beans on the others. The Feds were letting the local police run those cases, were only interested in the online activity.

Denny le Roux had been arrested in Durban. There was talk that the barmen were plea bargaining, would turn state witnesses. There were bigger fish to fry.

The Feds had been particularly interested in Robbie's recount of his meeting with Sylvana at Gorky Park and the subsequent discovery of her "body" at the house in Rondebosch.

Robbie continued down the corridor and hobbled down the stairs. The sun was bright but weak. He smiled as he viewed a text from Vusi Mahlaba, skipper of his rugby team.

Anything to get out of a game against
Maties, huh Rob?

His phone was crazy. There was another, this one from a friend in Kopano:

When I said you needed shots, it was figurative,
Rob. Figurative.

Robbie paused to enjoy the sunlight on his bare arms. He was coming out of one dark tunnel, entering another: exams. But they seemed like a walk in the park now—despite the ultimatum. Pass, and his Johannesburg-based bursars would be funding his final two semesters; fail, and he'd be farming with his father. Pineapples and chicory.

It's real dry.

Don't take a step back.

The day before, he'd met with Melanie, his ex, at the Josephine Mill. He pictured her expression, huge eyes, mouth wide open, as he related his story.

"A few months without me and look what happens to you," she'd joked.

She'd noticed his missing bracelet. Though she hadn't said anything, he'd sensed all was not well in Picasso-land.

Then he'd got her invite, a note in an envelope pinned on the notice board. "Come join us at Elevation, Friday night. Mel."

Us?

He wasn't sure. Exams were now an all-consuming priority.

But it was what accompanied the note that made up his mind. He twirled the new elephant-hair bracelet in his hand.

THE CAPTAIN'S INSTINCT

Robbie strolled across the car park to his Mazda, washed and polished.

He jumped in and started the engine. First time. The latest copy of The *Big Issue* lay on the passenger seat. Robbie was going for a quick drink at the Rugby Club, hadn't made up his mind about Elevation. A tap on the window startled him.

"Hello skattie," Captain Vermaak said, dressed in blue, carrying a leather briefcase. "Didn't mean to spook you."

Robbie raised his eyebrows, surprised, took a deep breath and wound down the window.

"Can I get in?" She walked around to the passenger door; Robbie leaned over and popped the lock.

"I know you work with the big boys now, but something still bothers me," she said, once she'd taken her seat. She smelled of stale cigarette smoke.

The big boys....A second interview with the FBI that morning, two clean-shaven suits had flown out to Cape Town and they'd joined him on the conference call.

Have you ever heard of Julian Lynch?

No.

Why do you think you were sent a CCTV photograph of Lynch's car entering his premises?

No idea. I didn't know anything about it, just delivered the note as per instructions.

They'd impounded his laptop. Robbie had complained about his exams, wondered if their influence stretched to his computer science department. They said they'd only keep it for a couple of days.

Vermaak pulled out a file from her leather briefcase, opened a hardcover notebook.

"I've made my head blunt on all this," she said.

Robbie smiled.

"The blood on your shoes. The girl we spoke to."

She was searching for the name.

"Sylvana," Robbie reminded her. He'd heard enough about her for a while.

This Ms. Natlova—the girl you know as Sylvana—had you met her before the weekend in Plettenberg Bay at Mr. Beacon's residence?

No.

To whom was she planning to sell the video?
I don't know.
Did she ever mention Julian Lynch's name?
No.
What happened to the blood sample you say you took from your shoes?
I don't know. It was taken from my room.

"Ja, Sylvana," Vermaak said. "The stripper girl. So they pretended she goes home to Ukraine then another girl takes her place."

Robbie nodded. None of this would have been known without the international assistance. As he'd suspected, it hadn't been Sylvana who'd answered the call when Vermaak phoned her number from the Wynberg Police Station on the day Robbie reported her supposed murder. Identity theft. The real Sylvana had been running Internet video scams, selling student videos—with or without consent—to websites like Uselessjunk and Watchit. The Feds believed she had crossed Dark Video and been murdered as a result. The new Sylvana was in custody facing deportation. Local forensics had been dispatched to the Lendell Road house, and found traces of blood-spatter, matching blood samples to a headless body washed up near Hermanus two weeks previously.

"So you was right," Vermaak said, looked up at Robbie and grinned. Robbie said nothing. He wanted to be done with this shit, move on. Seeing Vermaak reminded him of that terrible morning at the Wynberg Police Station.

"And the big American who killed her," Vermaak continued. "He comes after you, because you were her partner?"

Robbie pulled the seat belt and grimaced.

"As I understand it," he said. "They don't know that, uh, this Chester guy killed her. Dark Video thought I was working with, I guess, the competition. That's the theory, anyway."

Vermaak's yellow teeth showed. "Julian Lynch was a Dark Video client," she said.

She got one thing right, Robbie thought ironically. He'd also learned about Lynch from the Feds, about the abduction of Jacqui Simpson, the link to Dark Video, and that the photograph he'd given to Vermaak had saved the girl's life. Robbie was at least pleased that Tony Beacon's name had been cleared.

"All sorts of theories," Vermaak remarked. "We thought you were, maybe, working with the barmen."

"I know," said Robbie patiently.

"Who sent the tip-off? That picture of Lynch's red BMW?"

"I told you I don't know."

"No idea who?"

Robbie shook his head.

"No idea," he said. "Ask the FBI. They're chasing the same information in about twenty countries."

Robbie was keen to meet up with his mates at the rugby club. He pointed to the clock on the Mazda dashboard, which was half an hour slow. "I've unfortunately got to meet some people," he said.

"I'm sorry to be delaying you. Are you hitting the clubs tonight?" she said, looking intensely at him.

"Maybe. No dancing, though," he replied, indicating his injured side.

She smiled. "A few more minutes."

A car full of students hurried down the hill. Friday night. They would have an exciting evening ahead, Vermaak thought without resentment. For her, it didn't really matter whether it was Friday or Monday, except she wouldn't have to get up early tomorrow. She would go home to her flat in Bellville as she always did, feed the cat, and hope for something interesting on television.

"You see these barmen at Blue Venus. All we make is a big hole for someone worse. We must break the problem. Catch the organizers, the ones who fetch and carry the victims."

"I understand," said Robbie. "How can I help you?"

"Tell me. This Chester. Where he jumped you. How did he know?"

"Captain, I've gone over this before. It's in the report," Robbie replied, patience being tested. "He used a tracking device in my cellphone. I assumed as much and left it in a minibus taxi, which is how he ended up in Khayelitsha."

"Yes, I'm sorry. I don't read a lot. Now the cellphone. The calls you got on the night of the attack. Who did you say made them again?"

"Which calls?"

Vermaak consulted her files.

"There were two missed calls on your cellphone. At about quarter past eight."

How far should he one take his discretion? Robbie wondered. He imagined the drug busts at the Blue Venus must be attributable to Fallon's team. He wasn't going to blow her cover to this bumbling cop.

"My cellphone was never found."

Vermaak removed Robbie's battered Nokia from her jacket pocket.

"Unfortunately the contacts and numbers are different." She looked at the list. "I am sorry but I have to keep it."

Constable Rykens and Mgwena had enjoyed their stolen possessions for exactly eight hours. Back at Lingulethu West station, Rykens had flashed Chester's BlackBerry to a colleague, who jealously informed the station commander. Under immediate cross-examination, Rykens confessed and shopped Mgwena in the same breath. Both constables were suspended.

Robbie nodded and stared at his old Nokia. He'd got himself a second-hand Siemens in the meantime.

"Just a girl I was visiting. The missed calls on my phone were from her."

"Oh," said Vermaak.

"Why do you ask?"

Vermaak looked at her notes.

"You said....Yes, here it is...I presumed the warning message, 'Someone is going to kill you,' came from a barman at Blue Venus."

"Yes. I was wrong."

"Mr. Cullen. We are looking for the, uh....I can't think how you call it. The brains?"

Robbie narrowed his eyes. As he understood it, the brains were Dark Video. The FBI had made that much clear.

"Can you look at some pictures?" She looked down at an identikit then flashed one at Robbie. "Do you recognize this man?"

She showed a picture of Kryff to Robbie.

"No."

Vermaak held up another picture: a young man with a pointy chin.

"No."

A blurred image of an old woman wearing a scarf.

"No. Come on, that could be anyone. How much more of this is there?"

"Sorry, just one more. I've also got this."

Vermaak fumbled through her papers, produced an identikit sketch of a young woman.

"Do you know her?"

Robbie stared at the illustration.

"Recognize her?" Vermaak pushed.

Robbie shrugged and wound down his window. He stared out across the hockey field. "She looks like lots of people I know," he said eventually.

The last time Robbie had seen Fallon was the night he'd passed out in his room. She hadn't answered any of his calls. Then, just her voice briefly on that intercom.

Vermaak raised her hand. "The number that called your phone that night is not in use any more," she said, changing tack.

Robbie nodded. He'd tried Fallon's number numerous times, visited her flat. No response. The landlady of the Rosebank apartment block had told him number 15 was vacant, the previous lessee some attorney in Johannesburg.

Vermaak stared out of the window. She wasn't sure why she'd come to find the boy. Perhaps she was wasting her time. The day before she'd shown photographs of each item found in Lynch's memento box to the reported date-rape victims on the local database. Angie Dean's ID and bangle, Marianne Combrink's charm bracelet, Jacqui Simpson's cell-phone. She even had a hunch about the bloodied ring—from an eyebrow, not an ear, she reckoned. But she wasn't looking for recognition. She'd given up on that long ago. She wasn't looking for praise from her own people or the bloody American smart-asses in their shiny suits.

And she wasn't particularly trying to make amends for making fun of Robbie Cullen's report of Sylvana's death, and not believing his date-rape claims. She was just doing what she knew.

She had stayed in this job because she didn't know what else to do, how to fill her day if she didn't have the discipline of the force. She stayed in it because she was good at it, despite all the *kak* she had to put up with. She had plenty to give to it—but she no longer wished to give it.

Though she'd lost her enthusiasm, the instincts remained. Some of them. When she'd first met Robbie Cullen, she'd assumed he was mad. An attention-seeker. A prankster. But she hadn't been listening. Now that she was listening, he seemed not to be saying anything. She felt a need to protect him.

"The girl who phoned you. That you were visiting."

"Yes," replied Robbie.

"Does this girl look anything like this sketch?"

"Maybe," said Robbie. "Maybe."

Vermaak cleared her throat. She wasn't sure why she'd asked the question. Clearly Cullen was visiting a girlfriend when Chester struck. She felt suddenly tired. Wanted to put her feet up and sit with Kitty and drink Klipdrift.

"Did you actually bust that Lynch character?" Robbie asked to break the silence, regretting the question immediately, knowing it would only extend the Captain's enquiry.

"Ja," she replied without pride. Vermaak made to exit the car, paused. "You know, Mr. Cullen. He was fokken nuts, hey. Collected all sorts of shit, was a serial sex offender. In the end, he wanted to kill himself. You know, so he was in control at the end and could go out—how do they say?—on his own terms. He's in jail now, Pollsmoor, nice white guy probably being looked after by the gangsters, if you know what I mean. And when he gets into court they'll send him to Valkenberg or wherever and the shrinks are going to be fokken falling over each other to study him in his little cell for the next fifty years. Jissis, he was living in a complete fantasy. I'm told the correct term is 'delusional disorder.'"

Vermaak used her forefingers to signify quotation marks. Shook her head, smiled, before continuing.

Robbie fiddled with his keys.

"Turns out he had this fetish for young girls because he never got to see his daughter. Pretty little thing. Called Holly. Ex-wife was a total bitch, he said, got a restraining order so he couldn't contact either of them. Tragic, hey, because he loved her so much, had photographs of her everywhere, would secretly watch her playing sport at school, spent his life obsessing about her, that's how much he loved her. But you know what the best bit is?"

Robbie shook his head.

"She wasn't even his daughter. Lynch never had any children. After they got the divorce, the ex-wife met someone else and had the kid with him. Things aren't always like you think they are, hey?"

THE BITTEREST PILL

Robbie turned his back on the VIP bar and looked across the dance floor. After midnight on a Friday at Elevation and the nightclub was peaking.

He was excited, expecting a special guest.

He'd thought long and hard about Melanie's second message, the one that had appeared the day after the first. "Picasso over. Meet me at Elevation at 12. Love, Mel."

After his surprise visit from Captain Vermaak, he'd nursed a couple of beers at the UCT Rugby Club, then driven back to Kopano and hung out at the Verge Inn. Meet me at Elevation at 12. Decision time. Now he waited at the bar in anticipation.

The doors of the silver lift opened and a fresh batch of clubbers marched urgently into Elevation. Robbie fingered the new elephant-hair bracelet and leaned back against the bar. He wasn't much of a clubber, wore a creased pair of khaki pants and a pale-blue collared shirt, sleeves rolled below the elbow. Close to his best.

A barman tapped him on the back.

"Another?"

He had at least two sips left in a brown bottle of Castle lager.

"I'm good," he said, half turning his head.

The Black Eyed Peas were moving the clubbers. An endless supply of leggy models and suavely dressed men were grinding away. *Tonight's gonna be a good night.* Robbie felt the infectious excitement of the room course through his veins. *Tonight's gonna be a real good night.*

Robbie caught his breath as he spotted her, stepping out of the silver-plated lift and gliding across the room toward him. She wore a black leather mini skirt, paper-thin black top, buttons open, tied at the bottom to expose her belly button.

Robbie stared.

Tonight's gonna be a good good night. Woohoo!

The club vibrated with energy.

She smiled in acknowledgement and shifted the silver bangles on her left wrist.

"Fallon. Geez, what a surprise to see you here."

Robbie grasped her hand. She pushed her body against his, transferring heat, the intoxicating scent of vanilla perfume evoking an immediate reaction.

"You smell good," she whispered, nuzzling into his neck, slipping a wet tongue across his ear. "I won't ask you what you've got on. I can feel it."

Robbie straightened up, shifted backwards. *Lust was the most obvious of the seven deadly sins*, he thought.

"Oh my god," Fallon said, noticing the stitches above his right ear. He flinched as she reached out and touched the wound. "What happened to you?"

Robbie adjusted the bandage beneath his shirt.

"Long story," he said, his eyes searching hers.

Her frown remained.

"I'm serious, Robbie. What happened?" She ran her hand through his hair. "You've had a haircut."

"Where've you been?" he said, an accusatory tone.

"Nowhere," she turned and looked behind her then back at him, raised her eyebrows.

Robbie shook his head slowly.

"Why don't you answer your calls," Robbie stated.

"Oh that," she answered, reached into her handbag and pulled out a cellphone in a cute pink cover. "I lost my old one. Let me give you my new—"

Robbie caught her hand.

"You don't believe me?" she said, surprised. "What's the matter, Robbie? What happened to you?"

"You didn't get my message? Last week? You didn't hear the flipping shooting outside your flat?"

Fallon's eyes were wide.

"My flat? Where? In Rosebank?"

Robbie's jaw was set; he folded his arms.

"I haven't lived there for a month. That was temporary. I've got an apartment in Green Point."

Robbie stared out at the dance floor, chugged the remnants of his beer. It had been her voice on the intercom, he was sure of it. Just like it had been Sylvana's body in Lendell Road. He pulled out his Siemens and checked the time on the face.

"You meeting someone?" she asked, a hint of disappointment in her voice.

He nodded.

"Hey!" Fallon tapped Robbie, indicated over his shoulder to the waiting barman.

"What'll it be?"

Fallon reached into her Gothic handbag, extracted her wallet. "Jack and ginger," she said to the barman before Robbie could react. "Times two."

"Not for me," Robbie declined, but the barman had already taken the order and spun on his heels.

Fallon turned to him and took his hand lightly. Her proximity was like an electric charge, her pouting lips glossy under the club lights, the lacy edges of her black bra peeking out.

"I'm sorry, Robbie. Don't be angry with me." She smiled, sorry, seductive.

Robbie folded his arms again, tried to think with his head—the one on top.

The barman returned with their drinks; Fallon paid with a two-hundred-rand note.

"For old times' sake," she said, smiling again.

She reached into an ice bucket on the bar counter and scooped out a handful of cubes.

"You want?" she offered Robbie.

He nodded and she opened her palm and slipped a handful of cubes into his drink.

"So," he said, chinking his glass against hers. "You must be pleased with the outcome at Blue Venus."

"Yes. Very. A lot of bad bastards." Her fringe dipped over her eye as she sipped her drink.

"So, who you meeting?" she asked.

Robbie stared at her.

"You," he said.

Fallon looked confused, frowned back at him for a moment. Then her long eyelashes fluttered, irises black pinpricks in her green eyes.

"Melanie would never call her boyfriend Picasso," Robbie said.

He removed the glass of Jack and ginger from her hand, took a long sip, and exchanged it with his. "You can have mine," he said.

Then he raised his right hand and two plain-clothed policemen descended on them.

SNOWED UNDER

Carlos drew the blinds and stretched out on the narrow bed. He tried to imagine that the room was a tomb and when his eyes closed, he would never awaken.

But he couldn't sleep. The revelations of the past week, and his painful escape into Canada via the Pacific Highway border post at Blaine, poisoned any chance of repose. He'd driven for two days to get to Toronto.

And without sleep there could be no rebirth.

Outside, unseasonal snow like white mold gathered on the pathway of the guesthouse he'd found in Davenport, a quiet suburb north of the CBD. It would have to do for now. $71 per night, one bedroom, one bathroom, lounge and kitchen joined. He was paying cash for everything, didn't dare use a card.

Carlos dressed warmly and drove his rental into downtown Toronto, purchased a Sony VAIO laptop from the Future Shop on Yonge Street and a set of handgrips at the SportChek down the road.

He returned and unboxed the laptop in the lounge.

Not quite the surroundings he'd become accustomed to, but he'd started from scratch before and he could do it again.

He removed the precious red flash disk from a rubber condom and inserted it into the USB drive. The computer immediately recognized the device.

What do you want to do?

Carlos navigated to an install directory and selected rebuild. He'd tested the rebuild many times over. The computer beeped.

ERROR

The discordant clang of the message struck to his core.

He'd tested the upload religiously every month. Could it be the Sony? Surely not, it had an Intel processor and ran Windows 7.

He tried again.

ERROR

Nothing.

The realization came to Carlos like an ancient instinct; with it a quickening of the senses, the overwhelming threat of danger. If he couldn't reload from the flash disk...

Everything was gone, the electronic extensions of his brain lost forever.

Carlos picked up the handgrips and pumped violently.

It wasn't just his business. His system controlled everything, including his international bank accounts and overseas mailboxes.

Carlos dropped the handgrips; closed his eyes and took a deep breath. He'd have to rely on his memory—his trusted memory.

He logged on to Skype, his standard address without any security. No point. He had no way of locating Jacker's protected address, and Jacker wouldn't recognize him anyway.

One last chance: an email to Jacker the old-fashioned way. He logged into his old Hotmail address, tried to summon Jacker's address from the depths of his frazzled mind. His hacker ran the same system as Carlos had: if someone wanted to get hold of Jacker, they could email an address that he accessed by bouncing through various portals to avoid detection.

Got it!

He recalled the address, sent an email with his non-secured Skype information. This was urgent; it would have to do.

To his relief, Jacker came online within a minute in the guise of the laughing clown. He'd been waiting for his call. Carlos let out a gasp of air, increased the audio volume on the Sony.

"Jacker. I can't reload. The rebuild function, it's—"

"Tough break," Jacker interrupted. "Tell me where you are and I'll send an engineer over."

Carlos paused. It was as bad as he'd believed.

"You're kidding me."

"Wanna see the action I got from Yarrow Point?"

Video streamed onto his screen. Police and FBI agents congregating in his road, then bursting through the door, his wife in a nightie, kid in her arms. On screen, his wife screaming; an agent gripping her tightly by the arm.

It was like an ice pick through his heart; his perfect world crumbling before his eyes.

"Jacker, you must help me. We can get it all back. I will reward you handsomely."

"Retire and give me all your business?"

Carlos paused. He needed to soothe Jacker. Play for time. Then he'd engage every resource at his disposal to exterminate him.

"How did they find me?" he spoke softly.

Jacker laughed: "Bugger! A blasted tip-off."

"*You* found me?" Carlos spluttered. He closed his eyes. "How?"

"You really think I'd tell you that?" Jacker replied.

Carlos pulled at his hair. He was sweating profusely. He couldn't think, couldn't concentrate.

"Let's just say that I learned something from your previous operator in Cape Town," Jacker said, unable to resist blowing his trumpet. "The Gorillas gang. When I cleared the dead operator's hard drive, I found a reverse phone book. They were using it to decrypt GSM conversations—your mobile calls. You never found out how they nearly got to you. A big mistake."

His biggest mistake. Carlos thought about the pay-as-you-go cellphones, the little conversations he'd had with his wife. Suddenly it seemed to him that everything was a mistake. All the years of meticulous caution wasted.

Jacker laughed.

"They're amateurs. Verizon, Sprint, T-Mobile," Jacker gloated as he listed US cellular-network providers. "They think that they're secure because they encrypt the voice signal between the cellphone and base station."

Carlos looked back at the screen. His wife looked so small, vulnerable. The kid was screaming. *His* kid...

"But the end-to-end signal within the phone network..." Jacker continued but Carlos was not listening. "Fucking wide open."

Carlos eventually broke his silence—he could try one more approach.

"So, Jacker, you want to run Dark Video?" he asked.

Jacker laughed maniacally.

"Do I want to *run* Dark Video? I *am* Dark Video!"

"What?"

"You're a fool, Carlos. *I* have the list of the Dark Video clients."

"How?" gasped Carlos.

"The very way you hypothesized. Perhaps you're not such a fool then?"

"But....The cookie....You couldn't have..."

"Well, then I couldn't have," Jacker replied, his voice dripping with sarcasm. "*Ich liebe dich*, eh Carlos?"

Carlos's heart froze. The German scientist? Jacker?

"I bet you're wondering about the client busts?"

Carlos barely listened.

"A clean-up....Thought I'd rid the business of the rubbish. Before I took over. A few tip-offs here and there. Even stirred up the Mickey Finn barmen. We don't want that risky business, now do we?"

Carlos ground his teeth. He tore his gaze away from the screen of the Sony; it was like the FBI were crawling around inside him, stripping him of his life force.

"I have everything now, Carlos," Jacker continued. "Access to every secret you ever possessed. You're going to kick yourself until the day you die."

"I'll find you," Carlos hissed, his fists clenched, rage like a thunderstorm.

"Who will you find?" said Jacker. "I'm not just Dark Video, you know? I'm also Carlos. And you're nothing. You are shit."

"Jacker!" Carlos cursed.

"You always said you were a figment of the imagination, Carlos. Well—poof!—you're gone. Check it out!"

The Dark Video banner danced across his screen. Carlos pointed the mouse and clicked. Hysterical laughter burst forth from the sound card.

Jack-Jack-Jack-Jack-Jack!

Dark Video. Under new management...

ALSO BY PETER CHURCH

CRACKERJACK

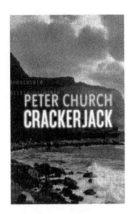

Young, bright and sexy, Carla Vitale has been handpicked to run Supertech, Africa's leading independent Engineering firm. Then one Friday afternoon in Cape Town, her dream is shattered. Her boss and mentor, Nial Townley, disappears, his luxury vehicle is found in a crevice at the bottom of Chapman's Peak and 20 million US dollars are missing from the Supertech's overseas accounts. Three months later and the police are no closer to solving the riddle.

No job, no car, no phone, Carla turns to the one person she believes can help: software hacker turned day trader, Daniel Le Fleur. But Le Fleur's maintaining a low profile in Bantry Bay and he's in no mood to ruin the serendipity.

"Crackerjack is a smart, cleverly plotted thriller that takes readers into the darker corners of the digital world. South African novelist Peter Church has created a great protagonist in hacker/day trader Daniel Le Fleur."
- JAMES LILLIEFORS, author of *THE LEVIATHAN EFFECT* and *THE PSALMIST*

"All the more impressive when considering that Crackerjack is author Peter Church's debut as crime novelist to an American readership, this impressively original and deftly crafted paperback will prove to be an immediate and enduringly popular addition to community library collections and the personal reading list."
- *MIDWEST BOOK REVIEW*

ALSO BY PETER CHURCH

DARK VIDEO

 A minibus taxi flipping spectacularly on its head; two teenagers engaged in illicit sex in a shopping mall rest room; a raunchy table dance in a Cape Town strip club. What have these scenes got to do with a beautiful young woman running through Newlands Forest early on a Sunday morning?

Alistair Morgan is the key. A gifted law student with a glittering career in the offing, Alistair seems to have it all: looks, charm and money—and the attention of the hottest girls on campus. But his privileged lifestyle is about to be turned upside down as he is lured deeper and deeper into the sinister online world of Dark Video, where reality blurs and morals unravel.

From the ominous slopes of Table Mountain and the murky depths of False Bay to a dusty Karoo farm and the limestone cliffs of Arniston, Dark Video is an intense thriller that will keep you spellbound from the word go.

"A roller-coaster ride into the dark world of online pornography and the horrors you can let yourself in for without knowing it! A local author with international potential"
- LOUISE MANN, *LEISUREBOOKS*

peterchurch.bookslive.co.za/dark-video

PETER CHURCH

Peter Church is a Cape Town-based writer.

After a successful career in Information Technology, Church's first novel *Dark Video* (2008) was published by Random-Struik in South Africa and New Holland Publishers in Australia. Reviewed as 'one of the best debuts in a long time' by Lindsay Slogrove of *The Natal Mercury*, *Dark Video* was a Sunday Times "Book of the Week."

In 2011, Church followed up with the "drink spiking" book *Bitter Pill*. *Cosmopolitan* magazine's "Hot Read of the Month," the plot was described by Gillian Hurst of The Drum as "adrenalin-laced, [the] gritty (plot) will keep you furiously turning pages long after your bedtime." *Bitter Pill* was nominated for the 2012 Sunday Times fiction prize.

In 2015 Two Dogs published *Blue Cow Sky*, a novella of sexual proportions.

Peter Church is a member of SA Pen and the Kimberley Club. His acclaimed sporting articles are featured on M&G's *Sports Leader* site.

A short story, *The One*, about compulsive love, appeared in a compilation of South African crime fiction called *Bad Company*. Another shortie, *My Side*, was selected for the annual Short Sharp Story collection *Bloody Satisfied*, edited by Joanne Hichens.

Peter lives in Cape Town with his wife Paula and three children Christopher, Megan, and Ross.